Murder Unveiled
A Detectives Daniels and Remalla Prequel Novel
J. T. Bishop

Eudoran Press LLC

Eudoran Press LLC

6009 W. Parker Rd. #149-913

Dallas, TX 75093

www.jtbishopauthor.com

Publisher's Note: This is a work of fiction. Names, characters, places, and incidents are a product of the author's imagination. Locales and public names are sometimes used for atmospheric purposes. Any resemblance to actual people, living or dead, or to businesses, companies, events, institutions, or locales is completely coincidental.

Author Photos by Nick Bishop and Mayza Clark Photography

Book Editing by P. Creeden and G. Enstam

Cover Design by J.T. Bishop

Murder Unveiled/ J.T. Bishop -- 1st ed.

Paperback 978-1-955370-39-4

Hardback 978-1-955370-40-0

To my sister Cathy.

Your unwavering strength, gritty determination, and powerful love make you a force to be reckoned with. You're the mother of all rockstars, and I love you.

Other Books by J. T. Bishop

Lexie Logan

The Forgotten Night

The Silent Sister

Chapter One

A CACKLE OF LAUGHTER traveled down the long hall from the front of the house. It joined the murmur of conversation slurred by a night of drinking, eating, and celebrating. Dominique walked down the hall, away from the shrill tune of the latest famous pop artist playing over the sound system, and wished she could go home. Rowan Laroche's parties lasted long into the night, though, and she suspected she'd be cleaning up after the messy and drunken partygoers until the early morning hours.

Spying an empty wine glass and its spilled contents lying on the gleaming wood floor, she pulled a rag from her pocket, wiped up what she could and picked up the glass. Looking up, she saw the immense painting adorning the wall beside her. It was a landscape of a lush valley and horses with golden hues of a distant sunset. It had a fancy name, but she couldn't recall the actual title or the artist. All she knew was that it was expensive and famous, and her boss showed it off to his guests whenever he had the chance. Rowan Laroche was famous for his downtown art gallery but perhaps even more famous for his private collection, which decorated the walls of his home and private gallery just down the hall from where she stood.

Rarely were guests allowed in this section of the house unless escorted by Rowan himself or for nights like these when Rowan liked to show off. He'd recently acquired a new piece sought after by many collectors, which he'd purchased for an exorbitant sum. Rowan loved to revel in his victories, so after the auction house had delivered the piece, he'd invited everyone to see his latest acquisition and gloat over his success.

His latest purchase had garnered more attention and a larger amount of jealousy than usual. Dominique recalled the guests' arrival. They'd been served plenty of drinks and a buffet of food prepared by Rowan's chef, Maurice. Rowan had appeared an hour later in his stylish and shiny suit, flashy jewelry, and over-styled hair. He welcomed his guests, made the rounds, flaunted his victory, drank a lot of booze, and annoyed every invitee with stories of his brilliance and cunning.

Dominique wondered why anyone bothered to come to Rowan's parties since he made it a point to celebrate his rivals' defeat. His influence, stature, and prowess in the art world, though, made him a formidable opponent, and his connections and authority could make you or break you as an artist, dealer, or gallery owner. Until that ended, Rowan's parties would continue to be the talk of the art world.

Satisfied with her clean up, Dominique stood and continued down the hall, picking up the trash as she went. The noise lessened as she headed toward the back of the house and Rowan's private gallery. The party guests had just left after Rowan had invited everyone to the gallery to unveil *The Crimson Tiger*, the acquisition coveted by everyone. Dominique had been serving champagne when he'd pulled a satin sheet from the painting sitting on an easel in the room. It had been smaller than she'd expected, but with an ornate frame. The subject was a large tiger standing amidst swaying grass, his body taut as if on the hunt, and his face turned toward the viewer. The artist had used elaborate swirls and dabs of color to capture the strength and power of the animal, and the grainy texture gave it a feel of movement, but its face and eyes were the allure. They seemed to stare through you, and Dominique had caught herself wanting to get closer and study it. The look of the animal was almost magnetic, and she supposed that's why it was so desired. Just as quickly, though, she recalled the rumor she'd heard from Maurice. This painting was supposedly cursed; its last three owners had died. She knew only that, but staring at the tiger's eyes, she shivered, and quickly looked away.

Before unveiling the tiger, Rowan had insisted everyone have a full glass of champagne, and Dominique had walked among the patrons, filling glasses and overhearing bits of whispered conversation. *Pompous ass, giant blowhard,* and *I can't believe he pulled this off again* were common phrases, but they were not new to her, except for a couple of *maybe he'll die next* remarks. She suspected most of Rowan's guests hated him, but they couldn't stop associating with him, like a nasty breakup with a lover who kept luring you back despite his betrayals.

Once everyone's glasses were full, Rowan had made a toast proclaiming his magnificence and delight in his purchase and had unveiled the painting. The reaction was not disappointing. The guests lingered near the work, staring, admiring, and gushing over it. Rowan soaked up the attention, drank more champagne, and after an appropriate amount of time, told everyone the show was over. The party was moving back to the front of the house where more alcohol and food would be served, the music would switch to something more contemporary and fast-paced, and there would be dancing and raucous behavior into the wee hours of the night.

The guests slowly left the gallery, leaving Rowan alone in the room, while he stood staring at the painting. Dominique, at his request, had closed the doors on her way out. Rowan liked to linger in his gallery before rejoining his guests. She suspected he took the moment to allow the partygoers time to gossip about him while awaiting his return. They'd drink loads of liquor, the noise and music would grow and then Rowan would enter yet again, and he'd entertain his guests until almost sunrise.

Eying the time, Dominique left the hall and entered the foyer outside Rowan's private gallery. Not seeing him, she guessed he was still inside, soaking up the accolades. She hoped he'd leave soon so she could get into the room and clean it. By this time tomorrow, the painting would be on a wall in the gallery wherever Rowan chose to display it. Dominique, as a trusted member of the staff, was one of the few allowed in the gallery alone. Not that anyone could get away with much in Rowan's house. He had an elaborate security system with cameras that tracked everyone's movements through the home and grounds, and Robert, Rowan's head of security, was on duty that night. Dominique didn't see him though, and suspected he was dealing with an unruly guest or two. That happened frequently at Rowan's parties and Robert, if he couldn't settle them down, would escort them to security outside, who would ensure they were removed from the grounds and taken home safely.

Stretching her tight shoulders, Dominique waited for her boss. The sooner she could get in and clean, the sooner she could leave once the party ended. No one else would be allowed in this area for the rest of the night, and once she finished cleaning, she'd lock the gallery doors behind her and return to the party.

Approaching the entrance, it surprised her to see the door slightly ajar. Wondering if he'd already left or was waiting for her, she pushed on it, and it swung silently open. She peered into the quiet gallery.

"Mr. Laroche?" Not seeing him, she stepped into the room, wondering why he wasn't there. *The Crimson Tiger* remained on its easel and the tiger stared back at her with its haunting eyes. More famous paintings adorned the walls and vases and statues on pedestals stood behind glass or velvet ropes. Rowan had moved his desk into his gallery so he could work amongst his most valued prizes. Passing the desk, Dominique studied the tiger and its face and almost tripped when her foot caught on something. Turning, she saw legs on the floor. Her heart rate escalating, she stepped around to the side of the desk and saw Rowan Laroche lying on his back on the rug, his eyes glassy and flat, and his lips purple. Saliva trickled down his chin and cheek and the fingers of one hand curled into the rug as if clawing at it and the other hand clawed at his throat. His stiff body, pale face, and frozen expression of terror told Dominique all she needed to know. Rowan Laroche was dead.

Her body trembling, Dominique gasped, clutched her stomach, and screamed.

Chapter Two

DETECTIVE AARON REMALLA PULLED up to the crime scene. He parked behind a police cruiser with swirling lights, and yawned. After rubbing his tired eyes, he looked for his partner's car, but with all the blazing lights, it was hard to see anything. After checking the time, he groaned, took a big gulp of his coffee from his thermos, and blinking back his fatigue, got out of his vehicle. His captain, Frank Lozano, had called Rem an hour earlier at two thirty a.m., and told him to get to this address immediately. Rowan Laroche had been murdered and Lozano had assigned him and Daniels to investigate.

Having no idea who Rowan Laroche was, Rem had rolled out of bed, quickly got the coffeemaker going, called Daniels to confirm they'd meet at the scene, and had jumped into the shower.

Now that he was here, he took a second to take in his surroundings. Aside from the multitude of police cars, a forensic van, and the coroner, there was a slew of press. Police had put up crime scene tape across from the house, and media vans lined the street. Despite the time, onlookers stood on the sidewalk and watched the activity. Reporters shouted questions at any officer in the vicinity.

Rem cursed quietly to himself. Whoever Laroche was, it was obvious he was well known, and Rem took a second to pull out his phone and search for the name. It didn't take long to realize that the victim was a prominent art dealer and gallery manager with ties to powerful people in the city. He was also a big benefactor of the police. He'd donated millions to law enforcement and other charities. His death was all over the headlines, which meant the pressure to solve this would be amped up to the tenth degree. Rem hoped his captain was mistaken, and the guy had died of a heart attack.

"Good morning."

Rem turned to see his partner, Detective Gordon Daniels, approaching. He wore his customary pressed khaki pants and collared, long-sleeved dark shirt and had combed back his gelled blond hair in its usual style. Rem had barely thought about what he was wearing. He'd tossed on a pair of jeans and a wrinkled shirt, which he hoped was stain free, pulled his long black hair back with a tie and had tossed on a jacket. He'd never been much for appearances, at least not for a while. After a hard couple of years, just getting dressed was an accomplishment.

"Morning," said Rem. He gestured at the surrounding activity. "Can you believe this?"

Daniels nodded. "It's Rowan Laroche. What did you expect?"

"I'd never heard of this Laroche guy until Lozano called. Then I looked him up. I guess the art world is pretty upset."

"I should say so. This guy has one of the premiere art collections in the world. He's known for his eye for talent and the priceless works in both his professional and private galleries."

"Not to mention his generous donations. He gave a lot of money to law enforcement charities recently."

Daniels ducked under police tape, and Rem followed. "Let's hope this case is open and shut," said Daniels, "or it's going to be hell until it's solved."

"Lucky us. Why couldn't Lozano have called Titus and Georgios?"

"Probably because he wants it resolved before the year ends."

Rem snorted. "Good point."

They flashed their badges as they approached an elaborate, contemporary-style mansion with stone walls and a lot of glass windows. Mature trees and manicured shrubs filled out the lushly landscaped grounds. They passed a large bubbling fountain where cherubs in a circle spewed water from their arrows, and entered the house. Rem immediately noticed all the art on the walls. To the left was a big room with big furniture and several people in it, all of them looking pale and in shock. To the right was another big room with a buffet of food set on a long table under a crystal chandelier. Rem spotted roast beef, shrimp, cheese, desserts, plus an assortment of other tasty treats. More people, most of them wearing uniforms, were sitting around the table, staring off into space.

An officer approached. "Hey, Daniels. Rem."

"Reynolds," said Daniels. "Why are all these people here? Shouldn't they be outside?"

Reynolds rolled his eyes. "They were in the house when I arrived. Our vic was throwing a party and his guests were wandering all over the crime scene. I got them in here and told them to stay put."

"Great," said Rem. "That doesn't bode well for our evidence."

"It sure doesn't help," said Reynolds. "Come on back."

They followed Reynolds down a long hall with a dark wood floor covered with a plush oriental runner. Rem admired the art on the walls as they entered another foyer area, where more art covered most of the wall space.

Daniels whistled. "They weren't kidding." He stopped in front of a large painting where two angels with huge wings were fighting a demon. "Look at this. I think this is a Diego."

Rem eyed the painting. "What's a Diego?"

"It's the artist. Samwell Diego. He died about ten years ago. His stuff goes for a lot of money."

Rem narrowed his eyes at the picture. "I don't see the appeal."

"It's all in the eye of the beholder."

Rem looked around. "I don't see any velvet paintings of dogs playing poker."

Daniels smirked. "Rowan Laroche wouldn't be caught dead with that in his house."

"My dad had one when I was a kid."

"Exactly." Daniels followed Officer Reynolds through a set of double doors and into a smaller oval-shaped room.

"This is the gallery," said Reynolds.

Rem followed Daniels and stopped short when he walked inside. He couldn't believe the amount of artwork. Colorful paintings, large and small, covered the walls. Statues stood on pedestals and smaller works were behind glass displays. In the center of the room, sitting on an easel, was a portrait of a tiger. Its gaze held Rem's attention, and the shades of red and gold the artist used gave the animal a majestic look. Its eyes seemed to follow Rem as he approached it.

Daniels stopped in front of the picture, his mouth open. "Is this what I think it is?"

"It's a tiger," said Rem.

Daniels stared, his eyes wide. "Wow."

Rem shrugged. "Haven't you seen a tiger before?"

Daniels sighed. "Of course I have." He pointed. "But this is *The Crimson Tiger*. Even I've heard of this."

"Great." Rem pointed. "How about we check out the body? Let's hope it isn't crimson, too." He headed toward Reynolds, who was standing next to the remains of Rowan Laroche, whose body was lying on the floor beside an ornately carved wooden desk. Rem stood over him, and Rowan's death stare told Rem that Rowan's last moments had not been good ones. "Damn. That's definitely not a heart attack."

"Heart attack?" asked Reynolds.

Rem straightened. "I was hoping."

Daniels leaned over the body. "We got a time of death?"

Reynolds flipped open a notebook. "Ibrahim says two to three hours ago. One of the staff members found him like this. Her name's Dominique Lorens. She's outside the room, talking to Gonzales. She's pretty shook up."

Rem squatted beside the body. "What's her story?"

Reynolds flipped to another page. "Laroche was throwing a party for a new painting he purchased. Something about a red tiger."

"Crimson," said Daniels.

"Sure," said Reynolds. "Laroche unveiled it in here and then stayed while everyone else went back to the party. Dominique came in to clean and found him like this."

"I don't see any marks on his neck," said Rem.

Daniels looked closer. "Look at his bloodshot eyes and purple lips. Plus, he's clutching his neck and has scratches on his skin, like maybe he was fighting to breathe."

"Maybe not strangled, but what about suffocation? Somebody could have put a bag over his head." Rem straightened and eyed the half-filled champagne glass on the desk. "Make sure Forensics bags that and gets a sample of the champagne."

Reynolds nodded. "Will do."

Daniels raised a brow. "You thinking poison?"

Rem gestured toward the door. "Crowd like this? Guns and knives are beneath them. Poison is right up their alley. No muss. No fuss."

"I don't think Laroche would agree." Daniels looked around the room. "We need to find out if anything in here was stolen."

Rem glanced at the painting on the easel. "I guess that fancy tiger wasn't the target."

"Maybe not, but it's a great distraction." Daniels walked over to the painting. "Think about it. Laroche throws a party to show off his latest acquisition, which is nothing to sneeze at. This painting is a huge feather in someone's art gallery cap. I can't imagine what he paid for it."

Rem studied the tiger. "It's just a picture."

"Not to an artist or dealer. Assuming Laroche threw this party to show it off and gloat, which I've heard is his style, then maybe our killer used this party as an opportunity."

Rem put his hands on his hips. "So, they wait until Laroche is alone, kill him, and return to the party like nothing ever happened?"

"Maybe."

Rem shot his thumb at the painting. "All because of this?"

"This could be just the catalyst. Maybe this isn't the first time Laroche bested his killer with a victory lap. The grudge may run deep." He looked around the room. "There. Look." He pointed up in the corner. "That's a camera."

Rem perked up. "Hey, Reynolds."

Reynolds walked over. "Yeah."

"That camera," said Rem. "We need to see the footage. Any idea who can get that for us?"

Reynolds eyed the camera. "Not sure. But I'll find out."

"Thanks," said Rem, as Reynolds walked off. "What are the odds our killer is on film?"

Daniels shook his head. "Don't count on it. It's never that easy."

"I can hope, can't I?"

"Feel free."

Rem glanced around at the other artwork and settled back on the tiger. "Well, we've got a room full of potential killers and Dominique, who found the body. Who do you want to talk to first?"

"Let's start with Dominique. Find out what she knows."

"What if she's the killer?"

"Then let's pray she confesses." Daniels turned to leave. "But something tells me she won't. Between the media, Laroche's connections and his fortune, this case has nightmare written all over it." He paused. "I hope you ate your Wheaties this morning."

"Wheaties?" asked Rem. "Try a big cup of coffee and that's it."

"I've got a sprouted vegan protein bar in the car if you want it."

Rem made a gagging noise. "I'd rather partner with Titus or Georgios."

Daniels offered him a sideways glance. "It wouldn't hurt you to eat something other than a donut for breakfast every once in a while."

"Maybe so, but anything with the words vegan or sprouted should be planted in dirt, not consumed. One of these days, your skin's going to turn green with all the veggies you eat."

"Better than neon white, considering all the sugar you eat."

Rem patted his stomach. "I'm as fit as ever."

They returned to the foyer. "You sure about that? I heard your breathing when we climbed those stairs the other day."

Rem dropped his jaw. "That was twelve floors."

"Thank God it wasn't thirteen."

Rem frowned as he followed Daniels toward a woman in a staff uniform, standing in the hall talking to an officer.

Daniels chuckled. "C'mon, partner. Let's talk to Dominique."

Chapter Three

DOMINIQUE LORENS WAS A petite woman with heavily lined narrow eyes, a pointed chin, olive skin and long, black hair pulled tightly into a bun on her head. She wore a black shirt and pants with a white apron, and she wrung her hands together. Her gaze darted toward the entrance of the gallery, as if she still couldn't believe what was happening.

Daniels approached her and Officer Gonzales, wondering if Dominique would be strong enough to suffocate Rowan Laroche. Based on her size, he guessed not. If poison had been the weapon though, then Dominique was still on the suspect list.

"Miss Lorens?" he asked.

She turned toward him, her eyes wide. "Yes?"

Daniels flashed his badge. "I'm Detective Gordon Daniels." He gestured toward Rem. "And this is my partner, Detective Aaron Remalla."

Rem raised his badge. "Hello."

"We know you've had a tough night and you've talked to Officer Gonzales here, but we need to talk to you as well."

Dominique nibbled her lip. Her pale face told Daniels she might need to sit. "Is there a place we can go, so you don't have to see all of this?" He waved toward the gallery, where Forensics moved through the area taking photos and dusting for prints. Two men appeared and rolled a stretcher into the room to collect Laroche's body.

She stared for a second and nodded. "We can go in here." She pointed to an adjacent room.

Daniels took her elbow. "We've got it, Gonzales. Thanks." Gonzales walked off and Daniels guided Dominique into a small music room with a piano, harp, and a large, colorful rug under a couch and two upholstered chairs. There were more pictures hanging on the walls, but not to the degree as the hall and gallery.

Rem followed and partially closed the door to block the view and muffle some of the noise.

Dominique sat on the couch and Daniels and Rem each sat in a chair across from her. "You okay? You need anything?" asked Rem.

Dominique shook her head. "I'm fine. Just exhausted and a little scared."

"That's completely understandable," added Daniels. "We'll try not to take too much of your time. Why don't you tell us what happened tonight, starting with the beginning of the party."

Dominique wrung her hands again as she told her story of what had happened that night, from the arrival of the guests to the unveiling of the painting and finding Laroche lying dead in his gallery.

"Did you see anything suspicious?" asked Rem. "Anything about the guests or Laroche that made you take notice?"

She pursed her lips. "That's hard to say. I could consider everyone here suspicious, but I wouldn't call that unusual."

Daniels pulled a small notebook and pencil out of his jacket pocket. "Why do you say that?"

"Because I think almost everyone here tonight hates Mr. Laroche."

Daniels glanced at Rem. "Interesting. Why do they hate him?" Daniels had an idea why, but needed Dominique to confirm.

She eyed the floor. "I've worked for Mr. Laroche for eight years and he wasn't a humble man. He belittled his adversaries and bragged to all the rest. He was brash, tacky, and impatient. He paid his staff well but didn't tolerate mistakes. I was the only staff member he trusted to work in his gallery. Tonight, while I was serving drinks, I heard chatter among his guests. They were petty and mean, and most were jealous of him. With good reason, I suppose. When Mr. Laroche set his sights on something, he usually got it."

Rem rested his elbows on his knees. "It sounds like you're saying he was unscrupulous in his business, and he'd betray others to get what he wanted. Do you think that painting of the tiger has something to do with that? Did it upset someone here tonight?"

"I'm not privy to most of what he does, so it's hard to say." She ran her palms over her knees. "But it wouldn't surprise me. I hear that painting is very valuable and was sought after by some at the party."

Daniels wrote in his notebook.

Dominique lowered her voice. "Of course, I've heard it's also cursed, so that could be part of it, too. Maybe that painting didn't like Mr. Laroche either."

Rem narrowed his eyes. "Excuse me? Cursed?"

Dominique nodded. "Maurice, Rowan's chef, told me. Mr. Laroche is the fourth owner of the painting to have died."

Daniels hadn't heard about any curse. "I didn't realize that." He made a note to investigate this supposed curse.

"Curses aside, Dominique," said Rem. "Let's assume a human being, and not the painting, killed your boss. How well do you know the guests here tonight? If you've worked here a while, my guess is you know some things. Is there anyone specific who you believe has motive to kill your boss?"

She clenched her hands together. "I'm not sure what I should say. It would all be pure conjecture."

"We understand that," said Daniels. "But we need as much information as you can provide. Everything will be checked and double-checked. But if you know something, you should say something."

She stared at the floor again. "And it won't get out?"

"Mum's the word," said Rem. "But we can't promise that once we make an arrest, that you won't need to testify against the perpetrator, but if protection is warranted, we can provide it."

"Hopefully, it won't come to that, though." Daniels tapped the tip of his pencil against the paper. "We'll do our best to prevent it."

Dominique sighed, closed her eyes, and paused. "Okay." She took a deep breath.

There was a soft knock on the door, and Daniels looked to see Reynolds standing over the threshold. He signaled that he wanted to talk to them.

Rem stood. "I'll go. You can finish up with my partner, Dominique." He walked over to Reynolds and they both left the room.

Daniels regarded Dominique. "Who do you suspect?"

She stared back with weary eyes. "I think the bigger question is who don't I suspect?"

Daniels shifted back on the couch and rested his notebook on his knee. "Let's start with your first, then."

Dominique started talking and Daniels started writing.

· · • • • • • · ·

Rem followed Reynolds back into the foyer outside Laroche's gallery. "What is it?" asked Rem.

Reynolds gestured toward a tall man with curly brown hair and broad shoulders wearing black pants and a beige shirt standing down the hall. "That guy is Robert Clifford, Laroche's head of security. He was here tonight during the party. Says he can show you the footage on the cameras."

Rem studied Robert. "He's security? Where the hell was he when Laroche was murdered?"

"Says there was a problem between Maurice the chef, and one of the guests. Someone was angry about the kitchen being out of caviar."

"I hate it when that happens."

Reynolds snickered. "No kidding. Anyway, Robert went to handle it. Says Laroche didn't need him during the unveiling, and preferred to be alone afterward and would rejoin the party later."

"What happened to the unhappy guest?"

"Robert escorted them out, and they went home. Apparently, they were pretty drunk. That was about the time the commotion started after Dominique found Laroche."

"Figures." Rem patted Reynolds' arm. "Thanks. I'll talk to him."

"They're taking the body soon. You need to see anything else?"

"No. We're good. Our guests still hanging around?"

"Some have gone home, arguing that unless we're going to arrest them, they don't have to stay."

"You get their names?"

"Sure. Robert says he's got a list of all the partygoers too. He gets their names when they arrive. Said he can give it to us."

"Great. That's something, at least. Thanks, Reynolds."

Reynolds headed off and Rem approached Robert. "Robert Clifford?"

Robert sighed and crossed his arms. "Who's asking?"

Rem sensed Robert's annoyance. He held up his badge and introduced himself. "I hear you were in charge of security tonight."

Robert clenched his jaw. "What are you implying?"

Rem hadn't had enough sleep to act nice. "It's a simple question, Robert."

Robert held Rem's stare. "Yeah. I'm in charge of security."

"What happened? Why weren't you with your boss?"

"Contrary to what you may expect, I don't stick to Rowan like glue. The art was my concern. Not him. And as far as I know, the art is just fine."

Not having the patience for a smart ass, Rem tensed. "That you know of. Where were you when he was murdered?"

Robert's gaze hardened. "I did nothing wrong."

"Your boss is dead. That never looks good on a resumé."

"I was doing my job."

"I heard. It sucks when you run out of caviar."

"A drunk guest was threatening Maurice. What was I supposed to do? Let a fight break out? Rowan would have been pissed."

"Well, good news. You don't have to worry about pissing him off anymore."

Robert cursed and looked away.

"I hear you've got a list of party attendees?"

"I do."

"Good. We need it. I also need to see your security footage. Based on the value of the items in this house, I'm guessing the security system is top-notch."

Robert perked up. "It's as good as Rowan would allow. But if someone murdered Rowan tonight, he, or she, is on video. I guarantee it."

Rem prayed he was right. "Then show me."

Robert pointed. "It's back here." He started walking, and Rem followed him past the gallery and down the hall. He stopped in front of a door close to the room where Daniels was speaking with Dominique.

"It's in here." Robert entered a dark room with a desk and computer and several monitors on the wall. Rem followed and studied the screens, seeing views of the front and back of the house, the entrance to the gallery and the gallery itself, and parts of the grounds.

"Pull up the unveiling," said Rem.

Robert pulled out a chair from the desk and sat. He dragged a keyboard over and started typing. A monitor on the counter flickered to life. "Give me a second." Robert clicked a mouse, and Rem saw a black and white view of Laroche's gallery displayed on the screen. Moving closer, he watched it.

"This is it." Robert tapped the screen. "There's Rowan."

Rem watched as Rowan stood beside the painting of the tiger and raised a champagne glass. "Is there sound?"

"No. Rowan did business there. He didn't want microphones."

Rem continued to watch as Rowan pulled a sheet from the covered painting. People approached, stared, and talked. "Can we speed it up? To after everyone leaves?"

Robert clicked the mouse, and just as the footage picked up in speed, it went dark.

Rem waited, but the screen remained the same. "What's wrong?"

Robert clicked, and the footage resumed at its regular pace, but there was nothing to see. "What the...?"

Rem stared at the blank screen. "Where's the footage?"

Robert clicked again, hit a few buttons, the footage backed up and played again. Rem saw the start of the unveiling once more and then it went dark. "What the hell is going on, Robert?"

Robert cursed and tried again, but with the same result. "I don't get it. This should all be recorded." Another view came up, but it was also dark. "This should be the entrance at the front of the house." He clicked again. "And this should be the back. It's all dark."

"Any other viewpoints besides these?"

"No," said Robert, clicking the mouse. "This is what Rowan wanted monitored." He tried again to pull up the video but failed. "It's not there."

"What are you saying?"

Robert let go of the mouse and slid his seat backward. He ran his hands through his hair. "I don't believe this. The footage is gone."

"Gone? What do you mean, gone?" Rem dreaded the response.

"I mean, it's erased." Robert sat up. "Someone tampered with it, Detective. Whatever was on here, it's not there anymore."

Chapter Four

DANIELS LOOKED FOR REM. After finishing his talk with Dominique, he asked Reynolds to arrange for someone to take her home. She didn't want to walk out the front door where the remaining guests could see her, so she left through the back with an officer.

He spotted Rem walking down the hall and Daniels joined him. "What's the update?" asked Daniels.

Rem's face fell. "You were right."

"Aren't I usually?"

"Almost as often as me." He massaged his neck. "I met Robert Clifford. Mr. Security Guy's got a chip on his shoulder bigger than Laroche's fortune, and he was sure we had the killer on video."

"Let me guess. We don't."

"Like you said. A case like this is never simple."

"Somebody tampered with it?"

"According to Robert, yes. There's no other explanation. He insists that no one else could access the equipment, but the room doesn't have a lock and its location isn't a secret."

"Could Robert have tampered with it?"

"He insists he didn't, but we can't rule him out. The guy thinks he's too smart to work for Rowan but can't protect the security system, much less his boss. With Rowan's kind of money, he could have done a lot better."

Daniels glanced at his notes. "Well, according to Dominique, Robert's definitely a suspect. He talks down to the staff and isn't well-liked. He and Laroche got into a shouting match last week, and she heard them argue tonight, but Dominique doesn't know what it was about."

"Maybe Laroche was thinking about making a change. I wouldn't blame him."

"It's something to check."

"Who else is on the list?"

Daniels read the names to Rem. "Robert's the only staff member listed. The rest are guests." He pointed at a name at the bottom that said *mystery guest*. "She knows all of them except this man. Said she'd never seen him before and didn't know his name. He's six feet, around sixty, has black hair with gray streaks and was wearing a tuxedo that was too small. Nobody else seemed to know him either, and he kept to himself during the party. We'll have to find his name on the guest list."

"Interesting."

"We should talk to whoever is still here."

Rem checked his watch. "It's four o'clock in the morning." He ran a hand over his face. "If our killer's hanging around, we won't find him tonight. We're not even sure how Laroche died or if anything was stolen."

"Let's introduce ourselves and ask a few questions. We'll tell them we'll be in touch, and not to go anywhere until this investigation ends."

Rem blew out a deep breath. "You mean put the fear of God in them?"

"Exactly."

"All right. Come on."

They headed up the hall toward the entry and stopped just before the main room. "Let's talk to the staff first," said Rem.

They entered the room with the long buffet table and a large crystal chandelier hanging over it. The food had been cleared and several of the remaining staff had paper plates containing cheese and bread and other items from the buffet. Daniels guessed they'd helped themselves to some leftovers. When Rem walked in with Daniels, a few staff members entered from the kitchen, including a large Black man wearing a white shirt and pants and a chef's hat. Daniels assumed it was Laroche's chef, Maurice. Emotional, he dabbed at his teary eyes with a napkin and wiped his nose. Rem introduced himself and Daniels and explained that someone would be in touch to speak with each of them within the next few days and not to go anywhere. While he spoke, a man with curly hair entered and sat beside a thin Asian American woman with long black hair that ran down her back.

Rem leaned closer to Daniels and whispered. "That's Robert, our security man."

Daniels nodded and made a note beside Robert's name on his list.

After Rem's speech, the staff said little. A few asked questions about Laroche and some wiped tears from their cheeks, especially Maurice, but most didn't say a word and quietly left.

"One room down," said Rem. "Let's go hit the guests."

Daniels crossed the hall and stopped outside a set of closed doors. He held out the list of names Dominique provided. "Let's see if we can put some names to faces." He opened a door and walked into a large, ornate room with big mirrors, elaborate wall sconces, and colorful wallpaper. About twenty people were in the room, some sitting on a long white leather couch or on tall-backed upholstered chairs, and others were sitting on the floor on an extravagant oriental rug. The rest milled about in small groups, talking to each other. Dressed in fancy clothes with lots of leather, lace, satin, and silk, and wearing expensive jewelry, they looked stunned and out of place, like captured wild animals pacing in a small enclosure at the zoo. Some were drinking from half-filled glasses, and champagne flutes were sitting on the mantel above an enormous fireplace, and on small tables set up around the room. Daniels had to assume the drinking and partying had come to an immediate stop at the discovery of Laroche's body. Some women had streaks of mascara running down their cheeks and most of the guests' pale faces implied they were still struggling with the news.

Everyone turned when he and Rem entered. Daniels introduced himself and Rem, and they showed their badges. Daniels looked for the mystery man in the snug tuxedo, but didn't see him. He made a note on his paper.

"It's about time someone came to talk to us," said a woman in the back of the room. She wore a lot of makeup, a long-sleeved black dress that sparkled in the light, and her dyed black hair was severely pulled back into a low bun on her neck. "We've been waiting for hours."

"We apologize for the wait," said Rem.

"Why did they close the doors?" asked a younger Black man with an afro wearing a lavender suit. He looked to be in his thirties. "Are we not allowed to leave?"

"Closing the doors prevents everyone from contaminating the crime scene," said Daniels.

"You can't force us to stay, you know," said a younger woman with long, dark brown hair, wearing a leather dress with plenty of exposed cleavage. "It's ridiculous you made us wait this long."

"Several already went home," said an older man with salt and pepper hair wearing an oversized navy suit. He eyed the other guests. "And if you all hadn't wandered around the crime scene, they wouldn't have shut the doors."

"Oh, be quiet, Henry," said the woman in the black dress. "What did they expect us to do? Rowan was murdered. Should we just stand around and do nothing? What if he'd still been alive? We could have performed CPR or something."

Another man in the back of the room, wearing a red suit with wide lapels and a white shirt unbuttoned almost down to his navel, chuckled. "The day you put your lips on Rowan's to save his life, Evelyn, is the day I'll sell you my Matisse."

Evelyn glared. "The rate you're going, Roger, you're going to need that Matisse to get out of bankruptcy."

Roger glared back and someone else in the room chuckled. Roger shot a look at Rem and Daniels. "If you two are looking for suspects, you've come to the right place. This room's full of them, and you can start with Evelyn."

Evelyn gasped, and a man standing beside her wearing black pants with a purple and white striped shirt, with several diamond rings on his fingers put his hand on her elbow. "Don't listen to him, Evelyn." He spat back at Roger. "You better include yourself on that list, Roger. I know how badly you wanted *The Crimson Tiger*."

"Maybe that's what killed Rowan," said a woman sitting on the couch. She wore a slim-cut white suit, spike heels and her thick auburn hair was softly pulled back with clips. "The tiger was cursed, after all."

The room hummed with conversation, and Rem held up his hand. "Um, excuse me." He rapped loudly on a table beside him. "Everybody quiet down."

The conversation slowed and stopped.

"Listen," said Daniels. "We appreciate you all staying. We know it's been a long night. We do want to speak to each of you, one at a time. We know it's late, though, and you'd like to go home. But before you go, we'd like to learn your names and how you know Mr. Laroche. And if anyone saw anything suspicious tonight, we'd like to know that too."

"Victoria is wearing pearls with that atrocious dress," said Roger. "Is that suspicious enough for you?"

The woman in the leather dress scowled at Roger. "And Roger brought his lover to the party tonight while his wife stayed home. How's that for suspicious?"

Roger's eyes flared. "Becca and I are separated, you cow."

Victoria started yelling, and Roger yelled back. Evelyn chimed in with the man in the purple shirt, and then everyone was all talking at once.

Rem put his fingers between his lips and whistled loudly. Everyone stopped chattering. Rem raised a brow at Daniels, who shook his head. Looking at his notebook, he saw two of the names on Dominique's list were Evelyn Sinclair, who was in the black dress and Victoria Laroche, who was wearing the leather dress.

"Before you all come to blows over your devastation," said Rem, "why don't we take this one step at a time."

A man standing beside one of the tall-backed chairs made a snort. He had black hair slicked back with gel and wore a well-cut designer chocolate-brown suit with gold and diamond cuff links. He put his hand on the shoulder of a woman sitting in the chair. Her thick blonde hair brushed her shoulders, and she wore a shimmery pink satin dress with a diamond necklace, and mascara ran down her cheeks. When the man put his hand on her shoulder, she visibly pulled away and swiped a tear from her eye.

"My wife is very upset about Rowan, and I'd like to take her home," said the man.

"It's fine, Carlo," said the woman. "If I can stay and help the police, then I will."

Carlo frowned at her. "We need to get home to Mateo, Isabella." Daniels eyed his list and saw the names Carlo and Isabella Vespucci.

"What about the guests who've already left?" asked the man in the red suit. "Are you going to talk to them, too?"

"Of course," said Daniels. "We have a guest list. We'll be talking to each of them, plus the staff."

The man in the purple shirt crossed his arms. "I would hope so. That Maurice is crazy. You make one small comment about his crab dip, and he goes insane." He huffed.

"Be quiet, James," said Evelyn. "The less we interfere, the sooner we can get out of here."

James sighed. "You're right. Sorry. No more remarks about the crab dip. Or those truffles." He rolled his eyes. "Personally, I think Maurice dug those out of the alley. Atrocious."

"Sssh." Evelyn poked James in the arm. "Stop complaining."

"Asking the sun to stop shining would be easier," said Roger.

Daniels raised his hand before James could offer another ugly retort. "Yes. We're talking to everyone, but not about the food." Daniels eyed his list and saw the name James Montrose, who was Evelyn Sinclair's gallery manager.

"Pity," said James with a scowl at Roger.

Daniels didn't know who Roger was, and Dominique had not mentioned him, but he made a note to consider him a suspect.

The woman in the tailored white pant suit stood from the couch. "I apologize for my friends." She gestured at the group. "I know we sound awful, but it's been a hellish night. Rowan is dead." She paused and looked around the room. "And most of us knew him well. It's shocking that this has happened, and right under our noses."

Everyone slumped, and the energy left the room.

"We'd like to know who did this," she said. "And if it means answering your questions now or later, I'm sure we'll be happy to do it."

"Well said, Maria," said a man leaning against the mantel. He wore leather pants and a black narrow-cut silk shirt, which emphasized his muscular arms and narrow waist. A silver and diamond watch on his wrist sparkled in the light. "Rowan deserves better from us."

Roger snorted. "Says the man Rowan made rich."

"Be quiet, Roger," said Maria. "Hendrix is right. Rowan deserves better. He's dead, for heaven's sake. Can't we take five minutes to mourn him?"

Daniels studied the people in the room, who suddenly appeared sheepish. Isabella, who'd deflected her husband Carlo's touch, sniffed again, and wiped away another tear. "I can't believe he's gone."

Carlo set his jaw. "It doesn't surprise me at all."

"What's your name, Miss?" Daniels asked the woman in the white suit.

"I'm Maria Rossi. A long-time acquaintance of Rowan's." She stepped forward. "And I'd be happy to talk to you."

Daniels recognized the name. Maria Rossi was also one of Dominique's potential murderers. The name Hendrix wasn't on the suspect list, but he added it.

Victoria stood and smoothed her leather dress. "Are you sure, Maria? You don't have to say anything."

Maria patted Victoria's hand. "It's okay, Victoria. No need to worry." She looked around. "We all need to tell them the truth. Okay?"

No one would look her in the eye.

"Great," said Rem. He gestured toward the door. "Then let's get started."

Chapter Five

REM PRINTED OFF THE lists of names of both the staff and guests from Laroche's party. Sitting at his desk, he sipped some coffee and tried not to think of all the legwork in front of him.

After speaking to him and Daniels, the remaining guests at the party had gone home. Other than James Montrose, Evelyn's gallery manager, suggesting Laroche may have died from Maurice's less-than-impressive food, none of the guests had provided a smoking gun nor seen anything suspicious. On the positive side, Rem and Daniels now knew their potential suspects, assuming Dominique was trustworthy. As a member of Laroche's staff who was present at the unveiling, though, she would also have to be checked.

After the guests and staff had left, Rem and Daniels stayed until the body was removed, and Forensics finished their testing. The media and onlookers remained outside until the early morning hours. The driveway had lit up with the number of flashbulbs going off when the body had been taken out on the stretcher. While Rem and Daniels waited, Reynolds had informed them that a man named Brian Klein had called after hearing the news. He was Laroche's assistant and business manager who had not attended the party. Daniels spoke to him on the phone. Klein was distraught but offered to help in any way he could. He agreed to send a staff list and a full inventory of Laroche's gallery pieces as soon as possible. They'd been in Rem and Daniels' inboxes by the time they'd made it to their desks later that morning. Daniels had quickly forwarded that information to Captain Lozano and had provided a quick update on what they'd learned at the crime scene. With the amount of attention this case was receiving, Lozano was expecting frequent updates and progress reports. Rem expected long workdays ahead until they figured out who killed Laroche.

After leaving Laroche's, they'd taken a little time to get some breakfast on the way in and the rest of their morning had been talking to the coroner and Forensics, gathering information, writing reports, and organizing tasks. Even though it was early, the case had been given priority and information was trickling in. Based on his preliminary examination, the coroner agreed someone had poisoned Laroche with a delayed-onset toxin, but they'd have to wait for the lab to determine the type of poison.

Robert had provided a copy of the video footage from the party that hadn't been deleted, and Rem and Daniels had watched it. The party guests had arrived around eight p.m. and had enjoyed food and liquor until Laroche had appeared around ten. He'd mingled and had plenty to drink until almost midnight, when he'd disappeared and gone to his gallery, where *The Crimson Tiger* sat on an easel, covered by a black cloth. He'd found a female staff member alone in the room peeking behind the tiger's covering. He'd spoken to her, and she'd left hastily. Not long after, Robert entered, and he and Laroche appeared to argue. Robert left as the guests convened in the gallery. They mingled and Laroche spoke. Based on what they could see before it went dark, Dominique had poured everyone a fresh glass of champagne, including Laroche. Just before the unveiling, he'd set his glass down, walked to the painting, made a speech, and pulled the covering off. The guests' expressions revealed their amazement and gathered around the portrait just before the footage ended. Rem and Daniels' logical conclusion was that the killer had spiked Laroche's drink after the unveiling while everyone focused on the tiger. Laroche continued to drink his champagne, but the effects of the poison didn't take effect until after everyone had left the gallery and returned to the front of the house.

Daniels had also noticed that while the angle of the camera showed most of the room, the far side was in shadow and harder to see. Just after everyone had gathered in the gallery but before the video ended, he pointed out a lone figure standing in the back, watching. It was too difficult to make out any facial features, but the figure appeared to be wearing a tuxedo. Daniels guessed that was their mystery man that Dominique had mentioned.

Groaning at the list of suspects and debating where to start, Rem stood and added more coffee and generous helpings of cream and sugar to his thermos. He sat again, eyed the lists of staff and guests, and was about to read through them when Daniels entered the squad room. He looked as weary as Rem felt.

Holding a couple of bags, he sat at his desk and handed one to Rem. "Ham and cheese and some chips."

Rem took it. "Great. Thanks. You talk to the lab?"

"I stopped on the way up. They confirmed poison. They mentioned a few chemical names that were too long to remember, but they'll send a report as soon as they have it." He dug into his own bag and pulled out his sandwich and an apple. He set a third bag on his desk.

"Please tell me that's got cookies in it," said Rem, eyeing the third bag.

"Sorry. No such luck. That's for Lozano. He's on his way up and asked me to get him something. He hasn't eaten much today."

"I bet. The way the press is all over this, Lozano's likely getting an earful from the chief."

"There's going to be a press conference this afternoon."

Rem's heart sunk. "Please tell me we don't have to be there."

"Nope. That's Lozano's area of expertise. But he's going to want the latest and greatest before then. Apparently, the chief and Laroche were friends."

His stomach grumbling, Rem unwrapped his sandwich and opened his bag of chips. "As if this case wasn't hot enough."

"Tell me about it. We're going to need some help with this one if they expect this to be solved quickly."

"Too bad Wonder Woman isn't available. We could use her Lasso of Truth."

"She has a Lasso of Truth?"

"And an invisible jet." Rem popped a chip into his mouth. "Didn't you read comic books when you were a kid?"

"Are you kidding? Dad called comic books trash. At best, I got to read the Hardy Boys and Nancy Drew. I think that spurred my interest in solving crimes."

"I bet he's regretting that now."

"Probably."

The squad doors opened and their captain, Frank Lozano, entered. He wore a navy suit with a light-yellow shirt which complemented his dark skin. He'd loosened his tie, and the top collar of his shirt was unbuttoned. Carrying his jacket, which covered his round belly, he passed by their desks. "You two. In my office. You get my sandwich, Daniels?"

"Sure thing, Cap." He stood. "We'll be right there."

Lozano grunted and walked away.

Rem stood and picked up his food and coffee. He placed the guest and staff lists in a folder and picked that up, too.

Daniels grabbed the third bag, his sandwich, and water. "Ready?"

"As I'll ever be."

They headed into Lozano's office and sat across from his desk. Daniels handed Lozano his food and set his own wrapped sandwich on the edge of the desk. Rem did the same on his side.

"How was your morning, Cap?" asked Rem. He ate another chip.

"Take a wild guess, Remalla." Lozano draped his jacket over his chair, pulled his tie off and draped it over his jacket. "You'd think the world was ending based on the reaction to Laroche's death."

"I'm a little surprised at the reaction myself. It's not like he was a celebrity." Daniels unwrapped his sandwich.

Lozano sat with a sigh. "On the contrary. He's more of a celebrity than we realize. The chief wasn't the only friend of Laroche's. He ran in some pretty famous circles. And that Maria Rossi you met? She's an actress. Or at least she was. Back in the day, when she and Laroche were an item, their faces were all over magazines and in gossip columns."

Rem had a sudden recall of a monster movie he'd seen as a teenager. The lead actress had spent most of the movie in a bikini and he'd crushed on her for months, and even had a poster of her in his room. "You don't mean Maria Rossini, do you?"

"I don't know, Remalla." Lozano opened his bag. "All I know is she was an actress."

Rem recalled the woman in the white pantsuit with her wavy hair pulled back with clips. "Holy... That was her?" He fell back in his chair.

"She obviously made an impression," said Daniels.

Rem chuckled. "To a teenage boy with raging hormones, she certainly did. I was sure I would marry her one day."

"Maybe she's single," said Daniels. "That wish could still come true."

Rem deflated, recalling his last two years. "No thanks. I'm swearing off women for the foreseeable future, celebrity or not."

Lozano grabbed a bottle of water from a nearby shelf. "Well, between Laroche's celebrity status and that supposed curse on the painting he unveiled, it's like the perfect story for the press. They can't get enough."

Daniels picked up his sandwich. "You get a chance to look over what we sent you?"

"I did." Lozano pulled out his sandwich and chips. "You still think your list of suspects stands? Can you trust this woman? What's her name? Dominique?"

Rem took a bite of his sandwich and spoke through a mouthful. "Yes. And we think she's legit."

"She's worked for Laroche for eight years," said Daniels, "and he trusted her enough to work in his gallery. Plus, she's got a six-year-old daughter. Laroche paid Dominique well, too. He was a tough boss, but working for him paid the bills. Dominique doesn't have motive." He took a bite and chewed.

"That you know of," said Lozano. He unfolded a napkin and set it on his desk. "Just make sure you check her out. She was pouring the drinks at the unveiling. If anyone had access to Laroche, it was her."

"We'll do our due diligence," said Rem, "but that suspect list is getting long." He tapped on the folder he'd set in his lap that was catching his crumbs. "Did you see both the guest and staff lists?"

"I glanced at them." Lozano bit into his sandwich and sighed with satisfaction. He popped a chip into his mouth. "Don't tell Sheila I'm eating chips."

"I almost got you some carrots," said Daniels, "but it seemed like a chip kind of day."

"More like a chocolate and alcohol kind of day," added Rem.

"They limit the alcohol selections in the cafeteria." Daniels chewed another bite of his sandwich.

"Not the chocolate ones." Rem was already looking forward to eating a chocolate bar later.

"I'll stick to my fruit." Daniels took a swig of water and replied to Lozano. "We're going to need help talking to these people."

Lozano nodded. "I'm working on it. I'm thinking Mel and Garcia can check out the staff. Silvers and Edmund can help with the guests. Georgios and Titus are busy with another case, but I'll ask them to help if they can. I want you two to focus on our primary suspects."

"Anybody in that gallery during the unveiling is a primary suspect," said Rem.

"The staff is unlikely. They were all in other parts of the house, other than Dominique." Daniels set his water bottle on Lozano's desk.

"It's got to be one of the guests," added Rem, licking mayonnaise off his finger. "Considering the timing, it seems to me someone was upset over Laroche's latest acquisition."

"I did some checking online while I was downstairs," said Daniels. "That *Crimson Tiger* was supposed to go up for auction, but somehow Laroche got around that. I'm sure that upset some potential buyers."

"Some of whom were at the unveiling." Rem ate a chip. "Evelyn Sinclair owns a gallery. I think that Roger guy, too."

"Don't forget Victoria Laroche," said Lozano. "The chief told me she was planning on publishing an exposé on Laroche. It supposedly reveals her father's years of backstabbing, lies and betrayal that apparently led to his success in the art world."

"Seems like a happy family," said Rem.

"Laroche has never been known as a family man," said Lozano.

"I read a little about that too." Daniel wiped his mouth with a napkin. "He and Maria Rossi dated for a long time. During their relationship, he got another woman pregnant, and Victoria was born. Laroche and Maria broke up, but Laroche was never the doting father. He basically paid child support, and that's it."

"If Victoria was planning to expose Laroche's crimes, wouldn't that make her the target?" asked Rem.

Lozano chewed a chip and drank some water. "Not if Laroche somehow squashed the exposé, which is entirely possible. He had the clout to do it. That's something you two need to check."

Rem eyed Daniels. "Did you notice Victoria seemed pretty chummy with Maria? Are they friends?"

Daniels nodded. "I noticed. You think Maria could still hold a grudge against Laroche? Maybe her 'we all want to help' act is just a ruse and she and Victoria got rid of him. She is an actress, after all."

Rem pointed. "Laroche's will could tell us a lot. If one or both of them benefitted from his death, that moves them up on the list of suspects."

"Good point," said Daniels.

"What about Robert?" asked Lozano. "Our security man."

Rem shrugged. "He wasn't at the unveiling, so he couldn't have poisoned the drink, but it doesn't mean he didn't play a role in the murder. Based on the footage that we saw before it went dark, Dominique was right about Robert and Laroche arguing just prior to the unveiling. We'll have to ask him about that. But he could have erased the footage to protect someone."

"He's the obvious person to tamper with the security footage. But would he be stupid enough to implicate himself?" asked Daniels.

"Based on my conversation with him, yes," said Rem.

"Then he definitely stays on the list," said Lozano.

"Agreed," said Rem.

Daniels pointed. "There's also that female staffer who Laroche kicked out of the gallery after he found her peeking at the tiger. We need to find her, too."

Rem shrugged. "She was probably just curious, but we should talk to her."

"Can you tell who she is?" asked Lozano.

"We can't see her face. But she's wearing a uniform, and her hair is up in a bun. The footage is grainy, but she shouldn't be that hard to find once we talk to the staff," said Daniels.

"All right. Who else is on Dominique's main suspect list?" asked Lozano.

"The Vespuccis. Carlo and Isabella." Daniels took another bite of his sandwich.

"They were an interesting couple," said Rem. He sipped some coffee. "Did that last name ring a bell for you?" he asked Daniels.

"It does for me," said Lozano. "Any relation to the Vespucci crime family?"

"I recognized the name too." Daniels swallowed. "That would be interesting, wouldn't it?"

Rem recalled Isabella's tears. "Isabella looked pretty stricken over Laroche's death."

"And Carlo seemed pretty annoyed by it," said Daniels. "We'll dig into their story."

Rem munched a chip. "We should add the assistant, Brian Klein, to the list. I know Dominique didn't mention him, but he should still be checked."

"I added him plus Roger, Henry, and Hendrix," said Daniels. "Although Hendrix arrived late and almost missed the unveiling, and Klein's been pretty cooperative. When I asked him about why he wasn't at the party, he said Laroche didn't invite him. He told me art was never his thing."

Lozano arched a brow. "The man works for the most affluent gallery owner in the state and he's not into art?"

Rem shrugged. "I guess it's possible. Laroche did the art deals and Klein just handled whatever Laroche gave him. But as the assistant, he must know things. If Laroche was a tough boss, maybe Klein has a motive to kill."

"There's one problem with all of this." Daniels sat back in his seat. "How do we know who to believe? If Laroche was as conniving in the art world as he seems, he had enemies. These people run in the same circles and could protect each other." He wiped a crumb from his shirt. "Rem and I are not art experts. I know a few things, but only because Marjorie was an art history major. Outside of that, we're fish out of water."

"Marge is into art?" asked Rem. "I didn't know that."

Daniels narrowed his eyes. "You went with us to that Jackson Pollock exhibit downtown. Don't you remember? He's one of Marjorie's favorite artists."

Rem thought back. "The pictures with all the scribbles and drips?"

Daniels rolled his eyes. "Yeah. That one."

"I think I blocked that from my mind."

"Apparently."

Lozano snorted. "If you took him to an art exhibit, Daniels, then you should have expected as much."

Daniels sighed. "I guess I figured a little exposure to a world outside of velvet paintings and figurines made with popsicle sticks might help."

Rem recalled the art class he took at the rec center with Jennie. "That figurine I made of you was spot on."

"You think I look like a stick with hay for hair, glued-on clothes, and googly eyes?"

"It bore a resemblance."

"The one Jennie made of you was far more accurate. It had clothes with holes in them, long black yarn for hair and chocolate drops on its shirt, mouth, and hands."

Wondering where that figurine was, Rem smiled softly. It was probably in one of the boxes where he'd put her things after her death over two years ago. "She was pretty proud of that." He'd tried to go through those boxes on the two-year anniversary of losing her, but that had not gone well. His hangover the next morning had not been a good look when he'd shown up for work. If it hadn't been for Daniels, Lozano might have fired him that day. Rem scratched his knee at the memory, and the familiar grief bubbled up.

Daniels glanced over at him. "One of these days, we'll compare figurines, if I can find mine. Marjorie may have tossed it," he used his finger as quote marks, "by accident."

As he so often did, Rem shook off the past as best he could. "That work of art was better than anything by that potluck guy."

"Pollock," said Daniels.

"Whatever."

Lozano wiped his fingers on his napkin. "Speaking of needing some help, I agree with you, Daniels. You two need some, which is why you'll be working with Phoebe Reinart."

Rem frowned. "Phoebe who?"

"Reinart. From the Southern Division." Lozano ate a chip. "Her partner is on sabbatical, and she's got the time. I figure we can slide a desk over like we did for Jacobs."

Hearing Jill Jacob's name, Rem's gut took another punch. Jill had been a detective and his only serious relationship since losing Jennie. After investigating a hard case where they'd confronted a serial killer out for revenge and revelations regarding Jill and her past, their relationship took the hit and they'd broken up soon after. That had only been three months ago, and Rem was still adjusting to their breakup.

"Earth to Remalla."

Rem snapped back to the present and saw Lozano and Daniels staring at him. "What?"

"I asked what you thought?" asked Lozano.

"About what?"

Lozano arched a brow. "About Phoebe Reinart?"

Rem glanced at Daniels, who helped Rem out. "Do we need her, Cap? I mean, it's nice to have the extra hands, but if she has no more art knowledge than me or Rem, what's the point?"

Lozano grabbed another napkin from his lunch bag. "Phoebe Reinart's mother works in the FBI's Art Crime division. Reinart's got degrees in Art History and Criminal Justice, and she's forgotten more about art than you two will ever know. I'd say she's qualified."

Rem tossed his crumpled napkin on Lozano's desk. "Well, when you put it that way..."

"I guess it makes sense," said Daniels.

"Good," said Lozano. "Which is why I've already sent her to Laroche's home with the list of his inventory. She can verify if everything is where it should be, and nothing's been stolen."

Rem widened his eyes. "She's there now?"

"No," said Lozano. "She's going next week." He strengthened his tone. "Of course, she's there now. What part of *this case is a priority* did you miss?"

"I guess we just figured there'd be an introduction." Daniels sat up. "And maybe some discussion on who does what."

"You can have your meet and greet when she gets here," said Lozano. "Right now, you need to get some legwork in. While she handles the art stuff, you two start divvying out the workload to Mel, Garcia, Silvers, and Edmund. Get them out there. The sooner we can eliminate suspects, the better." He eyed the folder in Rem's lap. "Is that the list of guest names?"

Rem brushed crumbs off the folder and opened it. "Yes." He pulled out the papers. "Staff too."

"Break it up however you want, but you two take the prime suspects." Lozano swiveled in his seat. "Find out what you can about Dominique and Klein, too." He checked his watch. "I'll be prepping for the news conference but keep me posted." His phone rang, and he eyed the display. "I've got to take this."

Daniels stood and picked up the remains of his food. "We'll let you get back to it."

Lozano answered the phone.

Perusing the lists of names, Rem stood too, wondering if it was better to give Silvers and Edmund the staff and Mel and Garcia the guests. Grabbing his trash and walking out of Lozano's office, he read through to the bottom and reached the last name on the guest list. He stopped cold and his stomach flipped.

"What's wrong?" asked Daniels, closing Lozano's office door behind him. "You find another celebrity?"

Rem pointed at the paper. "Is this accurate?"

Daniels leaned closer. "It's the list Klein sent over. Why?"

Wondering if his eyesight was off, Rem blinked his eyes and reread the last name. *Carmine Remalla*. "I don't believe this." He sputtered and poked a finger at Carmine's name. "That's my uncle."

Chapter Six

Daniels pulled up to the curb in front of the small white A-frame house. The overgrown grass and peeling paint suggested Carmine Remalla wasn't big on home maintenance, at least not in the front yard.

Rem opened the door.

"Hold up." Daniels grabbed his arm. "Why don't you stay here? Let me talk to him."

Rem held the door open. "I know Lozano would want me to keep my distance, but this is my uncle."

"All the more reason for you to stay put. You shouldn't interview your family. We can't even be certain it's him. There're bound to be other Carmine Remallas in the world."

"None that wear a too small tuxedo to an A-list party. That's got Uncle Carmine written all over it." He glanced at the house. "I can't believe this. What was he doing at Laroche's?"

"We could have called him first. Asked if it was even him."

Rem shook his head. "He wouldn't have answered. He and I bump heads. Aunt Betsy's nice though. She makes a mean cherry pie."

"If you and Carmine don't get along, all the more reason for you to stay here."

Rem frowned. "Number one, he's not going to talk to you. Number two, if you think because he's family that I'm going to protect him or have an issue sending him to jail if he's the killer, you're wrong."

"How do you think Aunt Betsy's going to feel if you send her husband to prison?"

Rem paused. "If Carmine's a killer, then she'll have to deal with it. But do I really think Carmine has the guts or brains to poison Rowan Laroche? No."

"Then why was he there? Does he have any interest in art?"

Rem shrugged. "Not to my knowledge, but that velvet painting my dad had when I was growing up? He left it to my uncle in his will. That should tell you something." He swung the door out. "C'mon. Let's go." He got out of the car.

Daniels got out and shut his car door. "At least tell me why you two bump heads." He walked around the front of the car and joined Rem on the sidewalk. "You two start jawing at each other, and we won't get anywhere."

Rem hesitated and studied the house again. "You know my dad was a drinker. Well, so was Carmine. As brothers, they enabled each other. I can't tell you how many times Dad promised Mom he'd pull it together and then he'd go out with Carmine, and it would all fall apart. Dad would come home roaring drunk, and he and mom would argue, and I would listen to the whole thing from my bedroom. After a while, I held a grudge against my uncle and blamed him for my dad's problems. Then, when I became a teenager, it got worse because I stopped backing down to Dad and Uncle Carmine. When I turned eighteen, I booked it out of the house and never went back, except to see Mom. I saw Dad and Uncle Carmine occasionally, but not often. After Dad died, Uncle Carmine and I didn't even speak at the funeral. He was mad at me for abandoning his brother and I was mad at him for enabling Dad's drinking." He waved his hand at the house. "And he's still alive and Dad's dead. I'm mad about that too."

Debating what to do, Daniels hesitated. "Do you honestly think that you should be the one questioning him, then? I know you and your temper."

Rem sighed. "It's been a while since Dad died. Uncle Carmine and I can be civil when we need to be. This shouldn't be any different."

"You're about to question him about the murder of Rowan Laroche. I'd say it's a little different."

Rem put his hands on his hips and paused. "Fine. If this goes in the wrong direction, I'll excuse myself and let you talk to him, okay? But at least let me start the conversation."

Glad that Rem had at least offered to back off if needed, Daniels nodded. "Okay. Just don't let him get to you."

"I'll do my best."

They headed up the front walk to the door. Rem pulled the squeaky screen door back, knocked and waited. There was no answer, and he knocked again. "Uncle Carmine? It's Aaron. I need to talk to you."

The lock turned, and an older woman opened the door. She wore a flowery house dress with a blue apron tied around her waist. Her graying hair was up in a messy bun and wavy tendrils hung in her face. She smoothed them back and smiled. "Aaron? What are you doing here?"

"Hi, Aunt Betsy. Sorry for the unexpected visit, but I need to talk to Uncle Carmine. Is he here?"

Betsy glanced at Daniels, who said hello. Rem introduced him and Betsy eyed Daniels again. "Is this an official visit?" she asked.

Rem furrowed his brow. "Why do you ask?"

Betsy didn't answer, but stepped back. "Come in."

They stepped into a small living room with a brown couch, a big TV on the wall, two worn red leather chairs, and a small coffee table. A threadbare rug covered the floor.

Daniels shut the door behind him. He could smell something good and wondered what Betsy was cooking.

Rem sniffed the air. "Is that your cherry pie in the oven?"

Betsy smiled. "You and your nose. I think you could out smell a bloodhound."

"Especially when it comes to food," said Daniels.

Betsy laughed. "You know Aaron well. You're the partner we keep hearing about?"

"I'm guessing so," said Daniels. He spoke to Rem. "Unless you've been sneaking around on me."

"One partner's enough," said Rem. "I can't imagine handling two of you."

"The feeling's mutual." Daniels looked around the house. "We're sorry to bother you, Betsy, but is Carmine here? We need to talk to him."

Her face fell, and she softened her voice. "Is this about last night?"

"What happened last night?" asked Rem.

"I'm not exactly sure." Betsy wrung her hands as if worried. "But Carmine came home so late, and he wasn't himself."

Rem glanced at Daniels. "Was he wearing a tuxedo?"

Her eyes rounded. "How did you know that?"

"It's a long story." Rem glanced down the hall. "Where is he?"

Betsy adjusted her apron. "When I saw him in that tux, I couldn't believe it. He hasn't worn that thing in years. I told him to get rid of it a long time ago. But he refused. He said he was saving it for when you and Jennifer got married."

Rem stilled and his face clouded. "I bet he couldn't wait."

Betsy put her hand on Rem's arm. "I'm sorry. I didn't mean to bring up hard memories."

"It's okay, Aunt Betsy." Rem took a deep breath. "Is Carmine in the back?"

She nodded. "He slept late this morning and woke up with a hangover. He's out on the porch, drinking some coffee."

"Did he tell you where he went last night?" asked Daniels.

"No. He wouldn't say." Betsy put her hand to her chest. "But he seemed so upset."

"Do you mind staying here while we speak to him?" asked Rem. "It's better if we talk to him alone."

She lowered her hand to her stomach. "If you think so."

"I do. Thanks." Rem started walking past a small dining table and toward the kitchen, but Betsy took his wrist and he stopped.

"If he's in trouble," she said, "you'll tell me, won't you?"

"Of course I will." Rem patted her hand. "I'm sure everything's okay, though."

"He's fragile, you know." Betsy paused. "I know after what happened with your dad that you don't think so, but he is."

Rem hesitated and Daniels wondered what was going through his friend's mind. Rem softened his tone. "Don't worry. Daniels and I won't be mean. We save that for the murderers."

Betsy chuckled slightly. "Good."

Daniels smiled at Betsy to ease her worry and prayed Rem's uncle wasn't their killer. Rem continued through the kitchen and Daniels followed. They passed a small laundry room and Rem pushed open a back door and stepped out onto a screened-in porch, although screened-in was saying a lot. Most of the screens were gone or falling apart. An older man with thin, graying, uncombed hair sat at a small table drinking a coffee. He wore pajama pants and an old sweat-stained T-shirt. When he saw Rem, he sat up and glowered. "Well, look who the cat dragged in. What are you doing here? If you wanted a piece of Betsy's pie, you should have just called."

Rem stood beside the table. "Good to see you too, Uncle Carmine."

Carmine stared at Daniels. "Who the hell is this?"

Rem introduced Daniels. "Nice to meet you, Mr. Remalla," said Daniels.

Carmine scoffed. "It's Carmine. And don't blow smoke up my ass, Detective. I know what my nephew thinks of me." He sipped some coffee and made a face. Daniels suspected Carmine had spiked his coffee with alcohol. "Ain't no love lost between us, especially after Duke died."

"Duke?" asked Daniels.

Rem put his hand on the back of a chair. "My father. Duke was his nickname growing up." He pulled out the chair and sat in it. "We didn't come here to talk about Dad. Daniels and I need to know where you were last night, Uncle Carmine."

Carmine chuckled. "That's none of your business."

"Actually it is," said Rem. "We're investigating the death of Rowan Laroche, and you were listed as a guest at his party. We saw you on video in your snug tuxedo at the unveiling of *The Crimson Tiger*." He leaned forward. "You care to explain that?"

Carmine straightened in his seat. "Where I go and what I do with my time are nobody's damn business but my own."

"Not when the host of that party is murdered," said Rem. "Everyone who was there is a suspect. That includes you." He pointed.

"Hogwash." Carmine stood. "If you think I killed Rowan Laroche, then you're stupider than I thought, and that's saying something." He shoved his chair in. "How the hell Duke ended up with a kid like you, I'll never understand." He stepped away from the table. "I'm going inside for more coffee."

Rem stood too. "Listen, Uncle Carmine, you can't hide from this any more than you can hide from sending Dad to his grave."

Carmine threw the back door open and sneered. "You always were a son-of-bitch. That's the one part you got from Duke." He stomped inside the house.

Cursing, Rem followed, but Daniels put a hand on his shoulder. "Hold on there, partner. You're officially tapped out. I'm taking over."

Rem narrowed his eyes. "No way."

"Yes way. This is no way to talk to a suspect. You're too emotional."

"Daniels—"

Daniels spoke quietly to keep their conversation private. "Listen to me. This man is pushing your buttons and you're pushing his. I get it why you're upset. How could you not? The man's an asshole, but if you think yelling at him and dredging up old wounds is going to get him to talk to us, then you need to take another interrogation class."

Rem cursed again. "I'll keep my cool."

"Until he opens his mouth again. Let me talk to him, okay? You stay quiet. If he can't get to you, he may open up. All we need to do is find out why he was at Laroche's last night."

Rem blew out a deep breath. "You realize he's drinking, don't you? There's booze in that coffee."

"I suspected as much, and he's probably adding more right now. Something tells me he drinks a lot when you're around."

Rem took a step back. "I think that has more to do with Dad. I remind Carmine of him." He paused. "And it makes him feel guilty."

Daniels deduced that much was true. "All the more reason for me to question him." He patted Rem's shoulder. "Just hang back on this one." He paused. "And I don't think Carmine's the only one feeling guilty."

Rem clenched his jaw and his shoulders slumped. "Fine. You talk to him."

Glad to have won a minor victory, Daniels pushed the back door open. "Thank you." He stepped inside and Rem followed him in. "Mr. Remalla?" No one was in the kitchen.

"In here," said Betsy.

Daniels heard what sounded like the TV come on. He walked through the kitchen and saw Carmine sitting on the couch and holding the remote. Betsy was standing beside the dining table at the side of the room.

"You two still here?" asked Carmine. "I was hoping you'd left out the back." He bumped the volume up and dropped the remote on the coffee table.

Rem's face tightened, and he opened his mouth, but Daniels shot him a look. Rem paused, made a groaning noise, and shut his mouth. He went and stood next to Betsy, who looked at Carmine with worry. "How's that pie coming along, Aunt Betsy?"

She startled as if she'd forgotten all about the pie. "Oh, it should be close to done."

"Let's go check." Rem guided her into the kitchen.

Satisfied he could talk to Carmine without interruption, Daniels sat beside him on the couch. He studied the baseball game on the screen. "Who's playing?"

"No idea," said Carmine. "I'm just biding my time until you and my nephew leave." He took a drink of coffee from his mug, which was now substantially fuller than it was before. Carmine grimaced and set the mug down.

"We'll happily get out of your hair after you answer a few questions."

Carmine glanced at him. "Am I under arrest?"

"Should you be?"

Carmine looked away with a huff. "How long have you known my nephew, Detective?"

"A long time."

"He drive you as nuts as he drives me?"

"He has his moments, but don't we all?"

"Moments are one thing. Grudges are another. He blames me, you know. For Duke's death."

Daniels sat up, wondering how to best approach this situation. Maybe it wouldn't hurt to let Carmine get a few things off his chest. "Why would he do that?"

Carmine scoffed again. "Don't play stupid. If you've known Aaron for as long as you say you have, you know why."

Daniels picked up the remote and lowered the volume enough to talk. "His father was a heavy drinker. That can be a hard on a wife and son."

Carmine gripped his mug. "Go play the violins somewhere else, Detective. Life is what it is. Getting a few drinks after work doesn't make you a demon."

"No, it doesn't. But if you've got a wife at home who's trying to hold the family together and a desperate son who wants nothing more than to have a dad that doesn't let him down, it doesn't help."

Carmine's eyes narrowed, and he studied the TV screen.

Daniels told himself to move on, but his conscience wouldn't let him. "I think you know it was way more than a few drinks after work. And something tells me Betsy would agree."

Carmine's lips tightened, and he swiveled toward Daniels. "You leave my wife out of this. Who the hell do you think you are, any-way? Coming in here and accusing me? You don't know shit about me or my family."

Daniels eased off. "That's true. It's none of my business."

"Damn straight."

"But what is my business is Rowan Laroche." Daniels rested his elbows on his knees. "Why were you at his party last night? Did you know him?"

Carmine stared at the TV. "I knew him."

When he didn't elaborate, Daniels pushed harder. "I'm going to need more than that. How did you know him?"

"I didn't kill him, if that's what you're asking. But if I knew who did, I'd buy him a beer. Rowan got what he deserved."

Daniels interlaced his fingers. "Rowan, huh? You two on a first name basis?"

Carmine shifted in his seat. "In another life and a long time ago." He drank some coffee.

"If you want me and Aaron to leave, then tell me why you were at the party."

Carmine scratched his neck. "Because Rowan invited me."

Daniels didn't know what to think. Was Carmine playing with him? "He sent you an invitation to the unveiling of *The Crimson Tiger*?" Daniels was glad Rem was in the kitchen.

Carmine snorted. "Hell, no. I hadn't seen Rowan in years. But I bumped into him on the street two days ago." He went quiet and didn't elaborate.

Daniels tried to hide his frustration. Getting Carmine to talk was as difficult as getting Rem to eat a vegetable. "Why don't we start at the beginning? When did you first meet Rowan?"

Carmine picked at a fingernail. "If I tell you this, you'll get the hell out of here and take my nephew with you?"

Daniels raised three fingers. "Scout's honor, unless you know who the murderer is."

Carmine settled back on the cushions. "I wouldn't tell you even if I knew. That person deserves a medal. Not prison."

"So start from the beginning."

Carmine hesitated but finally spoke. "We were in our twenties. Back then, I was in art school. I used to dabble with painting and did it for fun. Rowan was also a student, but he wasn't Mr. Fancy Pants back then. He worked in a retail store in a local museum, and I worked at a mechanic's shop. We used to meet up after class, go get a few drinks, and hit on women. At the time, he was saving money to open his own gallery and trying to sell his own stuff. Nobody would buy it though. I was painting for fun but didn't take it seriously. I'd finish something and stick it in storage. My dad wouldn't have thought much of his son being a painter."

Daniels thought of his own father. "I'm familiar with that."

"Hell. I didn't even tell Duke. Anyway, about a year went by and suddenly Rowan has some money. He's all excited and plans to buy a little studio. Thinks he's on his way. I asked him where he got the money, and he told me he was finally selling some pieces." He paused. "It surprised me because, to be honest, I didn't think he was all that talented. But I figured he got lucky. Then he ends up selling more and opens his studio. I'm thinking good for him and wondering if I should sell some of my work. I go to my storage unit and start looking and I realize some of my pieces are missing." Carmine clenched his jaw. "I put two and two together, go to his studio, and low and behold, one of the paintings for sale is my own. Rowan had taken it, removed my initials and added his. He was selling my work and taking the credit."

Daniels listened with surprise. Not only was he shocked that Rem's uncle was a wannabe artist and apparently a good one, but that Laroche had stolen from him. "What did you do?"

"I went after him. I found him in his office and beat the crap out of him. Someone called the police, and I got hauled off to jail. By the time I got out, Rowan had everyone convinced that I was jealous of his success and had stolen from *him*. Since nobody believed I was an artist, almost everyone believed Rowan, and those that didn't, didn't bother to defend me."

"What about that art class you took? Someone from there could have vouched for you and your work."

Carmine watched the baseball game. "I didn't make friends easily, Detective. I kept to myself and wasn't a joiner. The only reason Rowan and I hit it off is because we both liked to party and meet the ladies. Otherwise, Rowan would have been just another loser."

"So, Rowan took credit for your work and sold it without your knowledge, which bankrolled his studio. And after you beat him up, Rowan fabricated a story about you lying and stealing from him. No one believed you and Rowan got away with it?"

"That pretty much sums it up. Except that they tossed me out of the art class because they accused me of being a fraud, even though they had to know Rowan was lying. By then, though, Rowan had made friends I hadn't and was likely paying off anyone who might have talked. I changed the locks on that storage unit and didn't pick up another brush after that. I spent several years at the mechanic's shop, which eventually became my own, and I didn't see Rowan again until two days ago, when we bumped into each other on the street."

"What happened then?"

Carmine chuckled. "He acted like a saint. Said it was good to see me and that it was sad we'd drifted apart. I stood there like a damn mule, doing nothing but wanting to shove him in front of the next passing truck."

"So, you wanted to kill him?"

Carmine glanced at him. "Wanting and doing aren't the same things. I'm sure Aaron has thought of killing me a time or two."

"But you're still walking around. Laroche isn't."

"If I drop dead tomorrow, would you accuse Aaron?"

"Of course not."

He sipped some coffee. "I rest my case."

Not sure how that argument helped anything, Daniels moved on. "Rowan invited you to the party? When you bumped into him?"

Carmine nodded. "Yup. I was about to tell him to take his fancy tiger and shove it up his ass when I reconsidered. I knew he didn't really want me there, so I said yes. His face expressed exactly what I thought, but he wasn't going to rescind the invitation. I'm sure he thought I was bluffing."

"What was your plan? To show up and embarrass Rowan?"

Carmine shrugged. "I had a few ideas. But when I got there, I just hung back and watched everyone, realizing that I wasn't the only one who hated Rowan. He'd made plenty of enemies. I was just his first." He picked something off of his T-shirt and flicked it to the floor. "I walked through his fancy house and watched the unveiling. I thought about defacing the painting but changed my mind. Rowan isn't worth prison. But seeing him up there, lording over his success, knowing it was all based on lies and deceit, it made me sick. And then I realized I'd let him destroy the one thing I truly enjoyed. Maybe it would have only been a hobby, but it was a hobby that offered some meaning, and I'd let him take that from me, and that pissed me off even more." He blew out his cheeks. "I left after that. If I'd spent another second in that house, I was going to throw up." He stared at his coffee. "I stopped and had a few drinks and came home. I didn't know Rowan was dead until I heard the news this morning."

Glad that Carmine didn't appear to be a killer, Daniels sat back. "While you were there, did you see or hear anything that might give you an idea of who might have killed him?"

Carmine rubbed his thumb over the side of his mug. "Based on the conversations I overheard? Anybody there could have done it." He scratched his stomach. "And if you and Aaron are the ones who have to find the killer," he smiled, "then good luck. I'm kind of happy Aaron's on this case."

"Why?"

Carmine set his coffee mug on a side table, then picked up a framed black-and-white photo. He stared at it and handed it to Daniels. "You see that?"

Daniels took it. He saw two young men smiling with their arms over each other's shoulders. One man was obviously a much younger Carmine, and the other was almost the spitting image of Rem. He had Rem's eyes and smile, but his hair was much shorter.

"That was taken not long after Duke married Natalie. You probably know, but they had their issues with having kids."

Daniels nodded. "I heard."

"When Aaron finally came along, Duke couldn't have been prouder. He beamed like a damn school kid with a straight-A report card and showed Aaron off to strangers on the street. He loved that boy."

Daniels set the photo on the coffee table. "I'm sure he did."

"Duke was a good dad. He gave everything to Natalie and Aaron. And what did they do? Judge him at every turn. Duke couldn't do anything right. And Aaron thought he knew everything. That boy needs a dose of humility. Maybe this case will help with that." He chuckled and reached for his coffee again.

Daniels eyed the picture again and felt the stirrings of anger. He told himself to stay out of it, but even he had his limits. "You're right about one thing, Carmine. I don't know your family or what's gone on between you and Rem, but what I do know is that your nephew is the best man I know. He's courageous, wicked smart, protects the weak, is loyal to a fault and when he loves someone, he gives his whole heart."

Carmine watched the TV, but his jaw tightened, and he didn't answer.

"Something tells me he got that from Duke, even though you don't dare admit it, especially to Rem."

Carmine shot him a look. "Are you done?"

"Not quite." He stood. "That nephew that you're so condescending to has been through hell and back since he lost Jennie. He's had moments where he lost himself in a bottle of liquor, but never once has he used booze as a crutch or an excuse to stop living. He pulls himself up, puts one foot in front of the other, and keeps going no matter how hard it is or how miserable he feels." Daniels stopped to take a breath. "You can blame Rowan for taking your hobby away and you can blame Rem for Duke, but the only one responsible for your life is you, Carmine." He leaned closer and made eye contact with Carmine. "Rem doesn't blame anyone else for his problems. Maybe *you* could learn a little something from *him*."

Carmine's gaze hardened and Daniels saw the tick in Carmine's cheek. Hearing the clearing of a throat, Daniels looked over to see Rem and Betsy standing near the dining table. Rem was holding a plate with a half-eaten piece of cherry pie and Betsy had her hand over her mouth. Daniels wondered how much they'd overheard. He straightened. "How's the pie?"

Rem swallowed a bite. "It's delicious."

Carmine stood and glared at Daniels. "I don't have to listen to a—"

"Carmine," said Betsy, her voice stern. "That's enough."

Carmine shut his mouth, but Daniels could imagine the colorful retort Carmine was suppressing. "You two know where the door is." He turned and strode away, but stopped beside Rem. "And give me that pie." He took Rem's plate. "You want some? Go make your own."

Rem gaped as Carmine stomped into the kitchen and dropped the plate on the counter with a clang. Then he stomped away again, and Daniels heard the back door bang open and closed.

"I'll get you another piece," said Betsy.

Rem shook his head. "It's fine, Aunt Betsy. I had plenty." He patted his stomach. "I don't need it, anyway."

Betsy waved a hand. "You're as fit as a fiddle." She looked him over. "You could stand to gain a few."

"I'll take a raincheck," said Rem. "I know where to find you."

She glanced toward the back of the house. "Is he in trouble?"

"Not with the law, he isn't, as long as he told me the truth," said Daniels. "Tell him if he remembers anything from last night, he should get in touch."

"What did he do?" asked Betsy.

"I'll let him tell you that," said Daniels. He eyed Rem. "You ready?"

"Yeah." Rem kissed Betsy on the cheek. "Thanks for the pie. I'll see you."

She walked them to the door. "I'll bring you some brownies next time I make a batch."

"Don't tease me." Rem walked out the door with Daniels. They said their goodbyes and Betsy shut the door. Neither of them spoke until they were back in the car. "Well?" asked Rem. "Is my uncle a murderer?"

"Jackass yes. Murderer no." Daniels started the car. "I'll tell you his story on the way to our next stop."

"I heard some of what you said. I thought we were supposed to leave emotion out of it."

"I meant every word. I probably said too much, but he needed to hear it."

"Talking to Uncle Carmine is like talking to a giant brick wall. It's gonna take a big boulder to knock it down." He glanced at Daniels. "But I appreciate you trying."

"That's what friends are for." He rested his wrist on the wheel. "Sorry about the pie, though."

"It's fine." Rem waved his fingers in front of his face. "I burned the hell out of my tongue on the first bite. I could barely taste the rest."

"Can you still talk?"

"Seems so."

"Good. Where do you want to go next?"

Rem's phone rang, and he pulled it out of his pocket. "It's Lozano." He answered and spoke to their captain for a few minutes. Phoebe

Reinart's name came up and Rem nodded. "Okay," he said. "We'll head that way. Thanks." He hung up. "Guess what?"

"What?"

"Phoebe found something of interest at Laroche's while going through his inventory. She wants to talk to us about it. Says it's important." He buckled his seatbelt. "Head to Laroche's."

Daniels checked the street and pulled out into the lane. "I guess it's time to meet our new partner."

Chapter Seven

PHOEBE REINART STUDIED THE inventory list and checked off another item. Running her finger down the paper, she set her pencil down, took her glasses off, and rubbed her eyes. Taking a few minutes to rest, she sat back in the office chair, satisfied that everything listed was present in Laroche's gallery. She looked around the room, still in a state of shock that she was here. Across from her, still on its easel, was *The Crimson Tiger*, staring back at her as if contemplating his next meal.

She couldn't believe that twenty-four hours ago, she'd been considering turning in her badge. After a lousy year, she'd summoned the courage to write her resignation letter and had planned to turn it in that morning, but her captain had come in late and once he did, told her he had a new assignment for her. Phoebe had been stunned to hear the news of Rowan Laroche's death that morning, but didn't think for a second she'd be assigned to assist with the case. With the amount of media attention and Laroche's notoriety, though, they apparently needed her expertise. She guessed her mother's connections didn't hurt either, not that Phoebe was going to ask for her mom's help.

Putting her glasses back on and listening to the quiet, she studied the other pieces in the room, most of them easily recognizable. Laroche owned some remarkable works of art. His home remained a crime scene; a patrol car sat out in the driveway, and they had posted officers at the front and back of the house. Because of the media onslaught and public curiosity, the police chief had to ensure that they protected the home until private security could take over. The department could ill afford a break-in and lost art on their watch. Phoebe had to flash her badge and provide the approvals to get into the house. Now that she was here, though, she soaked it all in. Once she left, she might never return. If her mother could see her now, she'd be as shocked as Phoebe was. Not even Special Agent Karla Reinart of the FBI had seen Laroche's private collection. Few had, which is what made it so special.

She stood, walked around the desk, and walked past and admired the variety of paintings on the wall. The detectives they had assigned her to work with, Daniels and Remalla, would be there soon, and then it would be all business. According to her captain, the detectives needed her knowledge of the art world and the players in it. Her role would be to assist as needed. She wasn't sure what that would entail, but she'd find out soon enough. She just hoped Daniels and Remalla weren't a couple of know-it-alls who saw this case just like any other and bull-dozed through it with the finesse of a bucking bull. Having worked with detectives like that before, Phoebe knew if she complained, they could make it a miserable experience. Her mother had told her many times to deal with it, though. As a woman in a male-dominated job, it came with the territory.

She thought of her partner, Thomas Barry, who was currently on a leave of absence from work. Stopping in front of a striking watercolor entitled *Seascape*, she debated calling him, but just as quickly admonished herself. That was the last thing she should do, but her heart thudded at the thought of talking to him.

She finished her walk through the room and stopped in front of *The Crimson Tiger*, still in awe of it. When the news had leaked that Laroche had purchased the painting before it could go to auction, the art world had been abuzz, but Phoebe had not been surprised. The business side of art could be every bit as unsavory and conniving as any other business, and many knew of Laroche and his mastery at manipulation. She often wondered why he was so popular with his peers, but supposed it was like anyone else noteworthy. Fame and wealth attracted friendships like flowers attracted bees. It was as natural as nature.

Studying the tiger's face, she admired its eyes. They stared back with an intensity that surprised her. For a moment, she wondered if the painting could actually be cursed. Could the tiger see into her mind, read her thoughts, and arrange for her untimely death? Lost in the gaze, Phoebe shivered but blinked, shaking off the strange sensations. It was an amusing story that got a lot of clicks, but it was still just a story.

Hearing voices outside the door, she guessed Daniels and Remalla had arrived. She straightened her jacket, smoothed her hair back and tightened her ponytail, ran her fingertips over her turtleneck to pull it up, and pushed her glasses up on her nose, trying to look authoritative. Her mother had taught her that first impressions were the most important, so she flattened her expression and put her hands on her hips. Feeling foolish though, she crossed her arms instead, then dropped them to her sides.

The gallery door opened, and two men walked in, looking like opposites. Other than their similar heights, one was blond with short gelled-back hair and the other had long black-hair, tied back with a band. The blond wore pressed pants with a long-sleeved shirt and the other looked like he'd thrown on the first thing he'd found in a pile of wrinkled clothes. She didn't miss the fact that they were both handsome, though, and maintained healthy physiques. The blond wore a wedding ring, but his partner didn't.

Seeing her, the blond approached. "You must be Phoebe Reinart." He held out his hand. "I'm Detective Gordon Daniels."

She shook his hand. "Nice to meet you."

"And this is my partner, Aaron Remalla."

"Hey," said Remalla. "Nice to meet you."

She shook his hand as well. "Same."

"We hear you're the art expert," said Daniels.

"I know a few things," said Phoebe. "I hope I can help."

"You're familiar with Rowan Laroche and his collection?" asked Remalla.

"Anyone who's anybody in the art world knows about Laroche and his collection." She gestured at the walls. "Most collectors would give their left arm to be standing where we're standing."

Remalla did a circle and eyed the art. "Seems a little extreme if you ask me."

"That's because you don't have a discerning eye," said Daniels.

Remalla raised a brow at him. "Who's the one that caught Joey Quick Fingers lift that guy's wallet?"

"That's not the discernment I'm talking about." Daniels gestured toward *The Crimson Tiger*. "If you'd seen this painting in a gallery, what would you have thought?"

Remalla tipped his head at the painting. "Nice kitty?"

Daniels pursed his lips. "How much would you have offered to pay for it?"

"Fifty bucks, tops."

"I rest my case," said Daniels.

Remalla sighed. "Why would I buy a cursed painting that doesn't match a thing in my house?"

"Nothing matches in your house. Why would this be any different?"

Remalla smirked and spoke to Phoebe. "I promise. He's not always this bad."

Daniels rolled his eyes. "I could say the same."

Watching the interaction between the two detectives, Phoebe didn't know what to think. Were they always like this? Or was this some sort of test? "Would you like to go through the inventory? I can show you what I've done so far."

"Sure. Why not?" said Remalla. "Let's see what you got."

She walked to the desk and picked up the sheet with the list of Laroche's items. "My captain sent me this, and from what I can tell, nothing's missing." She went through the list and pointed out various art in the room.

"That's something, at least," said Daniels. "Robbery wasn't the motive."

Remalla leaned back against Laroche's desk. "Then what was? Revenge?"

"Considering the suspects, it's definitely possible." Daniels spoke to Phoebe. "What do you think?"

Surprised he'd asked her, Phoebe hesitated. As they waited for an answer, she gathered her thoughts. "Well, considering what I know about Rowan Laroche, revenge wouldn't surprise me at all. Who are your suspects?"

Daniels pulled a small notebook from his jacket pocket and flipped it open. He read through a list of names and told her a staff member named Dominique, who'd worked during the party, had provided the chief suspects.

"We've got teams checking the entire staff and guest lists though," said Remalla. "No one is excluded until they're ruled out."

Phoebe pointed at a name on the list. "Is that Phillip Hendrix?"

Daniels eyed the paper. "Yes. He wasn't on Dominique's list, but we spoke to him last night, or should I say this morning. He was one of the guests who stuck around."

Phoebe imagined meeting him. "Wow. He's a big deal."

Rem glanced at the name. "Don't tell me. He's famous?"

"He's one of the most successful mainstream artists to date. Think Thomas Kincaid in the nineties."

"That's him?" asked Daniels. "My mother has a print of his in her bathroom. I didn't know he was that Hendrix."

"He's mostly known for his eclectic style of landscapes. Think Georgia O'Keefe with a touch of Picasso." Phoebe ran her fingers over her turtleneck. "It doesn't hurt that he's movie-star-handsome either."

"Sounds like you're a fan," said Remalla.

"From afar," she said. "As most are. I like his lesser-known pieces more, though. He paints with intense colors and light. His work can stir a lot of emotion."

"Never heard of him," said Remalla.

"How does he know Laroche?" asked Daniels.

"Laroche was largely responsible for Hendrix's career. Laroche invested money into Hendrix when no one knew his name, and in return, Hendrix only displayed his work in Laroche galleries. As Hendrix's fame grew, the two had a falling out. Most think it was because of Hendrix's drinking. He went to rehab though, and he and Laroche mended fences." Phoebe looked around the gallery. "I'm actually surprised there isn't a Hendrix piece in here."

"Probably because there isn't enough room," said Rem.

"I'd be surprised if he's involved. Never say never though," said Phoebe.

"He arrived late and almost missed the tiger," said Daniels, "but that doesn't mean he's innocent."

"You've confirmed Laroche died from poison?" asked Phoebe.

"Hundred percent," added Remalla. "Someone doctored his drink. And it wasn't pretty either. Laroche's last breaths weren't pleasant ones."

"He died after the unveiling," said Daniels. "Over here." He pointed at the floor beside the desk. "Dominique found him."

Phoebe hadn't stopped to consider that Laroche's last moments had been in that room. "At least he died looking at his new painting."

Remalla scratched his jaw. "Somehow, I think that was the last thing on his mind."

"Maybe that's what the killer wanted," said Phoebe. "For Laroche to see what he was losing."

Daniels eyed *The Crimson Tiger*. "That's a good point. Laroche purchasing and displaying that tiger may have been the straw that broke the killer's back."

"Well, since it's cursed," said Remalla. "Maybe it gave Laroche the evil eye."

Impressed by how far they'd come in a short period, Phoebe glanced back at the list of names. "Based on your list of suspects, I'm more inclined to believe one of them did it."

"Me too," said Daniels. He lifted his notebook. "Anyone stand out based on what you know?"

Pleased they seemed happy to incorporate her into the team, she nodded. "Right off the bat, there's Evelyn Sinclair. She's a major art dealer and gallery owner with plenty of clout. She and her gallery manager, James, have made a dent in the art world and she has an impressive collection of her own. I can imagine she had plans to purchase the tiger at auction. She and Rowan have been rivals for years."

"What about that Roger guy?" Remalla asked Daniels. "What's his last name?"

"Roger Deveaux," said Phoebe. "He's a possibility. Laroche and Devaux have always been at odds. One was always trying to outdo the other, and Laroche usually won. Roger would have hated that Rowan purchased the tiger."

"What about Rowan's daughter, Victoria? You know anything about her?" asked Daniels.

Phoebe thought back to what she knew about the daughter. "Not much, unfortunately. She didn't follow her dad's footsteps into the art world. From what I've heard, they didn't like each other very much."

"We've heard the same," said Remalla. "Apparently, she's written a revealing exposé on her dad. We're wondering if that has something to do with Laroche's death."

"I can do some digging on that," said Phoebe.

"You heard of the Vespuccis?" asked Daniels. "Carlo and Isabella?"

Phoebe nodded, recalling the gossip surrounding Laroche and his love life. "I have. Isabella's family is no slouch in the art world. Her grandfather is Enrico Rimaldi, who's famous in Italy for his oil paintings, and her aunt is Sophia Rimaldi, who's gaining popularity as well with her sculptures. Isabella and Rowan were an item for a few years, but it didn't end well. Not long after their breakup, Isabella married Carlo Vespucci in a surprise wedding. People speculated she only married him to make Rowan jealous."

Rem frowned. "That's a great reason to get married."

"What's worse is six months later, Isabella gave birth to a son, Mateo. The gossip was rampant that he was Rowan's child." Phoebe sighed. "That's plenty of motive for Carlo, if that's true."

Daniels' eyes widened. "That's good to know."

"Jeez," said Remalla. "No wonder Victoria was writing an exposé."

"That leaves Maria Rossi, former actress." Daniels glanced at Remalla. "And future Mrs. Remalla."

Rem snorted. "If only."

Daniels closed his notebook. "We hear she's another old flame of Laroche's, but based on our initial observations, she doesn't strike me as a killer. Although she and Laroche had a nasty breakup too. But that was a long time ago."

"It was," said Phoebe. "But it doesn't mean she can't hold a grudge. Rowan got another woman pregnant with Victoria while he and Maria were together. And she gave up her acting career for him."

"That's definitely a crime," said Remalla. "That lady had some acting chops."

"She didn't look bad in a bikini either, did she?" asked Daniels.

Remalla smiled. "Not at all."

"She came to his party," said Daniels. "Based on what she told us, she and Laroche were on good terms despite their history. Plus, she seemed to be close to Victoria, which is also odd."

"I wonder how Victoria's mother fits into all of this?" asked Rem.

Phoebe tapped her jaw. "I'll have to double-check my recollection, but her mother was a bit of a mess and used Victoria to get back at Rowan. Victoria grew up just as screwed up as her mom and dad."

"Maybe that's why Maria and Victoria are close," said Daniels. "Maria may have been the only stable figure in Victoria's life."

"Why would you befriend the child of the woman your significant other slept with?" asked Rem. "That seems unlikely."

"It's a good question to ask both Maria and Victoria," said Phoebe. "But before you label Maria Rossi as a forgiving ex and kind-hearted benefactor, there's something you should see." Phoebe gestured toward the far wall.

"Our captain mentioned you found something interesting." Daniels tucked his notepad into his pocket. "What is it?"

Phoebe walked to a far wall near a window with thick, partially closed curtains. "I caught it during the inventory." She stopped in front of a long narrow painting near the window. Delicate brush-strokes combined with heavy swirls of vibrant colors of red, orange and blue moved in circles and arches all over the canvas. To Phoebe, it looked like it was a portrait of the sky aflame. "You see this? It's called *Fury and Fire*. It's by an artist named Toby LaRue. Not that well-known nowadays but, in his heyday, he was a big deal. He was a recluse, though, and never showed his face. Sort of like Banksy today."

"Who?" asked Rem.

"I'll tell you later," said Daniels.

Phoebe pushed her glasses up her nose. "Rowan discovered LaRue and made him famous during a difficult time when the economy was down, and Rowan had made a few risky investments. He needed cash. Selling a couple of LaRues kept him afloat. When LaRue died, the value of his paintings jumped significantly. Laroche had this piece and two others in his public gallery downtown."

Rem pointed at the painting. "How much is this thing worth?"

Phoebe crossed her arms. "I'd say just shy of eighty grand."

Rem dropped his jaw. "This thing?"

"This thing," repeated Phoebe.

"Hell," said Remalla. "I'm in the wrong line of work."

"I don't think your popsicle figurines would generate that kind of cash," said Daniels.

Remalla made a face at him.

"Why is this painting interesting?" asked Daniels, stepping closer to the painting to observe it.

"Check out the bottom right corner." Phoebe pushed back the curtain. "This curtain was partially obscuring it. I pulled it back, and that's when I noticed it."

Daniels squatted. "What am I looking at?"

Remalla got closer and leaned over. He squinted. "Are those initials?"

"They are," said Phoebe.

"They're pretty faint," said Daniels. He stared for a second and frowned. "You said this is by Toby LaRue?"

Phoebe nodded. "I did."

Rem squinted some more. "But that's not a T.L."

"That looks like M.R.," said Daniels.

"Exactly," said Phoebe. "As in Maria Rossi."

Remalla straightened and Daniels gaped. He stood and eyed the painting. "What are you saying? That Maria Rossi painted this?"

"And Laroche claimed it was by another artist, took the money and the credit?" Remalla glanced at Daniels.

Knowing the rumors about Laroche, Phoebe took the leap that her theory was correct. "That's exactly what I'm saying. And if I'm right, then that, Detectives, is plenty of motive."

· · · • · • · · · ·

Rem looked again at the painting and the initials. "If that's true, why didn't Maria say something at the time?"

"It's possible she may not have known," said Phoebe. "She was an actress and an artist, but she never went public with her artwork until years after she and Laroche broke up."

"You're talking like this isn't a surprise to you," said Daniels. "Was Laroche known for this? Taking credit for others' talent?"

"I've heard accusations of it. Years ago. An artist that Laroche had mentored claimed Laroche had taken one of his paintings and sold it under a false name and taken the money. Laroche said it was a big misunderstanding and paid the friend back. I don't remember the man's name, but he never said another word about it. The speculation was that Laroche not only paid his friend for the painting but also to keep his mouth shut."

"Where is this guy now?" asked Rem.

"Dead," said Phoebe. "Drug overdose. He had a history of abuse, which is why I think Laroche got away with what he supposedly did. It was hard to take the word of an addict over Laroche's credentials."

Rem thought of Carmine. "Looks like my uncle's story is making more and more sense."

"Your uncle?" asked Phoebe.

Rem told her about his uncle's history with Laroche and that he was a guest at the party, and unfortunately, a potential suspect.

"Then he's definitely got motive, too." Phoebe crossed her arms. "You think he could do this?"

"I know how it looks," said Rem, "but no, I don't. That poison was a sophisticated concoction designed to kill. My uncle has the sophistication of a drunk man in a bar fight. Plus, he didn't even know he was going to the party until two days prior. It's not a lot of time to plan a murder like this."

"What if someone gave him the poison?" asked Phoebe. "And told him to drop it into Laroche's drink? Would your uncle have done it?"

Rem's belly clenched at the thought. "I doubt that's what happened." He met Daniels' gaze. "Who would trust a newcomer dressed in a tux a size too small to poison Laroche and then expect him not to talk after Laroche winds up dead?"

"Money talks, Detective." Phoebe looked around the gallery. "As you can see, the art world has plenty of it. Have you checked your uncle's bank account?"

Rem didn't like her implication. "My uncle didn't kill Laroche."

"But can you be sure?" she asked.

Rem set his jaw, not sure whether to be mad.

"She's got a point, partner," said Daniels. "Not that I think Carmine did it, but just like any other suspect, we need to be certain."

Considering his relationship with his uncle, Rem didn't know why he cared, but even after their earlier altercation, Carmine was still family. "Fine, but I think one of our other suspects is a more likely choice."

"I tend to agree," said Phoebe. She stepped toward the painting with the suspicious initials. "The only way to be sure about this is to bring in an expert and have him look at it, plus look at other paintings of Laroche's. It needs to be confirmed by someone other than me."

"If this is Maria's painting, then why hasn't she said anything after all these years?" asked Daniels. "Even if she didn't know initially, she must know now."

"That's another important question for Maria," said Phoebe. "And if Rowan defrauded her and Remalla's uncle, then who else did Laroche defraud?"

"What about Isabella?" asked Daniels. "Is she an artist?"

"Not to my knowledge, but Isabella is a more recent flame," said Phoebe. "Rowan's success and affluence were well entrenched when they got together. He would have had no reason to steal anyone's work."

Rem shook off his concern about Carmine. "So the theory is when Rowan broke up with Isabella, she married Carlo Vespucci, a mobster, to get back at Laroche?"

"He's a mobster?" asked Phoebe.

"Haven't you heard of the Vespucci crime family?" asked Daniels.

"I have, but there's bound to be more than one Vespucci family in town." Phoebe ran her fingers under her turtleneck. "But if Carlo is a mobster, then that makes this even more interesting." She shook her head. "I wouldn't want to be the person who asks Carlo if he thinks his son's father is Rowan Laroche."

"I'll leave that to Rem," said Daniels.

Rem narrowed his eyes. "You'll be right beside me, sport."

"Says who?" asked Daniels. "My plan is to talk to Maria Rossi. Ask her about that bikini."

Rem chuckled sarcastically. Phoebe looked as if she didn't know what to think about either of them. "Are those all your main suspects?" she asked.

"There's another." Rem recalled Robert. "Our security expert, Robert. The whole reason we don't know who our murderer is, is because someone tampered with the video footage of the unveiling, and Robert swears it wasn't him. Until we verify it wasn't, he's on the list. Plus, he had an argument with Laroche the night of the murder."

"That's a lot of people to talk to." Phoebe scratched her head. "There's something else to consider, though."

"What's that?" asked Daniels.

Phoebe walked back over to *The Crimson Tiger*. "This," she said.

Rem followed Daniels back to the painting.

"Why this?" asked Daniels.

Phoebe took off tortoiseshell glasses, blew on one lens, and put them back on. Rem noticed the faint smattering of freckles dusting her nose and cheeks, and an image of Jennie flashed in his mind. She'd had similar freckles, and the memory took his breath away. Trying to stay focused as his emotions swirled and grief flared, he closed his eyes, and 'sat with it' as his therapist had taught him. A second passed, and he collected himself. It always surprised him how the smallest detail could hit him at the most unexpected times.

Hearing Phoebe talking, Rem opened his eyes and saw Daniels staring at him with a knowing look. After two years of hell, his partner knew when he was having a moment. Rem took another breath and nodded at his partner to show he was fine.

Daniels eyed Phoebe. "Sorry. Can you repeat that?"

She stopped and looked between them again.

"The tiger's eyes distracted me," said Rem. "It looks like he's hungry." His emotions still swirled, but he had it under control. Phoebe and her insights were proving to be a helpful distraction.

"They're intense," said Phoebe. "The whole painting has a vibe, don't you think?"

"That probably doesn't help with the whole curse thing, does it?" asked Rem.

"No, it doesn't." Phoebe studied the painting. "Do you two believe in the supernatural?"

Rem made eye contact with Daniels again, recalling their interactions with Jacobs and her siblings, plus a few other unexpected encounters in previous investigations.

"If you were asking anybody else," said Daniels, "they'd be laughing at you."

"You're working with two detectives who've had a little experience with the unexpected." Rem let go of a long sigh.

"A little?" asked Daniels.

Phoebe narrowed her eyes. "You two putting me on? It's fine if you want to laugh at me."

"We're not laughing," said Rem. "What's your point? You think this tiger is actually killing its owners?"

"Haven't you heard of the Hope Diamond or King Tut's curse?" asked Phoebe.

"Sure," said Daniels, "but I don't think there's proof that either of those things killed anyone."

"It's not about proof, Detectives. It's about belief." Phoebe stepped closer to the painting.

Rem stepped closer too. "Unless this tiger stepped out of this frame and added poison to Laroche's drink with his paw, I think the curse is a moot point."

Phoebe grabbed a heart pendant that hung from a delicate gold chain around her neck and slid it along the chain. "Maybe so, but what if someone wanted to perpetuate the story? It's hard to call this cursed if an owner keeps on living."

"Laroche didn't own it for long," said Daniels. "Who was in such a big hurry to confirm the curse?"

"Whoever else wanted *The Crimson Tiger* for themselves," said Phoebe. "Think about it. If Laroche dies, what happens to this painting?"

Rem frowned. "It goes to whoever Laroche left his fortune to."

"We don't know who that is yet," said Daniels.

Phoebe stepped back and leaned against Laroche's desk. "Would you want to own this thing after every other owner has died?"

"You think someone killed Laroche to perpetuate the curse?" asked Daniels. "And encourage whoever gets it next to sell it?"

"Which would allow our killer to snap it up at a lower price?" asked Rem.

Phoebe tapped her lip with a fingertip. "It's something to consider."

"That's a hell of a motive." Daniels eyed the painting again. "What exactly is the history of this thing?"

"The artist is Dru Dunberry," said Phoebe.

Rem eyed the initials in the painting's corner. "I see a DD, so that's a good sign."

"Dunberry was eccentric," said Phoebe. "He painted in many styles and various techniques. Some of his work was terrible, but not all of it. He made a name for himself after doing a series of sketches featuring a water hose."

Rem wasn't sure he heard right. "A water hose? Are you joking?"

"I'm not. They were not your typical sketches, though. Let's just say they were highly erotic."

Daniels furrowed his brow. "I'm afraid to ask."

"It's better you don't. At the time, they were scandalous, but they drew a lot of attention when he exhibited them. He eventually sold them to a wealthy collector from Europe for an undisclosed amount. Not long after, Dunberry introduced *The Crimson Tiger*. There wasn't much interest at first. People were more curious about the erotic stuff. But eventually, interest grew because Dunberry wouldn't sell it. Plenty of galleries displayed it and Dunberry's other works, but no matter what anyone offered, Dunberry refused to let go of the tiger."

"Why did anyone care?" asked Rem.

"Because the offers got so big," said Phoebe. "Collectors were offering tens of thousands of dollars, but Dunberry refused. People wondered why. What was so special about the painting? The more word spread, the more people wanted to see it."

"The art world is strange," said Rem.

"It is." Phoebe crossed her arms. "Interest would have likely waned, but Dunberry died of a heart attack when he was forty-two. He dropped dead at an exhibit right in front of the tiger."

"You're kidding," said Daniels.

"No. I'm not. After that, the tiger went up for auction to pay off Dunberry's debt. Finally, collectors got the chance to purchase the painting. It sold for a ridiculous amount of money. The new owner was a collector named Stephan Fry. He held on to the tiger for two years before he died in a car accident on his fifty-sixth birthday."

"Jeez," said Rem.

"Where'd the painting go next?" asked Daniels.

"To Fry's ex-wife, Daniella. They'd divorced, but Fry hadn't changed his will. She took it and hung it over her fireplace mantel, thinking she'd bested her ex by inheriting the piece, until eight months later, when she fell and hit her head on the edge of that same brick fireplace. She died a week later from a brain hemorrhage."

Rem dropped his jaw. "Holy shit."

"No kidding," said Phoebe. "After that, the curse rumors gained steam for good reason. After Daniella's death, her daughter Jane inherited the painting, but she didn't want it because she believed it had something to do with her parents' deaths. She wanted it gone and immediately put it up for auction. That's when Rowan Laroche stepped in, and you know the rest."

"That's a bizarre story," said Daniels. "But now that I hear it, I can see why people think it's cursed."

Rem admired Phoebe's knowledge and recall. "How do you remember all of that? It's a lot of detail."

Phoebe shrugged. "I'm lucky to have a good memory. Plus, I did a little online searching before you guys got here. I needed to brush up on Laroche and his personal life, plus the painting's background. If we're going to find a killer, we're going to have to be familiar with both."

Rem noted how she used the word *we*. "To be honest, I wasn't sure how this collaboration would work, but now that you're here, I'm glad. Your insight is going to help a lot. I'm a fish out of water with this stuff." He gestured at the paintings in the room.

"He's much more knowledgeable when it comes to food," said Daniels.

"You ever have a Taco del Fuego?" asked Rem.

Daniels groaned.

"Can't say that I have," said Phoebe.

Rem glanced at his watch. "Well, you're in for a treat. How about taking a break from all this art education and get a bite? I'm buying."

"I don't think treat is the right word," said Daniels. "More like indigestion. And you just had a sandwich at the station."

"That was a couple of hours ago. And if you want my brain at its best, I need to eat. Uncle Carmine and this curse stuff are making me hungry."

Daniels sighed. "What do you think, Reinart? You up for a bellyache and an antacid later?"

Phoebe hesitated. "You sure? I could head to the station and get settled in. I can start looking for an expert to verify *Fury and Flame*, plus dig into our suspects' backgrounds."

"*Fury and Flame* isn't going anywhere, and neither is our scary tiger here." Rem pointed toward the painting. "Grab your stuff and let's go. While we're eating, Daniels can catch you up on everything else because, knowing him, he'll just have a glass of water."

Phoebe straightened. "I...well...okay." She seemed flustered, but walked around the desk and gathered her notes and picked up her purse. "I guess I could eat."

"Don't forget," said Daniels. "I warned you. I think owning *The Crimson Tiger* would be safer."

His mouth already watering, Rem headed to the door. "I don't know what you were thinking when you got this assignment, Reinart, but I bet it wasn't this."

Phoebe shook her head and seemed a little wistful, but she smiled softly. "No. It wasn't. To be honest, I...," she set her jaw, "...well, never mind. It doesn't matter."

Rem wondered what she was about to say. He reached the gallery door and pulled it open. "Taco del Fuegos, here we come."

Chapter Eight

DANIELS HUNG UP HIS phone, and carrying his bottled water, walked over to the outdoor table. He sat with Rem and Reinart. As usual, the Taco del Fuego food truck was doing a brisk business and Daniels still wondered how that was possible.

Rem took a big bite of his taco and spoke through a mouthful of food. "Who was that?"

"Forensics," replied Daniels. "Laroche's champagne glass had his fingerprints on it, along with Dominique's."

Reinart chewed a bite and swallowed. "That's the staff member who found him?"

Rem nodded. "It is." He licked a smear of sauce off his finger. "But she served the drinks at the unveiling, so that's not unexpected."

"Still," said Reinart. "That shows opportunity."

Daniels uncapped his water bottle. "Other than Robert, all our suspects were in that room and any of them could have poisoned Laroche's drink. They all had opportunity." He sipped some water and grimaced when Rem took another bite and the sauce oozed out of the taco and splattered on his paper plate. Daniels glanced at Reinart, who seemed to enjoy her own taco. She'd limited herself to one, though, while Rem was devouring his third. "How is it?" he asked her. "Have the stomach cramps hit yet?"

Rem frowned and Reinart chuckled. "It's not bad. I can see why they're popular. It's great comfort food."

"See?" Rem said to Daniels. He drank some soda. "Too bad we can't have a beer."

"We can save the beer for when we find our killer," said Daniels. "It'll be worth celebrating." He waved at a fly that buzzed near the table.

"So, who's our next stop?" asked Rem, after swallowing a bite. "You two have a preference?"

"I say Robert," said Daniels. "Personally, I don't think his story adds up. How did someone delete the video footage without him knowing, and why was he arguing with Laroche before the party?"

Rem licked another finger. "I think Maria should be next. I want to know why she didn't call out Laroche for his crimes if he really stole her work." He took another bite and smiled. "And maybe get an autograph." He chewed. "What do you think, Reinart?" he said through another mouthful.

Reinart wiped her messy fingers on a napkin. "I'm thinking Evelyn Sinclair. I know Roger was always trying to best Laroche, but the rivalry between Evelyn and Rowan was legendary, and she wanted that *Crimson Tiger*. I wonder if she would murder Laroche to get it."

"All good places to start," said Daniels. "You want to flip a coin?"

Rem swallowed and took the last bite of his taco. "How about the next person a fly lands on wins?"

Daniels slumped his shoulders. "Only you would suggest that." He waved at another fly. "But based on the number of them, somebody should be victorious soon."

"If you'd stop swatting at them, you might get lucky." Rem grinned.

Daniels sighed. "If it means we can get out of here, I'll refrain."

Reinart sipped some iced tea. "How long have you two been partners?"

Daniels shook his head. "Way too long."

"Tell me about it," said Rem. He crumpled the wrapper from his tacos and tossed it on his plate.

"I can imagine you have some stories to tell," replied Reinart.

"More than you can count on your fingers and toes," said Rem. "What about you? How's life over on the south side? We heard your partner is on sabbatical."

Reinart tensed and gripped her cup. "He is." She paused. "He's got some family issues and needed to take time off."

"I hope everything's okay," said Rem.

Reinart nodded, but eyed her drink. "It is. It's fine."

The tone of her voice told Daniels that all was not fine. "How long have you two worked together?"

Reinart looked up. "Not long. Almost two years."

Rem rested his forearms on the table. "We hear your mom is some FBI big shot. She works in the FBI's Art Crime Division?"

"She leads it, actually." Reinart fidgeted with the edge of her turtle-neck.

"Really?" asked Daniels. "That should come in handy with a case like this."

Reinart shrugged. "I suppose."

Rem studied her and Daniels could see his partner's wheels turning. "Does she even know you're working on this case?" asked Rem.

Reinart shook her head. "No."

"The plot thickens," said Rem.

"You plan to follow in Mom's footsteps?" asked Daniels.

"Based on what we've seen so far, you're certainly capable," added Rem.

"I've considered it, but..." Reinart paused. "I don't know. My mother and I have a complicated relationship."

"We understand how that goes," said Rem. He tilted his head toward Daniels. "Only we have dad issues." He pulled another napkin from the holder and wiped a smear of sauce from the tabletop. "Where's your dad? He still in the picture?"

"My parents divorced when I was a teenager," said Phoebe. "Dad remarried and had a couple of other kids. He lives in Phoenix."

"How'd you end up in San Diego?" asked Daniels.

"I was raised in LA while Mom rose in the ranks of the FBI. I moved here when I joined law enforcement. Mom's in New York now."

"You could have joined the FBI right off the bat," said Rem. "Why didn't you? It seems like you had an easy in."

"That's exactly why I didn't do it." Reinart waved at a fly that landed on her paper plate. "I felt like I needed to prove myself. Mom wasn't thrilled. Said I was wasting my talents working for a city PD."

Rem scoffed. "Well, that's insulting."

"I thought so too." Reinart shifted on the bench. "I've learned a lot as a cop." She stared off.

Daniels glanced at Rem, who lifted his brow. "Is that a good or a bad thing?" Daniels asked her.

Reinart smoothed back a loose strand of hair that had escaped from her ponytail. "I'm not sure I'm a good fit for law enforcement."

Rem furrowed his brow. "You seem to do just fine."

"You've known me less than three hours," said Reinart.

"You do this job long enough and you sense things," said Daniels. He wondered about her lack of confidence and where it stemmed from. "Rem would have never suggested bringing you here if we hadn't given you a thumbs up. Believe it or not, this is sacred ground."

Rem pointed. "Only those considered worthy are allowed at the Taco del Fuego food truck."

She smiled softly. "Have you seen the people in line? I don't think that bar is set very high."

"I didn't invite those people," said Rem.

Reinart set her crumpled napkin on her plate. "I appreciate it. I get a good sense about you guys too. But not everyone's lucky enough to have a partnership like yours. Barry and I, we've had some difficulties, and I've done some stupid things..."

Daniels pursed his lips. "You do this job long enough and you'll make plenty of mistakes."

"He's right," said Rem. "This job requires sacrifices. And just because you've bumped heads with your current partner doesn't mean you can't find a new one or make it work with Barry."

Daniels recapped his water when a fly almost landed on the edge of the open bottle. "And if you really want to join the FBI, don't let your mother intimidate you. Just because she's a bigwig doesn't mean you can't find your way. But if the FBI isn't for you, then don't let her pressure you, either."

Reinart shifted again. "I didn't expect all the helpful advice."

"That's all it is. Advice," said Rem. "You can take it or leave it. But sometimes it helps to get another opinion. Daniels and I are good at that. He tells me what to do all the time."

Daniels snorted. "And he does the exact opposite."

Rem's eyes widened at Reinart. "Looks like Evelyn Sinclair wins. A fly just landed on your shoulder, Reinart." He smiled at Daniels. "Sorry, sport. You lose."

"I'll live," said Daniels.

Reinart waved the fly away. "I don't know if I should be happy or not."

Rem picked up his plate. "Take the victory, Reinart. You don't get 'em often in this line of work." He stood and tossed his plate into a nearby trashcan when his phone rang. He pulled out his cell. "It's Lozano." He answered. "Hey, Cap. What's shakin'?"

Daniels picked up Reinart's dirty plate. "He's right, you know. Celebrate your victories." He tossed her plate in the trash.

"I have a hard time celebrating," said Reinart. "I tend to be naturally pessimistic."

"It's hard not to be in this line of work," said Daniels. "But if you don't make the effort, this job will kill you before old age does. Something to consider if you stay in law enforcement."

"Believe me. I hear you." She rubbed her neck again.

Rem hung up his phone with a sigh. "Sorry to rip the thrill of victory from your clutches, Reinart, but Evelyn Sinclair will have to wait." He slid his phone back into his pocket.

"Why? What happened?" asked Daniels.

Rem picked up his soda cup and tossed it. "Isabella Vespucci just shot her husband, Carlo."

Reinart dropped her jaw. "Is he alive?"

"Isabella's in custody, and Carlo has a bullet in his shoulder." Rem pulled out his car keys. "Care to take a ride to the hospital?"

· · • • • · • • · · ·

Daniels heard a booming male voice from the hallway and commented. "I think we found Carlo."

They'd arrived at the hospital to a bustle of activity. A city bus had overturned and there was a steady stream of arriving patients, most of whom were not seriously injured, but the ER was busy. They'd finally tracked down a nurse who told them where to find Carlo. On their way to his room, they found an officer sitting in a chair in the hallway. After speaking to him, they learned an ambulance had brought in Carlo, but his injury wasn't severe. He would require surgery and was waiting to be brought upstairs, but with the bus accident, his condition had taken a back seat, and Carlo wasn't a patient man.

The officer pointed out Carlo's room, and they heard Carlo complaining as they stopped outside a pulled curtain. "This should be fun."

Rem peeked behind the curtain, reached up and pulled it back. A nurse was standing beside the bed, checking the IV, and Carlo looked around her.

"Who the hell are you?" he asked. "Ever heard of privacy?" He wore a hospital gown, his heavily bandaged shoulder was visible, and a sheet was pulled up to his waist.

Daniels caught the nurse rolling her eyes.

"Remember us?" asked Rem, holding up his badge. "From Rowan Laroche's party? We talked to you and your wife before you left this morning."

Carlo eyed Daniels and Reinart, who also raised their badges.

"Oh, you guys." Carlo fell back in his bed. "Fred and Barney." He sneered at Reinart. "Who's this? Wilma or Betty?"

"Try Phoebe," said Reinart. "But you can call me Detective Reinart."

They approached the bed. "How is he?" Daniels asked the nurse.

She tapped something on a tablet and stepped away. "Unfortunately, he's conscious."

Carlo sneered at her, too. "If you people would get your act together, I could get this bullet out of my shoulder. At this rate, I'll die from an infection or gangrene."

"If only," the nurse muttered under her breath.

"What?" asked Carlo.

"I said I'll be back when they're ready to take you up." She reached for the curtain. "Have a nice chat." She closed the curtain abruptly.

"Since when do nurses cop an attitude?" asked Carlo. "I'm the patient here." He pointed at himself.

"Obviously you're a lousy one," said Rem. "Maybe if you lightened up a little."

Carlo scowled. "Who the hell are you to tell me what to do? Mind your business."

"I'd be happy to," said Rem, "but your wife shot you, so that sort of makes it our business."

Carlo snorted. "It's a flesh wound. No big deal."

"Based on your bitching, it sounds way worse than that," said Daniels.

"If you guys came down here just because of this," he gestured at his shoulder, "you've wasted your time. I'm not pressing charges against my wife. We got into an argument. Shit happens."

"What were you arguing about?" asked Reinart.

Carlo studied Reinart. "Since when does it take three of you to talk to someone?" He looked Reinart up and down and smiled. "You could do better things with your time, sweetheart."

"She asked you a question," said Daniels.

"I suspect you call a lot of women sweetheart," added Reinart. "Most men with colossal egos do. Is that what you and your wife were arguing about?" Reinart crossed her arms. "Or was it about Rowan Laroche?"

Carlo narrowed his eyes. "What the hell does that mean?"

"Do we need cue cards?" asked Rem. "We want to know if this incident has anything to do with Laroche's murder. If your wife can shoot you, could she kill Laroche?"

Carlo laughed. "My wife? Isabella? Kill Laroche?" He laughed harder and held his stomach. "You guys ever consider going into comedy?"

"Tempting," said Rem, "but somebody's got to catch the bad guys...or girls."

Carlo kept laughing. "You're barking up the wrong tree, boys...and girl. My wife wouldn't kill anyone, especially Laroche."

"Why not?" asked Reinart. "Because she was still in love with him?"

Carlo stopped laughing.

Daniels appreciated Reinart's ability to get to the point. "And if that's true, maybe you killed Laroche, Carlo."

"You'd certainly have motive," said Rem, "if your wife's in love with another man." Rem tilted his head. "We saw Isabella's reaction to Laroche's death. She was pretty torn up, and she didn't seem interested in being comforted by you. In fact, she seemed annoyed by it. Did you poison Laroche, Carlo? Because you were sick of your wife wanting someone other than you?"

Carlo's face twisted. "You don't know what the hell you're talking about."

Daniels put a hand on the bed rail. "Well, maybe Isabella will be of more help. We're talking to her next."

Carlo raised his voice. "Talk to her all you want. There's nothing to say. She didn't kill Laroche, and neither did I. He was an asshole, and there's plenty of other people who wanted him dead."

Reinart walked to the foot of the bed. "There's a nasty rumor going around, Carlo. One you might not enjoy hearing."

Carlo chuckled sarcastically. "What's that, Wilma?"

Impressed that Reinart was about to ask the big question, Daniels braced for Carlo's reaction. Rem instinctively moved closer to Daniels.

Reinart stared back at Carlo with a calm expression. "Is it possible your son Mateo could be Laroche's child and not yours?"

Carlo's jaw tightened and the tendons in his neck bulged. "You bitch." He sat up with a grimace and gripped his shoulder. "Do you know who you're talking to? You better watch your mouth."

Daniels and Rem stuck close to the side of Carlo's bed in case he jumped out of it. "Who exactly is she talking to, Carlo?" asked Daniels, hardening his tone. "Are you threatening her?"

"We know the Vespucci name," said Rem, his own tone stern. "You're a prominent member of a crime family. And the mere suggestion that you're threatening an officer or that you're not Mateo's father is plenty of reason for us to suspect you of murder."

Carlo's face turned red. "We're done talking. Get the hell out of here." He glared at Reinart. "And take Detective Barbie with you."

Reinart smiled softly. "We'll leave, Carlo, but we're not done."

"Yes, you are." Carlo pulled up his sheet. "From here on in, you can direct your dumbass questions to my attorney. That goes for Isabella too."

"That's up to Isabella," said Rem. "And if she's mad enough to shoot you, maybe she's mad enough to tell us the truth about her and Laroche, Mateo, and what really happened at that unveiling."

Carlo directed his glare at Rem. "Be careful what you ask for, Detective. Don't open a can of worms you can't close."

"We'll take our chances." Daniels directed his own glare at Carlo. "But I'd suggest you take your own advice."

Carlo held Daniels' gaze. "Did I stutter?" asked Carlo. "I said get the hell out of here. Now."

Daniels paused, but then stepped back from the bed. Rem and Reinart joined him. "We'll be seeing you, Carlo," said Rem. "Good luck with the surgery. We'll give Isabella your regards just in case something goes wrong."

"One can only hope," muttered Reinart. She turned toward the curtain.

Carlo shouted at them. "I'll be talking to your captain. I'll have your damn badges when I'm done with you."

"Promise?" asked Rem.

"We could use the time off," said Daniels.

Rem reached for the curtain. "See you, Carlo." While Carlo cursed, Rem slid the curtain closed.

Chapter Nine

PHOEBE ENTERED THE SMALL house where she would stay while she was helping with the Laroche investigation. Normally used as a safe house, the small home sat empty, but Captain Lozano had received the required permissions for her to use it. Since she might work with Remalla and Daniels for the foreseeable future, the commute from her own place was impractical.

After shutting the front door behind her, she set the key on a small side table, put her bag down, and looked around. She flipped on some lights and checked out the small living area and kitchen, and down the hall were two bedrooms and a bathroom. More than adequate for her needs, she thought as she brought her bag into the first bedroom and set it down.

After checking out the kitchen, she went outside and grabbed the groceries she'd picked up on the way over and brought them in. She took a couple of minutes to put them away in the kitchen and, yawning, she pulled out a ready-made meal, and set the oven temperature. While the oven preheated, she walked into the bathroom and turned on the shower. After a busy afternoon, she couldn't wait to clean up and change her clothes, have a glass of wine, eat a quick meal, and sleep.

She emptied her suitcase, put her clothes in various drawers, and thought about the events of her day. After visiting Carlo in the hospital, they'd attempted to talk to Isabella, but she'd refused to speak to them, insisting she had nothing to say. If Carlo did not press charges, Phoebe guessed his wife would be released soon. Unless something changed, Phoebe doubted they'd get any more useful information out of either Carlo or Isabella.

After leaving Isabella, they'd picked up Phoebe's car, which they'd left at Laroche's, and returned to the station so Phoebe could get settled in and they could get progress updates. By the time she'd arrived, a desk and computer had been set up for her beside Remalla's and Daniels' desks. Captain Lozano had introduced himself and welcomed her to the team, and she'd met some of the other detectives who were assisting with the investigation. Before she knew it, they were nose-deep in information and planning their next steps. Since Remalla and Daniels had been up early that morning, Lozano had told them and Reinart to go home and get some sleep, but to be ready to start early the next morning.

Her belongings organized, Phoebe left a cozy pajama set on the bed and got into the shower. As the hot water sprayed her body, she let out a long sigh, still surprised to find herself where she was. That morning, she'd been prepared to resign, and now she found herself working with two new detectives trying to solve the murder of Rowan Laroche. The turn of events was hard to believe.

Not only that, but she was enjoying herself. Remalla and Daniels were easy to work with, shared information liberally, valued her opinion, and didn't treat her any differently than the other detectives on the squad. Running her head under the shower, she wondered why this experience was so different, but in her mind, she already knew. They didn't really know her and her history, and if they did, they'd likely treat her the same as her colleagues from the Southern Division.

Glad that at least she'd found a brief reprieve, she told herself to relax and not overthink it. Maybe once she had some time away from sitting at a desk and could actually work on a case where she could be of benefit, she might change her mind. The time away from Barry was helping; the more distance she got from him, the better. As much as she thought she'd loved him, she began to reconsider. Maybe she'd never really loved him at all, but had only fallen for the idea of him, which he'd created rather effectively, and she'd bought hook, line, and sinker.

Finishing up with her shower, she turned the water off and stepped out, grabbed a towel, and dried off. Seeing the pink scar running along the side of her neck, she lightly touched it, her stomach tightening at the memories and thinking again of her failure, but she forced herself not to dwell on it. There were other things to focus on, like their day tomorrow, which would start with talking to Evelyn Sinclair and her gallery manager, James. Distracting herself, she considered the questions to ask them.

Getting comfortable in her pajamas, she flipped off the bedroom light and returned to the kitchen, where she put the meal in the oven and set the timer. She opened the bottle of red wine, found a glass and half-filled it. After smelling the wine, she swirled it and took a drink. Appreciating the bold flavors, she sighed and pulled out a chair from a small round dining table when there was a knock on the door. Wondering who would stop by at that hour and why, she put her wineglass down and walked to the door.

The knocking came again, and she heard a male voice. "Phoebe? It's me. Barry."

Not sure she heard right, she flipped on the outside light and looked through the peephole. Sure enough, she recognized her partner, Thomas Barry, standing on her porch. Shocked, she undid the lock and opened the door.

Barry stood there in his customary pair of jeans and a long-sleeved sweatshirt with a bulldog on it. A lock of his brown wavy hair fell in his face, and she had a brief urge to brush it back. "What are you doing here?" she asked.

He ran his fingers through his hair and brushed the errant lock back. "Hey, Pheebs. Can I come in?"

Seeing him, her heart rate picked up. She'd made a concentrated effort to keep her distance, and he was supposed to do the same. It had been difficult, but she'd honored their commitment. "How did you know I was here?"

"I made some phone calls. It wasn't that hard."

She hesitated, recalling their complicated past. "You shouldn't be here."

Barry released a deep breath. "I need to talk to you."

"Go home to your family, Barry." She started to close the door.

Barry put his hand on it. "Please, Pheebs."

Studying him and seeing the familiar sadness in his eyes, Phoebe's heart raced faster. "Barry..."

"Just a few minutes."

Phoebe held the door and, for a moment, almost shut it, but then her heart won the battle. "Fine." She stepped aside to let him in.

· · · • • · • · · ·

After getting a bite to eat and taking a long, hot shower, Rem threw on a pair of sweatpants and a T-shirt. Tired, he stared at himself in his bathroom mirror, debating whether to go to bed or watch a cheesy movie. Thinking about the next day's busy schedule, he smoothed his wet hair back and sighed, deciding a cheesy movie and a beer would allow him to decompress. He flipped off the bathroom light but before leaving his room, stopped beside a chest of drawers across from his bed. A lighted lamp reflected off a framed photo of him and Jennie taken at a local park. They stood on a bridge that spanned a large pond, and

Rem had his arm around her. He'd teased her and poked her in the ribs just as Daniels had taken the photo and caught the look between Rem and Jennie. They were smiling at each other, and it was Rem's favorite photo of the two of them. After her death, he'd put the picture in a box so he wouldn't have to see it, but he'd recently felt the pull to return it to his bedroom. His heart thumping, he picked it up, his thoughts traveling back to memories of better times. Reinart's freckles flashed in his mind, triggering the familiar grief. Feeling the wave build, he put the picture down. Taking a second, he sat on his bed and took a deep breath. His shrink's advice echoed in his mind, and he took several more breaths. He considered scheduling another appointment with his counselor since he hadn't been to see him in a couple of months. He'd been feeling more stable recently, so he'd taken some time off, but this challenge was a good test to see how he would handle future ones. In the past, he hadn't handled them well, but he'd been feeling stronger since his breakup with Jacobs and their life-altering encounter with the killer they'd called Rutger.

His heart rate slowing and feeling calmer, he stood, thinking he might need vodka instead of beer, when his cell rang. He picked it up from his nightstand, saw Daniels' name on the display and answered. "Hey."

"Hey," said Daniels. "You awake?"

Rem heard a muffled baby's cry. "Yeah. I'm about to go find something on TV and get a drink. Is that J.P. crying or is our day catching up to you?"

"It's J.P. I cried on the way home."

Rem chuckled. "I hear you. What's wrong with the little man?"

"It's his teeth. He's been cranky all evening. I came home to Marjorie about to pull her hair out. I told her to take a break and go to bed since I'm likely to be pretty busy for the next several days. She's resting and I'm in the nursery, trying to put him down."

Rem sat on the bed and stifled a yawn. "Seems like everyone's having a hard day."

"Seems so. How are you?"

Rem rubbed his eyes. "Oh, you know me. I'm hanging in there."

"I noticed that moment in Laroche's gallery today."

Rem pinched the bridge of his nose. "It was Reinart's freckles. They reminded me of Jennie's. It kicked me in the gut for a second, but I held it together."

Daniels paused. "Funny what can trigger those memories."

"It still surprises me."

"What do you think of Reinart?"

Happy to change the subject, Rem sat up. "I like her. She's smart and certainly capable. She handled Carlo's antics without a sweat. I think she'll be a big help."

"I think so too, but she also seems hesitant, like she's surprised to be included. She doubts herself."

"I noticed that. Something tells me there's more going on with her and her partner and this sabbatical of his."

"I'm thinking the same."

"It's not our business though, and she won't be around long enough anyway to worry about it."

"Assuming we solve this thing sooner rather than later."

Rem sighed. "Let's pray we do. This kind of pressure gets old fast." J.P. cried again and Rem heard Daniels speak softly to his son to soothe him. "J.P. getting sleepy yet?"

Daniels whispered. "He's exhausted. He's just fighting it. Sometimes just walking with him soothes him enough and settles him down."

Rem stood and left the bedroom. "Is this conversation helping?" He entered his kitchen and took a beer out of the fridge.

"Uncle Rem's voice always calms him."

"Or makes him shriek."

"That too."

Rem smiled and opened his beer.

"I talked to Marjorie about our case before she went to bed." Daniels paused while J.P. gurgled. "Guess what? She knows Evelyn Sinclair."

"Really?" Rem tossed the cap of his beer in the trash. "How does she know Sinclair?"

Daniels spoke softly into the phone. "When Marjorie was in college, Sinclair was the professor in one of her art classes. Apparently, they got to know each other. Marjorie had an old boyfriend and when she broke up with him, he didn't take it too well, and he stalked her."

Holding his beer, Rem walked into his living room. "Seriously?"

"Seriously. One day, this guy followed Marjorie into her art class and when it was over, he stuck around and Marjorie told Sinclair what was going on. Sinclair took Marjorie into her office and called the campus police. They showed and spoke to the ex-boyfriend who was compliant and left, but the police couldn't do much more."

"Did you know about this?"

"No idea. This is the first I heard about it."

"What happened to the boyfriend?"

"Two days later, he got assaulted in an alley. Spent two days in the hospital. Never bothered Marjorie again."

Rem sat on the couch. "You think that was a coincidence?"

"No idea. But it's interesting. Could Sinclair have had something to do with his assault?"

"If she did, that would make her an interesting suspect. She doesn't put up with bullshit."

"Especially from asshole men, and I think Laroche fits that description. Something to consider when we question her."

"Definitely. What does Marjorie think? Did she suspect Sinclair's involvement with her stalker?"

"I think she did, but she never came out and asked." He paused. "She mentioned something else of interest, though."

"What's that?" Rem picked up the remote and flipped on the TV. It flickered on and he turned down the volume.

Daniels hesitated. "She said Sinclair had a big impact on her. After the stalker incident, Sinclair became a friend and mentor to Marjorie. It disappointed Marjorie that they hadn't stayed in touch. Then she sighed and said something about what could have been."

Rem detected the change in Daniels' tone. "You think she was implying something?"

"I don't know," Daniels said with uncertainty. "She went to bed, and I've been in here thinking about it, wondering if she's wishing she'd made different choices."

Rem set his beer on the coffee table. "What? You think Marjorie's regretting her decisions to become a wife and mother, and would have rather pursued an art career?"

Daniels took a second to respond. "Hell. I don't know. I'm sure I'm just tired and overthinking it. She was tired too."

"Of course she was. I wouldn't take a comment made after a long day at work and dealing with a cranky son too seriously."

"I know." Daniels made a soothing sound to his son, and Rem could imagine him in the dark nursery, pacing and patting J.P.'s back. "I can't help but wonder, though. Did we jump into marriage too soon? Does she regret it? And you already know J.P. was a surprise to both of us."

Rem sat back on the couch. "Daniels, you're getting way ahead of yourself. You two just tied the knot. You barely had time for a honeymoon, and you came home to a teething ten-month-old. I'm sure you've had a few of your own what-the-hell-have-I-done moments, but they always pass. Especially when you realize how lucky you are to have what you have. Marjorie is no different, so cut her some slack."

Daniels took a second to respond. "I'm overreacting. Is that what you're saying?"

"Completely. And I'm sure if you asked Marjorie about it tomorrow, she'd completely agree. You just need some sleep."

Daniels paused. "Speaking of sleep, I think the little man finally succumbed."

"It's because of me. I have the magic touch."

"You do have a knack for making Lozano's eyes cross."

"I consider that a skill to be proud of." Rem heard a soft coo, heavy breathing, and some shuffling.

"He's down and out like a light," said Daniels. "Now it's my turn."

"Good. Get some rest. You and Marjorie will both feel better tomorrow."

"Yeah. Okay. You get some rest too."

Rem fought back a yawn. "I'll probably fall asleep on the couch in about two minutes." He glanced at the TV and saw Michael Myers chasing Jamie Lee Curtis through a dark house. "We'll find out tomorrow what Evelyn Sinclair has to say about Laroche, and maybe a stalker from Marjorie's past."

"Should be interesting."

"Should be." Rem stifled a yawn. "See you in the morning."

"See you, and thanks for the pep talk and helping with J.P."

Rem picked up his beer. "I'm here to help. My office hours are always open, and I owe you."

"You don't owe me a thing. We're partners."

Rem thought back on some hard memories. "I owe you anyway, but if you want to call it even-steven, I can do that."

"Even-steven, then. And turn off that horror movie."

Rem dropped his jaw. "How did you—?"

"You're not the only one with magic powers. Get off the couch and go to bed. I'll see you tomorrow."

Rem groaned. "Good night."

"Good night."

Rem hung up and watched the movie for a few minutes. After taking a few more drinks of his beer, he settled back on the couch, closed his eyes, and while Jamie Lee screamed, he fell asleep.

Chapter Ten

REM, DANIELS AND REINART stepped onto the sidewalk outside the Sinclair gallery near the design district. The ground shook as a large delivery truck drove down the busy road next to the gallery. They'd started their morning meeting with Lozano and the other detectives to discuss updates and their goals for the day. Reinart had seemed distracted and quiet after arriving at the station, but as the morning went on, her focus returned, and she seemed eager to get started. Rem noticed she'd worn another turtleneck. Not that he knew much about women's fashion, but another turtleneck on a warm day seemed odd. Smoothing his semi-wrinkled shirt, he was glad he didn't have to worry about what to wear. He was happy just to get out of bed in the morning and get to work on time, especially since he'd fallen asleep on the couch. He'd woken up around three a.m. to an infomercial and a stiff neck and had dragged himself to bed.

As more traffic rumbled down the street, Rem looked through the windows of the swanky art gallery. Seeing the variety of paintings and sculptures, he dug his fingers into his tight neck and grimaced.

"You fell asleep on the couch, didn't you?" asked Daniels.

Rem frowned. "Maybe. How'd you sleep, Reinart? That house comfortable?"

Reinart ran her hand over her turtleneck. "It was fine."

"I'm guessing you didn't sleep on the couch," said Daniels.

Reinart shook her head. "No. I didn't."

Daniels glanced at Rem. "Smart lady."

Rem ignored him and opened the gallery door. "How about we talk to Evelyn Sinclair instead of me?"

"That's why you shouldn't sleep on the couch," said Daniels. "It makes you grouchy." He followed Reinart into the gallery, and Rem entered and let the door shut behind him.

Looking around, Rem whistled. "Wow." He'd been to museums and the occasional art show with Jennie, but he'd never seen anything quite like the Sinclair gallery. It had the most bizarre work he'd ever seen. Pictures with odd shapes and patterns bulging out from the canvas, some with color and others black and white, huge paintings with thick gobs of paint splattered and dripping down the canvas, bizarre sculptures with various limbs and nude people in strange positions, and in the center of the room was a twirling circle with a painted mannequin standing in the center, spinning. The artist had draped heavy metal chains over the mannequin's shoulders and neck and what looked like gold bars hung from the mannequin's wrists and earlobes.

Daniels looked around too, his eyes wide. "It's definitely unique."

Reinart approached the spinning mannequin. "Sinclair sees exceptional talent in unexpected places. Many of her artists have become very sought-after talent."

Rem stared at the spinning mannequin. "You call this exceptional?"

Reinart nodded. "To the right person, yes."

"I definitely don't run with that crowd." Rem fought the urge to reach out and touch the mannequin.

"Not with that shirt, you don't," said Daniels, stepping up beside them.

Rem pulled on his sleeve. "I'll take this shirt any day over that." He pointed at a framed picture of a red triangle intersecting a blue circle over a black background.

Reinart glanced at the picture. "That's a Delavigne. It's worth probably around twenty grand."

Rem dropped his jaw. "That?"

"And that's one of his less expensive pieces."

Daniels shook his head. "I'm more into landscapes."

"He has those too," said Reinart. "That'll set you back almost thirty grand."

"I think I've stepped into another dimension," said Rem.

"This is normal, especially for a Sinclair Gallery piece," said Reinart. "You won't find anything under ten grand in here."

"I could paint a coffee cup," said Rem. "How much would that get me?"

"About ten bucks, if you're lucky," added Daniels.

"Not based on what I'm seeing in here." Rem studied a statue of a naked woman twisted into what looked like a pretzel.

"If Sinclair displayed it, you'd make a pretty penny." Reinart stopped in front of the female pretzel. "But don't expect that to happen. Sinclair has a critical eye."

"That's one way of describing it." Rem frowned at a painting depicting an apple lying in a naked man's lap with a knife protruding from it. The position of the knife suggested it was a central part of the man's anatomy. "Unbelievable."

A male voice interrupted their conversation. "Detectives. Nice to see you again."

Rem looked over to see James, Evelyn Sinclair's gallery manager, emerge from an office at the back. He wore a dark pink suit with pearl buttons and a purple shirt with a striped collar and tie.

James approached and spoke to Reinart. "I don't believe we've met." He held out his hand. "James Montrose, Manager at the Sinclair."

Reinart shook his hand. "Detective Phoebe Reinart. I'm assisting with the case."

"How nice," said James. "I'm sure these handsome fellows are happy to have your help. We can't have Laroche's killer walking around without consequences, although it's tempting." He walked over to Rem and gestured at the painting with the apple in the man's lap. "Do you like it, Detective?"

Rem knitted his brow. "It's one way to slice an apple. But it's not exactly my cup of tea." He glanced at the spinning mannequin. "I'm still trying to figure out this thing."

James turned and approached the mannequin. "This is my favorite piece. It's a Ragsdale, and it's one of a kind."

"I can see that," said Rem.

"How much does that cost?" asked Daniels.

"If you have to ask," said James, "you can't afford it. But I'd give you a deal at a hundred twenty grand."

Rem almost choked. "Are you serious?"

James crossed his arms. "I don't kid about money, Detective."

"Do you actually sell these things?" asked Daniels.

James smiled and adjusted a gold and silver pinky ring. "We sold another Ragsdale last month for over two hundred. And we've got two interested buyers for this piece." He nodded at the mannequin. "I suspect I'll sell it by the end of the week."

Rem put his hands on his hips. "No wonder the art world is so dangerous."

James raised a brow. "It's the most cutthroat world I know." He pointed toward the back. "I assume you're here to discuss Laroche? Let's go to the client office and sit. Can I get you all some sparkling water with lemon?"

Reinart and Daniels both agreed to the sparkling water and Rem asked for tap. James showed them to a bright office with big glass windows and a wide glass table with metal chairs. They sat and waited while James got the drinks.

Rem almost didn't want to put his hands on the table for fear of leaving fingerprints. "This is quite a place."

"I didn't see Evelyn," said Reinart.

"Maybe she's in her art fortress talking to this Ragsdale guy," said Rem. "The rate he's going, I'd be sticking to him like glue."

"Ragsdale is just one of many," replied Reinart. "She's got a slew of artists in her pocket. Most would sell their souls to get into her gallery, but there's always a few she courts to keep them from going elsewhere. Ragsdale would be one of them."

"You mean she wants to keep him away from Laroche?" asked Daniels.

Reinart nodded. "She and Laroche were highly competitive. Between the two of them, they can make or break an artist. Judging by the prices of these works, you can see why."

Rem wiped at the table with his sleeve after leaving a print. "I get it from a business standpoint, but *The Crimson Tiger* was going into Laroche's private gallery and I'm guessing if Sinclair had purchased it, she would have done the same. Neither wanted to sell it for big bucks, so why the furious competition?"

Reinart leaned back in her seat. "They didn't want to make money from it. They wanted it for its notoriety. In the art world, your private gallery is almost as important as your public one. Laroche has always been the big daddy and *The Crimson Tiger* put a bigger feather in his cap. That painting would have gone a long way to pushing Sinclair's gallery up that hill and closer to Laroche's."

"How does killing him help her, though?" asked Daniels. "She still wouldn't get *The Crimson Tiger*."

"Maybe. Maybe not," said Reinart. "It's possible Laroche's estate could sell it, especially with the supposed curse, or this might just be about good old-fashioned revenge. Killing Laroche means a lot more opportunities for Sinclair."

James returned, carrying a tray with the waters. He handed them out with napkins and sat at the head of the table. "I apologize for Evelyn's absence, but she'll arrive soon." He smoothed his tie. "I hope you don't mind talking to me for a few minutes."

"We don't mind. We just have a few questions," said Daniels, pulling his notebook from his jacket pocket. "Can you tell us more about the party? What happened before, during, and after the unveiling of the tiger?"

"Of course," said James. He leaned back and crossed his legs. "Evelyn and I arrived suitably late. We mingled with the other guests and ate what Maurice called food from the buffet." He rolled his eyes. "Rowan eventually showed, pompous and flashy as usual. He spoke to his guests, and we all ate and drank until Rowan was ready for the unveiling. Then, as his dutiful guests, we all filed back to the private gallery and waited until Laroche graced us with his presence again. Dominique handed out champagne, and Laroche made a trivial speech about his brilliant acquisition and unveiled the tiger. Everyone played their part, gasped in awe, and gathered around it." He tapped on the table and a diamond ring on his finger glimmered in the light. "The painting is really quite extraordinary, don't you think? I have to say, I can see why Evelyn wanted it so badly. I wasn't supportive at first because I believed its value was over inflated, but once I laid eyes on the tiger, I wanted to have it myself." He sighed and waved a hand. "Anyway, once we exclaimed enough and lauded Laroche for his prize, we were all escorted out and returned to the front of the house where the party continued. Laroche never showed though and then we heard screaming. We rushed to find out what was going on, and Dominique was in a state. She kept screaming he was dead, so several of us returned to the gallery, and that's when we saw him." He clenched his eyes shut. "Such a sight. I'll never forget it." He opened his eyes and sighed.

"How was Laroche acting during the party?" asked Rem. "Anything unusual stand out, like an argument or maybe an intense conversation with another guest?"

James stared off. "Let's see. He spoke to several people. I couldn't say one way or the other if anything stood out. Rowan was always an intense man, though, and we'd all been drinking." He paused. "Wait. He and Isabella talked for a while, and that husband of hers, Carlo, didn't seem too pleased about it."

"Did Carlo talk to Laroche?" asked Daniels.

"He interrupted the conversation between Isabella and Rowan, which appeared somewhat intense, and Isabella wasn't happy." James sighed. "That woman's been carrying a torch for Rowan for years. I think if Rowan had given her any sign that he was still interested, she would have dropped Carlo like a rock." He shook his head. "I suppose you've heard the rumors?"

"About Laroche being the actual father of Isabella's baby?" asked Reinart.

James smiled. "You're good."

"You think it's true?" asked Rem.

James shrugged. "All I know is that Mateo was born six months after Isabella abruptly married Carlo after breaking up with Rowan. Make your own conclusions."

"Why marry Carlo if she's pregnant with another man's child?" asked Daniels.

"Isabella's not stupid, unless it comes to men." James sipped his water. "Rowan was her meal ticket and when she got pregnant, he didn't plan to marry her or raise the child. It was all on Isabella. Marrying Carlo was her security, and she probably hoped it would make Rowan jealous. It didn't, though. After Mateo's birth, I think she hoped there would still be a chance with Rowan, which is why she stuck close to him during the party, much to Carlo's dismay."

"Why even invite Isabella if they're no longer together?" asked Rem.

James chuckled. "Because that's Rowan. He loves to stir things up. It's what makes his parties fun."

Daniels wrote in his notepad. "So Carlo never spoke to Laroche?"

"All I saw was Carlo approach Isabella and speak to her in her ear while she talked to Rowan. She looked annoyed but left Rowan and stayed close to Carlo for the rest of the evening. If Carlo spoke to Laroche later, I didn't see it."

"Do you think Carlo could become violent?" asked Daniels.

James pursed his lips. "Considering his family name, I think that's a given, and when it comes to love, Detectives, or seeing your wife talk to the likely biological father of your child, it's certainly possible. If Carlo's paternity was questioned, who knows what he would be capable of?"

Recalling Carlo's outburst in the hospital, Rem guessed Carlo would be capable of plenty. "Anybody else at that party that you think might want to kill Rowan Laroche?"

James faced Rem. "That is a far more interesting question, Detective. It's one thing to have actually seen something, but entirely different if you suspect someone."

"Like who?" asked Reinart.

"That daughter of his, Victoria, for one. She's always held a grudge against her father."

"He was an absentee dad," said Reinart. "What do you expect?"

James set his water glass down. "I'm not saying it isn't deserved. Laroche got to where he was by putting himself first and made enemies along the way. Victoria being one of them."

"We heard she wrote an exposé on her father," said Daniels. "Had you heard that?"

"Who didn't hear about it?" asked James. "Everyone wanted to read it. Apparently, a big-name publisher approached her to turn it into a tell-all book about her father."

Reinart sat up. "Which publisher was that?"

"No idea." James leaned back in his seat. "I suspect Maria Rossi would know. She and Victoria are close. It wouldn't surprise me at all if Maria encouraged Victoria to write that exposé or even the book. Maria may have contacted the publisher herself. She has connections of her own."

Surprised to hear his opinion of Maria Rossi, Rem sat up. "Maria appeared upset after what happened to Laroche. Are you saying that wasn't genuine?"

James snorted. "Maria? She can play the game as well as anyone. You know she used to be an actress?"

"I'm aware," said Rem.

"Well, Rowan used her, broke her heart, and left her career in tatters. If anyone has reason to want Rowan dead, it's her."

"She's done well for herself though," said Reinart. "She's become a respected artist all on her own, and despite Rowan's manipulations, she survived and even thrived. Why come after Rowan now?"

James removed a fleck of lint from his jacket lapel. "I hear Victoria's book reveals Rowan's mistreatment of Maria and how he may have stolen her work and possibly taken credit for it. If that's true, then Maria hasn't quite let bygones be bygones."

"If she aired her secrets to Victoria, then why kill Rowan?" asked Daniels. "The whole point of the book would be to expose and humiliate him. That's hard to do if he's dead."

James nodded. "Yes. That's true. But Rowan, like Maria, also had friends in high places, and if he tried to kill the book deal, then who knows what that might have triggered?" He raised his hands. "I realize this is all pure conjecture, but Rowan had a way of getting under your skin. He would have loved flaunting Victoria's and Maria's failure to discredit him, and the party would have been the perfect opportunity to do it if he hadn't done it already."

Daniels took more notes. "Are you saying he invited them to the party to revel in their defeat?"

"That's one way of looking at it."

"Then why would they attend?" asked Rem.

James tipped his head. "Why indeed, Detective."

Reinart reached for her water glass. "Laroche's parties were legendary." She took a drink. "He invited friends, enemies, rivals, colleagues, and people off the street. Even the occasional member of the press. Victoria's and Maria's presence doesn't make them killers." She set her glass down.

Rem thought of his Uncle Carmine and hoped Reinart was right.

"I never said they were," answered James. "But if you want my opinion, then you have it."

"Anybody else you would consider a suspect?" asked Daniels. "What about the staff?"

James shook his head. "I can't help much there. Other than the chef, Maurice, I don't know many of the others."

"How do you know Maurice?" asked Rem.

"I met him when I worked for Laroche." He interlaced his fingers.

Rem glanced at Daniels. Reinart raised her brow. "You worked for Laroche? When?" she asked.

James widened his eyes. "It's no secret, Detective. I was Laroche's gallery manager until Evelyn hired me away last year."

"How long did you work for Laroche?" asked Reinart.

"Just over three years." James adjusted his cufflink. "Laroche was a tough boss, but I expected that going in. I adjusted to his management style, but he was rigid in his ways, and I felt restricted. Evelyn came along and offered me more pay, a bigger role in decision making and more opportunity. I couldn't pass it up, so I left Rowan and came to work for Evelyn." He waved his hand. "And before you jump to conclusions, the transition was amicable and there were no hard feelings between me and Evelyn, and Rowan."

Reinart frowned. "Rowan's biggest rival steals his gallery manager, and you want us to believe it was all harmonious and friendly?"

James sighed. "Steal is a strong word, Detective. I gave Rowan plenty of chances to meet or beat Evelyn's offer, but he declined. Said he could do it on his own, which he did for a while, until he hired Brian, who was exactly what he wanted. Someone who could be told what to do with no opinion of his own." He shrugged. "Like they say in *The Godfather*, it's not personal, it's business."

"And we all know how well that turned out," said Rem.

"I'll admit," said James. "My departure didn't thrill Rowan, but he managed."

"I bet Evelyn was happy," said Reinart.

"Why wouldn't she be? She and I have maintained a good partnership. We work well together and I'm worth every penny she pays me." He smiled.

"I'm guessing humility wasn't part of your job description," said Rem.

"No. It was not." James eyed his suit. "Does a man who wears pink with purple come across as humble to you?" He ran his hand down his tie. "And if you're thinking I have some sort of motive to kill Rowan, you'd be wrong. We may not have been friends, but we remained business associates."

"And rivals," said Reinart. "Evelyn wanted *The Crimson Tiger*, which suggests you played a part in trying to get it for her, but you failed. That probably didn't go over too well with Evelyn."

James' body language shifted. "No, it didn't. But that's the way the wind blows in our world. Like I said, it's a cutthroat business, and Rowan could play that game better than most."

"How badly did Evelyn want that tiger?" asked Rem.

"The tiger would have been a nice acquisition for any gallery, but as I said earlier, I thought it was overpriced. But if you think Evelyn would kill for it, you'd be wrong. Evelyn may have hated Rowan's games and showmanship, but she respected him. Without him, she would have never become the proprietor of the largest female-owned private gallery, one which is envied by the most revered art collectors in the world."

"Surpassed only by Laroche," said Reinart.

"And a few male owners in Europe, and a couple in Russia, but I see your point," replied James.

Rem studied James, debating if he could be a killer. "Anybody or anything else strike you as odd during the party?"

James rubbed his jaw. "As a matter of fact, yes. There was a man there. I'd never seen him before. He stood off by himself, didn't speak to anyone, and just watched everything." James narrowed his eyes. "Now he could be your man." He pointed. "And he wore a tuxedo. It was obviously too small and well past its expiration date."

Rem tensed and gripped his armrest.

"Did he do anything strange besides just stare at people?" asked Daniels with a glance at Rem.

"No. He barely spoke to Rowan when he made his rounds at the party. I lost sight of the man until the unveiling and then I spotted him in the back of the room, just standing there. He definitely gave off a vibe. I'd say if you want to catch a killer, start with that guy." James shivered. "Definitely creepy."

"Thanks," said Rem. "We'll look into it." He changed the subject. "Do you know Robert, the security guy at Laroche's?"

James rolled his eyes. "If you can call him that. I expressed my concerns when Rowan hired him, but as usual, he ignored me and hired Robert anyway. I suppose if Rowan had listened to me, he might still be alive."

"Why didn't you like Robert?" asked Daniels.

"He's smug, overconfident, and cheap, which is why Rowan liked him. But as they say, you get what you pay for." He paused. "I told Rowan many times that the house needed more security and to add more guards and cameras, but he didn't listen to that either. Said Robert could handle it." He sat forward. "And Robert likes the ladies. I know at the time I left, there were rumors he was sleeping with someone on the staff. I didn't trust him then and I don't trust him now." He rested an elbow on the tabletop. "Let me guess. He's taking zero responsibility for his boss' death."

"We're talking to him too," said Rem.

"He's a loser with a capital 'L.'" James leaned back with a look of disgust. "Evelyn will tell you the same."

"Speaking of Evelyn, where is she?" asked Reinart.

James checked his diamond-beveled watch. "I expected her by now. I can call her." He reached for his phone.

Reinart leaned up and rested her forearms on the table. "Before you do, why don't you think Evelyn could kill Laroche? She had the means and the opportunity, and her motive is obvious."

James scoffed. "You think she'd kill over *The Crimson Tiger*? That's absurd."

"Is it? She's a woman in a man's world, working twice as hard to get half as far. Laroche beat her again when she lost the tiger. Maybe she got tired of losing." She paused. "And if she got tired, maybe you did too. You are her partner, after all."

Surprised by Reinart's assertiveness, Rem watched James' reaction. He went quiet but held Reinart's gaze. Daniels lowered his pencil and watched too.

"I'm Evelyn's gallery manager, not a partner," answered James.

"You implied you were partners," said Reinart. "Is that not true?"

James twirled his pinky ring around his finger. "I see what you're doing, Detective. My ambition is obvious, but I have my limits, and murder is one of them."

Reinart didn't back down. "You sure about that? You worked for Laroche. You're familiar with the house and its security, and Rowan's habits. You even know Robert and Maurice. And you work for Rowan's biggest competitor. You say you thought the tiger was overvalued, but maybe besting your former boss who didn't listen to or value your opinion was worth far more, until that failed, too."

James clenched his jaw.

Reinart spoke in a level tone, but remained serious. "Did you kill Rowan Laroche, James?"

"No, I did not," said James. "And neither did Evelyn."

"Maybe you should let her speak for herself," said Reinart.

James' shoulders bunched. "You strike me as a woman with a chip on her shoulder." He sighed and seemed to relax. "I hope you won't let that guide your judgment in this case."

Reinart's eyes darkened, and she opened her mouth to respond when the office door opened. Rem turned to see Evelyn Sinclair enter. She wore a stylish red suit, high-heeled black pumps, and her dyed midnight-black hair was teased high and hair-sprayed.

"Hello, Detectives. I'm so sorry I wasn't here sooner." Her flowery perfume filled the air, and she took the seat next to James and across from Rem. "What'd I miss?"

· · • •• • ••· ·

Tapping the tip of his pencil against his notebook, Daniels eyed Reinart, whose flash of annoyance cooled when Evelyn arrived. Evelyn looked between James and Reinart and raised a brow. "Obviously I missed something."

James cleared his throat. "This is Detective Phoebe Reinart, Evelyn. She's helping with the case. I think she believes one of us killed Rowan."

Evelyn put her hand on her chest. "My word. Are you serious?"

Rem spoke first. "It's a question we have to ask of everyone at the party, and Reinart has a good point. Both of you had means, motive, and opportunity."

"Along with several others," replied Evelyn. "And Rowan was poisoned. Believe me, if I wanted to kill Rowan, poison would not be my first choice."

"Nor mine," said James.

"What would be your first choice?" asked Daniels. He picked up his water glass and took a drink from it.

Evelyn hesitated. "Whoever murdered Rowan had the balls to do it during the unveiling of the tiger amidst a slew of people. If I'd planned to murder him, it wouldn't be a secret, and I'd be in jail. The murderer was sending a message."

"What message was that?" asked Rem.

Evelyn crossed one leg over another. "That Rowan's dominance in the art world was over. He died amidst his priceless works, none of which he could take with him. They were the last things he saw before he left this earth, and his relentless pursuit of them couldn't save him. And that the tiger is supposedly cursed, provided the killer with the perfect opportunity."

"You think the killer thought the painting would be blamed?" asked Rem.

Evelyn smoothed her skirt. "It perpetuates the curse theory, raising the value of the painting. If it's sold, it will probably go for twice what Rowan paid for it."

"You want that painting," Reinart said to Evelyn. "Would you buy it if it goes up for sale?"

Evelyn shook her head. "Not now. After everything that's happened, I wouldn't put that painting in my gallery, public or private." She rubbed her arms. "It gives me the willies."

"Maybe you should consider someone on Rowan's own team," said James. "By selling the tiger after Rowan's murder, they could make a pretty penny. Is Victoria a beneficiary in his will? Or someone else? Would Brian Klein benefit?"

"Good point, James," said Evelyn.

James rested his hand on his knee. "Thank you, Evelyn."

"We appreciate your detective skills," said Reinart, "but I think we've got that part covered."

James shot her another look. "Just a suggestion, Detective."

Evelyn sighed. "Listen. I understand your suspicions and concerns, but let me put your fears to rest. James and I had a history with Rowan, and it wasn't all pleasant. Rowan could be a son-of-a-bitch and he loved to rub his success in our, and others', noses. It's no secret I wanted the tiger, and it pissed me off when I didn't get it. Rowan has been a perpetual thorn in my side for my entire career. Add to that the rumors of his cheating and stealing from others and how the art world kissed his ass despite all that, and I can see why you'd think I'd want to kill him. Believe me, I've considered it more than once. It wouldn't have been poison, though. I'd have shot him or hired some thugs to do it."

Daniels thought of Marjorie. Rem glanced over and Daniels knew he was thinking the same.

Evelyn sat up. "But as a woman in the heavily male-dominated art world, that solves nothing. Another Rowan will pop up to replace him and nothing will change. You'll see. Eventually, another ambitious and wealthy dealer will take his place and the tiger will somehow end up in his hands. It happens all the time."

Reinart regarded her. "Let me ask you something. Laroche got the tiger because he arranged to buy it before it could go to auction. Would anyone else have been able to do that other than him?"

Evelyn's face fell, and she glanced at James, whose expression also fell flat. "I tried it myself," said Evelyn, looking back at Reinart, "and was denied. I was told it needed to go before the public, where it would fetch the best price. Two weeks later, we learned Rowan had accomplished the very thing I wanted and got the tiger."

Daniels took more notes.

"That sounds like a motive to me," said Rem.

"It is," said Evelyn. "I was angry and I doubt I was the only one. But I've learned to accept that this world isn't fair, and killing Rowan was never part of the plan. It's much more satisfying to watch the person you've bested react when you've bested him."

"So you had plans to take the tiger from Rowan?" asked Daniels.

Evelyn rested her elbows on the chair's armrests. "Rowan's like most other men. They love the thrill of the chase, but they get bored easily. I just needed to bide my time. Plus, with James on my team, who used to work with Rowan, I felt I had an edge."

"Or a detriment," said Reinart. "Rowan would never sell the tiger to his rival's gallery manager, who used to work for him." She eyed Evelyn. "Or to you either. And I think you know that."

Evelyn squinted at Reinart. "That's an assumption, Detective, and one you should be careful about making. You're also a woman working in a man's world. You should never assume or underestimate your peers and what they might do. It's much better if they underestimate you."

The two women stared at each other, and it went quiet until James spoke. "There is someone else I think they should consider as a suspect, Evelyn." He paused and Evelyn looked over at him. "Hendrix."

Evelyn's eyes widened. "Hendrix? Why on earth would he kill Rowan? You, of all people, know how loyal Hendrix was to him."

James flattened a palm on the table. "Hendrix is loyal only to himself."

"Rowan took good care of him. Hendrix owes his career to him."

James offered a look of impatience. "I'm sure you've noticed that Hendrix is doing just fine on his own."

"Maybe for his mainstream work, but he's much more passionate about his personal projects, and Rowan supported those. And if he's doing so well, what reason would Hendrix have to kill him?" Evelyn swiveled her seat toward James. "Now I know you don't like the man, but you better prepare to work with him."

Taking notes, Daniels watched the exchange with interest, as did Rem and Reinart.

James sat up. "Are you talking to him? Already? Rowan is barely cold."

"You don't think Deveaux has already contacted him, and God knows who else? I left a message earlier and I plan to call again soon. If we don't strike now, we'll lose him. Every gallery owner is going to want to work with him, and I intend for his next exhibit to be in this gallery."

James set his jaw and leaned back rigidly in his seat. He glanced back at Daniels. "Perhaps we should table this discussion for another time, Evelyn."

Evelyn looked around the group. "I think that's wise." Returning to her poised self, she smoothed back a loose hair. "Any other questions, Detectives?"

"We have other detectives talking to Hendrix," said Rem. "No one is excluded as a suspect yet."

"Good to know," said James.

Evelyn sighed and shook her head.

Daniels debated whether to ask more about Hendrix, but since neither Evelyn nor James had anything substantial to offer other than assumptions, he asked about something else instead. "I have another question. I'm curious about your tactics, Evelyn. You mention you'd have hired thugs to do your dirty work. How do we know that's not what happened with Laroche?"

Evelyn took her attention off James and smiled. "Believe me, if I'd hired someone to hurt Rowan, I would tell you. But as much as I hate to admit it, Rowan served a purpose. Despite our differences, we maintained a respectful business relationship. And I'm not that stupid."

Rem rested his hands on the glass table, leaving plenty of fingerprints. He raised a brow at Daniels and Daniels picked up on the silent communication. He regarded Evelyn. "You used to work as an art professor, didn't you?"

Evelyn's eyes widened. "Why, yes. It's been a while though. Why do you ask?"

Reinart furrowed her brow at Daniels.

"I believe you know my wife," said Daniels. "She took one of your classes. Her maiden name is Marjorie Benson."

Evelyn's jaw dropped. "Marjorie Benson? She's your wife?"

Daniels nodded. "She is."

"Who is Marjorie Benson?" asked James.

Evelyn touched her jaw. "She's a former student and protégé. We fell out of touch, though, and it's been years since we've spoken." She leaned forward. "How is she?"

"She's well." Daniels shifted in his seat, unsure why he was uncomfortable. "We have a ten-month-old son."

"Is she working in the art world?" asked Evelyn. "At a gallery or as an artist? I haven't heard her name if she is."

"She's a high school counselor, and a very good one," said Daniels.

"A high school what?" asked Evelyn. "But she showed such promise."

Daniels gripped his pencil. "She still does."

Evelyn sucked in a breath. "I apologize, Detective. I didn't mean it to sound demeaning. I'm sure she's very good at what she does. She was an excellent student and very devoted. I just thought she'd...she'd..."

"She'd what?" asked Daniels.

Evelyn shook her head. "Never mind. What I thought doesn't matter. Just as long as she's happy, and it appears she is, which is what's important."

Daniels picked up on the BS. Evelyn had expected much more from Marjorie besides marriage and motherhood. "Marjorie mentioned to me you helped her once, with an ex-boyfriend who stalked her. Said you called the campus police."

Evelyn stared off. "That's right. I recall that." She frowned. "Terrible man. He was scaring the hell out of Marjorie and the damn police couldn't do a thing about it."

"She said a few days after calling the police, they found her stalker in an alley, beaten to within an inch of his life. He never bothered her again."

Evelyn nodded. "Yes. That's true." She sat back but didn't elaborate.

Daniels waited and Rem finally asked the obvious. "Did you have anything to do with that?"

Evelyn shot him a look. "Absolutely, Detective." She tipped her head. "Sometimes, a woman has to take matters into her own hands, don't you think?"

Daniels, Reinart, Rem, and even James stared at her in surprise. No one said a word.

Evelyn stood with a slight smile. "I'm going to get some hot tea. Can I get anyone anything?"

Chapter Eleven

REM DROVE DOWN THE street, following the navigation system on his dash to Maria Rossi's apartment. "That was the strangest questioning I think I've ever had with a suspect."

Daniels glanced at him from the passenger seat. "What about the sumo wrestler we arrested for fencing stolen merchandise? Who dared you to arm wrestle while his girlfriend sang songs from *The Sound of Music* in the other room?"

Rem flashed back on that unique interrogation. "Aside from that one."

Reinart sat up from the backseat. "Evelyn Sinclair is a cool customer."

"No kidding," said Rem. "She spends a good part of the time trying to convince us she couldn't kill Laroche and then admits to hiring people to beat the hell out of a stalker."

"You buy her story?" asked Daniels. "That Laroche and a stalker are two distinct problems that required two different solutions?"

"I can see her point," said Reinart. "But I don't buy that she wouldn't kill Laroche. And James is still high on my suspect list."

Daniels looked back at her. "You came on pretty strong with him."

Reinart huffed. "I don't like him. He's pretentious, egotistical, and a narcissist."

"Gee," said Rem. "What made you think that?"

"That doesn't make him a killer though," said Daniels.

"It sure doesn't rule him out," said Reinart. "I think he's hiding something."

"He's not hiding his disdain for Hendrix," added Rem. "Although Evelyn can't wait to get her hands on him."

"She can't wait to get her hands on the money he'd bring in," replied Reinart.

"Maybe after we talk to a few more suspects, we'll get a clearer picture of James," said Rem. "What do you think about what he said regarding Maria and Victoria, and Isabella and Carlo?"

"He didn't tell us more than what we already knew. Same with Robert," said Daniels. "Other than Victoria's exposé becoming a potential book deal and Maria's contribution to some of the book's juicier details."

"I'd like to know what Isabella and Laroche were talking about during the party," said Reinart.

"Something tells me Isabella isn't going to share," said Rem. "But if Laroche rejected her again, we have to consider she could have killed him."

Daniels raised a finger. "Or she might have been talking to him about Mateo. What if she was asking for child support or some sort of recognition from Laroche that he's the father? If he told her no, that could have set her off."

"The more likely scenario is that Carlo got pissed," added Reinart. "He wanted Mateo's biological father out of his, Mateo's and Isabella's life. With his connections, he could certainly make that happen."

"There's a problem with that," said Rem. "The mob doesn't kill with poison. They take you to a secluded spot and shoot you in the back of the head."

"Maybe Carlo didn't want that," said Daniels. "It would be too obvious that he was involved."

"I still don't buy him as a poison guy. He's more of a leg-breaker," said Rem, stopping at a red light. "This conversation with Maria Rossi will hopefully reveal a few things. Is she really the worried, heartbroken ex or is she out for revenge against the man who dumped her, stole her work, and ruined her career?"

"I think there's more to Rossi's story," said Reinart, "and Victoria's too."

"I'm not sure I buy the whole publishing deal gone bad," said Rem. The light turned green, and he drove through the intersection. "A tell-all book with Laroche as the subject would make plenty of money. Even if one publisher dropped it, another would be right behind him, ready to scoop it up. I doubt Laroche had the clout to kill every deal."

"Maybe there's more to that story," said Daniels. He rested his elbow on the door's armrest. "If Laroche had dirt on Victoria and Maria, maybe he threatened to use it if they went public."

"And if he didn't have dirt, he could certainly make something up," said Reinart. "He could plant some of his own seeds to discredit Maria's claims. Don't forget. She's become a decent artist all on her own. If Rowan threatened her career, which he could do, maybe Maria took matters into her own hands."

"If that's the case, then it's possible Victoria helped her," said Daniels. He glanced at Reinart. "I know James has a lot of inside knowledge about Laroche and his home, but so do Isabella, Victoria, and probably Maria. Robert too."

"That helps my Uncle Carmine's case then," said Rem. "He doesn't know any of that stuff."

"Well, I hate to tell you, but that doesn't rule him out," said Reinart. "He could have come to the party with the poison in his pocket, hoping to get an opportunity."

Rem scoffed. "The chances of my uncle getting hold of a poison to kill Laroche within two days of his invitation are slim to none."

"I'm sure you would have said the same about your uncle even being at the party," said Reinart.

Rem shot a glare at her. "You're all heart, Reinart."

"Just stating the obvious," she said. Her cell rang, and she sat back and answered it.

"Just for the record," said Daniels, "I don't think Carmine killed anyone, but she's right."

Rem sighed. "Yeah. I know."

"He's still a suspect for now, but I think we'll find our killer is one of Laroche's supposed friends. It's just figuring out which one."

Rem stopped at a stop sign. "Let's hope Maria has some insight into that."

"Unless she's the killer."

"I hope not." Rem rested his wrist on the steering wheel. "I'm rooting for my teenage crush."

"Those heartbreaks hurt the most, partner." Daniels shook his head. "So try not to get your hopes up."

"Believe me," said Rem, thinking back, "I've learned that the hard way."

Daniels offered him a knowing look, but didn't respond. Reinart finished her conversation and hung up. "Good news," she said, sitting forward again. "I've got a guy coming tomorrow to check out the *Fury and Fire* painting at Laroche's. If Maria Rossi is the actual artist, then he'll be able to tell us."

"That should be enlightening," said Rem. He turned into a swanky apartment complex and flashed his badge at a gate with a security guard. After being allowed in, he found the right building, parked, and unbuckled his seatbelt. "Let's go talk to the lovely Miss Rossi."

· · · · • · • · · · ·

Daniels knocked on the door of Maria's apartment. It was in a ten-story building with a small lobby and sitting area with large furniture and a big stone fireplace. The elevator was all gleaming mirrors and when they reached the sixth floor, they stepped into a wood-paneled hall with an oriental rug running down the length of it. It smelled of wood polish and flowers, and Daniels spotted a huge bouquet of fresh ones in the middle of the hall, near to Maria's door.

"She's definitely doing pretty well for herself if she's living in a place like this," said Rem.

"She's a successful artist," said Reinart, looking around, "but I didn't think she was this successful. Guess I need to brush up on Maria Rossi's work and what it's worth these days."

"Probably a good idea," said Daniels.

The door opened and Maria Rossi stood at the entrance, wearing a form-fitting navy-blue pantsuit with a low-cut neckline and a large silver and turquoise necklace. Her auburn hair was down and softly brushed her shoulders. "Hello, Detectives." She stepped back. "Please, come in."

"Thank you," said Daniels. They stepped inside and Daniels introduced Phoebe, who showed her badge and shook hands with Maria.

"Thank you for taking time to talk to us," said Rem. He smiled and Daniels could tell his partner was a little starstruck. "I can imagine you're busy," said Rem.

"Not at all. If I can help with the investigation, then it's time well spent. Have a seat." Maria gestured toward a chocolate brown leather couch with two end tables, each with a lamp on it, on either side of the couch. "Can I get you some water or tea?"

Daniels requested tea, and Phoebe and Rem asked for water. Maria disappeared into a kitchen with lots of granite and stainless steel, and

Daniels and Rem sat on the couch. Reinart sat on a loveseat beside the couch. She pointed at a painting on the wall. "See that?"

Daniels glanced at the painting, which featured a large colonial ship with billowing masts sailing across a stormy sea. Dark storm clouds and vast waves gave the painting a look of desperation and gloom. "Is that famous?"

"I like that," said Rem. "It's more my style."

"It's called *Rage of the Sea*," said Reinart. "The artist's name is Willow Hathaway. She's British and lost much of her work in a warehouse fire. Private collectors own the ones that are left, Laroche being one of them. Last I heard, this one was supposedly his."

"Then what's it doing here?" asked Rem.

"Good question," said Reinart. "Maybe we should ask."

Rem looked toward the kitchen. "Is it wrong to want her autograph?"

"What are you? Sixteen?" asked Daniels. "She's a murder suspect."

Rem whispered. "And a former actress who was largely responsible for getting me through my formative years with a big smile on my face."

Daniels spoke to Reinart. "I apologize. He's usually not this unfiltered."

"Since when?" asked Rem.

"I had a Brad Pitt poster on my ceiling," said Reinart, "much to my mother's dismay. She was more of a Tom Selleck fan."

"See?" said Rem. "Who was your childhood crush?" Rem asked Daniels. "And don't tell me you didn't have one because I know you too well."

Daniels rolled his eyes, amazed at his partner's unique ability to stray into bizarre subjects at unlikely times. He thought back to his own teenage years and felt his cheeks flush. "That's not important."

Rem's eyes widened. "Now I have to know. Who was it?" He tapped his jaw. "Don't tell me." He narrowed his eyes. "Heather Locklear? Or Brooke Shields?" He paused. "Halle Berry?"

Daniel shook his head. "No to all three."

"You strike me as more old school," said Reinart. "Marilyn Monroe? Or Elizabeth Taylor?"

"Nope," said Daniels.

"We can't be that far off," said Rem. "Give us a hint."

"It's not important." Daniels pulled out his notebook and pencil.

Rem snapped his fingers. "Jessica Rabbit."

Daniels scoffed. "Hardly."

"Wonder Woman?" asked Rem. "I had a poster of her too."

"No."

"Then who?" asked Rem. "You know I'm going to hound you until you tell us."

Daniels hesitated, knowing Rem would do exactly that. "Fine." He sighed. "Princess Diana."

Rem dropped his jaw, and Reinart chuckled. "I can see that," said Reinart.

"Seriously?" asked Rem. "But you were just a kid when she died."

"I was, but Dad was never big on us watching TV or movies, and I saw her on magazine covers all the time and I remember thinking how pretty she was. When I was around fourteen, my sister got a book from a friend that was all about Diana and her life and it was full of pictures. My sister never read it, but I did, and I couldn't put it down."

"Let me guess," said Rem. "You kept that book under your bed."

"Plus a few magazines with Diana on the cover, but that's none of your business," said Daniels. "Can we get back to Laroche now?"

Rem grinned. "I am going to have so much fun with this."

Daniels almost responded when Maria entered the room with two water glasses. She set them in front of Rem and Reinart. "Here you go. Sorry to keep you waiting. Let me get the tea." She returned to the kitchen and brought out a small tray with a teapot, two teacups, and a small box. She set it on the coffee table and offered Daniels the box, which contained assorted teas. He picked one while she poured hot water in his cup. She poured herself some hot water in a cup with a tea bag already in it.

She sat in a chair across from Reinart. "Have you made any progress in finding Rowan's killer?"

"Nothing definitive yet," said Rem.

"I can imagine you have several people to question and evidence to sort through." Maria leaned over and bobbed her tea bag in her water.

Daniels opened his packet of tea and added the bag to his cup. "We do. We'd like to talk to you about Laroche's party and what you remember. Can you tell us what happened while you were there?"

She nodded. "Yes. Of course." She sat back and recounted the events of the party, which were similar to James' recounting.

"Did you and Rowan's daughter Victoria arrive together?" asked Rem.

Maria nodded. "Yes, we did."

"You two must be close," said Reinart.

"We are," said Maria.

"Isn't she the daughter of the woman Rowan cheated on you with?" asked Reinart.

Maria stilled. "You've done your homework."

"Sorry to be blunt," said Reinart, "but it seems to be an unusual relationship."

Maria studied her fingers. "I understand why you'd think that, but I never held a grudge against Victoria's mother. I didn't blame her for the affair."

"Did you blame Rowan?" asked Rem.

"Of course I did. Once I found out about it, of course. She wasn't the only one he slept with. I had blinders on when it came to him. I was in love with a ridiculous dream, but I couldn't see it until it became impossible to ignore. By the time I figured it out, I'd lost my career, my reputation, and my friends. After he dumped me, I basically started over. And strangely enough, I befriended Kendra, Victoria's mother. We could commiserate with each other after he dumped her too, even though she was pregnant with his child."

"What happened after Victoria was born?" asked Daniels, taking notes.

"Kendra and I actually roomed together while I tried to get my life in order. I helped her with Victoria, and we supported each other until she remarried. We stayed in touch as Victoria got older and she and I grew closer, especially after Kendra died a couple of years ago from breast cancer."

"Sorry to hear that," said Rem. "I'm sure Victoria appreciates having you in her life, especially since you know her father so well."

Maria reached over and picked up her teacup. "It hasn't been easy. Kendra kept no secrets from Victoria. She's always known who her father was, and she tried several times to develop a relationship with him, but he failed her each time."

"If he constantly let Victoria down, and treated you so poorly," said Daniels, "then why did he invite you both to the unveiling? And why did you go?"

She sipped her tea. "Rowan and I have always had a complicated relationship."

"You stayed in touch after your breakup?" asked Rem.

"Not at first." She sipped some more tea and returned the cup to the table.

"What changed?" asked Reinart.

She ran a hand down her thigh. "On a whim, I walked into one of his galleries one day, and saw one of my paintings in there, only it was credited to another artist."

Reinart straightened. "Was it Toby LaRue?"

Maria gripped her knee. "How did you know?"

"I saw *Fury and Fire* in Rowan's gallery with what looked like your initials," said Reinart. "I made an educated guess."

Maria shook her head. "I couldn't believe it. I'd taken up painting while dating Rowan, thinking it would somehow please him, and found that I actually enjoyed it. My teacher said I had a real talent but Rowan," she snickered, "he told me I was mediocre, and it was fine to pursue as a hobby, especially since it was more respectable than acting, but it could never be anything more." She smiled softly and rubbed her forehead. "And I believed him. I'd paint and then hide my work in a closet, never thinking for a second that it was worth anything, much less that Rowan would use it for his own gain."

"What did you do after you found out?" asked Rem.

"I confronted him." Her voice took on a stronger tone. "I accused him of theft and threatened to go public. He denied it, of course, and told me I couldn't prove a thing, and I realized he was right. How could I prove the work was mine? How could I fight a man of Rowan's stature? And even if anyone believed me, who would want to cross Rowan?" She leaned back and crossed a leg over her knee. "But I didn't back off completely. I put pressure on Rowan and insinuated I had friends who would back me up and could prove that Toby LaRue was me. It scared him just enough to pay me a handsome sum, which bankrolled my new career. I started painting again. I went to school and honed my craft and started over, telling no one the truth about the nonexistent Toby LaRue. By then, Rowan had moved on, newer artists replaced Toby LaRue's works, and Rowan and I got along whenever we crossed paths. I'd even say we maintained a strained friendship, and when he purchased the tiger, it didn't surprise me at all that he invited me to the unveiling."

Reinart tapped on the armrest of her seat. "It had nothing to do with Victoria's exposé?"

"Or a supposed book deal revealing all of Rowan's deceit and lies?" asked Rem.

"Which you supposedly recounted to Victoria, so she could out Rowan?" asked Daniels. "And ruin his career and reputation?"

"Seems like a good way to exact revenge," said Rem.

"Unless you murdered him instead," said Reinart.

Maria's gaze bounced between the three of them, but she maintained her cool façade. "That's quite a story."

"Is any of it true?" asked Daniels. He reached for his teacup and took a sip.

Maria bounced her foot. "Victoria wrote an exposé, and a big publisher approached her about turning it into a book, but that had nothing to do with Rowan's death. Neither of us murdered him."

"He must have known about the book," said Reinart. "And wasn't happy about it."

"Did he threaten you or Victoria if you went public?" asked Rem.

Maria sighed. "He made some threats, yes, but we expected that."

"What threats?" asked Daniels.

Maria crossed her arms. "He told us no one would publish it after he called in a few favors and when we didn't back off, he got personal, and said if we published, he'd use every means at his disposable to discredit us. He said the book might sell, but my future in the art world would be ruined and he would cut Victoria off from any inheritance he might leave her in his will." She chuckled. "Both of which were ludicrous."

"So you didn't take him seriously?" asked Rem.

"Oh, no. He meant it, and he might have discouraged a few galleries from showing my work, but let's be honest, the attention the book would have received would likely have boosted my sales, and did he honestly expect Victoria to believe he'd put her in his will?"

"So, what's the status of the book? Is it going to be published?" asked Reinart.

Maria fidgeted in her seat, and Daniels picked up on her first signs of discomfort. "Victoria and I discussed how to best handle the situation. We talked to Rowan and attempted an amicable agreement."

Reinart raised her brow. "And how did that turn out?"

Maria scratched her neck and fiddled with her necklace. "We agreed to hold off on publishing the book. Temporarily."

"In exchange for what?" asked Daniels. "Money?"

She frowned at him. "I don't need money, Detective."

Rem eyed the room. "Apparently not." He met her gaze. "What did you want?"

Reinart pointed at the painting *Rage of the Sea*. "Did you want that?"

Maria bounced her foot up and down faster. "I've always loved that piece. Rowan offered it to me."

"Offered it?" asked Rem. "Interesting terminology. Anything else?"

Her face tightened, and Daniels sensed her annoyance. "He put in a good word for me to get this apartment, plus paid the first year's rent."

Rem whistled. "That sounds like money to me."

"You blackmailed Rowan?" asked Reinart.

Maria tensed. "Blackmail is hardly what it was, Detective, and Rowan knew it. He owed us both."

"What did Victoria get?" asked Daniels.

"He put her in his will."

Daniels straightened. "Really? That's interesting. Any proof of that?"

"He showed it to her. It was witnessed and signed."

"What did he leave her?" asked Reinart.

Maria met Reinart's look, and her expression didn't change. "Everything, Detective."

Reinart paused. "Rowan's entire estate?"

Maria shrugged. "He has no other heirs. At least none that he's claimed. Why shouldn't she inherit it?"

"That's a hell of a twist," said Rem.

"And a hell of a motive," added Reinart.

"Before you jump to conclusions," said Maria, "Victoria did not kill her father. Yes. They had a tumultuous relationship, but she would never take his life."

"How do you know?" asked Rem. "Were you with her the entire time at the party?"

"Yes, but we took time to speak to other guests. We weren't connected at the hip." Maria brushed her hair off her shoulder.

"Who else knew about the changes Rowan made to his will?" asked Daniels.

"I don't know," said Maria. She reached for her tea again and held the cup in her lap.

"Anyone you can think of that might have been unhappy if they knew about the changes to the will?" asked Reinart. "Who was the beneficiary before Victoria?"

Maria sipped some tea. "My guess is that Rowan would have left his art to a museum and the rest of his estate to charity. I don't know who else he could have left it to."

Rem sat forward and put his elbows on his knees. "I can appreciate you supporting Victoria, but if what you say is true, you just made her, and possibly yourself, prime suspects. If Victoria gets his estate and she's friends with you, that's a lot of change coming your way. Add to that your 'book deal,'" he made air quotes with his fingers, "and his past treatment of you and Victoria, and you've got plenty of reasons to kill."

Maria gripped her cup. "We did not kill him, no matter how bad it looks. And there are plenty of other suspects with motive."

"Like who?" asked Reinart.

Maria shot a look at Reinart. "Evelyn Sinclair and that manager of hers. They've never liked Rowan. It's no secret Evelyn wanted that tiger and when Rowan snatched it out from under her, the word was she was furious. I even heard that she almost fired James."

"That may be," said Daniels. "But killing Rowan doesn't get them any closer to the tiger."

"They may not have thought so. And who says his death has anything to do with gaining the tiger?" Maria shook her head. "Somebody could have killed him just because he pissed off the wrong person at the wrong time." She pointed. "You should look at that Carlo, too. Isabella's husband. Don't tell me he's not capable of killing the supposed biological father of his son. He's a mobster, for heaven's sake. And that wife of his, Isabella? She's a money-hungry opportunist. Don't underestimate her either. She's as good an actress as me."

"That's an interesting point," said Rem. "You were a talented actress. I remember one of your horror films. You ran around in a bikini for most of it."

She held her head. "Don't remind me."

"I loved that movie." Rem smiled.

She looked up. "Thank you, but that was a long time ago. I've changed since then. My bikini days are behind me, at least the ones on film."

"Maybe so, but as you say, you are an actress." Rem's smile fell. "How do we know you aren't acting now?"

She hesitated. "All I can tell you is that I'm not. Whether you believe me is up to you."

Reinart studied her. "Anyone else you think is capable of murdering Rowan Laroche?"

"You should talk to Robert, the security guy. I saw him snooping around at Rowan's before the unveiling. He looked like he was up to something."

"Snooping around?" asked Daniels. "What does that mean? He's security. Shouldn't he be snooping around?"

"I'm familiar with that house, Detective," said Maria. "I saw him coming out of a side room before the unveiling. His shirt was untucked, and he looked flustered. And he was nowhere to be found during the unveiling, the most important part of the night."

Daniels took more notes. "We'll be talking to him."

"But if he wasn't present during the unveiling, then he couldn't have poisoned Rowan," said Reinart.

"That doesn't mean he's innocent," said Maria. "He could have been working with anyone at that party."

"Including you?" asked Rem. "Or Victoria?"

Maria pursed her lips. "There was also a strange man at the party who looked totally out of place. He was wearing a terrible tuxedo, and he kept staring, like he was up to something. If you ask me, he and Robert could have been working together."

Rem sighed.

Reinart glanced at him and spoke to Maria. "Did you talk to this man? Did you get his name?"

Maria shook her head. "No. I didn't. But Victoria did. She was curious about him and went over to speak to him." Maria sucked in a breath. "In fact, she told me something he said that I'd forgotten until now."

"What's that?" asked Rem, his face a little pale.

"You'll have to check with Victoria to make sure I'm accurate, but she asked him who he was, and he told her he was Rowan's past coming back to haunt him. Victoria asked what that meant, and he said something about karma." She held her chest. "What do you think he meant? Could he be the killer?"

Rem groaned and dropped his head.

Chapter Twelve

REM DROVE UP A long street with a steep incline as they neared Victoria's address. She lived in a hilly area of the city and as they approached her apartment building, Rem drove past an overlook. "If she wanted a place with a view, she's got a good one."

Daniels eyed the navigation screen. "She lives around the corner."

Rem rounded a curve and slowed at a turn into a set of apartments. "These are nice, but not at the level of Maria's." He pulled into the complex and looked for the building number.

Reinart spoke from the backseat. "She hasn't inherited any money yet."

"If she's in Laroche's will," said Daniels. "She will soon."

Rem found an open spot and parked. "I wonder if Laroche told Victoria the truth. Based on what we know about him, it wouldn't surprise me if he lied to her and showed her a phony will."

"I wondered about that too," said Reinart. "But you'd think Victoria would expect that."

Daniels unbuckled and opened his door. "After everything Maria told us, I don't blame them for extorting him, but if we brought what we know to Lozano right now, he'd be eager to bring them in and pushing even harder for us to find the smoking gun."

Reinart exited the vehicle along with Rem. "Once we talk to everyone, the poison that killed Laroche may be our only link to the killer. We're going to have to find out who made it or purchased the ingredients."

Rem shut his door. "One thing at a time, Reinart."

"She's right," said Daniels. "With the media attention the way it is, the online sleuths are all over this. The sooner we can crack this, the better before someone else sticks their nose in and interferes."

Rem walked down the sidewalk. "One thing at a time, Daniels."

Daniels glanced at him. "Since when are you the voice of reason?"

"Since we don't have a choice. We rush this, we'll make a mistake, and Lozano will be pissed."

"And if we don't rush it, he'll still be pissed," said Daniels.

"So we pick our poison, so to speak. Let's see what toxicology says and we'll go from there." Rem pointed toward a door. "That's it." They approached the door and Rem knocked.

"Let's hope she's as forthcoming as Maria," said Reinart.

Rem sighed. "I'm still trying to get over the fact that my teenage crush is an extortionist."

"Cheer up." Daniels patted his arm. "It could be worse. She might be a murderer."

Rem smirked. "Gee. Thanks."

"At least she's still alive, which can't be said of Daniels' teenage crush," said Reinart.

Daniels slumped his shoulders. "Don't remind me."

Reinart smiled. "At least Brad Pitt is alive and well and still dream-worthy."

"Let's hope you never have to interrogate him," said Rem.

Daniels knocked too. "Victoria Fordham? Detectives are here to speak with you."

"She knows we're coming, doesn't she?" asked Reinart.

Rem nodded. "I called earlier and told her we would stop by. She said she'd be here." He knocked again. "Hello?"

"Looks like she made other plans." Reinart's phone rang, and she slid it out of her pocket. Eyeing the display, her face fell, and she hesitated.

"Something wrong?" asked Rem.

She rubbed her temple with her finger. "I need to take this." She stepped away and answered the phone.

Watching her, Rem couldn't make out the conversation, but based on her rigid stance, she was agitated. "Hope it's not bad news."

"Doesn't look like good news." Daniels turned back toward the door. "Well, what do you want to do? Victoria's either ignoring us or isn't home."

"Why would she ignore us?"

"Maybe Maria called her after our visit, and now she's not too eager to help."

Rem considered that. "You think she'll lawyer up?"

"Based on what Maria told us, wouldn't you?"

"If she really is the beneficiary of Laroche's estate, I'd certainly be talking to an attorney."

Daniels rested his hands on his hips. "That's what worries me." He paused. "We need to talk to Brian Klein and find out about Laroche's will. And we need to talk to Robert."

Rem nodded. "Yeah. I suspect he hasn't told us everything. He had access to the house, the security system, the gallery, and other members of the staff. If anyone knows anything, it's him."

"Klein's got to know some things, too. You can't be Laroche's manager and not have inside information."

Reinart's voice rose, and Rem glanced over at her. She was pacing on the sidewalk. Her back was still rigid, and her fingers were clenched around her phone. She shot a look over at Rem and Daniels.

Rem made out her next words.

"I have to go. I can't talk right now." Reinart stopped on the sidewalk. "Barry, please. Stop calling me."

"Did she say Barry?" asked Rem.

"Isn't that her partner who's on sabbatical?"

"Guess they're having some issues."

"Fine," said Reinart. "I've got to go." She lowered the phone and hung up. Rubbing her fingers over her turtleneck, she put the phone back in her pocket and returned. "Sorry about that."

"Everything all right?" asked Rem.

Reinart blew out a breath. "It's fine." Her tone suggested she didn't want to talk about it.

Daniels didn't probe further. "Since Victoria's not answering, we thought we'd talk to Robert next. Or Brian Klein."

Reinart stared off. "Yeah. Sure. Sounds good."

Rem debated asking what was up, but decided against it. If it were Daniels, he'd be all over it, but he didn't know Reinart well enough to dig deeper into her personal life. He spoke to Daniels. "You got Robert's address?"

"I do," said Daniels. "Let's go."

"Maybe we can get a bite to eat soon. My stomach's rumbling." Rem headed down the walkways and back toward his car.

Daniels followed. "No Taco del Fuegos. Something lighter, please."

"How about a hot dog?" asked Rem. He walked through the lot.

Daniels groaned. "How about a salad?"

Rem reached the car and opened the door. "You mean like lettuce on the hot dog?" Rem slid into the front seat.

Daniels got into the passenger seat and Reinart got into the back. "No," said Daniels. "Like lots of lettuce in a bowl with other veggies and maybe some chicken or steak."

"Now a steak I could go for." Rem started the car. "What do you think, Reinart?" He looked in the rearview mirror. "You hungry?"

Reinart stared out the window. "No. Not really."

Seeing she was still distracted, Rem buckled his seatbelt and backed out of the spot as Daniels punched in the address to Robert's place. "What do you think about that expert coming to check that painting at Laroche's tomorrow?" asked Rem. "Do we still need him after what Maria told us?"

Reinart appeared to refocus. "I think so. It never hurts to get a second opinion. Let's see what he has to say."

"I agree," said Daniels. "Just because Maria says Laroche stole from her doesn't mean she's telling the truth."

Rem drove out of the lot. "My uncle said Laroche did the same to him, which corroborates her story."

"Then let's be sure," said Daniels. "Maybe we should have him look at some of the other paintings while he's at Laroche's. You never know what he might find."

Rem turned onto the street. "We should call Victoria. Let's find out why she isn't home."

Daniels pulled out his phone. "If she's lawyered up, she likely won't answer."

"One way to find out." Rem stopped at the corner and turned, heading back down the hill. He approached a four-way stop and hit the brakes. The car slowed slightly, but continued forward. Alarmed, he hit the brakes again, but his car sped through the intersection, narrowly missing a passing car, which blared its horn.

Daniels lowered his phone. "You just shot through the stop sign."

Rem hit the brakes, but the car picked up speed. "I know."

Reinart sat forward. "What's wrong? Slow down."

Rem pumped the brakes several times, but his car raced forward. His heart rate zoomed, and he gripped the steering wheel. "Hold on. We've got no brakes."

"What?" Daniels dropped his phone and put on his seatbelt. "Buckle in, Reinart."

Reinart cursed and sat back. Rem tried the brakes several times with no result and then shifted into a lower gear. The car jolted, slowed, but didn't stop. That they were on a road with a decline didn't help. He swore as they approached a red light, and he swerved around a slower car.

"Try the emergency brake," said Daniels, gripping the dash.

Rem applied pressure to the emergency brake. The car groaned and slowed a little, but the red light was nearing. He pulled harder, there was a grinding sound, and the car's speed decreased only slightly, but then picked up again. "Shit." He flipped on his red lights and hazards and started honking his horn. "Hold on."

They flew through the intersection just as one car drove past, and a van entered it. It swerved and halted, and Rem narrowly missed its front bumper. Rem cursed loudly as the car picked up speed. "I've got to get off this street."

"There," said Daniels, pointing to a grassy area just ahead and to the right of the road. Rem passed another car and moved over. "Am I clear?"

Reinart yelled from the back. "There's a jogger up ahead."

"Shit." Rem swerved back into the lane. He'd been so focused on getting off the road that he'd missed the jogger. The car swerved and his tires squealed, and Rem fought to keep control. If he lost it, they could flip and roll. He held the wheel and tried the emergency brake again, but it didn't help. Approaching another light at a busier intersection, he cursed again.

"Up ahead," said Daniels. "There's a spot where you can pull off."

Their speed increasing, Rem saw what Daniels was talking about and eyed the area for pedestrians. He saw a construction crew up ahead working on the side of the road. The busy intersection nearing fast, Rem knew he wouldn't make it safely across without endangering the construction crew. Out of time, he pulled the wheel to the right and braced. "Hold on," he yelled again. The car swerved abruptly, the tires protested and slammed into the curb. The car bounced and hit the ground with a hard jerk, headed into a grassy section of rocky terrain, and bounced again. Rem fought to maintain control as the car raced forward toward a grove of trees. Rem swerved to avoid them, but their momentum and a dip in the ground caused the car to tip. Reinart shrieked, Daniels cursed, and Rem jerked the wheel, trying to stop the roll, but it was too late. The car flipped to its side, slid through the dirt, rolled over onto its hood, and slammed into a tree. Rem's air bag deployed, the seatbelt pulled hard against his body, and the car came to an abrupt stop.

·· • • •• • • •• ··

Breathing hard and feeling dizzy, Reinart blinked to clear her head. Hanging upside down and held in the seat with her seatbelt, she tried to focus. After the sudden departure from the road and the terror of the car tipping, sliding, and landing upside down, every-thing had gone eerily silent other than the hissing of the engine. Grateful they hadn't hurt innocent bystanders, she eyed the front seat. Daniels and Remalla were both hanging upside down and she saw Daniels' head move.

"Rem? Reinart?" he asked in a gruff voice. "You okay?"

Her lower body pulling uncomfortably on her seatbelt, Reinart reached to unbuckle it. "I'm okay."

Rem grunted. "Yeah. I'm alive." His head was lying against the ceiling of the car, and he pushed up with a free hand. "You all right?"

"I think so," said Daniels. He shifted his position.

Reinart undid her belt and fell onto the top of the car with a thud. "You guys need help?" She righted herself and moved toward the front of the car. She heard the click of Daniels' belt, and he fell out of his seat with his own grunt. "Damn," he said.

"Can you get my belt?" asked Rem. "I can't reach it."

Reinart looked up. "I'll get it." She reached up and unbuckled it. It let go and Rem fell onto the ceiling and to his side.

A man's face appeared at Rem's window. "You guys okay?"

Another man appeared at Daniels' window, and he tried to open the door. "Unlock the doors," he said. Reinart saw they were construction workers.

Daniels clicked the unlock button, and the worker pulled Daniels' door open. Daniels got to his hands and knees and crawled out. "Thanks," he said as the worker helped him out of the car. The worker at Rem's window yanked his door open.

Reinart crawled into the front seat and out the same side as Daniels and the worker helped her out.

Rem got out and stood with a moan. Blood streaked down his temple, and he rested a hand against the side of the car.

Daniels had a scrape on his cheek, and he rubbed his neck. Reinart checked herself over. Her body ached, but she didn't see any serious damage.

"We called nine-one-one," said one worker, his eyes wide. "You guys flew off the road. You sure you're okay?"

Rem shook his head as if to clear it. "I think so."

"You're bleeding," said Daniels.

Rem touched his bloody temple. "I think it was the air bag. It's not bad."

"What the hell happened?" asked another worker. "Did you lose control?"

Sirens wailed in the distance.

Reinart leaned against the car, and Daniels and Rem exchanged a wary look. Rem sighed as smoke trailed out from the engine. "Yeah. Something like that."

Reinart picked up on their unspoken communication and suspected what they were thinking. The failing brakes were not accidental. Someone had tried to kill them.

Chapter Thirteen

Lying in bed in his dark bedroom, Daniels rested an elbow over his eyes. He'd been trying to sleep for the last two hours, but couldn't relax. His mind wouldn't stop replaying the events of their afternoon.

After EMS had arrived at the scene of the car accident, they'd taken Rem, Daniels and Reinart to the hospital to be checked out. Other than some cuts, scrapes, and bruises, none of them were seriously injured. Worried, Lozano and Marjorie had come to the hospital and, once released, Marjorie had insisted on driving Rem and Reinart home. She told them she would pick them up in the morning and get them to work where Daniels' and Reinart's cars remained. Ready to go home, none of them argued.

After dropping Rem and Reinart off, Marjorie stopped at her mom's house to pick up J.P. and drove home with Daniels. She got him some dinner and insisted he take a hot shower and go to bed. Grateful for the attention but knowing he was fine, he stayed up long enough to talk to her about what happened and put her mind at ease. He left out the part about his suspicions of being targeted. Until he knew for sure, he didn't want her to worry.

Once he tried to sleep, though, all he could do was stare at the ceiling. He thought about Evelyn Sinclair and her manager, James, Maria Rossi and Victoria, the terror of racing down a busy street with no brakes, and whether his wife was happy with the decisions she'd made in her life. Tired, he glanced at the clock, wondering if Rem was up. Daniels suspected he was sitting in front of his TV with a beer in his hand, watching another horror flick. Considering their day, Daniels couldn't blame him.

The bedroom door opened, and Marjorie entered. She kept the lights off and entered the bathroom. Daniels tried to relax, telling himself that tomorrow would be another busy day. He heard the sink running and after a few minutes, the bathroom door opened. He heard soft footsteps and felt her slide into bed.

He sighed and dropped his elbow. "Hey."

She glanced over at him. "You're still awake?"

"Yeah. I can't sleep." He paused. "How's J.P.? He go down okay?"

"Yes. He's feeling better. He went out pretty quickly." She studied him in the minimal light of the room. "You feel okay? Are you sore?" She pushed up on her elbow.

"It's not that. I'm just thinking."

"About your case?"

"Among other things." He recalled again his conversation with Evelyn Sinclair.

"What other things?"

He sighed and rubbed his forehead. "It's nothing. It's stupid."

She frowned. "Well, now I know something's bothering you. It's not like you to evade." She poked his shoulder. "Come on. Spill it."

Daniels debated what to say. He looked over at her. "Are you happy?"

Her brow furrowed. "That's a strange question." She rested her cheek on her palm. "Of course I am. Why wouldn't I be?"

Daniels shrugged and stared at the ceiling. "No reason."

"Are you happy?"

He held his stomach. "Of course."

"Then what are we really talking about?"

Suddenly nervous, Daniels' heart thumped. "I talked to Evelyn Sinclair about you today. I asked if she remembered you."

"You did? What did she say?"

"That you were a star student and a protégé that showed a lot of promise." He paused. "I told her you were a school counselor, and well, she implied you could have done more with your life. She acted disappointed."

Marjorie sucked in a breath. "She said that?"

Daniels nodded. "Pretty much." He rolled toward her. "She also said she was responsible for your ex's beating in the alley."

Marjorie's eyes widened. "I knew it." She sighed. "Something about Evelyn told me she was involved. Makes you wonder if she killed Laroche."

"It does." He studied her in the dark room and broached the subject that was keeping him awake. "Yesterday, when you were having a hard time with J.P., you said something to me about what might have been after I mentioned Evelyn's name." He paused. "It made me wonder if you had regrets."

She reached over and took his wrist. "Honey, I didn't mean anything by that. It had been a long day, and I was tired."

Daniels settled his head on his pillow. "I guess I just wondered if you were happy being a wife and mom, or if you wished you'd chosen a different path. Evelyn said how talented you were. She wondered if you were working in the art world."

Marjorie's eyes softened. "Babe, listen to me. I have zero regrets. I love my life with you and J.P. I wouldn't want to be anywhere else." She took his hand. "There's a reason Evelyn and I drifted apart. Back then, she was ambitious to a fault and her drive and will to succeed was admirable. I thought that's what I wanted too, but that life comes with a cost. The more I dipped my toes into her world, the less I wanted to be in it. She's built to wheel and deal and compete, and I'm not. I'd rather help others and contribute. That's why I became a counselor. Evelyn's not cut out like that, which is why we drifted apart. I couldn't be in her world, and she couldn't be in mine." She rested her head on her pillow. "You and J.P. are my world now, and I wouldn't want it any other way."

Daniels reached over and trailed a finger down her cheek. "You sure we're not holding you back?"

She smiled softly. "Honey, if I wanted to pursue art, painting, tennis, or skydiving, I'd tell you because I know you'd support me a hundred percent. I wouldn't hide it from you."

Warmth spread through his chest, and he caressed her soft skin. "Skydiving, huh? You might get a little pushback on that one."

She inched closer to him. "You risk your life every day and you're going to question my skydiving? I don't think so, bub."

He chuckled. "I suppose you have a point."

She ran her fingers over his arm. "I'm sorry if what I said implied that I wished I was somewhere else. I love you and J.P., and my life with you. We're pretty damn lucky."

Daniels leaned in and kissed her forehead. "I know we are. I wouldn't want to be anywhere else either."

She swept back a tendril of his hair that had fallen onto his face. "Good. Now go to sleep."

Daniels snuggled closer. "You sure you're ready to sleep?" He ran his hand down her neck and shoulder.

Her smile grew. "Oh, no you don't, Romeo. You were in a serious accident. No fooling around tonight. You need to take it easy."

He kissed her nose and stroked her arm. "A little hanky-panky with you may be just what the doctor ordered."

She sighed softly. "I don't think that's what the doctor said."

He trailed kisses down her cheek to her neck. "What he doesn't know won't hurt him." He ran his lips over a sensitive spot he knew she liked and heard her suck in a breath.

"You're bad, Detective." She inched closer and ran her fingers up his back. "Sometimes I think Lozano should be arresting you."

His body heating fast, he pulled her against him. "If anyone's going to put me in handcuffs, it better be you." He nipped at her skin with his teeth.

"Tempting." She moaned softly and tilted her head back. "If you're tired or sore tomorrow, I don't want to hear an ounce of complaint."

Daniels ran his hand into her hair and nibbled the skin below her ear. "That's a deal, Mrs. Daniels."

She moaned again, dragged her leg up over his waist, found his lips with her own, and kissed him.

·· • • • • • • • ··

Rem sat at his desk, eating a donut, and drinking some coffee. The squad room was quiet, although there were a few other detectives at their desks. After a crappy night's sleep where he'd dreamed about crashing his out-of-control car into a group of pedestrians, he'd gotten up in the middle of the night and flipped on the TV. After watching the last half of *The Notebook*, he'd found out the hard way how that had been a mistake when he'd fallen asleep on the couch and had another dream—only this one had been about him crashing into a jogger. He'd jumped out of his car, raced to the victim, and had seen Jennie's face. He'd awoke abruptly, his heart racing and his chest tight, and had barely held it together.

He'd given up on sleep after that, taken a shower, and made a big pot of coffee. After drinking a couple of cups, he'd called a rideshare and gone to work early, mainly because he needed the distraction. His last dream lingered, and he needed to focus on something else.

Tired and his body sore from the accident, he drank more coffee and tried to focus on the recent evidence. Since yesterday, the lab had

learned more about the poison. It included a variety of com-
pounds, and they didn't have exact proportions, but knowing the
ingredients helped. Silvers and Edmund were digging into where
they came from and who may have purchased them. The poison
spawned new questions, though. Had the killer bought it from
someone, or created it specifically to kill Laroche? Judging by its
effects on Laroche, it seemed tailor-made to make him suffer a
drawn-out and painful death.

Yawning, Rem sat back in his seat and rubbed his eyes. The
swirl of information fatigued him more, and he hoped he'd make
it through the day. Besides the poison, other detectives helping on
the case had provided reports on what they'd learned from those
they'd questioned. Most of them had learned nothing new from the
other guests and staff, but some interviews had sparked some interest—one with the chef Maurice, one with a staff member named
Emily, and two with Roger Deveaux and the artist Hendrix. Rem
made a note to talk to the detectives who'd questioned them.

Eyeing the time, he stood to get more coffee when the squad doors
opened, and Lozano walked in. He saw Rem and frowned. "Why are
you here so early? You're supposed to be getting some rest."

Rem poured coffee into his thermos. "Couldn't sleep, Cap. Bad
dreams." He slid the coffee pot back into the machine.

Lozano huffed and stopped at Rem's desk. "How's your eye?"

Rem touched his puffy eye and felt the small bandage just above
his brow. "It's fine."

"You sure? You're not hurting anywhere else? I don't need you to
be a hero, Remalla. This case needs detectives who are well enough
to solve it. You need to take time, let me know."

Rem shook his head, but Jennie's face from his dream flashed in
his mind. "I'm okay."

"You hear from Daniels or Reinart?"

"They should be here soon. You hear anything about my car?" He added a healthy dollop of sugar to his thermos.

"I'm about to find out. When your partners arrive, come see me in my office. I want to go over what we know."

"Can't wait, Cap." He added creamer to his coffee and stirred it.

"And Remalla."

Rem dropped his stirrer into the trash. "Yeah, Cap?"

"You had a close call yesterday. Trauma like that can stir things up. If you need help, ask for it."

Remalla stilled. While his captain had never been one to delve too deeply into his detectives' personal lives, his occasional insights surprised Rem. He nodded. "I hear you."

"Good." Lozano turned and strode into his office.

Rem sat again at his desk, wondering if the captain was right. Did he need to make that appointment with the shrink? Deciding to deal with that later, he flipped open another folder and started reading about additional forensic evidence found at the scene. They'd found fingerprints, hairs, and fibers in the gallery, but they could attribute most of it to Laroche and it didn't point to an obvious killer. And with the number of people who'd been in and out of the gallery, any evidence that didn't point to Laroche was unreliable. Rem thought again of the missing video evidence. If Robert wasn't lying and didn't erase it, then who did? He scribbled a note to remind himself to ask certain questions when they spoke to Robert. He also added that they still needed to speak to Brian Klein, meet with the art expert at Laroche's gallery, plus find Victoria and find out why she'd ditched them. If Rem's brakes failing right after they'd left her apartment turned out to be intentional, then she was a top suspect. He made another note to learn more about Laroche's will.

Reading through his list, he sat back with a sigh. It was going to be a busy day. Sipping his coffee, his head pounded, and he took out a bottle of aspirin from his top drawer, doled out two tablets and swallowed them with some coffee.

The squad doors opened again, and Daniels and Reinart entered. Daniels looked more rested, but the bruise on his scratched cheek had turned a darker purple. Reinart looked almost as tired as Rem felt. "Morning," said Rem.

"You're up early," said Daniels. "You should have told me before you came in. Marjorie and I were up with J.P. We could have picked you up." He sat at his desk and set a bottle of apple juice beside some folders.

Reinart set her small purse in a drawer. "I was up too."

"Glad we could all take advantage of the extra rest," said Rem.

"You couldn't sleep?" asked Daniels.

Rem shook his head. "Had nightmares about running people over with my car. You?"

Daniels cracked open his juice. "Slept okay once I finally crashed."

Reinart rubbed her shoulder. "I dreamed about getting stuck in the car. Someone came to help and then it burst into flames, and we couldn't get out."

Rem grimaced. "That's not much better."

She eyed the coffee machine. "Any coffee left?"

"Plenty," said Rem. "Help yourself. Cap wants to see us too."

As if on cue, Lozano stuck his head out of his doorway. "You three. I need to talk to you." He disappeared back into his office.

Rem stood and picked up his thermos. "Maybe we'll get lucky, and he'll reassign this case to someone else."

Holding his juice, Daniels stood, too. "And maybe Laroche will rise from the dead and reveal his killer."

"One can only hope."

Reinart filled a mug with coffee, and they headed into Lozano's office and sat.

Lozano typed on his keyboard, studied his monitor, and sat back. He'd taken his jacket off and had loosened his tie. "Before we get started, how are you all feeling? Any aftereffects from your accident?" He eyed Rem. "Other than bad dreams?"

"Feeling pretty good, Cap, considering we almost bought it yesterday," said Daniels.

"I'm fine, just tired," said Reinart. She set her coffee cup on her armrest.

"You're all damn lucky," said Lozano.

"Rem's driving saved us," added Daniels. "It could have been a lot worse."

Rem recalled the car flipping. "Yeah. Landing upside down and hitting a tree were all part of the plan."

"At least no one died," said Reinart. "That's what matters."

"Did our guys have time to look Rem's car over?" asked Daniels.

Lozano nodded. "I just got confirmation. The brake line was cut. This was deliberate."

His suspicions confirmed, Rem sat his thermos in his lap. "I guess I was hoping I was wrong."

Daniels sighed. "Why, though? It's not like killing us is going to stop the investigation."

"It would only make it worse," said Reinart. "The force would be looking for a cop-killer."

"It would have ramped things up, but it also would have slowed things down." Lozano scratched his jaw. "The press would have gone crazy, the city would be on edge, the chief would have triple the amount of pressure on his shoulders, and I would be in hell, trying to find Laroche's killer and yours. There's no evidence they're the same person."

"Logically it's the same guy," said Daniels. "But I see your point. You'd be so busy trying to calm the waters that the Laroche investigation would suffer."

"Giving our killer time to slip away," said Rem.

"But why not slip away now?" asked Reinart.

Rem had an idea. "What if it's Laroche's will? If our killer is in it and we get too close before he has time to get the goods, then bye-bye freedom and hello prison bars."

"Makes sense," said Daniels. "But since he failed with us, that puts that much more pressure on him."

"But even if he's in the will, he doesn't get the inheritance overnight," said Reinart. "This sort of thing takes time, especially with an estate like Laroche's."

"Our killer may not know that," said Rem. "And if he does, then all the more reason, in his mind, to come after us."

"It's a theory," said Lozano, "but a stupid idea on our killer's part if it's accurate."

"Well, if he was stupid enough to try something like this, let's hope he's not stupid enough to try it again." Daniels touched his bruised cheek. "Maybe once Laroche's will is revealed, we'll find our killer."

"We'll have to be careful and alert," said Reinart. She picked up her cup and sipped some coffee.

"I'll send Mel and Garcia to the complex to see if they have cameras. Maybe we caught this guy tampering with your car. In the meantime, we keep moving forward," Lozano pointed. "And Reinart's right. Watch your backsides." He rested his forearms on his desk. "Now let's go over what we know."

They spent the next several minutes discussing the latest updates on the case and their interviews with the suspects prior to their accident.

"I think your first task is to find Victoria," said Lozano, scribbling on a piece of paper. "I want to know her story."

Daniels nodded. "That's the plan."

"And find out what's in that will," replied Lozano.

Rem rubbed his temples. "We will."

"When are you meeting the art expert?"

Reinart checked her watch. "Couple of hours."

"Good." Lozano's desk phone rang. He answered. "Lozano." He listened and eyed Reinart. "He's downstairs?"

Reinart straightened.

"Sure. I'll tell her. Thanks, Shorty." He hung up. "Your partner, Thomas Barry, is downstairs. He's asking to speak to you."

Reinart dropped her jaw. "Barry? He's here?"

"He says it's important. You can use an interview room if you need to." Lozano set his pencil down. "Just tell him to keep it short. You've got things to do."

Reinart sputtered. "I...um...okay." She stood.

Rem recalled her agitated conversation with Barry outside Victoria's apartment. "You all right?"

She picked up her coffee cup. "Yes. I'll be right back."

Rem glanced at Daniels.

"Sorry for the interruption." She headed to the door. "It won't take long." Her face strained, she left the office and shut the door.

"What do you think that's about?" asked Daniels. "Barry obviously doesn't instill confidence."

"Whatever's going on, it's not good," said Rem. "You think we should ask about it?"

"Leave it for now," said Lozano. "They're partners. Let them work it out. Unless it affects Reinart's work, it's not our business."

Rem bobbed his foot. "Sometimes it helps to talk."

"She barely knows us," said Daniels.

"The three of us almost died yesterday," said Rem. "I'd say we're a lot closer."

"Point taken," said Daniels. "Let's see how their conversation goes." He spoke to Lozano. "Anything else, Cap?"

Lozano narrowed his eyes. "Actually, yes. Now that Reinart's not here, I need to discuss something with you both." He raised his voice. "You want to explain to me why you interviewed Carmine Remalla?"

Rem braced for the outburst. He'd hoped they'd dodged this bullet, but as usual, Lozano hadn't missed a step.

"He's a suspect and you have no business interrogating a family member." Lozano leaned in. "If he turns out to be a killer, you may have jeopardized this entire investigation. You two know better."

Rem shrank back in his seat.

Daniels cleared his throat. "Cap, we don't think he killed anyone."

"Since when are you the judge and jury?" yelled Lozano. "Did it escape you that he's a mechanic and your brake lines were cut?"

Rem scoffed. "Cap, my uncle wouldn't—"

"Spare me your opinion, Remalla." Lozano glared. "From here on in, you two play it by the book. If we need to bring your uncle in for questioning, give it to Mel and Garcia. You got that?"

Rem sat up. "Cap, I—"

"Stop talking," yelled Lozano. "Unless your next words are 'yes, sir.'" He narrowed one eye.

Rem shut his mouth. "Yes, sir."

"Yes, sir," said Daniels. He stood. "We'll go now."

"The sooner, the better." Lozano grunted. "Before I put Reinart in charge."

Rem got out of his seat. "Sorry, Cap."

Lozano waved his hand. "Your job is to find me a killer. You screw that up, and you can clean police cruisers for the foreseeable future."

Rem and Daniels headed to the door. "We hear you. One killer, coming up." Rem opened the door, and they quickly left.

• • • • • • • • • •

Daniels sat at his desk and put his apple juice down. "We took that bullet square in the chest."

"I was hoping he would overlook it. No such luck." Rem pulled out his chair and sat. "Let's hope we don't have to bring Carmine in, because he is not going to respond well to Mel and Garcia."

"He didn't respond well to you and me. What's the difference? But Cap had a point about the brake lines."

His head still pounding, Rem massaged his temples. "Carmine did not try to kill us."

Daniels held out his hands. "It's not me you have to convince."

Rem sat back in his seat. "Yeah. I know."

Daniels picked up his desk phone. "I'm going to try Victoria. See if I can arrange another meet up."

"Good idea." Rem reached for his phone. "I'll call Brian Klein and let him know we'll be stopping by."

"Call Robert too."

Rem nodded. "I will." He dialed.

Daniels dialed and listened as Victoria's phone went to voicemail. He left a message, telling her they needed to talk to her. After he hung up, he saw Mel and Garcia enter the squad room.

Rem hung up his phone. "Guess what? Brian Klein is the executor of Laroche's will. He's meeting with Laroche's attorney in Klein's office this afternoon to read the will. Apparently, Laroche requested that all the interested parties be together for the reading. They'll all be there."

Daniels perked up. "I hope you invited us."

"Sure did. Told him we wanted to talk to him, too." Rem read from a piece of paper. "Victoria, Robert, Isabella, Maria, and Evelyn are invited. Maurice too."

"Quite the crowd. This should be interesting."

"No doubt. Maybe we can talk to Victoria or Robert. And Isabella, if she'll agree to it."

"Don't hold your breath."

Mel and Garcia approached their desks. "Morning," said Mel. "Glad to see you guys alive and well after yesterday."

Rem lowered his paper and swiveled in his chair. "So are we."

"I'm surprised to hear your driving skills actually saved you guys, Remalla," said Garcia with a smile. "I'd have expected the opposite."

Daniels tossed a pen into his drawer. "You'd have been amazed, Garcia. He was a regular Dale Earnhardt."

"Dale would have made it all the way back to the station and parked in front of the entrance," said Mel.

"My evasive driving is a little rusty." Rem closed a folder on his desk. "Hopefully, I won't get any more practice."

Daniels snorted. "It better not happen again. I had enough yesterday."

"Chicken," said Rem. "Where's your adventurous spirit?"

"At home, in bed, with the covers pulled up." Daniels smiled. "I'll wake it up later when this case is over."

"I hear you," said Mel. "You read our report about our suspect interviews?"

"We did, or at least I did," said Rem. "You had some suspicions about Maurice the chef, and a staff member named Emily?"

"What suspicions?" asked Daniels.

Mel put his hands in his pockets. "Nothing too obvious, but based on experience, they seemed a little less forthcoming. Maurice didn't enjoy talking about his boss. He worked for Laroche for ten years and was pretty emotional over his death. He's superstitious too. Blames that tiger painting and the curse for what happened to his boss. He thinks anyone who comes into contact with that thing is in danger."

"Emily is a housekeeper," said Garcia. "She didn't want to talk at all and was super anxious. You'd think we were there to arrest her."

"Maybe she has reason to be concerned," said Rem.

"We don't think she's a killer," said Mel, "but we don't think she's telling us everything. She got especially squirrelly when we asked if she knew anything about a female staffer sneaking into the gallery and checking out the tiger prior to the unveiling."

"Maybe she and Laroche had a thing going," said Garcia, "and she doesn't want anyone to know."

"What makes you think that?" asked Daniels.

"Maurice suggested some members of the staff may have been fooling around, but he refused to elaborate. Said he didn't want to spread rumors."

"How nice of him," said Rem. He eyed Daniels. "Looks like we need to add Maurice to our 'talk to' list."

"Seems so," said Daniels. "Emily too." He sighed and rubbed his face. "Our list keeps getting longer."

"We talked to the guy with the afro, Henry LaPlace, but he's not your man. He's a philanthropist and his only reason for being at the party was to get another donation out of Laroche. Roger Deveaux and Hendrix, though, are a pair," said Mel. "I made the mistake of using Hendrix's first name, Phillip." He rolled his eyes. "Apparently, he goes by his last name only, like Beyoncé or Whitney."

"People in Laroche's realm live in their own little world," said Garcia.

"Tell us about it," said Rem.

"Roger did a lot of gasping and sputtering at the very thought of being accused of murder," said Garcia. "But he didn't deny that Laroche was an enemy, and his mourning period was brief. He's got a wife and kid and a huge mortgage, but his marriage is on the rocks and his business isn't even close to the size of Laroche's. He may have wanted that tiger, but he would have needed to leverage everything to get it. He talks a big game, but he's not in the same league as Sinclair and Laroche, and I doubt he could have planned this without caving in to police pressure or leaving a hell of a lot of breadcrumbs behind him."

Daniels leaned back in his chair and rested an ankle on his knee. "Good to know. What about Hendrix?"

"He's a much cooler customer," said Mel. "But seemed genuinely affected by Laroche's death. He arrived late to the party because he'd been in Europe for the last six weeks and had flown in that afternoon. Even showed us his tickets. He told us how Laroche discovered and supported him, and Hendrix gave him all the credit for his success. Said he'd made mistakes too, and almost lost everything, but Laroche stuck by him." He chuckled. "But he's also got the ego of a newly-elected politician. The guy showed us his studio and tried to sell us some of his stuff." He shot a thumb at Garcia. "Garcia almost bought something."

Garcia shrugged. "My wife loves his work and her birthday's coming up. He said he'd autograph it and give me a deal." He eyed Daniels and Rem. "Did you two know who that guy was when you spoke to him?"

"Not at the time, no," said Daniels.

"Why didn't you buy anything?" asked Rem.

Garcia pointed at Mel. "Because he was giving me the evil eye. I told Hendrix it would be a bad look if he's the killer. He told me to come back once the case was solved, and he'd offer me the same deal. I might take him up on it."

"Nothing like a good murder case to hook you up with a famous artist," said Mel. "I guess we take what we can get."

"No kidding," said Rem. "Anything else of interest?"

"Just that we're doing some more digging into the guest and staff backgrounds," said Mel. "If we find something, we'll let you know."

Rem sighed. "Maybe we can get somewhere when Klein reads the will."

"You need us to revisit a suspect, or talk to anyone else," said Garcia, "let us know."

Hesitating, Rem poked at the tip of a folder. "We, um, may need you two to talk to my Uncle Carmine. He was at Laroche's party."

Garcia raised his brow. "Since when does a Remalla get invited to a posh art dealer's party? Who'd he pay to get in?"

"No one. He got invited," said Rem. "He and Laroche have a history."

Daniels leaned an elbow on his desk. "We already talked to him once, and the captain didn't take it well. Neither did Carmine."

"I bet," said Mel.

"It's not necessary yet, but if we pull that trigger, you guys are up." Rem paused. "And I apologize ahead of time. He's not an easy guy to deal with."

"Just let us know." Mel tapped on Rem's desk. "And if he's anything like dealing with you on a bad day, we'll know what to expect."

"I'm a cakewalk compared to my uncle."

"I'm not so sure," said Daniels. "Now I think I know where you get your temper."

Rem picked up his thermos. "I get my temper from my mother. You should see her when the bartender at her retirement home makes her a bad Cosmo. It's not pretty."

Daniels smiled, and Mel and Garcia chuckled.

The squad doors opened and Reinart entered. Her flushed face told Daniels her conversation with Barry had not gone well. She strode to her desk, opened her drawer, and pulled out her purse.

Mel and Garcia excused themselves and returned to their desks.

"What's up, Reinart?" asked Rem.

Reinart slammed her drawer shut.

"Something Barry said?" asked Daniels.

Reinart glanced at the captain's office. Daniels could see the captain was on the phone. "You need to talk to him?"

She nodded. "I do."

"Something we can help with?" asked Rem.

She looked between the two of them, took a deep breath, and scratched her neck over her turtleneck. "I guess so." She paused and dropped her head. "I'm done."

"Done with what?" asked Daniels.

"The investigation. I'm leaving. I...I have to go."

Rem furrowed his brow. "What the hell's going on, Reinart?"

She shook her head. "I'm not cut out for this. I should have never agreed to help." She eyed the captain's office again. "Tell him I'm sorry." She clutched her purse. "And I apologize to you guys for wasting your time. I'll finish my reports and send them to you."

Daniels didn't understand her sudden change in behavior. "Wait a minute, Reinart."

"I can't wait, or I'll..." She paused and swallowed. "I'm sorry," she whispered. Composing herself, she turned and headed for the squad doors.

Chapter Fourteen

DANIELS WASN'T ABOUT TO let her leave without an explanation. He stood along with Rem. "Hold up," said Daniels.

She kept going and Rem raced over and took her by the elbow as she walked out the squad doors. "Wait one second, Reinart." He guided her down the hall.

"I need to go," she said.

"You can go in a minute." Rem walked her into an open interview room. Daniels followed and shut the door behind them.

"What's going on?" asked Rem.

"What happened between you and Barry?" asked Daniels.

Reinart paced like a restless tiger in a cage. "Nothing. It's nothing. I just need to leave."

"It's obviously not nothing," said Daniels.

"You've been a big help on this case," said Rem. "Your expertise has been invaluable. You've been doing a great job. Why the sudden change?"

"That's nice of you to say." She clutched her purse tighter against her. "But you don't have to lie to me."

Daniels frowned. "Why do you think we're lying?"

"If we thought you weren't working out, believe me, you'd know," added Rem.

Reinart gripped her temples. "It's better if I leave."

"Why?" asked Daniels. "Has Barry returned to work? Do they need you?"

Reinart shook her head. "No."

"Then why?" asked Rem.

Reinart stopped pacing. "Because...because if I stay...I'll just screw everything up."

"You're scared of making a mistake?" asked Rem. "Join the club. I make them all the time."

"It's true," said Daniels. "He does."

Rem smirked at him.

"And I've made my fair share too," said Daniels. "It comes with the territory."

"You don't understand." Reinart leaned back against a wall.

"Then help us understand." Rem took a few steps closer to her. "You've been all over this case from the beginning. You handled Carlo, James, and Maria like a pro. You know way more about art than all the detectives in this squad combined, and we survived a near-fatal car accident. You came in here this morning tired but ready to go and then you see your partner and suddenly you think you're incapable."

She put her hand on her head. "I'm a fool."

Rem pulled a chair over. "Sit." He pulled two other chairs over, and he and Daniels took a seat. "Let's talk."

"There is nothing to talk about."

"I disagree," said Rem.

"Me too." Daniels sat back. "Tell us what's going on and then you can go."

She looked between the two of them. "I don't believe you."

"See," said Rem. "Don't tell me you don't know what you're doing." He paused. "You tell us what's going on. We'll try to help, and then if you still want to leave, you can go."

She relaxed the hold on her purse. "You don't have to do this."

"What are we doing other than trying to help you?" asked Daniels. "Pretend you care."

Rem narrowed his gaze. "I don't know who did a number on you, Reinart, but you've got it all wrong. We care. If we didn't, we wouldn't be sitting in this room, and you'd be backing out of your parking space."

Daniels pushed her chair toward her. "Sit."

She eyed them both with hesitation. "Fine." She set her purse down on the table in the room and sat in the chair.

"Now what happened with Barry?" asked Rem.

Reinart eyed the floor. "We got in a fight."

"About what?" asked Daniels.

"About the car accident. He heard about it and was mad I didn't call him, and when he tried to call me, I ignored him. That's why he showed this morning."

"Why were you ignoring him?" asked Daniels.

"Because I didn't want to talk to him."

Rem crossed his arms and sighed. "Listen, Reinart. There's obviously a problem between you and Barry. Why don't we start at the beginning? Why is he on sabbatical? And why are you avoiding him?"

She clenched her jaw. "It's a long story and we…no you…don't have time for this."

Thinking of their to-do list, Daniels eyed his watch. "Then you better start talking."

He and Rem stared at her while she shifted uncomfortably in her chair. "Anybody ever tell you guys that you're pushy?"

"Almost every day," said Rem.

She nodded. "I get that." After a second, she straightened and cleared her throat. "Okay. Here goes. Barry and I had an affair." Her face paled, and she stared at them like she was preparing to be scalded in hot water.

"You wouldn't be the first," said Rem. "Partners get close enough where things happen."

"He's married with kids," she said. "His wife found out and threatened to leave him. He took time off to salvage his marriage, and it became pretty obvious to the rest of the squad that something went on between us. I've been getting the cold shoulder ever since." She ran her hands through her hair. "And I understand why. This will affect both our careers. I was stupid, but...," she nibbled her lip, "...I thought I loved him, and...," she crossed her arms, "I thought he loved me too." She blew out a heavy breath. "I'm such an idiot." Her eyes watered and she sniffed.

"You're not an idiot, Reinart, and it takes two to tango," said Rem. He stood. "Be right back." He walked out of the interview room.

A tear trickled down Reinart's cheek, and she swiped it away. "Barry was supposed to use this sabbatical to work on things with his wife and we agreed it was over, but he keeps calling me."

Rem returned to the room with a box of tissues. He sat again and held it out to her. "Here."

She took one and dabbed her eyes. "Thanks."

"Why does he keep calling you?" asked Daniels.

She raised her voice. "Because he says he misses me. I keep telling him it's not a good idea, but he doesn't listen, and then he came by my first night here and insisted on talking. I let him in because, damn it, it stirred stuff up and my heart gave in. And then I couldn't get him to leave. I think he expected to spend the night, but I told him we couldn't. He finally left after telling me again that I was right. That he needed to stop, but he couldn't let me go." She groaned. "I don't know what to do."

Rem set the box of tissues on the table. "Why did you two argue today?"

"He's mad that I didn't call him yesterday. I told him we're not together anymore, but he said we're still partners. I reminded him we're probably not partners after all that's happened. My captain hasn't come out and said anything, but I'm expecting a reprimand, and I can see the looks in the other detectives' eyes. Barry will probably be reassigned, maybe to a different division, and the other detectives will blame me, if they don't already."

"If your captain hasn't said anything to you, then I wouldn't assume anything," said Rem. "You don't know what's happening behind the scenes."

"I can read the writing on the wall." Reinart sniffed and picked at her tissue. "And Barry's said as much."

Daniels leaned in. "What has he said to you?"

She nibbled her lip. "That's what upset me. After I told him to go home and leave me alone, he lost it. He told me I should appreciate all he's done for me, and if it hadn't been for him, I'd never be a detective. He's gone to bat for me, and I owed him, and without him, I would never amount to much. And if anyone's going to be reassigned or lose their job, it will be me, not him."

Rem made a grunt and straightened. "He said that to you?"

"It's true though. He went to bat for me. He helped me out when I really needed it."

"That's what partners are for, Reinart. That's what they're supposed to do," said Daniels. "You don't owe him a thing."

"Yeah, I do," she whispered. "I wouldn't have a career if it wasn't for him."

Rem bobbed his foot. "Okay. I'll bite. Why not?"

She tensed and looked away. "Because..." she cleared her throat and slowly raised her hand. With trembling fingers, she pulled on her turtleneck. "...of this." She pulled it down enough to reveal a jagged pink scar running from just below her ear toward her throat.

Daniels eyed the injury. "What happened?"

She let go of her turtleneck. "I'd, uh, just been promoted to detective. I had another partner. His name was Sam Carter. He'd been on the job for seventeen years. After about six months into my first year as a detective, we went to talk to a couple about the murder of their next-door neighbor—a woman who'd been found with her throat cut. The husband wasn't home, so we talked to the wife. She seemed uncomfortable, but I assumed she was nervous about talking to us. The victim was her friend, and she was upset. The conversation was uneventful until the husband came out of nowhere with a knife in his hand, calling his wife a bitch and a liar. He stabbed her in the back right in front of us."

"Hell," said Rem.

Reinart squirmed and rubbed her neck. "Carter went for his weapon, but the husband was on him too fast. I tried to intervene, but he slashed out with the knife and caught me in the throat, then stabbed Carter." She clenched her jaw. "Carter managed to pull his gun though and shot the husband. He died, along with the wife. Carter survived, but his injuries forced him into early retirement." She paused. "We learned later that the husband was an abuser and an addict, and he killed the neighbor over a drug deal gone bad."

"How long ago did this happen?" asked Daniels. He eyed Rem. "I think I remember hearing about a domestic violence situation gone bad a few years back and a detective retiring because of his injuries."

Rem nodded. "Yeah. It sounds familiar."

"It's been three years." Reinart held her elbows. "I spent almost a month in the hospital and when I finally returned to work, I could sense the shift in the squad. I blamed myself for Carter, and I think the squad blamed me, too. Because of who my mother is, I was supposed to be this wunderkind, and instead, I almost get my seasoned partner killed. No one wanted to work with me except for Barry. He spoke to

the captain, and we teamed up not long after. He helped and supported me through it. I thought I would quit plenty of times, but my mom
and Barry refused to let me. They both told me to stay strong and stick
with it, and I did. And then, after several months with Barry, I started
to feel better about myself, and he made me feel like maybe I could do
this job. And after a grueling day dealing with a double homicide, we
got drunk, and ended up in bed together, and then it just went from
there." She fell back in her seat. "And it's been disastrous ever since.
The day I got assigned to help you guys? I was planning to resign."

"So now you think you're incapable of being a detective?" asked
Rem.

She straightened. "Come on. Look at what I've done. Ruined two
detectives' lives. Barry's right. I suck at this job, and if I stick around,
I'll ruin yours, too."

Daniels almost chuckled, and Rem did chuckle. "Well," said
Daniels. "I appreciate your concern, but if our jobs are at risk, it's
because of us, not you."

"We're pretty good at screwing up all on our own. We don't need
your help to do it." Rem put his hand on his knee. "Daniels and I have
worked with plenty of detectives, some good, some bad, but you're
up there with the best."

Daniels nodded. "Barry is selling you a crock of shit, Reinart."

Rem leaned in. "He's using your insecurities against you. My
guess? He enjoys having you right where he wants you. Guys like him
see a wounded soul and take advantage."

"That's not what he did," said Reinart.

"Isn't it?" asked Daniels. "Reinart, you are not responsible for what
happened to Carter. That scar on your neck is proof enough of that.
You almost died yourself."

Rem pointed. "And you sure as hell are not responsible for the mess
that Barry has created for himself. He made the choices that got him

into his current situation, and you are not some femme fatale who seduced him."

She held her head. "I thought he loved me."

"I hate to tell you this, but Barry has all the markers of a man who loves himself first at the expense of others," said Daniels. "If he really loved and respected you, he'd honor your decision to break it off, focus on his marriage, and leave you alone. Not pester you into seeing him and sure as hell not make you feel guilty and worthless for not doing what he wants."

"He's an asshole, Reinart," said Rem. "Partners are supposed to be there for each other, not make you feel worse or blame you for their problems."

"And you walking away from this assignment plays directly into his hands," said Daniels. "It keeps you scared and powerless and makes him feel strong. He'll keep playing you as long as you allow him to."

Reinart clutched her stomach. More tears surfaced, and she leaned over and held her head in her hands. "How did I get myself into this mess?"

"By not listening to your gut," said Rem. "You've been listening to everyone else for too long. Your mom, your captain, Carter, and now Barry. It's time to take the reins and start trusting your instincts." He leaned closer. "And that means not listening to me and Daniels, either."

She sniffed and looked up at him. "What do you mean?"

"He means that what you do next is up to you," said Daniels. "But whatever it is, do it because it's what you want. Not what Barry wants, or Lozano, or me and Rem, or even your mother."

She stared at them with watery eyes.

"The only one you have to please is yourself," said Rem. He sat back. "So, what's it going to be?"

Her eyes welled more, and she dabbed them again with her tissue. "Shit. No one's ever asked me what I wanted."

Daniels raised his hand. "Well, here's your shot. The ball's in your court, Reinart, and whatever you choose, Rem and I will support your decision, even if we don't agree with it."

"Hundred percent," said Rem. "Although I may yell a little."

"But you can just ignore him," added Daniels.

She picked at her tissue. "Okay."

"But make it fast because Lozano's going to come looking for us," added Rem. "And he won't be so easy to deal with."

Daniels' cell rang, and he pulled it out of his pocket. "Speak of the devil." He answered. "Hey, Cap." He paused and listened. "Yeah. We're still here. We're talking about the case with Reinart."

The captain responded, and Daniels sat up. "She's here? Now?" He paused. "Yeah. We'll be right out." He hung up.

"What was that?" asked Rem.

"Victoria is downstairs. She wants to talk to us." Daniels slid his phone back into his pocket. "Care to join us, Reinart?"

Reinart hesitated and wiped her nose. After a second, she stood, blew out a deep breath, ran her hands through her hair and picked up her purse. "I'd like that."

Rem stood. "Good. Then let's go." He slid his and Reinart's chair back and picked up the box of tissues.

"Nice to have you back on the team," Daniels slid his chair back to the table. "Let's go hear what Victoria has to say."

Chapter Fifteen

COLLECTING HERSELF, PHOEBE SPLASHED water on her face in the bathroom. She dried off with a paper towel and stared at herself in the mirror. Her argument with Barry echoed in her mind, but so did her conversation with Rem and Daniels. Was it true? Had Barry been playing her this whole time? Had he been using her insecurities to manipulate her into thinking he loved her? Had he ever really loved her, or had she been some sort of challenge to him to get her into bed?

Shaking her head in disbelief, she told herself she didn't have time to rehash her history with Barry. Rem and Daniels were expecting her. Her heart thumping, she smoothed her hair, took a long deep breath, and pulled it together. She had to get past Barry's cruel words and remind herself that she was an experienced and capable detective. Two detectives she'd worked with for only a short time believed in her, and it was well beyond time she did the same.

Composed, she finished her inner pep talk, tossed her paper towel in the trash, left the bathroom, and headed toward the interview room. She stood outside the door for a few seconds to bolster herself and walked in.

Victoria sat at the table wearing jeans and a casual sweater. Rem sat across from her and Daniels stood near the wall with his hands in his pockets. Victoria had an open bottle of water, and she eyed Phoebe when she entered.

"This is Detective Reinart," said Rem. "She's assisting with the investigation." He gestured at Victoria. "Victoria was just telling us why she ditched us yesterday, right before we had our accident."

"I didn't ditch you," said Victoria. She scowled at Rem. "I have a life, you know? I have other things to do with my time."

"You knew we were stopping by," said Daniels.

"You didn't give me an exact time."

Reinart sat in the chair beside Victoria. "We were coming to talk to you about your father's murder and you didn't think it was important enough to stick around and wait?" Her thumping heart slowed, and she slid into her detective role with ease. Thoughts of Barry and his ugly comments faded.

"It's not like I'm going anywhere," said Victoria. "Why do you think I showed up here today? I knew you guys would be all uptight about it."

Daniels leaned a shoulder against the wall. "Maybe you were worried that we might attribute our little accident to you."

Victoria gripped her bottle of water. "I didn't even know about your accident until I asked about his eye and your bruised cheek."

"Where were you yesterday?" asked Reinart. "What was so important that you couldn't bother to stick around to talk to us?"

"I had a meeting."

"With who?" asked Daniels.

"The pope." She sat up. "Who the hell cares who I was meeting? That's hardly important. You want to talk to me about my father? Well, here I am. Start asking."

"Okay." Rem rested his hand on the table. "Then let's start with the big question. Did you kill your dad?"

Victoria smiled. "God, no. I hated the man, but I didn't kill him."

"We heard about your exposé and potential book deal," said Daniels. "You obviously harbor ill-will toward him."

She shrugged. "He sucked as a father, as I'm sure Maria told you. I had no reason to protect him. My father made his bed, and it was time he slept in it."

"But that didn't happen," said Rem. "You never published."

"Not yet, I haven't." She crossed her arms.

"We heard he changed his will to prevent you from publishing," said Phoebe.

Victoria's brow furrowed. "Maria talks too much."

"But is it true?" asked Daniels. "Did your dad show you a copy of his updated will?"

"He did, but whether that really means anything is up for debate. I didn't trust my dad. This all happened six months ago. He could have amended it again for all I know."

"Then why agree to hold off on publishing?" asked Phoebe.

Victoria went quiet and looked away.

Rem tipped his head. "Maria got a sizable contribution toward her rent, plus a pretty painting. Surely you got something other than a supposed change in the will?"

"Not from Rowan." She shifted in her seat.

"What does that mean?" asked Daniels.

She closed her eyes for a moment and opened them. "It's not important."

"If it has some connection to why your father is dead, then it's very important," said Daniels.

She shot a look at Daniels. "I'm sure you'd love for me to tell you all my secrets, but that's not going to happen, Detective. I'm here to talk about my father and that's it."

Phoebe leaned in. "The will is going to be read this afternoon. You realize that if you are the beneficiary of his estate, that makes you a prime suspect?"

"I don't care how it looks. All that matters is what you can prove, and right now I'm guessing you can't prove a thing, otherwise someone would be in handcuffs." She picked up her water bottle and banged it on the table. "This is why I didn't want to talk to you because I knew you would try to scare me. I almost called an attorney, but I told myself no. Why should I? I did nothing wrong."

"Do you know someone who did?" asked Rem.

She scoffed. "Take your pick. Rowan didn't make friends easily, but he sure as hell knew how to make enemies. He stole from others and threatened them when they called him on it. He rubbed that *Crimson Tiger* in Evelyn Sinclair's face. He deserted Maria and my mother, and dumped Isabella when he found out she was pregnant. He could treat you like shit or shower you with gifts and compliments depending on his mood or whether he wanted something from you. Why do you think his manager, James, left and went to work for Evelyn? Rowan treated him like shit, too."

"Was all of that going to be in the book?" asked Phoebe. She wondered if Laroche would be the only one exposed in Victoria's manuscript.

"A lot of it, yes."

"Were you going to mention how you extorted your dad into changing his will to prevent publication?" asked Rem.

Victoria glared. "Publication was delayed. Not prevented."

"Delayed until when?" asked Daniels. "His death?"

"That's not what I said."

"But it's the only thing that makes sense," said Rem. "Laroche wouldn't change his will so you could publish a year later."

"Did he expect you to take certain things out of the book?" asked Phoebe. "Things that made him look less appealing?"

Victoria narrowed her eyes. "I came here to be helpful, and all you guys can do is try to pin this murder on me."

"All we want is the truth," said Rem. "Which you seem to be evading." He tapped his finger on the table. "What are you trying to hide?"

She glared again and stood. "You know what? I've answered enough of your questions. You have something else you need to know? Talk to my attorney." She picked up her water and her purse. "I'm leaving."

"If you didn't kill him, then why not talk to us?" asked Daniels.

"Because I can see where this is going." She strode to the door. "I know how this works. You want to blame this on whoever seems to make the most sense, truth be damned."

Rem swiveled in his seat. "That's not how this works, Victoria."

"Isn't it?" She opened the door. "I don't trust you three any more than I trusted my father."

"If you didn't kill him," said Phoebe, "then don't you want to know who did?" She watched Victoria's face fall. "Or do you already know who the killer is?"

She stood there with her hand gripping the doorknob. "I have to go. I've got a will reading to attend this afternoon."

"So do we," said Rem.

"We'll be there too," said Daniels. "Anxiously anticipating the news."

Victoria hesitated, but smiled. "As am I. And whether or not I'm the beneficiary, from here on, you can talk to my attorney instead of me. Have a nice day, Detectives." She walked out of the room and slammed the door shut behind her.

Rem leaned back in his seat with a sigh. "What do you make of that?"

Daniels walked over and sat in the seat Victoria had vacated. "You buy the indignant act?"

"She's definitely keeping something from us." Phoebe scratched her head. "Why not tell us what she was doing yesterday?"

"Is she protecting the killer?" asked Daniels. "And if she is, why?"

"She would if it's Maria," said Rem. "Maybe they worked together."

Reviewing the conversation, Phoebe shook her head. "The whole 'delay' of publishing the book makes little sense. If Laroche changed his will for her, he'd expect Victoria to kill the book, not postpone it."

Daniels rubbed his jaw. "Unless she did what you suggested, Reinart, and agreed to take a few of the less savory items out."

"Or," Rem raised a finger, "maybe she agreed to add a few unsavory items about someone else. That would also explain the delay."

Phoebe liked that theory. "I was wondering the same thing. What if she planned to expose someone else's dirty laundry besides Laroche's? Maybe that's what Victoria was referring to when she mentioned someone else giving her something to delay the book other than Laroche."

Daniels sat up. "So Laroche wanted her to discredit someone else and go easier on him. Meanwhile, Victoria's got another source who wants her to go after Laroche or someone else?"

"Maybe she planned to expose someone else all along, and Laroche added a little fuel to the fire." Rem bounced his foot. "Either way, it sounds like Victoria got a few perks from a mystery person."

"But she still plans to publish," said Daniels.

"Maybe she played both sides for maximum benefit," said Phoebe. "She agreed to what Laroche wanted, but also agreed to the mystery source's request."

"It's a dangerous game to play," said Rem. "If the killer got a clue what Laroche was up to, it might have gotten him killed."

Phoebe ran through the various options in her mind. "Which frees Victoria up to publish a scathing tell-all against Laroche with no repercussions."

Daniels interlaced his fingers. "But does she still publish what this mystery source wants?"

"I guess that depends on what they want and why they want it," added Rem. "If it's about Laroche, he's not around to complain, but if it's about someone else...," he paused, "then who knows?" He held up a finger. "What makes this even more interesting is if Laroche didn't lie about his will, then Victoria gets his estate, plus the book royalties," said Rem. "Not a bad way to wrap things up."

Phoebe crossed her arms. "Except the killer is still running around and if he knows Victoria benefits from both, maybe he'll want a piece of the pie."

"Maybe that's the deal she made," said Rem. "She'd share some of the pie with the killer."

"That makes her an accessory," said Reinart. "Especially if she had knowledge about or involvement with our accident yesterday."

"It's a narrow tightrope to walk," said Daniels. "But it would explain her reluctance to talk to us."

Rem sighed. "Well, right now, it's all pure conjecture. Until we hear what's in that will, we're going in circles." He stretched his neck. "How are we doing on time?"

Daniels eyed his watch. "Good. We need to head to Laroche's gallery soon to meet your expert, Reinart."

Phoebe stood. "Let's hope he can help expose some secrets, because at the rate we're going, I may be around a while."

Rem and Daniels stood, too. "You're always welcome, Reinart," said Rem. He gestured at Daniels. "If he ever joins the circus, I'd take you as a partner anytime."

"Try the other way around," said Daniels. "If anyone's going to make it as a clown, it's you."

Rem opened the door. "I see myself as more of a lion-tamer."

Daniels rolled his eyes. "Until the lion roared at you. That would be the end of your circus career."

"You got a point," said Rem. "I guess nobody's joining the circus, at least for now, Reinart."

Phoebe followed them out. "It's okay. You guys are way better as detectives anyway. And I appreciate your help this morning. You pulled me off the ledge and gave me a lot to think about."

"It's what partners are for," said Rem. "Support, guidance, friendship and the occasional lifesaving, and nothing else should be expected or assumed, and if it is, there's a problem."

Daniels scoffed. "Unless your partner has a sugar and Taco del Fuego addiction, then you're expected to keep him supplied."

"That's a given," said Rem. He eyed Reinart. "Got it, Reinart?"

She nodded at him. "Got it."

Chapter Sixteen

REM STUDIED *THE CRIMSON Tiger* while Daniels walked through Laroche's gallery. They waited for Reinart, who'd gone out front to meet the expert and escort him inside. "You really think this thing is dangerous?" asked Rem, pointing at the tiger.

Daniels walked over and eyed the painting. "It all depends on what you believe. If you think it is, then it is. The power of the mind is a formidable thing."

Rem raised his brow at him. "Have you been reading those self-help books again?"

"I'm serious. If you think the worst, the worst tends to happen."

"So you think Laroche died because of the curse?"

"No. I think Laroche died because he did crappy things to people, and it caught up to him."

"So it's karma?" asked Rem.

"Something like that."

Rem thought of Jennie. "Then how do you explain when bad things happen to good people?"

Daniels turned toward him. "I can't. It's life, buddy. And if I knew the meaning of it, I'd write a book, make a few million, and retire to my beachfront home."

Rem nodded. "Yeah."

"But you can't deny that if you're not contributing to this world, you're likely taking from it, and that skews the odds of good things happening away from instead of toward you."

"And what if you're contributing?"

"Then the exact opposite happens."

Rem sighed. "So you're saying there's hope for me?"

Daniels offered him a telling look. "There's always hope, and I'd be willing to bet that one day soon you'll see it for yourself."

"I don't know about that. I think it's better not to hope for much, then you won't be disappointed."

"I understand why you'd feel that way, but one day soon, that Re-malla spark and charm will kick in, something amazing will happen and you'll wonder why you ever doubted it."

"As usual, you're way more positive than me."

"If I have to be positive for you until you can do it for yourself, then I'm happy to help."

Rem wondered if that would actually make a difference. "They say it's always darkest before the dawn. I think I've gone as dark as I can go." He put his hands on his hips. "Or at least I hope so. I can't imagine it getting any worse." Jennie's face flashed in his mind and that familiar grief returned.

"Give it time. You've come a long way, but you're still recovering. Try not to think the worst, okay? One day at a time."

Rem bit back a groan. "I've said that to myself so many times, I should have it tattooed on my chest."

"We can arrange that."

Rem smiled softly and decided he needed to think of something else. "Hey. Did you talk to Marjorie about what Evelyn Sinclair said?"

Daniels nodded. "I did. We talked last night. And you'll be pleased to hear that Marjorie is very happy right where she is. She said Evelyn

Sinclair taught her plenty about what she really wanted. She's sticking with me and J.P. for the foreseeable future."

"Of course she is. That positivity of yours slipped, and you worried too much. You guys have what most only dream of having, and she knows that."

"Thank you. I appreciate it. And you're right. I overreacted. I'm glad I talked to her."

"She's a special lady. Few could put up with you the way I do, so count those blessings."

"I'm counting them every day." He paused. "And one day you're going to have the same. I hope you know that."

"Hope. There's that word again."

Daniels patted Rem's shoulder. "I can't wait for the day when you look back and realize I was right all along."

"And you'll expect me to tell you that, won't you?"

"I look forward to it."

"Yeah, well. Don't hold your breath."

The gallery doors opened and Reinart entered with a tall, skinny man wearing wire-rimmed glasses, brown slacks, and a brown shirt. His balding head reflected the light, and he carried a small knapsack slung over his shoulder.

"Dr. Douglas Patterson," said Reinart. "These are Detectives Daniels and Remalla."

Paterson walked over, and Rem and Daniels shook hands with him and showed him their badges. "We appreciate your help, Dr. Patterson," said Rem. "Detective Reinart says you know your stuff when it comes to art."

"Dr. Patterson works at the university," said Reinart. "He's one of the foremost experts in both ancient and contemporary art history and restoration."

"Nice to have you," said Daniels. "I hope you can help us."

"I'm happy to help and I'll do what I can." He glanced at Reinart. "I've worked with Detective Reinart's mother in the past. Formidable woman." He glanced behind Rem and his eyes widened. "Is that *The Crimson Tiger*?"

Rem turned. "The one and only."

"My God. It's magnificent." He stepped closer and paused. "Look at those eyes."

"It is impressive," said Reinart.

"Enjoy it while you can," said Rem, "because after today, it will have a new owner, and who knows where it goes from here."

Patterson eyed the painting and then looked around the room. "My word. Laroche has an astounding collection."

"Correction," said Rem. "Had."

"I hope this all ends up in a museum because that's where it belongs." He shook his head. "Well, before I get caught up in my amazement, why don't you show me what you'd like me to look at? I can save my ogling for later."

Reinart waved toward the window. "Right this way." She led him to the Toby Larue painting with the faint MR initials. "We're wondering if you could examine this." She pointed out the initials and mentioned her suspicions. "We're hoping you can tell us who the actual artist is?"

He studied the painting, held his chin, and squatted to eye the initials. "Give me a few minutes."

"Of course," said Daniels. "We'll get out of your way."

Douglas leaned closer to the painting and then reached for his knapsack. Rem stepped back toward Laroche's desk, along with Daniels and Reinart, to give Douglas some space. They watched as he pulled out various tools and used them to inspect the painting.

Rem sat back against the desk. "So if he confirms Maria Rossi is actually Toby Larue, then we have a motive for Maria."

"We'll know Laroche lied and took credit for her work, but does that mean she killed him?" asked Reinart. "She painted these things years ago and has moved on. Why kill Laroche now?"

"She either holds a grudge or our theory about her working with Victoria is still in play," said Daniels. "Personally, I'm voting for the latter."

Reinart shook her head. "If she really held a grudge, then why not continue to extort him?"

"Because of the will," said Rem. "If she believed Victoria was getting it all, then that adds up to a hell of a lot more than a year's rent and a nice painting on Maria's wall."

Reinart sighed, took her glasses off, and wiped them with the edge of her shirt. "I suppose."

They waited while Douglas continued to study the painting. After a few minutes, he collected his tools and returned them to his knapsack. He stepped back from the painting, stared at it for a few seconds, and then turned and approached Rem, Daniels, and Reinart.

"Well?" asked Reinart. "What's your opinion, Doctor?"

He slung the knapsack over his shoulder. "It's hard to believe, but that is a Maria Rossi. I studied her recent work before coming here. She's more polished now and has honed her skill, but that painting is still her signature style, and that is something an artist never loses. I'd be willing to testify to it in a court of law."

"We're not there yet, but that's good to know," said Daniels.

"It's hard to believe," said Douglas. "Why would Rowan Laroche perpetuate such an obvious charade? A man of his reputation and expertise should have known the same thing. If I recall, he discovered Toby Larue." His eyes narrowed. "Was this intentional?"

"We're still trying to figure that out," said Rem. "But this is a big help."

"We appreciate you taking the time to come here," said Reinart. "I'm sure you're busy."

"Actually, since I'm here, do you mind if I look around?" He turned. "Who knows when I'll see these works again?" He eyed *The Crimson Tiger*. "Especially the tiger."

"Of course," said Reinart. "Take your time."

"Actually," said Rem. "If you see anything else suspicious, let us know."

"I will. Thank you." He stepped away and started walking through the gallery, stopping at various pieces and observing them. "Remarkable," he muttered. "Rowan Laroche had quite the eye for talent and appraisal."

Rem watched Douglas move around and exclaim his amazement. "Something tells me I'm not appreciating enough where I'm standing."

"Well, now's your chance," said Daniels. "So soak it up."

"When's the will-reading?" asked Reinart.

"Couple of hours." Daniels checked his watch. "Maybe we can get a suspect interview in between now and then."

"Don't forget lunch," said Rem. "I'm hungry."

"God forbid you should have a hunger pang or two." Daniels eyed Reinart. "If I ever resign, he's all yours."

"I'll keep that in mind," said Reinart.

"Hey," said Rem. "I've been on plenty of stakeouts with plenty of hunger pangs. You know how cranky I get."

"Don't remind me," said Daniels.

Reinart shook her head. "I can only imagine what you've been through, Daniels."

"You have no idea."

Rem wondered about the turtleneck. "Hey, Reinart. It's probably not my business, but if you're wearing turtlenecks to hide your scar, there's no need. You should display that scar like a badge of honor."

Daniels narrowed his eyes at Rem. "You're right. It's none of your business."

Rem shrugged. "I'm just saying."

Reinart fidgeted with the neckline of her shirt. "It's fine."

"You can wear whatever you want," said Daniels. He paused. "But he's right. You have nothing to be ashamed of. You got that scar in the line of duty trying to save your partner. Be proud of it."

"See?" said Rem.

"I hear you," said Reinart. "And I appreciate it."

"That's all I'm saying," said Rem. "Mum's the word from here on in."

Daniels returned his attention to Patterson, who'd stopped in front of the tiger. "That'll be a first."

Douglas stepped closer to the tiger. "I saved the best for last." He paused. "Beautiful."

"I'm glad you like it, Doc," said Rem. "But be careful. It is supposed to be cursed."

"Nonsense." Douglas leaned in and his gaze swept over the picture. He went still, and his wide eyes narrowed. After a second, his brow furrowed, and he got even closer.

"Something wrong?" asked Rem.

Douglas didn't say a word, but pulled off his knapsack. "Shh. Give me a second."

Reinart glanced at Rem and Daniels, and Rem wondered what had Patterson concerned. None of them said a word while the doctor studied *The Crimson Tiger* with his tools from his knapsack.

Several minutes passed and the doctor finally stepped back from the painting, his face pale. "I'll be damned." He shook his head. "I don't believe it."

Reinart stepped forward, and Rem and Daniels joined her. "Don't believe what?" asked Reinart.

The doctor gaped at the painting and then at Reinart. "This is not *The Crimson Tiger.*"

Rem wasn't sure he heard correctly. "Excuse me?"

"Then what is it?" asked Daniels.

Douglas tipped his head toward the painting. "A forgery, Detective, and a damned good one."

Chapter Seventeen

DANIELS PARKED ON THE far side of the lot outside Brian Klein's office. After meeting with Dr. Patterson, the three of them took a moment to collect themselves and decide what to do next. They'd sworn the doctor to secrecy, and he'd agreed to keep the knowledge of the tiger's forgery to himself.

They'd returned to the station and immediately went into Lozano's office, updated him on the latest, and discussed their options. Lozano had called in Mel and Garcia and told them to contact the auction house and ensure that the tiger had been authenticated and that Laroche had received the genuine painting. They needed to know at what point the fake tiger had appeared. Had Laroche created the forgery, or had someone stolen the tiger from him? The latter seemed farfetched, but it couldn't be ruled out. Until they knew more, the truth about the tiger would stay with them.

The three of them got out of Daniels' car. Rem shut his door and put his hand on the hood. "You guys ready?"

"I think so," said Daniels. "Let's see what happens and go from there."

Rem leaned against the car. "If we assume Laroche didn't forge his own painting, we need to know who had access to the tiger between its arrival at Laroche's gallery until the unveiling."

Daniels walked around to the other side of the car. "How come we keep adding to our list instead of subtracting from it?"

"We'll just have to be discreet about why we're asking," said Reinart.

Another car pulled into the lot and parked in front of Klein's office building. Carlo, his arm in a sling, and Isabella exited the vehicle. Carlo glanced toward the three and sneered. Isabella looked over but stepped away as Carlo put his good arm around her, and they entered the office building.

"Something tells me they aren't too happy to see us," said Rem.

"If they get a healthy payout from Laroche, they're going to be even less happy to see us," said Daniels.

A second car pulled up to the building, parked and Maria Rossi got out. She wore a stylish red suit with a black handbag, didn't look their way, and entered the building.

"She and Victoria didn't come together," said Reinart. "I wonder if they're trying to distance themselves."

"Probably a good idea," said Rem. He glanced at his watch. "We should head in."

Daniels nodded. "Let's get this party started."

They walked toward the office building, entered the lobby, and took an elevator up to the fifth floor. The doors opened into a hallway and after finding Klein's office, they stepped inside.

A female receptionist with lots of red hair and bright white teeth smiled. "Can I help you?"

They flashed their badges, introduced themselves, and she escorted them into a large conference room. Two men in business suits sat at the head of a long table and they stood when the three of them entered. The shorter of the two with a thick head of dark blond hair whose suit looked too big introduced himself as Klein and the taller man wearing an expensive designer suit and sporting perfectly cut graying hair was Adam Dryer, Laroche's attorney.

After the introductions, Rem, Daniels and Reinart walked to the back of the room, where they could observe the proceedings. Carlo and

Isabella were already seated, and Carlo continued to sneer at them. Maria Rossi sat across from them, next to Evelyn Sinclair. Beside Evelyn was Maurice, Laroche's chef. He sniffed and Daniels saw him dab his eye with a tissue.

Daniels leaned close to Reinart. "That's Maurice, Laroche's chef."

"He's awfully emotional," said Reinart.

"Mel and Garcia said he was close to Laroche and pretty torn up about his death," said Daniels. "They weren't kidding." He eyed his watch. "Victoria and Robert aren't here yet."

"Robert doesn't strike me as a punctual guy," said Rem.

Reinart muted her phone and slid it into her pocket. "I'd have expected Victoria to be the first one here."

Dryer spoke to Klein, cleared his throat, and looked up from some papers on the table. "We're about ready to begin, but we're still missing some people. We'll wait a few more minutes."

Reinart glanced at Rem. "Let's hope your uncle doesn't appear."

Rem snorted. "He better not."

They waited a little longer, and the receptionist appeared again, with Robert behind her. She opened the door to the conference room, and he raced in. "Sorry," he said, breathless, and sat next to Maurice. He looked around and his gaze stopped on Rem, Daniels, and Reinart. Rem waved his hand, and Robert frowned and looked away.

"That's Robert?" whispered Reinart.

Daniels nodded at her.

Dryer straightened his papers and eyed the clock. "We'll get started."

Rem whispered. "Where the hell is Victoria?"

Daniels wondered the same.

Klein adjusted his tie and cleared his throat. "Thank you all for coming. I know this was last minute, but as the executor and after reading Rowan's will, I didn't want to draw this out. Normally, I would have contacted each of you individually, but Rowan's wishes were that I bring you all together as a group."

Carlo smirked. "Figures."

Klein eyed Carlo but continued. "I'll have Adam read the actual will, since he's the one who drafted it. We'll answer any questions you have after it's read, but just know that any assets left to you will take time to be distributed until the probate court approves it. Adam can explain more about that later." He glanced at Adam. "Adam?"

"Thank you, Brian." Dryer pulled out a folder and opened it. "As we all know, we are here to read the last will and testament of Rowan Laroche."

Daniels watched as Carlo shifted in his seat and took Isabella's hand. Robert removed his jacket, presumably because he was sweating. Composed, Maria crossed her legs and interlaced her fingers. Evelyn Sinclair looked as relaxed as a vacationer sitting next to her hotel's pool. Maurice continued to cry.

"I know this is a difficult time," said Dryer, "and I offer my condolences to all of you for your loss."

No one said a word and Dyer pulled a paper out of the folder. "Let's begin." He straightened. "To my loyal friend and chef, Maurice..."

Maurice pressed his tissue against his mouth and made a moaning sound.

"I have always enjoyed your company, service, and food. Thank you for your years of friendship. We've talked many times about you opening your own restaurant, and it's time for you to pursue your dream. In order to help with that, take anything you want from my kitchen, except for the major appliances. Those will need to stay, but to help you get started, I bequeath you seventy-five thousand dollars. That will buy you a refrigerator or two."

Maurice closed his eyes, his shoulders shook, and a sob escaped. Everyone looked at him with somber expressions.

Dryer moved his attention to Maria Rossi. "To my lovely Maria. We have a sordid history full of regrets. You know my secrets, and, in many ways, you are the one I let slip away."

Maria's interlaced fingers tightened into a grip.

Dryer scratched his nose. "I bequeath to you my Toby Larue paintings and an additional year's rent of your current apartment building. And accept my apologies for the hurt I caused."

Maria's jaw tightened, and she looked away.

Dryer regarded Isabella. "To Isabella, I leave you my apology but not regret. I think we all know you loved my money and not me. Marrying Carlo was wise on your end and foolhardy for Carlo, but he never struck me as overly intelligent."

Carlo glared at Dryer.

Dryer paused and cleared his throat. "But you carried my child, Isabella, and are raising him. Does Carlo know about Mateo? If not, you should tell him."

Carlo's face darkened. "That son-of-a-bitch."

Isabella, her face pale, sat back in her chair with her arms crossed. "Be quiet," she whispered.

Dryer continued. "Since Mateo is mine, I'll leave you twelve thousand dollars, Isabella, for your effort. I know your accidental pregnancy was no accident, but that should cover your pregnancy expenses."

Rem shot a wide-eyed glance at Daniels, who returned the look. Laroche was not mincing words and using this moment to its fullest effect.

Isabella scoffed and drew her arms tighter around herself. "Asshole," she muttered to herself. Carlo gritted his teeth.

Dryer faced Evelyn. "To Evelyn Sinclair, my lifelong rival and competitor. I admire your constant determination to undermine me. Your failure to do so provided endless motivation. Few had the courage to battle me as you did. I once bet you a thousand dollars that I would live long enough to see you shrivel up into a prune and die destitute and alone. I am man enough to admit when I've lost. To you, I leave one thousand dollars."

Evelyn chuckled and swiveled in her chair. "I'm going to miss the bastard," she said. "But I'm so pleased I won that bet."

Dryer glanced at Robert. "And to Robert, my less-than-adequate but capable security consultant. Many have wondered over the years why I kept you on, but now that I am gone, the truth should come out."

Robert, unable to sit still, fiddled with a button on his shirt.

"I've always admired you for keeping our little secret, but now is a good time to reveal that you are my illegitimate son."

A collective gasp filled the room. Reinart gaped at Robert, along with Rem and Daniels, and the others in the room stared in wide-eyed silence.

Robert stared at the table and Carlo snickered. "You've got to be kidding me," he said.

Dryer read from the paper. "You have never asked for much from me other than a job, which I gave you. You inherited my ego and arrogance but not my relentless ambition. You, Victoria, and Mateo are my rightful heirs."

Robert didn't look at anyone but bounced his foot up and down, and Daniels thought he looked like he needed a big drink.

Dryer studied the room and continued to read. "Victoria, you and I have never been close. Being a father took a backseat to my career and despite your efforts, I disappointed you. I understand your need to destroy me. You inherited my spite and ruthlessness. I admire that. I made some promises to you, but after some thought, I've made some changes to our agreement, but I think you'll understand why."

Dryer turned to another page. "I bequeath my public and private art collection to the Art Institute of Chicago, in my hometown, to be displayed and appreciated by the public. The remainder of my estate, minus any assets distributed in this will, I leave for Victoria and Robert to be divided equally between them."

Robert sat up. "What?" he said.

Maria looked back at him in surprise and Isabella glared. "What about my Mateo?"

Dryer lowered the paper. "Rowan added an amendment to his will last month." He read again. "To Mateo, my youngest. I leave you *The Crimson Tiger*."

Isabella sucked in a breath and Carlo grinned. "Damn straight."

Dryer continued. "Since you are too young to appreciate this rare gift, the tiger is to be placed in a trust managed by Brian Klein until you reach the age of twenty-five, at which point Klein will transfer the trust to your name. At no point is your mother or Carlo ever to own or benefit from the painting."

Isabella's face fell and Carlo smacked his hand on the table. "Are you fucking kidding me?"

"My best wishes to all of you, even though your lives will be far less interesting without me in them." Dryer laid the paper on the desk. "That's it. Those are Rowan's wishes."

Carlo cursed again and Isabella, her face pinched, sat in silence. Daniels absorbed the implications and watched as Robert, his face white, didn't move. Maria stared at her hands, Evelyn smiled, and Maurice sobbed into his tissue.

• • • •• • • • • •

Rem's heart thumped after Dryer finished. Reinart appeared equally surprised.

Carlo stood. "This is bullshit."

Dryer tucked the paper back into his folder. "I can assure you that it isn't."

Klein sat up. "As I said before, the assets will not be distributed until the will is settled in court, but hopefully, that won't take long."

Carlo pointed at him. "You did this, didn't you?"

Klein furrowed his brow. "What did I do?"

"Was that your idea?" asked Carlo, "To keep the tiger away from me and Isabella?"

Klein shook his head. "I had nothing to do with Rowan's decisions. He rarely listened to me when he was alive. I certainly had no sway with him when it came to his death."

Carlo whirled on Robert. "And you. You're his son? How long have you known?"

Isabella finally shook off her shock. "Carlo. Stop."

"Leave him alone," said Maria.

"What if he's not his son?" asked Carlo. "Don't you think he should prove it? What if the little bastard is lying?"

"I'm not lying," said Robert. "I went to Rowan after my mother told me who I was. You think he would have believed me without a DNA test? I consented, and it was confirmed. I'm his son."

"I can concur that the DNA test was done," said Dryer. "Rowan confided in me, and I can provide the DNA results in the event there are any accusations that Robert is not his child."

Carlo yelled. "That little shit and his whiny sister split Laroche's estate and Mateo gets nothing until he's twenty-five?"

"I get half his estate minus the art," said Robert. "Most of his wealth was in his collection."

"On the contrary," said Klein. "Rowan was a savvy investor. His house alone is worth several million. The government will take their share, but you and Victoria will each receive a healthy sum."

Carlo leaned over the table and glowered at Robert. "You killed him, didn't you?"

Robert dropped his jaw. "What?"

"You and Victoria," said Carlo. "You both conspired together." Carlo's tone hardened. "You killed your father."

Robert shook his head. "I did not."

"You were supposed to be head of security. What a joke." Carlo jabbed out his finger. "You had the perfect opportunity." He aimed a hard gaze at Rem, Daniels, and Reinart. "What are you three standing there for? You want your murderer? There he is."

Robert shot out of his seat. "If anyone killed him, it was you. Everyone knows you're a mobster and that Mateo isn't your son. You probably killed Rowan hoping Mateo would get everything. That or your wife did it. It's no secret she loved Rowan's money."

Isabella straightened. "How dare you."

Daniels stepped forward. "Maybe we should adjourn this meeting for now and let everyone cool down."

"I'd like to know where Victoria is," said Maria. "I've called and texted, and she hasn't responded."

"He probably killed her too," shouted Carlo.

Rem raised his hands. "Everyone needs to calm down."

Isabella stood. "Excellent advice, Detective." She took Carlo's elbow.

Evelyn got up from her seat. "As enjoyable as all of this is, I should go." She eyed Klein. "You'll let me know when I can get my money?"

"Of course," said Klein.

Evelyn nodded. "Wonderful. Thank you all for an entertaining afternoon." She picked up her handbag and left the conference room.

Maria Rossi also stood. "I'm going to check on Victoria."

"I bet you are," said Carlo. "Something tells me you might have had a little insight into Laroche's death too. Did Victoria promise you a cut of her share if you helped kill Rowan?"

"Carlo, that's enough," said Isabella.

Maria didn't flinch. "I won't dignify that horrible question with an answer. And before you go accusing everyone else, maybe you should look in the mirror. This bluster and overreaction are good ways to divert attention from yourself." She spoke to Isabella. "You should be careful, Isabella. You married a bully."

"I can take care of myself," said Isabella. "I don't need your advice, nor do I want it." She spoke to Klein. "What I do want is my twelve grand."

Klein nodded. "Once the court approves it, you'll get your money."

"You need anything else from me?" asked Robert.

"How about the truth?" asked Carlo.

"We'd like to talk to you before you leave," said Daniels. "Maurice too."

"And Isabella," said Reinart.

"Screw that," said Carlo. He pulled Isabella's arm. "Let's get out of here."

Robert faced Daniels. "That's fine," said Robert, narrowing his gaze at Isabella. "I have nothing to hide."

Isabella stared back at Robert and hesitated. "I have nothing to hide, either." Her face taut, she spoke to Carlo. "Go wait in the car."

"You can't talk to them," said Carlo.

"Afraid something will slip out, like how she killed Rowan?" asked Robert. He smirked at Isabella. "Don't forget. I was around while you and my father were together. I know things."

Isabella's eyes flared. "That goes both ways." She looked at Rem. "You want to talk? Let's talk. Because after today, I'm not saying another word."

"Isabella—" Carlo tugged her wrist.

Isabella freed her arm but met Carlo's gaze. "I know what I'm doing. Trust me."

Carlo paused, and the muscle in his jaw twitched. "You remember what I told you?"

"Of course." She smiled softly and set her gaze on Rem. "Let's talk outside."

Her look told Rem to be careful. Isabella was proving to be a worthy adversary and not someone to take lightly. "After you." He gestured toward the door.

"I'll talk to Robert," said Reinart.

Daniels walked toward Maurice. "I guess that leaves me with you, Maurice." He walked over, pulled out a chair, and sat beside him. Maurice blew his nose and didn't argue.

Maria grabbed her purse. "I'm going to find Victoria." She left the conference room as Dryer and Klein stood.

"Feel free to use the room as long as you need," said Klein. "I'll be in my office if you wish to speak with me as well."

"Thank you," said Daniels.

Reinart gestured at the seats vacated by Klein and Dryer. "Let's sit over here, Robert."

Rem followed Carlo and Isabella out of the conference room. Isabella stopped in the waiting area. "I'll meet you downstairs," she said to Carlo.

"I think you should reconsider," said Carlo. He jabbed a meaty finger toward Rem. "You can't trust him. He'll twist your words."

"I'm not going to twist anything," said Rem. "I'm not the mob."

Carlo took a step toward Rem, but Isabella stopped him. "Go downstairs, Carlo. Now."

Carlo continued to stare, but finally backed down. He stepped away, kissed Isabella on the cheek, glared at Rem again, and stomped out of the office.

Grateful Carlo had left without resorting to violence, Rem gestured to the empty chairs in the waiting area. The receptionist was not at her desk, and Rem hoped she'd be gone long enough for him to talk to Isabella.

Isabella sat in a chair and crossed her legs. She wore a straight black skirt and a silky blue blouse, and when she sat, the skirt rode up over her knee, revealing her shapely legs. Her thick shiny blonde hair brushed her shoulders as it had the night of Laroche's death, and Rem could understand why a man like Laroche would have tolerated a woman like Isabella.

He sat in the chair beside her. "Thank you for talking to me. After our previous discussion with Carlo, I was doubtful this would happen."

"I shot him in the shoulder. He was in the hospital and understandably angry. Plus, you threw Mateo in his face." She pointed at him with a long red fingernail. "Is that how you got your shiner? You piss somebody else off?"

Rem touched his bruised eye. "Something like that. And I didn't throw Mateo in Carlo's face for fun. Your ex-boyfriend was murdered, and it's my job to find out who did it. That means I ask questions people don't like."

"Is that what you're going to do now?" She ran her hand through her hair. "Ask me questions I don't like?" She lowered and softened her voice.

"That depends. If you've got nothing to hide, you'll be just fine."

Her gaze traveled over him. "I'm not the only one who's just fine."

A sultry and alluring suspect had replaced the cold and abrasive woman from the conference room. Rem debated playing along to see if he could get more out of her. "You want to tell me about your relationship with Laroche?"

She put her hand on her knee. "What's to tell that you don't already know? We met at a fancy party on a yacht. I was wearing my low-cut, hip-hugging Vera Wang dress. Rowan and I exchanged a glance, he came over to talk to me, and I was living with him a week later. Rowan and I were like fire and ice. I was the fire, and he was the ice. One minute we'd be fighting like mortal enemies and the next we'd be making passionate love against his desk in front of all his works of art." She smiled and rubbed her knee. "That turned him on."

"Good to know." Rem turned sideways in his chair to face her. "When did it end?"

Her smile dropped and her eyes clouded. "I got pregnant. He accused me of doing it deliberately so he'd marry me. I disagreed, and he kicked me out."

"Did you do it deliberately?"

Her smile returned. "That's none of your business."

He smiled back. "If you did, then that suggests motive. You wanted Laroche for what he could give you, namely money and marriage, and when he refused, you got pregnant." He relaxed in his seat. "And when that didn't work, you married Carlo, the mobster, who's tough enough and certainly manly enough to compete with Laroche. Did you think Laroche would want you then?"

She played with a thread on the couch. "You make a lot of assumptions, Detective."

"I've been in this job way too long to think you weren't trying to manipulate him." Rem rested his arm on the back of the chair. "After Mateo was born, did you return to Laroche, asking him to take you back and claim Mateo as his?"

Her eyes sparked. "Why would I do that? I was happily married."

"Were you? How was Carlo feeling about Mateo's paternity? Or did you even tell him?"

"He's not stupid, Detective."

Rem debated arguing otherwise but held off.

"When Mateo was born, Carlo took one look at him and fell in love. There was no question from that point on who Mateo's father was."

"That didn't stop you from using Mateo to get money out of Laroche, though, did it?"

She straightened. "Mateo is Rowan's biological son. I didn't ask him to claim him publicly, but I expected him to contribute."

"And did he? Contribute?"

"Not without considerable effort. He knew how much Carlo loved Mateo and he knew Carlo's pride wouldn't allow him to admit that Mateo wasn't his."

"But everyone else knew."

"They were rumors, never confirmed or denied. I left it at that, but Rowan threatened to make it public. I didn't care either way, but Carlo was less enthusiastic."

"He didn't like another man claiming to be Mateo's father. Or was he angry about you wanting Laroche instead of him? Mobsters tend to frown on problems like that."

Her eyes flared again. "I didn't want Rowan."

"You sure about that? Those rumors you mentioned? A lot of them were about you leaving Carlo and returning to Laroche."

"Why would I go back to a man that dumped me after I got pregnant and refused to accept any responsibility for Mateo?"

Rem leaned in. "Money. That seems to be the universal reason for most crimes, other than love. And if you loved Laroche, then that gives you two good reasons to kill him."

"I wasn't in love with him, and I had no reason to believe I'd get any money from him, alive or dead."

"Maybe it was just good old-fashioned revenge, then. You strike me as a woman who believes in revenge."

"Oh, Detective." Her face relaxed. "If I or Carlo wanted Rowan dead, we wouldn't use poison to do it. I married a mobster, remember? They're very good at those sorts of things. They're more of a beat you up, shoot you in the head, and leave you for dead sort of group."

"Exactly my point."

She twirled a shiny tendril of hair through her fingers. "My husband and his friends don't know the first thing about poison."

"Except this is Rowan Laroche. If they shot him in the head, it would attract too much scrutiny. They don't like that kind of attention." He pointed. "You, however, might have had other ideas."

She swiveled sideways, leaned back, and rested her elbow on the armrest and her chin in her palm. "You have an active imagination, Detective, but I can appreciate that. Rowan had one too. It's what made him so good in bed." Her gaze lingered. "Something tells me you're the same."

Despite his realization that she was deliberately trying to distract him, heat bloomed in his gut. He played it cool, though, and didn't react. "Is that what you tell all the detectives who question you?"

"Only the handsome ones."

Rem held her gaze. "Did you murder Rowan Laroche?"

"No."

"Do you know who did?"

"No."

"If you knew who killed him, would you tell me?"

"Depends on who killed him."

"Who do you think did it?"

She paused. "After that will reading? I'd say your obvious suspects are Victoria and Robert."

"You have any evidence to support that?"

She shook her head. "No, but I think that's your job, not mine."

"You insinuated you had dirt on Robert. Is that true?"

She shrugged. "He was smug and full of himself, as most men his age are. I've heard Robert and Rowan argue plenty of times. They were more alike than they realized, and now I know why."

"Did you overhear anything of interest that might suggest Robert killed his dad?"

She sighed and stared off. "There was one time when I passed by the gallery, and they were shouting at each other. Robert called Rowan an old fool and Rowan said something about Robert being an impudent bastard. That wasn't the unusual part. They often argued mostly about Robert's job. This time, though, I heard Robert yell at Rowan that one day he would regret not listening to him, and that all the art Rowan held so dear could easily be stolen right out from under his nose."

Rem thought of the forged tiger. "What do you think that meant?"

"I don't know. I took it as an idle threat, but maybe it wasn't. Maybe Robert has bigger balls than I think." She chuckled and whispered. "If he's anything like his dad, he probably does."

Surprised by her boldness, Rem chuckled at her. "If you ever seduce Robert because he has all the money, at least now you know you'll be satisfied."

Her smile fell, and she sat back. "Robert should be so lucky."

"Based on that will, he's plenty lucky."

She scoffed. "At least Mateo got the tiger."

"Carlo didn't seem so happy about that."

"Because Mateo doesn't get it until he's twenty-five. It's absurd."

"And if he'd gotten the tiger today? What would you and Carlo have done? Sell it?"

She smoothed her skirt. "I guess we'll never know." She eyed the gold and diamond watch on her wrist. "As much as I'm enjoying our time together, Detective, Carlo is waiting."

"One more thing," asked Rem.

She ran her hand over her thigh. "What's that?"

"Why'd you shoot Carlo?"

Her hand stopped moving. "We had an argument."

"I assumed. Was it about Laroche or Mateo?"

In her first sign of discomfort, she looked away.

"Or were you arguing about Laroche's murder? Were you afraid of getting caught?"

She looked back. "No."

"What did Carlo do that warranted you trying to kill him?"

Her voice raised. "I wasn't trying to kill him." She paused and softened her tone. "He and I both have tempers, and we both said things we shouldn't have said. He was angry with me and threatened to take Mateo away."

Rem raised a brow. "That was bold of him."

"Nobody touches my son."

"Especially the man who isn't his father."

Her eyebrows arched. "You're pretty bold yourself."

"That's my job."

She held his gaze. Her face relaxed, and she leaned in. "I find you very attractive, Detective."

Rem didn't flinch. "I'm flattered, but I don't think your husband would approve."

"What he doesn't know won't hurt him."

Rem didn't believe for one second she was actually interested in him. "What are you up to, Isabella? Do you think flirting with me is going to help? I don't distract that easily." He leaned closer. "So if you think batting those lovely eyes and running your fingers through your hair is going to sway me into believing your innocence, you're mistaken. Carlo and Rowan may have fallen for this act, but I'm not dumb." He sat up. "If you killed Laroche, I'm going to find out. And instead of wearing pretty Vera Wang dresses, you'll be wearing an orange jumpsuit for the foreseeable future."

Her composure slipped, and her face tightened, but she quickly recovered. "You're used to being right, aren't you, Detective?"

"I wouldn't be a good detective if I was used to being wrong."

Her smile returned, but it held an edge of menace to it. "Were you right when your girlfriend died?" She pouted her lips. "Because I think maybe you made a few mistakes when it came to her death. Am I right?"

Rem stilled in shock. His heart pounded and his chest constricted. "What the hell are you talking about? How do you know—" He couldn't bring himself to say Jennie's name.

"Jennifer?" she asked. "You forget who I'm married to. Mobsters do their research and when you pissed Carlo off, he did some checking."

Rem went mute and broke into a cold sweat.

She whispered. "Remember who you're dealing with, Detective. I'm not easily manipulated, and Carlo doesn't enjoy being disrespected."

Rem forced himself to speak. "I don't care what you or Carlo like or what you know about me. It won't stop me from doing my job."

"Good." She stood. "Just so long as you do it properly, and it doesn't get anyone killed." She paused. "Or should I say, anyone *else* killed?"

Rem pictured Jennie's colorless face that he'd held in his hands on the day of her death. His guilt surged, and he wanted to wrap his fingers around Isabella's throat.

She stared at him for a second and headed for the door. "You have anything else you need to ask, talk to my lawyer. Enjoy your day, Detective." Smiling like she'd just been named the full beneficiary of Laroche's will, she pulled the door open and walked out.

Chapter Eighteen

R<small>EINART SWIVELED HER SEAT</small> toward Robert, who sat next to her. "Congratulations on the will. Your dad took good care of you."

"If you think I knew he was going to do that, and I killed him because of it, you're wrong. I never expected that in a million years."

"How come you never told anyone that Laroche was your father?"

"I didn't want anyone to know, and neither did Rowan. It would have caused too much drama."

"When did you find out he was your dad?"

Robert rested his elbows on the table. He glanced at Daniels and Maurice at the other end, who were quietly talking. "My mother told me when she deemed I was old enough to handle it. She'd never told Rowan, and he didn't know I existed. I didn't believe her at first, but as time passed, I got over my disbelief and got angry. I wrote Rowan a letter he never responded to, so I confronted him one day while he was leaving a restaurant. He tried to ignore me until I mentioned my mother's name. He reconsidered and invited me to his house, and we talked. He asked for and I agreed to a DNA test and once the results confirmed I was his kid, he asked me how much money I wanted." Robert studied his fingers. "It shocked the hell out of him and me too when I told him I didn't want his money. I just wanted to get to know him."

"How'd you get the security job?"

"I was working with a security firm and learning the ropes. I was doing pretty well and thinking one day I might open my own business. When Rowan fired his security guy, he offered the position to me. Said he'd pay me more, I'd learn more about his world, and we could work together. It sounded like the perfect solution. We both agreed to keep our relationship secret and I would handle security at the house."

"When did it stop working so well?"

He chuckled with derision. "It didn't take long for me to realize that he fired the other guy because the other guy didn't want to listen to him. Rowan did things his way, made up stupid rules that everyone else had to follow except him, and took dumb risks. I told him constantly that he needed to upgrade his security and he laughed at me."

"Why didn't you leave?"

"I thought about it. Came close a few times, but when he knew he'd pushed me too far, he'd cave to a small request, or he'd up my salary, or he'd take me to a fancy dinner at some expensive restaurant. He didn't want me to leave, and I didn't really want to go. He was my dad, and despite our disagreements, we were forging some sort of strange bond." He sighed and lowered his head.

Reinart watched him for any signs of deceit. "What happened the night of the unveiling?"

He looked up. "I told the other detective. I was doing the rounds, checking guests in, handling problems, the usual stuff."

"Why weren't you at the unveiling?"

"There was a problem with a guest who was yelling at Maurice. I went to handle it. The guy was drunk enough that he'd missed the unveiling because he was upset about caviar. I had to get him out without causing any more commotion."

"Couldn't you have given that to someone else? Wasn't the unveiling more important?"

Robert tensed. "It was an unveiling. All Rowan did at those was gloat over his prize and rub his victory into his guests' noses. He'd done it plenty of times with the same people, none of which I would have considered a murderer, so no. I didn't think Rowan was in danger. Besides, my job was to protect the art, not Rowan."

Reinart thought of the forged tiger. "Has the art ever been at risk? Any attempted robberies? Any threats or concerns about a guest or staff member?"

Robert shook his head. "No. Never. We've had plenty of annoying people around that I didn't think should be near the collection, but as usual, Rowan didn't take my concerns seriously."

"Like who?"

Robert rapped his knuckles on the table and sighed. "I never liked Isabella. Her motives were obvious, and she was mean to me and the staff. I gave as good as I got, though. When Rowan wasn't around, I let her know what I thought of her. I told Rowan what I thought too, but he said he understood women like her and could handle her." Robert snorted. "He was wrong."

"Did Isabella ever threaten Rowan, or suggest she might steal or damage his collection?"

"Not in so many words, but I always had the sense she was dangerous. I was thrilled when they broke up."

Reinart nodded. "Anybody else concern you?"

"Evelyn Sinclair and that nosy manager of hers, James."

"Why them?"

Robert scowled. "They always act so entitled, like they are royalty or something. When Evelyn was around, she'd looked at Rowan and his art like it should have belonged to her. And James, I was glad when he quit. He thought he was shit on a stick. Before he left, he acted like he was in charge. Annoyed the hell out of me and the rest of the staff. Except for Maurice."

"Why Maurice?"

"I think they dated for a while."

Reinart glanced toward Maurice, who was talking to Daniels. "James and Maurice were in a relationship?"

Robert nodded. "Yeah. I know James bitches a lot about Maurice and his food, but Maurice just ignores him."

"What about James and Rowan? Any arguments there that you saw?"

"James dealt with the same crap with Rowan as I did. He would try to do his job and Rowan would interfere. Rowan was always right and everyone else was wrong. It didn't surprise me when James left. I just wish it had been sooner. He looked down at me and everyone else who worked for Rowan."

Reinart tapped her fingertip on the tabletop. "How long was it between the delivery of the tiger to the gallery and the unveiling?"

"I don't know. Six weeks?"

"Who had access to the painting during that time?"

Robert scoffed. "Rowan was never good at being humble. If someone visited, he'd often take them into the gallery to show off the tiger."

"Is there a log of who visited? Or entered the gallery?"

"Just the cameras."

Reinart nodded. "Did anyone who was here for the will reading visit Rowan in the six weeks prior to the unveiling?"

Robert squinted. "That's an odd question."

"It might be important."

Robert paused. "Victoria and Maria came over to meet with Rowan. Isabella, too. I can't be sure if Rowan took them into the gallery, though."

"When was that?"

Robert shook his head. "Hell if I know. My mind's not thinking too clearly now."

"I'm not surprised. Did anyone else visit?"

"His friend, Hendrix, usually did, but I think he'd been out of town." Robert paused. "Brian Klein came by, but that's normal, and they'd typically meet in the gallery."

Reinart used her phone to take some notes. "Anyone else?"

"Not that I can think of at the moment."

"If you recall another visitor during that time, we need to know."

"The cameras are your best bet. Rowan had other business associates over and I didn't know their names. Plus, someone could have stopped by when I wasn't around."

"Okay. We'll check it." Reinart recalled another incident. "We've learned that you and Rowan had a fight prior to the unveiling. What were you arguing about?"

Robert shifted in his seat and scratched his jaw. "I...uh...I'm not sure. It was probably just another security issue."

For the first time, Reinart sensed deception. "You don't recall the problem?"

Robert shrugged. "I walked past the gallery and the door was open. I got pissed and when Rowan confronted me, I called him on it."

"Why'd he confront you?" Robert squirmed and Reinart caught him tighten his grip on the armrest of the chair. "What are you not telling me?"

Robert blew out a deep breath. "It's not important. It's got nothing to do with this case."

"Why don't you let me be the judge of that?"

Robert dropped his head into the palm of his hand. "Because you'll make a big deal out of it."

"Robert, someone murdered your father, and we need to find out who did it. I have to investigate every angle, and if you want me to clear your name, you need to tell me everything."

Robert hesitated and blew out a heavy breath. "Okay." He looked at Reinart with weary eyes. "Just before the unveiling, he found a female staff member in the gallery looking at the tiger, and Rowan was angry. I yelled at him that it was his own fault for leaving the gallery door open. He blamed the staff member and threatened to fire her. I defended her but...but...he said he knew I was sleeping with her."

Reinart tipped her head. "Were you sleeping with her?"

Robert nodded. "Yeah. Rowan had a weird thing about not co-mingling with the other employees. He told me to break it off, or she'd lose her job. I called him a few choice names and stomped out." He paused. "That was my last conversation with him."

"Did he have a problem with James and Maurice when they were together?"

"I don't know."

Reinart recalled Maria Rossi mentioning how, during the party, she'd seen Robert leaving a room in the house looking flustered and unkempt. "Who were you sleeping with?"

Robert groaned. "Is that important? Can't we leave her out of this? She's scared."

"No. Unfortunately, we can't. I need to know."

"She doesn't want anyone to know we're...together."

"You're still seeing her?"

"I hope so. After all this, though," he waved hand, "who knows?"

"I'll do my best to keep it quiet, but I can't promise anything." She waited. "What's her name?"

Robert set his jaw. "Some detectives already spoke to her, and it freaked her out. Are you going to talk to her again?"

"Probably."

"Oh, man. Do you have to?"

"Once we can rule you and her out, we won't bother her again. But we can't do that until we talk to her."

He sighed heavily and closed his eyes. "Fine." He opened his eyes. "Just go easy on her, okay? She's upset about all of this."

"I promise to do my best."

He paused. "Her name's Emily Chang. She's a housekeeper at Rowan's, or at least she was."

"Did she know you were Rowan's son?"

Robert straightened and smacked his palm on the table. "Don't you dare insinuate she had anything to do with this."

"I'm not insinuating anything, but I have to ask."

Angry, Robert stood. "I should have never said anything."

Daniels and Maurice looked over. "Everything okay?" asked Daniels.

Robert yelled at Reinart. "She did nothing wrong. You leave her out of this, you hear me?"

"Robert, sit down."

"No. I should have never said a word. Now you're going to screw it all up."

"Screw what up?" asked Reinart.

Robert shoved his chair back. "I'm out of here."

"Robert—"

He ignored her and walked out of the conference room.

· · • • • · • • • ·

Daniels and Maurice watched Robert leave. Reinart stood too, glanced toward Daniels, walked over, and sat beside Maurice.

"I think I hit a nerve," she said.

"Apparently," said Daniels.

Maurice was slowly collecting himself. The moment Daniels started asking questions, Maurice's emotions had spilled over, and the tears had come faster. Daniels had let Maurice do all the talking to let him work through his grief. He'd learned over the years that sometimes patience worked better than pushing. Maurice needed to feel heard, and Daniels listened as Maurice told him about his friendship with Rowan—how they'd met, how Maurice had worked for him, how their friendship had grown, and how Rowan had become a mentor and source of support to Maurice. After several minutes, Maurice's nerves settled and his tears slowed. Daniels sensed he could dig deeper when Robert had angrily stood and left the conference room.

Maurice sniffed and wiped his nose. "Robert's always had a temper."

"How bad of a temper?" asked Daniels.

Maurice fiddled with his tissue. "He's young and Rowan knew how to push his buttons. I wondered why Rowan put up with Robert's temperament, but now I know why."

"He never told you Robert was his son?"

"No," said Maurice. "Never."

"Did anyone else ever argue with Rowan?" asked Daniels. "Is there someone you think would want to kill him?"

Maurice shook his head. "No. I can't think of anyone. But it wasn't just a person who killed Rowan, it's what influenced that person."

"What do you mean?"

"It's that tiger." Maurice swiped his cheek with the tissue. "The minute that painting came into the house, I knew it was bad. It's not just bad for whoever owns it, it's bad for whoever comes into contact with it. I never went into the gallery once the tiger arrived. I don't even like speaking about it."

Daniels glanced at Reinart. "We've heard of the curse. Are you saying that's why Rowan died?" asked Daniels.

"I know it is," said Maurice. "I told Rowan it was a mistake to purchase it, but he wouldn't listen to me. He told me I was overreacting, but I wasn't. That tiger is bad news, Detective."

"I can understand how you might think that," Daniels kept his voice gentle to keep Maurice relaxed, "but the painting didn't poison Rowan. Someone at the party did."

Maurice showed the first spark of anger. "I know that. Someone took my friend's life and I pray you find him or her. But if it hadn't been for that painting, Rowan would still be alive."

Daniels had pulled out his notebook when he'd sat with Maurice, but he had yet to write anything. "Who do you think killed him?"

"I wasn't privy to his business dealings. I know it thrilled him that he'd taken the tiger from Miss Sinclair and James. He opened a very expensive bottle of wine that night to celebrate. And Rowan had confided his frustrations to me about Victoria and Maria. He hated that book Victoria was writing and didn't want it to be published. And it disappointed him that Maria told Victoria about sensitive things that had happened between them. He felt betrayed by both of them."

Daniels took some notes. "The night of the party, did you see anything suspicious?"

Maurice paused. "No, but I was in the kitchen, working my butt off. Just before Rowan revealed the tiger, I had an intoxicated guest express his fury over the choice of caviar, but thankfully, Robert escorted him out."

Reinart set her forearm on the table. "Was the unruly guest before or during the unveiling?"

"Just before. It was awful timing because I had to get the next course out before the unveiling ended. That's when the real party started."

"So Robert had left the kitchen around the time of the unveiling?" asked Reinart.

Maurice rubbed his jaw. "Yes. I know because James was being his usual picky self. He stopped by on his way to the gallery to bitch about the canapés, and I told him to get out of my kitchen." He rolled his eyes. "He's such a prima donna."

Reinart frowned and Daniels wondered what was on her mind. She asked another question. "Robert mentioned that you and James were involved."

Daniels perked up when he heard that. "Is that true?"

Maurice nodded. "We were together for a while. I thought he was so handsome. Still do I guess, but ultimately James' ambition did us in. He works all the time, and he's so driven. So am I, but not at the expense of the people I love. I took a backseat to his dreams, and I wasn't one of them. I deserve more, and I let him know. We ended it, but we remain friends. He still insults my food though, but I hate his clothes, so I call it even." He smiled softly.

Reinart leaned against the table. "Robert mentioned Rowan didn't like the staff fraternizing together. Did he have a problem with you and James?"

"Not that he said, but I knew of his issues with the staff fooling around, so I didn't discuss it with him much and James and I were low key about it. I think because of my friendship with Rowan, he didn't say anything." His eyes welled. "He respected me, and my choices, and I tried to do the same with him." He pressed the tissue to the corner of his eyes.

"When did you and James break up?" asked Daniels.

"Not long before he quit." He sighed. "I was sad when he left, but not surprised. Evelyn made him an excellent offer."

"Other than the unruly guest, did anything else happen at the party?" asked Daniels.

Maurice held the tissue against his lips. "I don't think—" His eyes narrowed. "Wait a minute. Yes. Something odd did happen." His face furrowed. "It was after the unveiling."

"What was that?" asked Daniels.

"One of the staff, Emily, came into the kitchen. She was very upset."

Reinart raised a brow. "Emily Chang?"

"Yes," said Maurice. "She's a housekeeper. She worked that night to make a little extra money. I asked her what was wrong, and she started crying. She kept saying that she'd made a big mistake. I asked her what she meant, but she wouldn't tell me. I told her to take a break and go splash some water on her face, and she left. It wasn't long after that Dominique...," he held his chest, "...found...Rowan." He scrunched his face as fresh tears fell.

Reinart patted his wrist. "I'm very sorry for your loss."

"Thank you," said Maurice, his voice cracking.

"Can I ask you something else about Emily?" asked Reinart.

Maurice composed himself and nodded. "Yes."

"Was she seeing anyone?" asked Reinart.

Maurice pulled another tissue from a packet of them in his pocket. "I don't like to speculate about those things. It's not my business." He wiped his nose.

"I understand, but it's important," said Reinart.

"We'll be discreet about any information you give us," said Daniels. "If Emily is in trouble, we may be able to help her."

Maurice cleared his throat. "I'm not sure, but I think she and Robert were together. They were always talking, and she smiled a lot around him. A few weeks ago, I saw them come out of the security room together and they both looked flushed. It wasn't hard to put two and two together."

"The security room?" asked Daniels. "Emily was in there with Robert?"

"Yes," said Maurice. "And if I'm honest, it's happened more than once." He lowered his tissue, and he caught the glance between Daniels and Reinart. "Is that a problem?" He gripped his tissue. "Did I get her in trouble?"

Daniels scribbled in his notebook. "Not at all."

More tears threatened to spill, and Maurice held his head. "I think I need to take a break. This is all so difficult to deal with. I'm overwhelmed."

"Just one more thing," said Daniels. "Do you recall anyone coming to see the painting prior to the unveiling? Did anyone request access to it other than Rowan?"

"I have no idea," said Maurice. "I avoided that gallery and stuck to the kitchen."

Daniels expected as much and set his pencil down. "That's fine. You've been very helpful."

"We appreciate your honesty," said Reinart. "Are you okay to get home?"

Maurice let go of a deep breath. "I'll be okay. I'll pull it together before I drive. The memorial service is going to kill me, though. I'm going to cry through the whole thing." He stood, and Daniels and Reinart stood, too. "If you need anything else," he said, "you know where to find me."

"Thank you again for your time," said Daniels. He patted Maurice's arm. "Take it easy."

"Thank you, Detective. I'm going to go home and eat a giant bowl of ice cream and make a batch of chocolate chip cookies. They're my specialty."

"I don't blame you," said Reinart. "I bet they're delicious."

"Maybe I'll bring you some as a thank you for all you're doing for Rowan." His voice caught as more tears threatened.

"We're only doing our job," said Daniels, "but Detective Remalla will be your friend for life if you bring him chocolate chip cookies."

"I'll remember that." Maurice smiled, said goodbye, and left the conference room.

Reinart waited for him to leave. "What do you think?"

Daniels closed his notebook and put it back in his pocket. "We need to gather our info and figure out where to go from here. It wouldn't hurt to ask Klein a few questions, too. Let's find Rem." He followed Reinart out of the room and into the waiting area. The receptionist was at her desk, but Rem wasn't there. "Where's Detective Remalla?" he asked the receptionist.

She smiled at him. "Oh, he was here when I returned, but he said to tell you he needed some air and he'd wait for you at the car."

Daniels frowned. "He left?"

The receptionist nodded. "Yes." Her phone rang, and she answered it.

"Why would he leave?" asked Reinart.

Daniels headed toward the door when Brian Klein came around the corner. "All done?" asked Klein. "I hope you could get some answers."

"Yes," said Reinart. "Thanks for letting us use the room." She paused. "Since you're available, Mr. Klein, do you mind if we ask you a few questions?"

"Not at all. Come on back." He gestured down the hall.

Sensing something was off, Daniels stifled the urge to go look for his partner. He and Reinart followed Klein into his office, and Reinart took over the questioning.

"This shouldn't take long," she said. "We know you're busy."

Klein sat at his cluttered desk in his modest office. To Daniels' surprise, there wasn't a single painting on the walls.

"How can I help?" asked Klein.

"How long did you work with Laroche?" asked Reinart.

"Rowan hired me not long after James Montrose left."

"How well did you and Laroche get along?" she asked.

"Pretty well. Our working relationship was simple, though. Laroche told me what he wanted, and I did it. I'm not an art expert and he didn't hire me as one."

"Why was that?" asked Reinart.

"That's the way he preferred it. Laroche valued his own opinion above all others."

"Were you involved in the purchase of *The Crimson Tiger*?" asked Daniels.

"I was. I assisted with the negotiations with the auction house and worked with Dryer on the legal issues. Once the purchase went through, I ensured the tiger was safely delivered to Rowan's gallery."

"Any issues with the transportation or delivery?" asked Daniels.

"No. Everything went smoothly." The wrinkles at the corner of his eyes creased deeper. "Why do you ask?"

"We're just checking all our boxes." Reinart adjusted her glasses. "Did you know about the amendment to Laroche's will?"

"You mean me managing the trust?" Klein shook his head. "Only that Rowan mentioned it to me after he made the change. I told him I was fine with it."

"So now that the tiger is yours," said Reinart, "what does that mean?"

Klein arranged some papers on his desk. "It's not actually mine. I'll handle the trust and the tiger until Mateo takes over when he's twenty-five."

"What do you plan to do with it?" asked Daniels.

"I'm not sure yet. I may just put it in storage for now until all of this hubbub dies down."

"Are you worried about the curse?" asked Reinart.

Klein smiled. "Not really. I'm not a superstitious man. Plus, I don't really consider myself the owner, just the temporary caretaker."

"You think that matters?" asked Daniels.

Klein smoothed his tie. "What are you suggesting, Detective? That I'm in danger because I'm currently in charge of the tiger?"

"The previous owners are all dead," said Reinart. "That doesn't concern you?"

"The tiger didn't kill them. Life did." Klein sat back. "I'm sure I'll be fine."

"Life didn't kill your boss," said Daniels. "He was murdered."

"My boss had enemies," said Klein. "Everyone knew that. I'm not Laroche and I stay under the radar. Why would anyone target me?"

"What happens to the tiger if you die?" asked Reinart.

Klein stilled. "You are direct, aren't you?"

"It's a good question," said Daniels.

Klein rubbed his jaw. "I'm not sure. I assume I'll have to amend my own will and assign another trustee."

"Who might that be?" asked Reinart.

"I haven't thought that far ahead, but in accordance with Rowan's wishes, it won't be Mateo's parents."

So far, Daniels thought Klein was giving them all the right answers, but there was still a big question to ask. "Who do you think might have killed your boss?"

Klein interlaced his fingers. "Laroche was a complicated man. He could be as cold as an Imperial Trooper and as generous as a country preacher. He didn't care about what people thought of him and enjoyed stirring the pot. I'd say any one of the people who were just in that conference room could be your killer, including Victoria."

"What about you?" asked Reinart.

Klein steepled his fingers. "I wasn't at the party."

"It's called being an accessory," said Daniels. "You could have helped anyone in that conference room." Daniels had to wonder about the forgery. Could Klein have been involved?

"I suppose," said Klein, "but I didn't. Why would I? I didn't benefit from his death."

"Do you get any compensation as the trustee?" asked Reinart.

"I do if I choose to display it," replied Klein. "Fifty percent of any proceeds. The other fifty percent would go into the trust for Mateo."

"That sounds pretty lucrative," said Reinart. "Plenty of museums would love to display it." She paused. "Maybe even offer you a little kickback to get priority access."

Klein remained unfazed. "I make plenty of money, Detective. Laroche paid me well. And if I choose to display the tiger, it would be on loan only. And any money received would go into the trust for Mateo to claim when he came of age."

Daniels studied Klein, but if Klein was lying, he was good at it.

"Anything else?" asked Klein.

"Yes," said Reinart. "After the delivery of the tiger, did it remain in Laroche's gallery?"

"Did it go anywhere else?" asked Daniels.

"No. It sat exactly where it is now."

"Did anyone else see it before the unveiling?" asked Daniels.

Klein furrowed his brow. "I did, and whoever Rowan showed it to. I'd say Robert would know better. I wasn't at the house often." He sat back in his chair. "Why all the interest in the tiger?"

"Like we said, we're covering our bases." She glanced at Daniels. "You good?"

Daniels nodded. "For now, but we'll be in touch if we have more questions."

"Of course. You have my number." Klein stood.

"Thanks for your time." Reinart headed for the door.

Eager to find Rem, Daniels followed Reinart out of Klein's office.

Chapter Nineteen

Looking for Rem, Daniels walked into the parking lot but didn't see his partner near the car.

"Over there." Reinart turned and pointed.

Klein's office building and the one next to it shared a small court-yard with a modest fountain, a tall sparse tree, a patch of grass and a bench. Rem was sitting on the bench. His elbows were on his knees, and he was staring at the ground.

Daniels and Reinart jogged over. "Rem?" asked Daniels. "What's wrong?"

"Why'd you leave?" asked Reinart.

Rem, his face pale and somber, straightened. "Sorry. I had to get some air. It was getting a little claustrophobic in there."

"Since when are you claustrophobic?" asked Daniels.

Rem blinked and Daniels caught the almost imperceptible tension in his partner's neck and shoulders. It was a movement he'd become familiar with as Rem worked through his grief after Jennie's death. He was about to pretend that everything was all right and deflect Daniels' concern.

"Oh, you know me," said Rem. "Antsy as usual." He scratched his knee. "How'd it go with Maurice and Robert?"

Daniels and Reinart each sat on either side of Rem. "Fine," said Daniels. "How'd it go with Isabella?"

That same tension returned to Rem's shoulders. "She's, uh, a piece of work."

"She certainly seems capable of handling Carlo," said Reinart.

"What did she say?" asked Daniels. It was obvious to Daniels that whatever was bothering Rem had occurred during, or after, his talk with Isabella.

"She denied killing Laroche, and she hit on me." He poked at a small hole in his jeans. "Her boundaries are a little iffy, to say the least."

Reinart widened her eyes. "She hit on you?"

Rem smiled, but it didn't reach his eyes. "I think it's the Remalla charm. It gets them every time."

"What else did she do?" asked Daniels. He debated how far to push. Would Rem want to express what was on his mind with Reinart present?

Rem met Daniels' look. The exchange between them communicated clearly that Rem knew he wasn't fooling Daniels at all. Rem sighed and went back to studying the ground. "All right. I'll tell you. Isabella didn't pull any punches. She mentioned Jennie."

"Who's Jennie?" asked Reinart.

"What the hell did she say?" Daniels tried to stay cool, but inside he was raging.

Rem cleared his throat. "Not much, but enough. Carlo did some digging after our visit with him in the hospital. He didn't appreciate our attitude, apparently. Isabella knew where to strike. I wouldn't underestimate that woman."

Daniels muttered a curse and clenched his fingers into fists. "I can't believe this."

"It was a distraction tactic more than anything, but she aimed well. I had to take a second after she left." He shook out his hands. "I'm doing better now."

Reinart looked between the two of them, her expression one of confusion.

Rem rubbed his face, glanced at Reinart, and spoke softly. "Jennie was my girlfriend. I loved her and would have married her, but she...uh...died in a car accident."

Reinart's face fell. "I'm so sorry." She shifted to face Rem. "When did this happen?"

"A little over two years ago," said Daniels.

"Two years, three months, and about," Rem stared off, "eight days." He blew out his cheeks. "It about killed me. There's more to the story, but that's all that really matters, and it's about all I can muster the courage to talk about."

"I can't believe Isabella would say something like that," said Reinart.

"It shocked me into silence," said Rem. "She implied I'd made mistakes and hoped I wouldn't make them again on this case."

Disgusted, Daniels stood and cursed again. "I may need to visit this lady and tell her what I think about her and her husband's research."

Rem sighed. "It wouldn't do any good, and you'd probably just slug Carlo, and they'd love that. If we end up arresting one or both of them, it won't look good if one of us is accused of police brutality."

Daniels paced. "I don't like it. It's a veiled threat."

"But not an actual one," said Reinart. "Isabella's not stupid."

Looking a little better, Rem stretched his neck. "Not by a long shot. She's manipulative and dangerous, which makes her a suitable candidate for killing Laroche."

"You think she or Carlo could have cut your brake line?" asked Daniels.

Rem made a soft chuckle. "I wouldn't doubt it. And we should all be careful. If they checked my background, they sure as hell checked both of yours." He eyed Reinart. "Which means they know about your attack and maybe Barry."

"Great," said Reinart. "That's good to know."

"Not sure what they could use against me," said Daniels.

"You're in the most vulnerable position of all," said Rem. "You've got a wife and kid."

Daniels stopped pacing, and an icy chill traveled up his spine. "They wouldn't dare."

Rem swiped back a loose piece of hair. "I don't know what they'll do. Maybe nothing, but the gloves are off as far as I'm concerned."

"They're trying to intimidate us," said Reinart. "Like Maria said, Carlo's a bully, and it seems Isabella is too. That's what bullies do. Belittle and degrade."

Daniels put his hands on his hips. "If they think this is actually going to make us back off, they haven't done enough research."

"It has to make you wonder," said Rem. "Why go to the trouble? Are they guilty of something or are they just being assholes?"

"Either way, we have to be careful," replied Reinart. "We question either of them again, we don't do it alone."

Daniels stopped pacing, but his anger percolated. "I'm sorry she did that to you, partner. You okay to keep going? We've got plenty to do."

Rem nodded. "I'm okay. I just needed a sec. And I need to keep busy, anyway." He relaxed his shoulders. "You two learn anything of interest?"

"We did," said Reinart. "Robert is having an affair with one of the staff. Emily Chang. Rowan found out and wasn't happy about it. He confronted Robert the night of the party after he caught Emily in the gallery. That's what their argument was about."

"Maurice said he'd seen Robert and Emily come out of the security room together more than once," said Daniels.

"That's interesting," said Rem.

"And Robert lied about where he was during the unveiling," said Reinart. "According to Maurice, Robert escorted the unruly guest out before Rowan revealed the tiger."

"So where was he during the unveiling?" asked Rem.

"My guess?" asked Reinart. "With Emily Chang."

"Sounds like we need to visit Emily," added Rem.

"Robert is super touchy about us talking to her," said Reinart. "He's protective of Emily and said we could mess it all up, whatever that means."

"Robert has strong feelings for Miss Chang," said Rem.

"Sure does," added Daniels. "And if he lied about his whereabouts during the party, what else would he lie about?"

"All right," said Rem, standing. "Sounds like we know where we're heading next. Let's go see Emily."

They started walking toward the car. "We spoke to Klein too," said Daniels. "He's pretty blasé about being the tiger's trustee for the next twenty-plus years. He's not worried about the curse."

"He should be more worried about Carlo and Isabella," said Rem. "And he doesn't need to worry about the curse because he's currently the trustee of a forgery."

"Good point," said Daniels. "Which means whoever's got the real deal better be careful."

Reinart kicked a loose rock. "Maybe the curse will help solve this crime. If one of our suspects dies, maybe they're our culprit."

"Assuming whoever stole the tiger is also Laroche's killer," said Rem.

Daniels stopped beside the car. "You think we're dealing with two crimes?"

Rem dropped low and looked beneath Daniels' vehicle. "It's possible."

"You going to do that every time?" asked Daniels.

After looking beneath the car, Rem stood, brushed off his hands, and opened his car door. "Better to be safe than sorry."

"Until we solve this case, being cautious is a priority." Reinart opened her door as Rem's cell phone rang.

He pulled it out of his pocket. "It's Lozano." He answered. "Hey, Cap. You missed a rousing will-reading. Wait till we fill you in." He stopped, listened, and his expression darkened. "What? When?" He eyed Daniels and Reinart. "Hell." He gripped his head. "Yeah. Text me the location. Thanks, Cap." He paused. "Yeah, we will." He hung up.

"What is it?" asked Daniels. "Something bad?"

Rem rested his palm on the frame of the passenger seat window. "Now we have three crimes to solve. Victoria is dead. Car accident. Cap wants us there."

Shocked, Daniels gaped at Rem. Reinart did the same. After taking a second to absorb the news, Daniels opened his door. "Let's go."

Chapter Twenty

REM STOOD JUST INSIDE the police tape, along with Daniels and Reinart. Police and firefighters milled around the accident scene as smoke billowed from an upside-down crumpled car lying in the middle of the busy intersection Rem had barely avoided the previous day.

Firefighters sprayed water on the vehicle and a coroner's van carrying Victoria's body drove away. When the three of them had arrived, the body had already been bagged, and before being carried off on a stretcher, they'd viewed it and confirmed it was Victoria. The officer in charge had met with the three of them and explained that, based on witness statements, the car had flown into the intersection at high speed and hadn't braked. Another car had broadsided it, causing Victoria's car to flip into an oncoming van, which had hit the car head on. Flames had erupted and a few brave bystanders had attempted to help the driver, but it was too late. At that point, there was little they could do. Once the police and EMS arrived, they'd pulled the license plate info and had identified the deceased driver as Victoria Fordham. The other drivers involved in the accident had thankfully sustained only minor injuries and had been taken to the hospital.

Thinking about their near miss the previous day, Rem gave thanks they were all still alive. Looking at the mess that was Victoria's car, he realized that could have easily been them. "Do we want to take a wild guess and assume her brakes failed?" he asked.

"We'll have Forensics check to be sure," said Daniels, "but I'd say it's likely."

Reinart put her hands in her jacket pockets. "Who would want to kill her? You think someone knew Laroche had put her in his will?"

"It certainly benefits Robert," said Daniels. "He's now the sole beneficiary."

"Did you see his face at the reading?" asked Rem. "He didn't look like he knew any of that was coming."

"He showed up late though," said Reinart. "Is that because he was busy cutting Victoria's brake line?"

Rem crossed his arms. "Three hours passed between us seeing Victoria at the station and the reading of the will. If she came straight home, that's plenty of time for someone to mess with her car and still get to the reading. It could have been anyone."

"Especially if our culprit hired someone to do their dirty work," added Daniels.

"We sure as hell can't rule out Isabella and Carlo," said Reinart. "Do we think Maria's capable of this?"

Rem shook his head. "I don't think so. She was worried about Victoria."

"She could have been acting," said Daniels. "But I see your point. Victoria's death doesn't benefit Maria."

"We need to get some clarity on this will thing," said Rem. "At what point is Victoria considered the beneficiary of Rowan's assets? Does her estate still benefit because she was alive at the time of Rowan's death? If that's true, then technically Victoria's will would now designate who gets half of Rowan's assets."

"I wonder if the killer thought of that," said Daniels. "We'll have to ask Dryer, but something tells me Robert will get it all."

"I think we need to consider that this might be about Victoria's book," said Reinart. "If she really was going to publish and expose someone else besides Laroche, maybe that's what got her killed."

Daniels stepped out of the way of a firefighter. "Or the killer took care of her because she knew too much." He widened his eyes. "Maybe that's why she missed our meeting yesterday and came to the station instead. She didn't want the killer to think she was talking to us."

Rem believed that was a good possibility. "We need to get our hands on her manuscript and find out exactly what she planned to reveal."

"I'll call Lozano," said Daniels. "Maybe he can assign someone to help with that. Her apartment needs to be searched anyway." He pulled out his phone.

Reinart's cell rang, and she took it out of her pocket. Rem could see Barry's name clearly on the display. She stared at it as it rang again. Rem glanced at Daniels, who'd seen the name too. Neither said anything.

Reinart hit the *Decline* button and slid the phone back into her pocket. "There's another thing to consider with Victoria."

Rem almost gave her a fist bump.

Daniels held his phone to his ear. "What's that?"

The firefighters turned off their hoses as police directed traffic around the accident site. The construction crew that had been working the previous day were standing across the street. Victoria's car had narrowly missed their work zone.

"I'm afraid to ask," said Rem.

"Could Victoria have stolen the tiger? Is that why she's dead?" She paused and sighed. "Did the curse strike again?"

Chapter Twenty-One

THE NEXT MORNING, REM sat at his desk, doing the same as he'd done the previous morning, which was review what they knew and try to stay awake. After leaving the accident scene the previous day, they'd accepted the hard task of informing Maria of Victoria's death. They'd gone to her apartment and after learning the news, Maria had tried to remain stoic but failed and collapsed into a puddle of tears.

Rem had guided her to the couch, Reinart found some tissues and Daniels brought over a glass of water. They'd stayed until she'd calmed, and hoped to get some information from her regarding who might have killed Victoria, but Maria could barely hold a conversation without sobbing. It had been difficult, and Rem had flashed back to Jennie's death more than once. Between Isabella and Maria, he was mentally spent. After leaving Maria's and while Daniels got updates from Lozano, Rem had sat with Reinart in a much prettier courtyard outside Maria's apartment complex than the one outside Klein's office building.

While they'd waited, Reinart declined another phone call, but before Rem could ask her about it, Daniels returned. He told them Lozano had found and contacted Victoria's publisher, but they were reluctant to provide Victoria's manuscript prior to publication. Lozano was working to get a court order to convince them otherwise. A tow truck had taken Victoria's car to the station's garage to be examined, and Titus and Georgios had accompanied a forensic team to Victoria's apartment. So far, they'd found little other than a laptop that was password protected. They'd brought it back to see if they could access it. Lozano was also assigning a team to review the previous six weeks' security footage at Laroche's home to find the person who'd replaced the real tiger with the forged one.

Daniels had also discussed the reading of Laroche's will with Lozano, telling him about Isabella's knowledge of Jennie. Lozano had reiterated for them to be careful and suggested they go home and start fresh tomorrow. Rem sensed that Daniels had encouraged their captain that they wrap the day up because Rem's energy reserves were fading fast. It was an enormous benefit of working with a partner who knew him so well.

Once back at his house and after a quick TV dinner, Rem had showered and gone to bed, but another nightmare abruptly awakened him in the early morning hours. Shaken, he'd tossed on sweatpants and an old T-shirt and had gone for a long jog to clear his head before returning home, showering, and heading into the station with a fresh thermos of coffee. His insurance had provided a loaner vehicle, and he'd picked it up on the way home the previous day. Reinart had come in right behind him and Daniels had texted that he was running late but would be there soon.

Staring at his emails, Rem stifled a yawn and sipped some more coffee. Realizing he wasn't actually reading anything, he closed his email and stood to get more coffee from the machine. Reinart had been staring at an open folder but didn't seem focused either.

"How'd you sleep, Reinart?" he asked. He poured coffee into his thermos.

She looked up. "So-so. You?"

"So-so." Rem put the coffeepot back on its base. "This case has stirred up some stuff for me."

Reinart closed the folder. "Barry called again last night. He wants to see me, but I said no."

"How'd that go over?" Rem added sugar and cream to his coffee.

"How do you think?"

"He is persistent."

"He certainly is."

Rem eyed the collared V-neck shirt she wore that morning that left her scar visible. "I like the new style." He pointed toward her. "No more turtleneck."

She glanced down at herself. "I almost caved, but at the last second, I told myself to get over it." She touched her scar. "Just sitting here, I feel like I'm exposed."

Rem looked around the squad room. A few detectives were at their desks, but no one was paying attention to them. "I'd say you're doing just fine."

"We'll see how the day goes." She sat back. "How are you after yesterday?"

Rem stirred his coffee and raised a brow at her. "Was it that obvious?"

"You look pretty drained. I think Daniels was worried about you."

Rem dropped the stir stick in the trash. "He does that, but I understand why. It's been a rough couple of years." He sat at his desk. "It hasn't been easy for you either."

She rubbed her shoulders. "Yeah, maybe. But I didn't lose someone I loved."

"You came close to losing yourself."

"Somehow, that doesn't seem as bad. And I'm not feeling sorry for myself. I'm just guessing you'd switch places with Jennie if you could."

Rem nodded. "In a heartbeat." Thinking back on all that had happened, he sighed heavily. "But that's not the way it worked out."

"Did you have another nightmare last night?" She picked at a seam in her pants. "And if I'm asking too much, just tell me."

"You're not asking too much." Rem leaned back in his chair. "And yeah. I dreamed Jennie was in an out-of-control car, heading straight for that busy intersection. I was right behind her, screaming and running, but I...I couldn't get there in time." There was more detail to it, but Rem left that part out. He closed his eyes and took a deep breath.

"Does that happen a lot? The nightmares?"

Rem opened his eyes. "It was getting better. I was seeing a shrink but took a break to see how I'd do. I was feeling pretty good until this case, and now it's flooding back." He sat up. "I'm debating whether to call the shrink again, but then I wonder if this is what I need—to be tested. Life happens and I have to deal with it."

"I suppose." Reinart sipped some coffee. "There's been no one else since Jennie?"

Rem recalled his recent breakup. "There was. Jill and I met when she worked with me and Daniels on the Makeup Artist case."

Reinart dropped her jaw. "You and Daniels worked that? It was all over the news."

Rem thought back on the serial killer's capture with displeasure. "We get all the fun ones, don't we?"

"It seems so."

"Jill lost someone close to her too, and between that and the stress of the case, we connected. We were good for each other, but the timing was terrible and the baggage we were both carrying didn't help. We broke up, but we're still friends." He paused. "It's hard though. She helped me through some things, but I also think I was trying too hard to replace Jennie. I kept telling myself it was time to get over her and move on, but I wasn't ready."

Reinart poked at the folder on her desk. "After my attack, it took me weeks before I could actually leave my house. PTSD is real. I kept seeing Carter getting stabbed, and I'd have nightmares about me getting stabbed repeatedly. It's better now and I attribute that to Barry. He helped me get through some stuff, too. It never fully goes away, though. All it takes is a trigger."

"Don't give Barry the credit, Reinart. You did the work and you're still doing it."

"Same as you," she said. "Maybe we both need to go easier on ourselves."

Rem drank some coffee. "Good advice. Now if I could just take it."

She smiled softly. "Me too."

The squad doors banged open, and Daniels walked in. His red face implied he'd raced through the parking lot and sprinted up the stairs. "Sorry I'm late. It's been a morning." He set a juice bottle and a paper sack on his desk and slid his jacket off.

"Don't worry about it," said Rem. "Reinart and I were just mulling over the meaning of life. She was just about to tell me her insights when you interrupted."

Daniels draped his jacket over his chair. "That's about par for how my morning's going." He eyed Reinart. "So, what's the meaning of life?"

She shrugged. "Something about courage and giving yourself credit when it's due. And relying on friends when you need them." She made eye contact with Rem, who smiled.

Daniels looked between them. "Sounds like you and Rem have been talking. It's a clear sign to get out while you're ahead." He sat at his desk. "My partner's wise but slightly deranged."

Rem chuckled. "You wouldn't have me any other way."

"True," said Daniels, "but it's too late for me. You, on the other hand," he gestured toward Reinart, "still have time."

"I'll take my chances." Reinart stood with her cup and headed to the coffee machine. "Just so long as Rem doesn't drink all the coffee."

"No promises," said Rem. "So what happened this morning?" he asked Daniels.

Daniels huffed. "Well, let's see. Marjorie's mom called early. Her car broke down and she needed Marjorie to pick up her sister, who Marjorie's mom was supposed to drive to work because *her* car was in the shop. J.P. didn't sleep well last night, woke up cranky, didn't want to eat breakfast and spilled juice all over my shirt. Marjorie picked him up just as she was about to leave, and he had a blowout diaper and pooped on her."

Holding his thermos, Rem rocked back in his seat. "Ah, the joys of parenthood."

"I'm not done." Daniels opened his juice. "Marjorie had to change clothes, and I changed J.P., plus my shirt. No wonder we're always doing laundry. Then, Marjorie leaves to pick up her sister and I'm getting ready to take J.P. to daycare when the neighbor's lawn service guy shows up and blocks my driveway." Daniels blew out his cheeks. "It took them ten minutes to move their damn trailer." He shook his head. "Unbelievable."

"And I thought my nightmare was bad," said Rem.

Reinart returned to her desk. "I think I'd rather talk to Barry."

"And that's not even the best part." Daniels took a drink of his juice and set the bottle on his desk. "Guess who called Marjorie last night?"

Thinking, Rem pursed his lips. "An old boyfriend?"

Daniels smirked at him.

"Hopefully not a new one," said Reinart.

Daniels smirked at her, too.

Rem sat up. "The President of the United States."

"Batman?" asked Reinart. "That would be cool."

"Superman would be cooler," said Rem.

Daniels rolled his eyes. "Aren't you two supposed to be detectives? Try Evelyn Sinclair."

Reinart widened her eyes and Rem dropped his jaw. "Seriously?" he asked. "Why?"

Daniels threw out his hand. "I guess our little conversation with Evelyn stirred up the past. She wanted to catch up and get this...she asked Marjorie about her job."

"That was pretty forward of her," said Reinart.

"I agree," said Daniels, "but what's even better is she suggested Marjorie come work for her. Can you believe that?" Daniels scoffed. "How did this woman even get our number?" He sputtered. "I mean, first you," he pointed toward Rem, "with Isabella, and now me with Evelyn Sinclair. It's like these people are working together to get under our skins." He paused and narrowed his eyes. "You think that's possible? Are we dealing with some weird art cult that was under the spell of Rowan Laroche, and now they're all working together to confuse and derail us?"

Rem shivered. "A cult? How terrifying is that? Talk about nightmares." He took a second to collect his thoughts. "But let's not jump to any conclusions. How hard could it be for Sinclair to find Marjorie? Evelyn's certainly savvy enough."

"And Isabella working together with Evelyn and Maria? Or Carlo working with Robert and James? I doubt it." Reinart tapped her pencil on a file folder. "Isabella and Carlo only work for themselves."

Daniels held his head. "I know it's unlikely, but it's just weird." He looked up. "Marjorie had to use J.P. as an excuse to get off the phone. And Evelyn didn't even mention me or the investigation."

"What kind of job was she offering Marjorie?" asked Reinart.

"I don't know, but it paid well," said Daniels.

Rem adjusted the lid of his thermos. "I wonder what James would think of that?"

Reinart arched her brow. "You think Evelyn was giving away his job?"

"Maybe not, but what if Evelyn was open to grooming Marjorie for the role? That might put some sand in James' underwear."

Daniels' face fell. "That's one way to put it."

"It's something to consider as we trudge through this case," said Rem.

"Trudge being the operative word." Daniels rubbed his face. "So, now that we're up to speed with my morning, what's next? Where do we start today?"

Reinart picked up the folder she'd been looking at. "My suggestion? Emily Chang. I think it's time we find out exactly what's going on between her and Robert and how much she knows about Rowan Laroche."

Rem nodded. "I second that."

Daniels stood. "And I third it. And I like the shirt, Reinart."

Reinart touched her scar again. "Thanks."

Daniels grabbed his jacket. "Let's go."

Rem stood too and grabbed his own jacket. "You mind if we pick up some donuts on the way? I'm starving."

"Great idea," said Reinart.

Daniels groaned.

· · · ● · ● · · ·

Feeling better after eating a couple of jelly-filled donuts, Rem knocked on the door of Emily Chang's apartment. She lived in a less-appealing section of town in a building where the ground was mostly dirt instead of grass, the weeds needed pulling, and trash littered the parking lot. They didn't call before arriving to prevent Emily from leaving. If she was as anxious as Mel and Garcia had described, Rem didn't want her to pull a disappearing act.

Rem held his ear against Emily's door. "Somebody's home." He knocked again. "Emily Chang? Detectives are here to speak with you regarding Rowan Laroche. Can you answer the door, please?"

"I hope she doesn't sneak out the window," said Daniels.

"She's on the second floor," said Reinart. "It's a bit of a drop."

"Considering the overgrown weeds," said Rem, "she'd have plenty of cushion." He was about to knock again when the door opened a crack. The latched chain caught, and a woman's face appeared through the crack.

"Yes?" she said.

Rem, Daniels, and Reinart held up their badges and introduced themselves.

Her wide eyes darted to each of them. "But I already talked to the police."

"We just have a few more questions," said Daniels. "It shouldn't take long. Can we come in?"

She looked behind her and then back again. Nibbling her lip, she nodded. "Okay." She closed the door and Rem heard her undo the chain. The door widened and Rem recognized the woman from the night of Laroche's party. She'd been the one Robert had sat next to when Rem and Daniels spoke to the staff.

"Thank you," he said, walking into a tiny living room with a small kitchen. Dirty plates were sitting in the sink and on a square breakfast table with four wooden chairs around it. He noticed three coffee cups, an open newspaper, and a few pill bottles on the table.

Daniels and Reinart followed him in, and Emily shut the door behind her. Her long shiny black hair trailed down her back and she wore a worn brown bathrobe, which she pulled tighter around her. "I don't have a lot of time."

Rem stepped closer to the table and eyed the newspaper and glanced at the pill bottles.

"We'd just like to ask you about the night of Rowan Laroche's party," said Daniels. "We know you talked to other detectives, but can you go over again what happened that night?"

"Sure." As Emily described the night of Laroche's party, Rem spied the closed bedroom door. Judging by the size of the space, he could see she had a one-bedroom apartment, but spotting folded sheets on the back of her couch and the number of dishes in the sink, he suspected she wasn't alone.

After her recounting, which mentioned nothing about Robert or her being caught by Laroche in the gallery, Reinart tipped her head. "What's your relationship with Robert Clifford?"

Emily, whose grip on the edges of her robe tightened, sputtered. "Wh...what are you talking about?"

"Robert, who was in charge of Laroche's security," said Daniels. "He told us you and he were seeing each other."

She swallowed. "He did?" She tucked her hair back behind her ear.

"Did Rowan Laroche catch you in the gallery looking at *The Crimson Tiger*?" asked Reinart.

Emily nibbled her lip harder. "Am I in trouble?"

"Not if you tell us the truth," said Daniels.

Emily stared at the ground and Rem looked closer at one of the pill bottles.

"The door to the gallery was open," said Emily, "so I just got curious," she said. "I wanted to know what everyone was talking about."

"What did you see when you went in there?" asked Reinart.

Emily held the lapels of her robe. "Pictures. Art. The tiger painting was on an easel and covered. No one else was in there, so I peeked behind the cover. That's when Mr. Laroche came in." She tensed. "I swear I didn't do anything. He told me to leave, and I did."

"What happened after that?" asked Reinart.

She studied the floor again, and Rem took a few steps toward the closed bedroom door.

"Nothing." Emily crossed her arms and gripped her elbows.

"Did you see Robert?" asked Daniels. "Or anyone else after Laroche told you to leave the gallery?"

Her head shot up. "I didn't do anything wrong."

"Nobody said you did," said Reinart. "But we need to know what happened that night and every detail is important. We know you were seeing Robert, and that's fine. We're not here to judge."

Her face tightened. "I...I...we..." She shook her head. "It was a mistake. I should have never gotten involved with him. He argued with Mr. Laroche because of me and then Mr. Laroche died."

Daniels and Reinart exchanged glances. "Did Robert have something to do with Mr. Laroche's death?" asked Daniels.

Emily's hands flattened over her chest. "No. Of course not. That's not what I meant."

"Did you talk to Robert before or after his argument with Mr. Laroche?" asked Reinart.

"Do I have to talk about this?" She sighed. "I really have to go."

"We need to know," said Reinart.

She swallowed. "Yes. I saw Robert."

"Where?" asked Daniels.

She hesitated.

Hearing something, Rem leaned toward the bedroom door.

Emily shot a hard look at him. "What are you doing?"

Rem pointed at the door. "Thought I heard someone. Are you alone?"

Her nervous demeanor dissolved. "That's none of your business."

"Is Robert here?" asked Daniels.

"No," she said, glaring at Rem until he stepped away from the door.

"When's the last time you saw him?" asked Reinart.

Emily kept her attention on Rem. "The night of the party," she said. "When you spoke to us."

"What about before that?" asked Daniels.

She shut her mouth and gripped the edges of her robe again.

"Did you sleep with Robert that night?" asked Reinart. "During the party?"

Her jaw clenched, and she whispered. "It was stupid."

"Was it during the unveiling?" asked Daniels.

She didn't answer.

"Emily?" asked Reinart.

She closed her eyes. "Yes. We snuck away and met in the king's room."

"What's the king's room?" asked Rem.

"There's a portrait of a king in there," said Emily. "It's down the hall from the gallery."

"Is it near the security room?" asked Daniels.

She straightened. "Why do you ask that?"

"We heard that you two would occasionally meet up in the security room," said Reinart. "Is that true?"

"Who said that?" she asked.

"We can't tell you," said Rem. "But we need to know if it's true."

She looked away again. "We've met in various rooms, security being one of them."

"What about the gallery?" asked Reinart. "Did you ever meet in there?"

Curious to hear the answer, Rem moved closer.

She paled. "No. Never."

Daniels took a step closer. "Is that why you were in the gallery that night? To meet Robert for a tryst?"

Her eyes widened, and she wrung her hands. "I don't think I should say anything else."

"You're not in any trouble," said Reinart. "There's nothing illegal about having an affair, or even falling in love."

Emily's eyes watered. "I'm not in love."

"You sure?" asked Reinart. "Because, based on Robert's answers to our questions, he seems pretty protective of you."

Observing the exchange between Reinart and Emily, Rem considered whether Emily would open up to Reinart. "Hey, Daniels. Can I talk to you for a second? Outside?"

Daniels looked at him and then back at Reinart. "Sure," he said.

Rem walked over, opened the door, and Daniels followed him out. Hearing Reinart speak, Rem kept the door cracked so they could keep an eye on her.

"You think Reinart will get more out of her?" whispered Daniels.

"I hope. She's already on edge about whoever is in that bedroom."

"Could it be Robert?"

Rem shook his head. "Not unless he's over the age of sixty."

"Why's that?"

"Because there's a newspaper and pill bottles on the table. The pills are for sore joints. Young people rarely read newspapers, and Emily's joints look just fine. And there are folded sheets on the back of the couch."

"Somebody's sleeping on the sofa?"

"That's my guess." Rem scratched his jaw. "Robert told Reinart that we could mess something up if we talked to Emily. I wonder if whoever is in the bedroom has something to do with that."

"She's definitely hiding something, but is it about Laroche's murder or something else?"

"Let's hope Reinart can find out." He glanced back into the room and Reinart and Emily were still speaking.

They waited a few minutes until Rem heard Emily's voice. "That's all I'm going to say. Now I'm late and I need you to leave."

Rem pushed the door wider. "Everything okay?"

Reinart nodded. "We're good." She pulled a card out of her pocket and handed it to Emily. "This is my number. You call me when you're ready to say more."

Emily took it from her. "There's nothing more to tell."

Reinart spoke directly, but her expression remained one of empathy. "Your boss is dead, Emily, and we're going to find out who killed him. And if you're hiding something, we're going to find that out, too. So, the sooner you can tell us what you know, the better it will go for you."

Emily fiddled with Reinart's card.

"I'll see myself out." Reinart walked to the door, joined Rem and Daniels, and closed the door behind her.

"Well?" asked Rem, as they walked down the hall toward the stairwell.

"She and Robert are definitely an item," said Reinart. "They've been together for almost a year. They've been keeping it quiet because they knew Laroche wouldn't approve. They met in the security room more than once and on the night of the party, it was Robert's idea to meet in the gallery before the unveiling. He left the door open for Emily to get in. He got delayed though, and Emily got caught."

"Robert lied about Laroche leaving the door open," said Daniels. They headed down the stairs.

"He did," said Reinart. "After his argument with Laroche, he found Emily, who was terrified she was going to get fired. That's when they met in the king's room—during the unveiling. She insisted nothing happened after they separated. She went back to work and the next time she saw Robert was after Laroche was dead." Reinart paused on the stairs. "And she volunteered what happened after leaving the king's room before I could ask, which makes me think something happened that she doesn't want me to know." She resumed walking. "And she also confirmed that she spoke to Maurice in the kitchen just before

Laroche's body was found, and when she'd told Maurice she'd made a mistake, she was only referring to Laroche finding her in the gallery."

"I wonder how true that is." Rem stopped at the bottom of the stairs. "Did you find out who was in the bedroom?"

"I got her to tell me it was her parents, but she wouldn't say anything else."

"Why would she hide her parents?" asked Daniels, heading toward the exit.

"It scared her to death to talk about them. That's when she asked me to leave. I told her she could trust me, but she's not ready to go there yet."

They paused in the lobby. "You think she saw something at the party?" asked Daniels. "And someone threatened her to keep quiet?"

"Or maybe threatened her parents?" asked Rem.

"I don't know," said Reinart.

"What about Robert's inheritance?" asked Daniels. "Does she know Robert is Rowan's son?"

"She denied knowing anything about Laroche and Robert being related. I asked her if she'd talked to Robert since the reading and she hadn't. I get the sense she's keeping her distance from him." Reinart rubbed her nose beneath her glasses. "Laroche's murder has upset her, and she's scared, but I don't think she's our killer."

"She may not be, but she may know who is," said Daniels. "Could Robert have been using her as an alibi?"

"Robert has more explaining to do," added Rem. "Maybe it's time to bring him into the station to clear up a few things."

"If he's guilty, he didn't act alone." Daniels' phone rang, and he pulled it out of his pocket and answered. "Detective Daniels." Listening, his brows rose, and he eyed Rem and Reinart. "What can I do for you, James?"

Rem perked up at the name and Reinart appeared just as curious.

"Sure. We have some time." He checked his watch. "We can be there in thirty minutes. See you then." He hung up and put his phone away. "James Montrose wants to talk."

"Talk? About what?" asked Rem.

"Evelyn Sinclair. Says he has some concerns and needed to wait until he could talk alone. We're meeting him at Evelyn's gallery."

"That sounds intriguing," said Reinart.

"The plot thickens." Rem pushed the door open. "Let's not keep him waiting."

Chapter Twenty-Two

DANIELS OPENED THE DOOR to the Sinclair Gallery. Rem and Reinart entered, and he followed them inside. The same mannequin with the chains and gold bars continued its methodical spin, and the gallery was quiet. A back-office door opened, and James emerged, wearing a green polka-dotted shirt with a black jacket and pants and a bright yellow and green tie. He had uncharacteristically loosened his tie, and the bags under his eyes suggested he hadn't slept well. "Thank you for coming," he said. He gestured toward the shiny glass-walled office where they'd met previously. "Let's go in here."

They followed him in and sat at the table. "You said you have more information for us?" asked Daniels.

"I do," said James. "I had to wait until I could meet with you without Evelyn present. She's out with a client now."

Reinart settled back in her seat. "What can't you mention in front of Evelyn?"

James ran his fingers over his tie. "It's been bothering me and the more I think about it, the more I can't sleep. That's why I called."

"What's bothering you?" asked Rem.

James shifted in his chair. "It's Evelyn. She's been acting strangely."

"Strangely how?" asked Rem.

"Distracted. Distant. Not herself." James slid his jacket off and laid it on an empty chair behind him. The diamond pinky ring he wore glittered in the overhead light. "It started a couple of months ago, but

I thought little about it. Work's been stressful and business has been down, and the tiger was coming up for auction."

"And we know how that worked out," said Reinart.

"Losing the tiger upset her." He rubbed his jaw. "But it comes with the territory, especially when you're dealing with Laroche. But Evelyn hasn't been herself since. At first, she was coming in late or not coming in at all. Then it switched, and she started working long hours. Longer than me. And she hides things from me. She's kept me in the loop on everything since she hired me, but in the last month, she's been secretive. There have been meetings I'm not a part of. I've seen her talking on the phone and she'll move into her office if she thinks I can overhear. It's not like her."

Daniels pulled out his notebook and pencil. "Have you asked her about it?"

"I mentioned it, but she tells me I'm overreacting. That it's not a big deal, but then, last night, I heard her talking to someone on the phone about a job."

Daniels had started writing, but stopped.

"Who was she talking to?" asked Rem.

Daniels looked up and met Rem's gaze. Reinart was staring at him, too.

"I don't know," said James. "She wouldn't tell me." His shoulders tense, he sat back. "That's when I knew something was up. And then I put that together with her behavior at the party."

"What behavior?" asked Reinart.

James waved his hand. "Normally, at a Laroche party, she's catty and opinionated. She complains about Laroche and his business dealings, and we talk about how we can undermine him. It's what made his parties fun, but that night, she was quiet. I'd comment on something, and she wouldn't react. And then, during the unveiling, she left the gallery. I went to look for her, but she returned as I was about to leave.

She wouldn't tell me why she'd left during the most important part of the night."

"Maybe she had to use the bathroom?" asked Rem.

"She could have used the restroom at any point before or after, and she wouldn't keep that secret." He put his hand on his chest. "And I heard about what happened to Victoria." He shivered. "It's horrifying, but now I remember seeing Evelyn and Victoria talking that night during the unveiling."

"Do you know what they were talking about?" asked Rem.

"No. Evelyn wouldn't tell me, but it seemed like an intense conversation, which was odd because they're acquainted, but not friendly."

Reinart rested an elbow on the table. "Are you suggesting Evelyn had something to do with Victoria's death?"

James frowned. "No. Not at all."

"What about Laroche's death?" asked Rem.

James sighed. "I can't imagine that either, but considering her odd behavior before and during the party, I'm wondering what's going on." He sat up. "Listen. I hope I'm wrong. I like Evelyn and I don't want to get her into trouble, but I don't want to get into trouble either."

Daniels tapped his pencil against his notebook. "Are you concerned Evelyn could be a target?"

James' eyes widened. "I hadn't considered that."

"You're aware of the book Victoria was writing about her dad?" asked Reinart. "Did Evelyn contribute any information to that book?"

"Everyone's aware of that book," said James. "But if Evelyn provided anything to Victoria about Laroche, she didn't tell me." He paused. "Evelyn met with Laroche, though, a week prior to the party."

"About what?" asked Reinart. "The tiger?"

"She didn't tell me that either," said James.

"Did they meet at Laroche's house or somewhere else?" asked Reinart.

James paused. "I'm not sure. I just saw a meeting with him on her calendar. Normally, I would accompany her, but she didn't invite me."

Studying James, Rem leaned in. "Does this have something to do with Evelyn's phone call you overheard last night? Are you worried she's going to give your job away, and you're taking the offensive?"

James' face fell. "This is not some sort of retribution. I'm just telling you everything I know. I should have told you sooner, but I found it hard to believe that she would have anything to do with any of this, but now, I'm not so sure."

"We talked to Maurice," said Reinart. "He told us you and he were in a relationship."

James nodded. "We were, but that ended a while ago."

"How come you didn't mention that before?" asked Rem.

"I didn't think it mattered. Maurice and I had a complicated relationship, but we ended it as friends." He paused. "Is that a problem?"

"Did Laroche have a problem with you dating Maurice?" asked Reinart.

James shook his head. "Not that he mentioned to me."

Daniels took some notes. "Is there anything else about Evelyn, or anyone else, that you think we should know?"

"No." James twisted the ring around his finger. "Is Evelyn in trouble? Will you tell her I talked to you?"

"We'll keep it between us, for now, and we'll definitely speak with her again." Daniels slid his pencil into his pocket. "Any idea when she'll be back?"

James dropped his jaw. "You're going to talk to her now?"

"No time like the present, James," said Rem. "Before we go, let me ask you another question. Did you and Laroche have any issues after you left as his manager?"

"No," said James. "Like I told you before, he didn't like it when I quit, but he accepted it."

"Did you see Laroche at all in the six weeks prior to the unveiling? Or have plans to see him?" asked Reinart.

James pursed his lips. "See him? No. I didn't see him." He gripped his knee. "Are you still thinking I could have done this? Why do you think I called you?"

"We have to—" Daniels stopped when Reinart redirected her gaze toward the showroom and her eyes widened. "Is that...?" She pushed up out of her seat. "...who I think it is?"

Daniels and Rem turned to look, and James swiveled around and cursed. "I don't believe it." He stood.

Daniels recognized Hendrix, the famous painter from the party. "What's he doing here?"

Wearing a light camel coat that reached his knees, a black-collared shirt and black ironed pants, Hendrix walked over to the spinning mannequin, touched one of the gold bar earrings, and smiled. His wavy dark hair and stubbled jaw rivaled those of the latest heart throbs Daniels occasionally noticed on magazine covers in the grocery aisle checkout line.

James pointed. "He's exactly what I'm talking about. Evelyn has been blowing up his phone since the moment Dominique discovered Rowan's body. I keep telling her we don't need him, but she's convinced that Hendrix's next benefactor is going to be her."

Reinart kept staring. "Why is that a problem?"

James glared in Hendrix's direction. "Because he's as sleazy as they come."

"Why is that?" asked Rem. "I thought he and Rowan were friends."

James' glare didn't waver as Hendrix sauntered toward the statue of the naked woman twisted into a pretzel. "Rowan put him on the map and Hendrix took it for granted. He used Rowan and Rowan put up with it until Hendrix got too big for his britches. Rowan cut him off and Hendrix tucked tail, went into rehab, and came out all petulant and contrite and begged Rowan for another chance. I told Rowan to move on, but he didn't listen. And now Evelyn's falling into the same trap." He sneered in Hendrix's direction. "He's as slimy as the oil pooled on top of a hot pepperoni pizza."

"But pepperoni pizza is pretty delicious," said Reinart, her tone much softer.

Daniels and Rem looked back at her. "Sounds like Brad Pitt is old news," said Rem.

Reinart's cheeks turned pink. "Look at him. He's so handsome, and I admit, I'm fangirling. I've always wanted to meet him."

Hendrix, who'd moved on to study a portrait on the wall, turned, and saw them through the glass wall. He grinned and walked toward them.

"Well, now's your chance," said James. "Don't be surprised, though, if you feel the need to take a shower later."

Daniels caught Reinart smoothing her hair as Hendrix walked through the door. "James, my favorite ex-manager of Rowan's. How are you?"

James didn't bother to offer his hand. "What are you doing here?"

Hendrix continued to grin. "Good to see you, too. I thought I'd drop in and speak to Evelyn. Is she here?"

"No," said James. "She's not."

Hendrix faced Daniels and Remalla. "Hello, Detectives. I hope I'm not interrupting something important." His gaze traveled to Reinart. "And who do we have here?" He walked over. "I don't believe we've met. I'm Hendrix." He offered his hand, and Reinart shook it.

"Detective Phoebe Reinart."

"Phoebe." He pulled her hand up. "What a lovely name." He kissed the skin below her knuckles.

Reinart's cheeks turned a deeper pink, and James rolled his eyes.

"What are you doing in such a harsh profession, Phoebe?" asked Hendrix, letting go of her hand. "A woman like you should be the subject of my next masterpiece."

Reinart chuckled and shifted on her feet. "I'm flattered. I'm a big fan."

Hendrix narrowed his eyes. "Please don't tell me you have one of my landscape prints in your guest bathroom."

"Actually, I'm a fan of your less mainstream work. One of my favorites is *Dawn of Light*. It's extraordinary. I saw it last year at your exhibition downtown."

His eyes lit up. "Why, Phoebe, you've surprised me, and that doesn't happen often." He held her gaze, and Reinart smiled.

Rem cleared his throat. "I hate to interrupt this tender moment, but we were talking to James."

Hendrix took his eyes off Reinart. "My apologies for the interruption and for having to speak with him. I find the less time one spends with James, the better."

Looking like he'd just eaten a piece of rotten meat, James put his palm on the back of his chair. "Why do you want to speak with Evelyn?"

Hendrix put his hands in his pockets. "I think it's obvious. She and others have all been vying for my attention. I wanted to tell her personally that I'm happy to meet with her, but until Rowan's memorial service, I will make no decisions regarding my future. Let's at least allow a little time to respect Rowan's memory before everyone fights over me and money."

"Since when did you respect Rowan?" asked James.

"I could ask you the same."

James' hold on his chair tightened. "You should know, I'm advising Evelyn to steer clear of you."

Hendrix chuckled. "Judging by how often she's calling me, I can see how well she's taking your advice." He adjusted his expensive-looking black and silver watch on his wrist. "What exactly do you have against success, James?"

"I want nothing but the best for Evelyn and her gallery, which is why she shouldn't work with you. You've lied to Rowan, and you'll lie to her, and when your ship sinks, I don't want her going down with you."

Daniels watched the interplay between the two men with interest. Could there be more to Hendrix and his relationship with Laroche?

Hendrix sighed and straightened the cuff of his coat. "Did you advise Evelyn on that artwork out there, James?" He tipped his head toward the showroom.

"I did."

"I expected as much. That explains a lot about the value of your advice."

James glared again and Hendrix turned to face Reinart. "It was a pleasure meeting you, Phoebe. I hope once all this unpleasantness is over, we can see each other again."

Reinart's blush returned. "I...uh...well...I don't..." She shook her head and chewed her lip.

"She'd love to," said Rem. "But first things first. We need to find a killer."

Hendrix raised his hand. "Of course. I'll get out of your way. James, please tell Evelyn I stopped by and that I plan to wait before deciding my next steps. Detectives," he glanced at the three of them, "good luck with your search." He headed toward the door.

Reinart found her voice. "You mind if we contact you if we have questions?"

He stopped and smiled at her. "By all means, Phoebe. Or I should say Detective Reinart. My door is always open."

James rolled his eyes again as Hendrix opened the door, strode out, and left the gallery.

"God, I hate him," said James. "I pray Evelyn listens to me."

"What do you know about him and Laroche?" asked Rem. His cell phone buzzed, and he pulled it from his pocket. "Hold that thought." He answered. "Captain?" He listened and his jaw clenched. "He what? When?" Rem paused. "Today?" Rem groaned and held his head. "I don't believe this."

Noting Rem's reactions, Daniels put his pencil away and closed his notebook.

"No. I know that. I will." Rem hesitated. "But I have to talk to him, Cap." He nodded. "Okay." He blew out his breath. "We're on our way." He hung up.

"What's wrong?" asked Daniels, picking up his notebook.

Rem returned his phone to his pocket. "C'mon, we've got to go."

"What's wrong?" asked Reinart, her composure back in place.

"I'll tell you when we're in the car." Rem glanced at James. "Sorry, James. We've got to cut this short. We'll be in touch."

"I understand," said James. "I'll show you out."

Rem headed for the door. "No need." He was out of the office and headed for the exit, and Daniels and Reinart had to walk fast to keep up with him.

Once outside, Daniels jogged to the car where Rem was already getting in. "Hey, what is it?"

"We've got to get back to the station," said Rem. He shut his door.

Reinart got in the back and Daniels slid into the driver's seat.

"What is going on?" asked Reinart.

Rem stared out the windshield. "It's Uncle Carmine. He's been arrested."

· · • •· • • • · ·

Collecting his thoughts, Rem sat next to Reinart on a bench outside the holding cells. Daniels was talking to Lozano, presumably to convince him to let the three of them speak to Carmine. Carmine had shown up at Laroche's house in the early morning hours, drunk and angry. He'd argued with security and thrown rocks at the windows. Security had booted him from the property, but he'd returned, and they'd called the police who'd picked Carmine up for drunk and disorderly conduct. Once they heard his name though and realized he was Rem's uncle, they hadn't booked him but brought him to the holding cell instead to let him sleep it off. Carmine had reportedly cursed at them and told them not to call his nephew or his wife. They'd obliged and left him in the cell, where he'd passed out.

Wanting to see his uncle but dreading it, Rem held his head in his hands. He debated calling his aunt, but figured it would be better to talk to Carmine first.

"I'm sure it's fine," said Reinart. "He's got a hell of a hangover and is probably regretting his actions."

"You don't know my uncle."

Reinart paused. "Why do you think he went to Laroche's?"

Rem raised his head. "Demons. My dad had them, too. This whole thing with Laroche has messed with his head and he's not dealing with it well."

"You think this makes him look guilty?"

Rem groaned. "Well, it sure as hell doesn't help."

Daniels came around the corner and Rem sat up. "What'd he say?"

"He's giving us some leeway," said Daniels. "Mainly because he sent Mel and Garcia in to talk to Carmine earlier and he wouldn't say a word."

Rem sighed. "That just pissed him off even more."

Daniels nodded. "I bet. Lozano says we can talk to him, but if he opens up about the case, Reinart takes the lead, and if things get heated, you have to leave."

Rem hung his head. "I guess that's fair enough. At least he'll let me see him." He put his hands on his knees. "Well, let's get this over with."

Daniels checked his phone and slid it into his pocket. "The good news is Carmine didn't actually do any damage to the property or to anyone else, otherwise, he'd be in the county jail."

"I guess that's something," said Rem, standing.

"The bad news is he went to Laroche's house the morning after Victoria's accident, which suggests Carmine's unstable and feeling guilty. I'm not saying he did anything, but you know how it looks."

"Yeah," Rem said with a sigh. "I know."

"Shouldn't we call your aunt?" asked Reinart. "Won't she be worried?"

Rem almost chuckled. "My aunt has been dealing with this shit for years. I expect she's assuming Carmine's in jail, or he told her he was out of town. I'll call her when we're done talking to him. She can come pick him up."

"You sure you don't want me and Reinart to talk to him?" asked Daniels. "You don't have to go in there."

"If we want to get him talking, I need to be there. He won't shut up if I'm around. The tough part will be getting him to stick to the subject and not focus on me and our issues."

"Okay, but if it goes off the rails, Reinart and I will handle it," said Daniels.

"If all he did was get drunk and try to break a window," said Reinart, "then what are we asking him about?"

Weary, Rem put his hand on the wall. "He's obviously holding a grudge, and logically, we should ask him again about Laroche, the party, and I guess Victoria, and make sure he told us everything. This outburst suggests he's angry enough to have done something stupid. I hope he didn't, but we have to be sure."

Daniels walked to the entrance of the holding cells. "You ready?"

"No, but I'm willing." Rem walked over. "Let's get this over with."

Daniels opened the door. Reinart walked in, and Daniels and Rem followed. They stepped into a narrow hallway with three cells on each side of it. The first cell on the right was occupied, but not by Carmine, so they kept walking. They found Rem's uncle in the last cell on the left. He was lying on a cot in disheveled clothes; his hair was dirty and his eyes puffy. Seeing the three of them, he cursed and sat up with a grunt. "I told them not to call you."

Rem stopped outside his uncle's cell. "Who else did you think they'd call? The Ghostbusters?"

Carmine snickered and swiveled his legs over to rest his feet on the ground. "What the hell do you want?"

Daniels put his hand on one of the bars. "We'd like to know why you showed up at Laroche's house drunk, throwing rocks, and berating security."

Carmine belched and rubbed his stomach. "Seemed like a good idea at the time." He looked up and narrowed his eyes at Reinart. "Who's she?"

"Detective Phoebe Reinart," said Reinart. "I'm assisting with the Laroche case."

"Sorry about that," he said.

"Why?" asked Reinart.

"Anyone who's got to put up with my nephew for extended periods of time needs a badge of courage." He eyed Daniels. "You definitely deserve an award."

Rem gripped a bar on the cell door. "We're not here to talk about me. We're here to talk about you. Why'd you go to Laroche's?"

"That's none of your damn business," yelled Carmine.

Rem took a second before he answered. "I wish it wasn't, but Laroche is dead and so is his daughter. And the three of us are investigating their murders. You were at the party the night Laroche died, and now you show up at a dead man's house in a drunken stupor, raging at the world, the morning after his daughter's death. Personally, I don't think you have the brain capacity to pull this off, but that's not enough to clear you. Our captain needs to know that my uncle didn't kill one of the most prominent art dealers in the country or his kid, and you doing something like this makes him suspicious."

"I don't care what it makes him." Carmine rubbed his temples. "And why the hell would I kill Laroche's daughter?" He threw out his hand. "You and your partners are as stupid as you look. If your captain wants to arrest me for murder, he can go right ahead." He scowled at Rem. "But if he was dumb enough to hire you, then I hold very little stock in his opinion."

Rem's anger flared. His cheeks warming, he fought the urge to lash out and almost lost the battle when Daniels touched his arm. It brought him back to the present, and he clenched his jaw shut and turned away from the bars.

"Listen, Carmine," said Daniels. "Regardless of whatever feelings you have about my partner or my captain, we are actually here to help you. We want to clear you of this mess. Now I don't care if you showed up at Laroche's to have a weenie roast or to pee in his bushes, but we need to know if this has something to do with his death."

"You're obviously angry," said Reinart. "I don't know much about your family history, but your nephew told me about your background with Laroche, and to be honest, considering what he did to you, I wouldn't blame you for wanting to kill him."

Rem stepped back to the empty cell behind him and listened.

Carmine scoffed. "That asshole deserved to be murdered years ago. I wish I'd had the courage to do it."

"Is that why you got drunk and went to Laroche's?" asked Daniels. "Regret?"

"It's one of many," said Carmine, his voice softening.

"He took something from you that didn't belong to him," said Reinart. "Did you want to do the same to him?"

"Not last night," said Carmine. "Last night, I just needed to vent. Seeing Laroche at that party, I wanted to wring his neck, but I just stood there like a damn idiot, and watched him prance around like he was God's gift to the people in that room. You should have seen them fall all over him. It disgusted me." He ran a hand through his dirty hair. "The only one who stood up to him was that Victoria gal. The way she was talking to him, I could tell there was no love lost between those two." He shook his head. "It's a damn shame she's dead."

Rem straightened, and Daniels glanced back at him.

"You saw Victoria speaking to Laroche?" asked Reinart. "When?"

"At the damn party," he said.

"When during the party?" asked Reinart.

Carmine made a snorting sound and spit into the toilet next to the bed. "When he did the whole unveiling thing. Nobody was paying any attention to me, but I was paying plenty of attention to them. I was eyeing everyone like a hawk and listening to the things they said." He looked up. "His guests may have been acting like they admired him, but like me, they hated his guts. They were just all too cowardly to tell him." He eyed the ground. "Also like me."

"Who else did you see?" asked Daniels.

Carmine looked up. "Plenty of people. Most of them boring and stupid as hell, but a few were interesting to watch."

"Like who?" asked Reinart. "Did you learn their names?"

"I figured out who was who," said Carmine. "It wasn't hard, the way they were talking." He paused. "Most of the guests were gushing over the painting, but some of them definitely had other things on their mind."

"Like who?" asked Daniels. "Other than Victoria and Laroche."

Carmine shrugged. "There was a woman named Isabella. She argued with Victoria. And that husband of hers, I think his name was Carlo. He and Laroche exchanged a few words, but Laroche blew him off." He chuckled. "Carlo didn't like that." He scratched his shoulder. "If looks could kill."

Rem took a step closer but said nothing.

"You see anything else?" asked Reinart.

"That celebrity artist showed up late. What's his name? Hendrix? He was chatty with Rowan and everyone else. You'd have thought the tiger belonged to him." He wiped his sleeve over his nose. "Guys like that are so full of shit they stink." He paused. "There was a pretty lady there too," said Carmine. "I recognized her. She used to be an actress." He whistled. "Looked like a goddess in a bikini. Maria something."

"Maria Rossi," said Daniels. "What did she do?"

Carmine nodded. "Yeah. Maria Rossi. She was obviously friends with Victoria. They had their heads together for a good part of the night, especially after Victoria's arguments with Laroche and Isabella."

"Did you hear any of these conversations?" asked Daniels.

"Some. They would lower their voices. I think they were talking about a book that Victoria was writing."

Rem took another step closer.

"Anything more specific than that?" asked Reinart.

"Not really. I lost interest once I started watching two other people."

"Who was that?" asked Daniels.

"An older woman named Evelyn, and a man named James. They came to the party together, but they weren't a couple."

"Why'd they catch your eye?" asked Daniels.

Carmine rubbed his eyes and wiped his lips with his sleeve. "You think I could get some water?"

"Sure," said Reinart. "We'll get you some. What about Evelyn and James?"

Carmine blinked. "Uh, right. Evelyn and James. They were strange because everyone was there to see that stupid painting. Laroche unveiled it and everyone pushed forward and gathered around it, except for them. They stayed back, as if they couldn't care less about the painting. After Isabella had her little tiff with Victoria, Evelyn spoke to Victoria too, but only for a few strained minutes. Then Evelyn left."

"Did James go with her?" asked Reinart.

"No," said Carmine. "He wandered over and finally looked at the tiger. He stared at it like it was the Hope Diamond, then walked away. I was curious about Evelyn, so I looked outside the door, and saw her talking to a staff member down the hall."

Daniels' face furrowed. "Staff member? Can you describe him or her?"

Carmine wiped at his eye. "Uh, yeah. It was a lady. Young with long black hair. Asian." He made a face. "Or should I say Asian-American." He rolled his eyes.

Daniels looked back at Rem, whose heart was thumping.

"You saw Evelyn Sinclair speaking to an Asian woman out in the hall outside the gallery during the unveiling?" asked Reinart. "Did you hear anything they said?"

"Nah, not really," said Carmine. He held his stomach again. "The younger lady seemed real upset though, like Evelyn was telling her something she didn't like. The lady looked like she was about to cry." He straightened and stretched his neck. "They stopped talking, and I stepped back into the gallery. Evelyn came back right after and started talking to James again."

"Any sign of the Asian lady?" asked Reinart.

"Not after that," said Carmine. "Laroche ushered us out of the gallery not long after, and then I left. I'd had enough of that foolishness." He narrowed his eyes at them. "Is that enough? Am I cleared? Can I get my damn water now?"

Rem looked between Daniels and Reinart. "I'll get you some water," said Rem. "And I'll call Aunt Betsy. She can come pick you up."

Carmine grunted. "Don't do me any damn favors."

Frustrated but keeping his mouth shut, Rem walked away.

Chapter Twenty-Three

DANIELS TOOK A BITE of his sandwich and had a drink from his water bottle. Sitting at his desk, he flipped through his notes. Rem bit into his hamburger and Reinart sipped from her soda cup.

After talking with Carmine, they'd waited for Aunt Betsy to arrive to take her husband home. She'd apologized profusely for his behavior and Rem had done his best to console her, but Carmine hadn't made it easy. He'd cursed some more at Rem and told his wife he'd meet her outside. Embarrassed, Betsy continued to apologize as Rem walked her out. After she and Carmine left, the three of them stopped by the cafeteria for lunch and brought their food to their desks, where they could discuss what they knew and where to go next.

Rem spoke through a mouthful of food. "I know Carmine's an ass, but he's not our killer."

"I agree," said Reinart. "But thankfully he's observant." She ate a chip.

Daniels swallowed his bite. "Between what James and Carmine said, we definitely need to talk to Evelyn again."

"She obviously scared Emily enough to prevent her from mentioning her encounter with Evelyn outside the gallery." Rem sipped some of his soda.

"You think Evelyn knew about Emily's involvement with Robert?" asked Reinart.

"There's one way to find out," said Daniels. "Let's ask her." He read through his notes. "What do you make of Isabella and Victoria talking during the unveiling?" He flipped a page. "I don't have it written down, but I got the distinct impression those two didn't like each other."

"I got the same impression," said Rem. "Carmine heard them mention Victoria's book, so maybe Isabella is in it."

Daniels recalled his earlier conversation with Lozano. "Speaking of the book, Lozano's legal pressure got the publishing company to cave. They're sending over a printed copy of an early version of Victoria's manuscript. They didn't want to send a digital copy."

"Why not?" asked Rem. "They don't trust us to keep it secret?"

"Shocking, isn't it?" asked Daniels. "They also want it returned as soon as we're done reading it and Lozano had to agree that we wouldn't discuss the contents with anyone else."

Rem's shoulders slumped. "There goes my money from *TMZ*."

Daniels picked up his sandwich. "What's *TMZ*?"

"A celebrity gossip show on television." Reinart took a bite of her chicken salad.

Daniels scoffed at Rem. "I should have known you were using your somewhat limited brain power for useless trivia."

"Hey," said Rem. "I won ten bucks playing that celebrity trivia contest at Lenny's. You won diddly squat."

Daniels remembered the contest. "That's because you cheated and Googled the answers."

Rem shrugged. "Yeah, well, I bought you a beer with those ten bucks, so stop complaining."

Daniels raised his hand. "I stand corrected."

"I once won a contest," said Reinart, "but it was about art, so I had a slight advantage."

"Did you cheat?" asked Daniels.

"No."

"What did you win?" asked Rem. He popped a fry in his mouth.

"A velvet painting of Elvis Presley."

Rem's eyes widened, and Daniels rolled his. "You're kidding?" asked Daniels.

"I'd take one of those," said Rem.

"I'm sure you would," replied Daniels.

"Actually," said Reinart, "velvet art is gaining recognition as collectible pieces. Depending on the artist and subject, they could actually be worth something. There's an artist named Edgar Leetag who's known for his velvet Tahitian paintings. His use of visual effects makes his pieces highly sought after."

"Did he make the Elvis painting?" asked Daniels.

Reinart smiled. "No. He didn't. That was a much less skilled artist."

"I rest my case," said Daniels.

"I'd still hang it on my wall," said Rem. "It's Elvis."

"I put it in my bedroom," said Reinart. "Barry hates it, though."

"Barry's losing more and more points in my book," said Rem.

"He actually just gained a few in mine," added Daniels. "Can we get back to the case now?"

Rem dunked a fry in ketchup. "Now I know what I'm getting you for Christmas."

Daniels aimed the remains of his pickle slice at Rem. "Don't you dare."

Rem chuckled. "I know what Reinart wants under her tree. A hot artist named Hendrix."

She immediately blushed and rested her face in her hand. "Was I that bad?"

"It was only slightly obvious." Daniels smiled. "I'd say he's smitten with you."

Reinart sucked in a breath. "No, he's not. Hendrix only dates supermodels."

"Not anymore," said Rem with a grin. "I think he's ready to upgrade."

Reinart's cheeks blushed darker. "That's sweet, but unlikely. He was just flirting."

"That's where it all starts," added Daniels.

Reinart smiled back. "How about we solve this case first before we play matchmaker?" She tossed her napkin on her desk. "Especially since James implied before we left that Hendrix isn't as good a friend as we may think."

Daniels ate the rest of his pickle. "Could have been a random comment to piss off Hendrix."

"But what if it wasn't?" asked Rem.

Lozano came out of his office, slid his jacket on, and stopped at their desks. "How's it going? Any progress?"

Daniels made a quick note about Hendrix and closed his notebook. "Some. We need to talk to Evelyn Sinclair. We need to know why she spoke to Emily Chang."

"And why she's been acting strangely around James," said Rem.

"Any luck with Victoria's laptop?" asked Lozano.

"Her files are password protected, so they're still working on it," said Daniels. "But it's confirmed that, like Rem, someone cut her brake lines."

Lozano grunted. "I spoke to Silvers and Edmund. They reviewed the footage from Victoria's apartment complex. Your car, Remalla, was just out of frame and the camera near Victoria's space wasn't working, so no luck there either."

"Figures," said Rem.

"Now they're reviewing the last six weeks of security footage from Laroche's. There's nothing to report yet, but they mentioned that there's a day missing."

Daniels wiped his fingers with a napkin. "What day?" He opened his notebook.

"The Saturday before the unveiling, so check into that." Lozano straightened his jacket. "I've got to meet with the Chief about another press conference. I don't have to tell you that the pressure is mounting. Now that Victoria's dead, the media coverage has gone international."

"I saw the news," said Rem. "Laroche and his *Crimson Tiger* are all over the headlines."

"Then get to it," he headed toward the door. "And keep me posted."

"Will do, Cap," said Rem. He popped another fry in his mouth.

Reinart took the last bite of her chicken salad and tossed her container in the trash. "James said Evelyn met with Laroche the weekend before the unveiling. I wonder if that's related to the lost day of footage." She crumpled her napkin and tossed it in the trash, too. "Evelyn better have some answers. I'm ready to find this guy."

Rem took the last bite of his burger. "You're not tired of us, are you?" He crumpled the burger's wrapper and threw it away.

"No, I'm not." She sipped some soda. "I'm going to miss working with you two when this is done, but I still want to find our killer."

"It's always darkest before the dawn, Reinart." Daniels wrote a note about the missing footage, wrapped up the remains of his sandwich and stuck it in his drawer to finish later.

"That's why I keep him around," said Rem. "For his motivational speeches."

"You think we've hit the darkest point?" asked Reinart.

Rem ate his last fry. "Between our brakes being cut, Victoria's death and Carmine's drunken rage fest, I hope so." He tossed out his soda cup. "You ready, Watson?" He eyed Daniels.

Daniels swept crumbs off his desk. "Let's hope we're on our way to the light." He put his notebook in his pocket. "After you, Sherlock." He waved his hand toward the door and spoke to Reinart. "And you too, Nancy Drew."

Reinart smiled, and they headed out the door.

· · · • · • · • · · ·

Daniels walked down the stairs to the lobby of the busy station. Detectives, officers, and civilians came and went. Shorty, the tall and lanky officer who worked the front desk during the day, was talking to a man with brown curly hair and, as Daniels, Rem and Reinart walked past, Shorty yelled Daniels' name. Daniels turned and saw Robert standing at the counter.

"You have a visitor," said Shorty. "Name's Robert Clifford."

"We know who he is," said Rem.

Holding an open bottle of water, Robert glared at them and stomped over. "Why did you talk to Emily?"

"I told you we were going to speak to her," said Reinart.

Robert raised his voice. "She called me all upset and in tears. What did you say to her?"

"Whoa, whoa, whoa, hold up," said Rem, raising his hand. "Why don't we go upstairs and talk about this?"

"I don't want to go upstairs," yelled Robert. "I don't want to go anywhere with you." His gaze narrowed at Reinart. "You told me you would go easy on her. You lied."

"I didn't lie, Robert," said Reinart.

"She said you were snooping around." Robert's uncapped water bottle crinkled from the pressure of Robert's grip. "You were sticking your noses where they don't belong."

"If she's got nothing to hide, then what's the problem?" asked Daniels.

"Because it's none of your business," he yelled. "You cops. You're all alike. Say one thing and do another."

Daniels noticed the glances from the other officers in the lobby. "I think you should calm down."

"I don't want to calm down." Robert pointed at them. "You can't see the forest for the trees. Now she's even more freaked out, and she doesn't want to talk to me anymore."

"Is that why you're upset?" asked Rem. "Because she broke up with you? Your love life isn't our concern, Robert, but solving a murder is."

"You just need to leave her alone." Robert shot his hand out and water splashed out of the bottle and landed all over Rem's shirt and jacket. "She doesn't know anything."

Rem wiped the water from his shirt. "Watch where you're flinging that thing."

"Emily knows more than she's telling," said Reinart, "and until we find out exactly what's going on, we're not going anywhere."

"You don't know what you're talking about," yelled Robert. "She's a housekeeper. What could she possibly know?"

Daniels stepped closer. "How about how you're the one who left the gallery door open the night of the party and not Laroche, because you were hoping to have a little fun in front of the tiger? And how it's your fault Laroche caught her because you showed up late."

"And how about how Evelyn Sinclair confronted Emily outside the gallery during the unveiling?" asked Reinart. "Emily failed to mention that when we talked to her."

"Did Emily tell you what Evelyn said to her?" asked Rem.

Robert paled and went quiet.

Daniels pointed at Robert. "Don't blame us for your troubles, Robert. Maybe if you two would stop keeping secrets, Emily would be a lot less upset."

"We're just doing our jobs," said Rem.

Robert slumped his shoulders. "Neither one of us killed Laroche. Why can't you see that?"

"There's a lot of distance between here and capturing a killer." Rem leaned in. "And right now, Robert, you and Emily are adding extra mileage."

"You may not have killed anyone," said Reinart. "But what you know could help." She crossed her arms. "What did Evelyn say to Emily?"

Robert hesitated and looked away.

"Either you tell us, or we'll happily visit Emily again," said Daniels.

Robert moaned. "If I tell you, will you leave her alone?"

"That depends on what you say," said Rem. He swiped at a water droplet on his sleeve. "But it better be the truth."

Robert raked his hand through his hair and swallowed. "Evelyn saw me leave the king's room and when Emily followed, Evelyn made some assumptions. She told Emily to be careful."

"About what?" asked Reinart.

"About Laroche. Evelyn suggested that if Laroche found out about me and Emily, then it would get Emily fired." He hesitated. "Emily needed that job. She had responsibilities and...and...people to take care of."

"Does this have something to do with her hiding her parents from us?" asked Rem. "What's the big secret?"

Robert's face fell, and he sighed. "Her parents are in the country illegally. She's terrified you'll turn them in, and they'll get deported."

Frustrated, Daniels huffed. "That's what she's hiding from us?"

"We couldn't care less about her parents," said Rem.

"She doesn't know that," said Robert. "And after what Evelyn told her and what happened to Laroche, Emily's suspicious of everyone."

"Why would Evelyn say that?" asked Reinart. "Did she know Emily?"

Robert shook his head. "No, but I'm sure Evelyn has seen her working there. If she knew Laroche well enough, and since she's big on women's issues from what I've seen, maybe she thought she was helping?"

"Maybe. Did Evelyn say anything else to Emily?" asked Rem.

Robert hesitated. "She told Emily to be smart and to hide any evidence of us being together." He paused. "That's when..." He grimaced and his water bottle crinkled again. "Never mind."

"Don't stop now," said Rem. "You're on a roll. When what?"

He closed his eyes and took a deep breath.

"Tell us," said Reinart.

He opened his eyes. "After everyone left the gallery, Emily went into the security room and tried to delete the footage of us together. She ended up deleting all of it instead."

Daniels muttered a curse. "And that's why there's no video of the unveiling?"

Robert dropped his head. "Yes."

"Well," said Rem, "at least now we know what happened."

"She's not in trouble, is she?" asked Robert. "If she gets arrested, then her parents will have nowhere to go."

"Relax," said Daniels. "She's not in trouble. Unless there's something else that you two aren't telling us."

"No," said Robert. "That's it. I swear it."

"Unfortunately, your promises don't hold much value right now," said Rem.

"We'll leave her alone," said Reinart, "but if we catch you two in another lie, we can't promise anything."

Robert nodded. "I understand."

"One other thing," said Daniels. "Detectives are going through the security footage at Laroche's, and they told us the Saturday prior to the unveiling is missing. You know anything about that?"

Robert paused. "Yeah. I remember. The system went down that day."

"You know why?" asked Rem.

"It happens." Robert shrugged. "I had to call a technician, but we got it back up by the end of the day."

"Anything weird happen while it was down?" asked Reinart. "Anyone visit or go to the gallery?"

"I doubt it. Rowan was gone most of the day," said Robert. "And I was busy in the security room."

"If you remember anything, tell us, but for now, you and Emily stick close and don't go anywhere. You got it?" asked Daniels.

"Okay." Robert's angst diminished. "Sorry I blew up on you." He eyed Rem. "And sorry about the water."

"Just watch the temper," said Rem. "You have an issue with us, just call and ask. It'll go a lot easier on the clothes." He pulled on his damp shirt.

"Go see Emily and tell her to relax," said Reinart. "Once she does, maybe she'll take you back."

Daniels checked his watch. "We have to go, unless you want to yell at us for something else."

Robert apologized again, said his goodbyes, and left the station. "Jeez," said Rem. "This day is just getting better and better."

Reinart swiped another water droplet off Rem's jacket collar. "Tell me about it."

"Let's hope our talk with Evelyn isn't as dramatic," said Daniels.

"At least now we know what she said to Emily," said Rem.

Daniels started toward the door when Reinart stopped abruptly and stared at the entrance. "Son-of-a—"

Rem stopped too. "What's the matter?"

Daniels followed her line of sight and saw a slender man of average height wearing jeans, a blue long-sleeved shirt, and a windbreaker standing near the door. His short brown hair and tan, angular face gave him the look of a man who'd just stepped off a sailboat after a long day on the water. "Who's that?" he asked.

Reinart clutched her stomach. "That's Barry."

Chapter Twenty-Four

FEELING A LITTLE ILL, Phoebe cursed again. "What is he doing here?"

"My guess?" asked Rem. "He wants to talk to you."

"I told him not to come back here." Phoebe stared at Barry, who stood at the entrance and made eye contact with her. His eyes flicked over Rem and Daniels, but his expression remained flat.

"I think Barry plays by his own rules," said Daniels. "Go talk to him. We'll wait."

"I think we should just go," she said.

"And he'll be here when we get back," said Rem. "Looking like a lost puppy."

Phoebe debated returning upstairs.

"It's fine, Reinart. Don't worry about it," said Daniels.

"Just take care of it now so you don't have to worry about it later." Rem nodded toward the corner. "We'll be over here. Just yell if you need us."

He and Daniels stepped away, and Phoebe's stomach rolled. The mix of emotions made her head hurt, and she wished Barry would leave. She knew he wouldn't though, until she spoke to him, so she bolstered herself, straightened her back, and walked over to him. "What are you doing here?"

"You wouldn't answer my calls."

"That's because I am busy."

"You were injured in a car accident, and you don't expect me to check in on you?"

Phoebe hadn't told him the true cause of the accident because she knew he'd pester her more. "I don't need you to check in on me."

"Who else is going to do it?" He shot a look toward Rem and Daniels. "One of them?"

She bit back a rude comment. "Barry. Listen to me. You are not my mother and you're not my boyfriend. We broke up, remember? You need to worry about your wife. Not me."

His gaze softened. "That's just it. I do worry about you. We may not be together, but you're still my partner."

Her heart hammered and that familiar need returned, but she pushed it back. "You're on leave. We're not partners right now and after what's happened, I doubt we will be when you return."

"Don't say that."

She took a deep breath and made herself say the words. "I think it's better if we aren't."

His brow furrowed.

"C'mon, Barry. Don't tell me you don't think the same. This is a disaster. You have a wife and kid, and I need to put my life together."

"We can still be partners and do all of that."

She scoffed. "No. We can't. Look at you. We agreed to keep our distance, and you came to my house and now you've been here twice. And you keep calling me."

He dropped his head. "Only because I miss you." He reached for her hand. "I need to tell you something important."

She pulled away. "Don't, Barry. Please listen to me." She took a second to gather her thoughts. "Maybe I've been sending mixed signals and if I have, I apologize. I've missed you too, but us being apart has given me some added insight." Nervous, she rubbed her fingers over her scar. "It's good for me to be on my own."

"Phoebe—"

"Let me finish." She took hold of his wrist. "I need to make some decisions. I've been through a lot, and you helped me through a difficult time, but now I have to rely on myself. I haven't done a good job of that, but now I have to."

"You don't understand," said Barry, grabbing her hand. "You don't have to go it alone because I'm getting a divorce. That's what I've been wanting to tell you."

His fingers closed over hers and she held her breath. Six months ago, those words would have thrilled her, but now, her stomach rolled again. "Barry, if you're divorcing to be with me, then that's the wrong reason to do it. I...I..." She gathered her courage. "I don't want to be with you anymore."

His eyes widened. "You don't mean that."

After saying the words, a weight seemed to lift. "But I do." She took her hand back. "That's why you need to leave and go back to your wife. I'm not the answer to your problems and you're not the answer to mine."

He shook his head. "C'mon, Pheebs. You and I, we're meant for each other."

"No. We're crutches for each other. And the only way for me to stand on my own is to let go of the crutch."

He stared for a second, and then his expression darkened. "Is this because of them?" He tipped his head toward Rem and Daniels. "Are you sleeping with one of them?"

Reinart dropped her jaw.

"I did some digging on those two," he said. "Is it Remalla? I saw you touch him."

She couldn't believe what she was hearing. "He had water on his jacket."

"Or is it Daniels? We both know how you much prefer the married ones."

It took every ounce of her strength not to slap him. Clenching her fingers, she told herself to stay calm, and for the first time, saw Barry through fresh eyes. "You need to go home."

Barry's cheeks turned red, and he patted his chest. "I was the one who was there for you, remember? I took you as a partner when no one else would. You owe me."

Outrage rivaled her disbelief. "What do I owe you? Sex? A bed to sleep in when your wife kicks you out?"

"You owe me a chance."

"I owe you nothing." She glared at him. "Nobody told you to partner with me, and nobody told you to break your vows. You made your choices just like I made mine, and now we have to live with them. You and I are over. We're no longer partners, and we're no longer friends."

"Now you're being ridiculous."

"It's the first time I'm not being ridiculous. This is called being empowered." She stood tall and faced him. "I've learned a lot from you, Barry, so I can't have regrets. You taught me to stand up for myself and know clearly what I want, and that isn't you."

"Pheebs—"

"Go home and don't call me again. Ever." She held his gaze and didn't waver.

"You don't mean it."

"But I do."

"When I come back—"

"You'll have a new partner. I'm moving on, and I suggest you do the same."

He clenched his jaw. "I know you. You'll change your mind, and when you do, you know how to reach me."

"I'm not changing my mind."

He raised his voice. "I am not leaving here until—"

Rem and Daniels approached. "Everything okay?" asked Rem.

Barry shut his mouth.

"Everything's great," said Phoebe, her heart racing. "Barry was just leaving."

Nobody spoke as Barry fumed. He stood for a second, shaking his head, then he turned, flung the door open, and stomped out.

Daniels scratched his jaw. "That seemed to go well."

"We thought Barry's head was about to explode, so we came over," said Rem. "You okay?"

Taking a deep breath, Phoebe relaxed her shoulders. "I'm better than I've been in a long time." She watched the doors, worried Barry would return. When he didn't, she centered herself and shook out her hands. "How about we go talk to Evelyn Sinclair?"

"Sounds good to me," said Daniels.

"I'll bet she'll be more fun to talk to than Barry," said Rem.

"It certainly can't get much worse."

They started to leave when Shorty called Daniels' name. They turned to see Shorty behind the counter, holding a manilla envelope.

"Delivery for you," he yelled. "Courier just dropped it off."

Daniels headed over, along with Rem and Phoebe. "Thanks, Shorty." He took the package from Shorty and read the label. "Change in plans."

"What is it?" asked Rem.

Daniels ripped it open and pulled out a thick, paper-filled folder. "It's Victoria's manuscript." He held it up. "Care to do a little reading before we visit Evelyn Sinclair?"

• • • • • • • • • •

Rem flipped through another page and skimmed over the parts about Victoria's childhood. Once they'd returned to their desks, Daniels had divided the book into thirds and given a section to each of them. Rem had gotten the first third and so far, it had been about Victoria's younger years and her complicated upbringing. He stood to get a fresh cup of coffee. "You two learning anything?" He poured coffee into his thermos.

Reinart turned a page. "I'm reading about Maria and her relationship with Laroche. She didn't hold back. Victoria mentions the Toby LaRue paintings and how Rowan lied to and stole from Maria."

Daniels looked up from his section. "Victoria also mentions Laroche's rivalry with Evelyn Sinclair and how he'd threaten and manipulate other dealers and artists to get what he wanted."

Rem returned the pot to its base. "Did other artists comment or contribute? This book sounds like it's ripe for a libel suit."

"It's an early draft," said Daniels. "I'm sure the publishing company is covering its bases, but you're right. Victoria suggests Laroche is a liar and a fraud." He turned a page and continued to read. "I can't imagine Laroche wanted any of this printed."

Reinart rested an elbow on her desk. "I wonder what the new version looks like."

Daniels checked the front of the folder. "If there's a newer version, they didn't send it to us," said Daniels.

"Or Victoria hadn't sent it to them." Rem added cream and sugar to his coffee.

"We need to get into the files on her laptop," said Reinart.

"Let's hope our tech guys have some success," said Daniels. He took the last bite of the remains of his sandwich and sipped some water.

Rem sat again and flipped to another page. "This version could still hold a key to what caused Laroche's or Victoria's death, so keep reading." They read for several more minutes before Rem sat back and rubbed his eyes. "This section is a bust."

"I think mine is too," said Reinart, sitting back. "There's a lot about Laroche and how he started his business and grew his art empire. It's not flattering, but there's nothing specific enough to kill over."

Daniels studied a page.

Rem stretched his neck. "What about you, Blondie? Anything?"

Daniels narrowed his eyes as they tracked across the page, and he held up a finger.

Reinart sat up. "This looks promising."

Rem set his section of papers aside. "I haven't seen him this serious since I stole his green juice and hid it in the men's room."

Daniels ignored Rem and kept reading. "Get this." He pointed at the page and looked up. "Victoria mentions Isabella and her pregnancy." He moved his finger down the page and turned it. "She also brings up Isabella's breakup with Laroche, her marriage to Carlo and his ties to the mob."

Reinart leaned in. "Anything about Mateo?"

Daniels nodded. "Yes. She says Mateo is Laroche's son."

Rem whistled. "So Victoria dropped the bomb. Carlo won't be happy about that."

"There's more," said Daniels. He continued to read, and his eyes widened. "Victoria says Isabella and Carlo's marriage is combative."

"Well, I think that's obvious," said Reinart.

"It's more than that." Daniels looked up. "Victoria suggests Carlo is abusive."

Rem frowned. "Abusive? In what way?"

Daniels scanned the page. "Carlo can get violent. He threatens Isabella and her son." His brow knitted. "Isabella plans to leave Carlo, take Mateo, and return to Laroche."

Listening, Rem set his thermos down. "I'm not surprised this book ruffled someone's feathers. This is explosive stuff."

Daniels went quiet and flipped to another page. "Listen to this. Victoria says Isabella fears for her life and the life of her child, and even suggests Laroche is in danger." Daniels looked up. "That adds an extra element to this investigation."

"But is it true?" asked Rem. "Or is Victoria just trying to sell more books?"

"Either way," said Reinart. "If Carlo knows about this, is it enough for him to kill Victoria to keep her from publishing?"

"The bigger question is, how did Victoria know any of this?" asked Daniels.

"Could it be Isabella?" asked Rem. "She and Victoria spoke during the unveiling. Is she planting the seeds of her husband's demise?"

"It's a treacherous game," said Reinart. "Especially with a mobster." She set her papers aside. "But this isn't the final version. What changes did she make after she spoke to her father and made a deal?"

"Or spoke to someone else?" Daniels took Reinart's section and added it to the binder.

Rem picked up his papers and straightened them. "I don't know, but if it's any more revealing, this is going to be a bestseller."

"And it's going to piss people off." Reinart swiveled in her seat. "So, do we talk to Evelyn or go find Carlo and Isabella?"

Rem handed his section to Daniels. "I'd rather not talk to Isabella. I'll leave that to you two."

"You can have Carlo," said Daniels, returning Rem's papers to the binder.

Rem deflated. "Gee. Thanks. That's even better."

"That's what you get for hiding my green juice in the john."

Rem blanched. "That's where it belongs. That stuff is disgusting."

Daniels' cell rang, and he sighed. "Now what?" He pulled it out of his pocket and answered. "Detective Daniels."

"Maybe it's good news," said Rem. He sipped some coffee. "We're overdue."

Daniels frowned. "When?" He sat straight. "Now? How bad is it?"

"Doesn't sound like good news," said Reinart.

"Anyone hurt?" asked Daniels. He aimed a look at Rem and Reinart. "We'll head over. Just try to calm the waters until we get there." He stood and grabbed his jacket.

Rem and Reinart did the same. "Definitely not good news," said Rem.

"We're coming now." Daniels hung up. "It's Tommy Parsons. He's on scene at Carlo and Isabella's for a domestic altercation. He recognized the name and their connection to Laroche, so he called us."

Reinart hesitated. "Domestic altercation?"

"Yeah. Apparently, they were fighting badly enough for the housekeeper to call the police. Parsons is trying to talk them down, but they're not cooperating."

Rem could imagine what Reinart was thinking. "Don't worry, Reinart. Different case. Different people."

She paused for a second and nodded. "Okay. Let's go."

Chapter Twenty-Five

DANIELS PULLED UP NEXT to the police car in front of Carlo and Isabella's Spanish-style home. The tiled roof, stucco walls, wide front porch, and ornately carved wooden front door gave it a European feel. A wrought-iron gate surrounded a manicured front lawn with two full, leafy trees, and Daniels wondered how two people who had so much could make themselves so miserable. He got out of the car along with Rem and Reinart, and the three of them headed to the front door. He knocked and Parsons, the officer who'd contacted him, opened the door and swung it wide. "Come on in."

"How's it going?" asked Rem.

Daniels saw Parsons' partner, Jim Reagan, talking to Carlo, who was pacing in a far corner of the living room. He was wearing a blue tracksuit, his arm was in a sling, and he had a red scratch on his cheek.

"Better, I think," said Parsons. "When we got here, they were screaming at each other. The housekeeper didn't know what to do and their kid was crying his head off. I got them to at least stop yelling at each other long enough to convince them to let the housekeeper take the kid to the park to get out of the house. As soon as they left, though, the screaming started again."

"What are they arguing about?" asked Reinart.

"What aren't they arguing about?" Tony gestured toward Carlo. "He got slapped by his wife, which is why his cheek is scratched and she's got a bruised arm. She says he grabbed her and shoved her on the couch."

"Where is Isabella?" asked Rem.

"She took a second to collect herself and went into the bathroom."

Her shoulders bunched, Reinart stared down the hall.

"You okay, Reinart?" asked Rem.

Her pale face and taut lips told Daniels her anxiety was flaring. "You can wait outside if you want."

Reinart shook her head. "No. I'm okay." She took a deep breath. "It's better to keep an eye on both of them. In a situation like this, you never know what can happen." She looked at Parsons. "Have you checked the rest of the house?"

"It's just these two," said Parsons. "We've been trying to calm them down."

"Why don't you two check on Isabella," said Daniels. "We'll help Jim with Carlo."

Reinart nodded and followed Parsons down a hall off the living room.

Daniels stepped farther inside the house. The living room shared a sizable space with an adjacent kitchen. Sunlight from large windows brightened the room. A white fluffy couch with red pillows sat atop a thick black and white rug, and a coffee table with a fresh flower arrangement was in front of the couch. Toys were scattered on the floor and Daniels spotted a half-filled glass containing an amber-colored liquid on the coffee table. Had Carlo or Isabella been drinking?

Carlo spotted them and cursed loudly. "What the hell are you doing here?" He yelled at Officer Reagan. "Did you call them?"

Jim raised his hand. "Relax, Mr. Vespucci."

"Don't tell me to relax," said Carlo.

Daniels approached. "What's the problem, Carlo?"

Carlo glared at him. "My wife. That's the problem."

Rem stopped beside the coffee table, picked up the glass and smelled it. "You been drinking, Carlo?" He put the glass back on the table.

"That is none of your damn business," yelled Carlo.

Rem walked up. "Why don't you take a break, Jim? We'll talk to him."

Jim rested his hands on his belt. "I appreciate that." He turned. "I'll be outside."

He walked away and Daniels observed the rest of the kitchen. He noticed a broken dish on the floor and a hole near the baseboard on the wall. "What are you and Isabella fighting about, Carlo?"

"And don't tell us it's none of our business," said Rem. "Because the minute the cops were called, it became our business."

Carlo stopped pacing. "You want to know? It's her. It's always her."

"What about you?" asked Daniels. "You expect us to believe this is all one-sided?"

"I'm the one with a mark on my cheek." He pointed to his face. "She's insane."

"Then why did you marry her?" asked Rem.

Carlo yelled. "What the hell kind of question is that?"

"A logical one," said Daniels. "You two are like oil and water. You end up in the hospital after Isabella shoots you and now you're fighting again."

"You two stressed over something?" asked Rem. "Is this about Mateo or Laroche?"

Carlo loomed over Rem. "Don't you dare mention that jackass Laroche and my Mateo's name in the same breath. The day Laroche died was a reason to celebrate. I don't feel one iota of sadness for that miserable man's life."

"Sounds like someone with a motive to kill," said Rem.

"I didn't kill anyone," yelled Carlo. "You want to talk to the murderer? Then talk to my wife."

Daniels picked up a small plastic ball from the floor and tossed it on the couch. "You got evidence to back that up?"

Carlo curled his lip into a sneer. "How about months of living with her? I don't know how Laroche put up with her as long as he did."

"We need more than that, Carlo," said Rem. "Did she tell you she killed him?"

Carlo put his hands on his hips and paced again. "Why am I talking to Laurel and Hardy? You two couldn't find your way off my driveway."

"If you don't want to talk to us, then stop giving us reasons to speak to you." Daniels' impatience grew. "If anyone's to blame for this mess, it's you and Isabella."

"What's going on between you two?" asked Rem. "Why so much animosity?"

Carlo stopped pacing and glared at them. "Because she's trying to kill me. Just like she killed Laroche."

"Did she try to poison you?" asked Daniels.

"I saw her put something in my drink," said Carlo. "I didn't know what it was. I called her on it, and she got in my face and slapped me. That's when I shoved her."

Rem glanced toward the kitchen. "What did she put in your drink?"

"It was in a plastic bag." Carlo ran a shaky hand over his head. "Somewhere on the counter."

"Why did you think it was poison?" asked Daniels.

"Because she's already shot me," yelled Carlo. "After that, I had to suspect she wanted me dead."

"But why does she want to kill you?" asked Rem. "Is it the whole mobster thing?"

Carlo erupted. "My family is not involved in this. Leave them out of it."

"It's hard to do that, Carlo," said Daniels. "If anyone's likely to be threatened, it's Isabella. Your family could easily retaliate against her."

"I can handle my own problems," yelled Carlo. "I don't need my family's help."

"You sure about that?" asked Rem. "Because from where we're standing, you're not doing too great."

Carlo's face tightened. "I don't need to take advice from a man whose got plenty of his own demons to face. I know about you and your girlfriend."

Rem stiffened and Daniels' stomach knotted. He got up close to Carlo and hardened his tone. "Watch where you tread, Carlo. You got a beef with me and my partner, then be prepared to deal with the repercussions. You don't like us dealing with your mess? Then stay the hell out of ours, or I'll haul your ass down to the station so fast, you'll think you're in a time warp."

Carlo sneered back at him. "For what? Hurting your feelings?"

"How about domestic assault, for starters? I can add harassment, too," Daniels narrowed his gaze and spoke low. "And if you so much as flinch when I put on the handcuffs, I'll add resisting arrest."

"And if we get a warrant to search this house," said Rem, "we'll be looking in every nook and cranny. Are we going to find something to add to the list?"

Carlo's fury abated, and he stepped back.

"That's the smartest move you've made since we met you," said Daniels. "Now watch your mouth and get back to the subject. You think you can handle that?"

Carlo's anger returned. "Why aren't you questioning her?" He pointed down the hall. "If anyone's to blame, it's Isabella. She's threatened to divorce me and take Mateo."

"Haven't you threatened to do the same to her?" asked Rem.

"Mateo isn't safe with her," yelled Carlo.

"Are you saying he's safe with you?" asked Daniels.

"After everything that's happened," he said, "that's exactly what I'm saying."

Stepping closer, Rem seemed to have shaken off Carlo's comment. "We read Victoria's book, Carlo. We know what she said about you and your marriage. She reveals Mateo isn't your biological son. She even mentions your volatile relationship with Isabella. She suggests you're dangerous."

"I don't care what's in that book," yelled Carlo. "And I don't care if Rowan is Mateo's father. I'm raising that child. I'm the one who will mold him into the man he will become."

"Did you kill Victoria?" asked Daniels. "To prevent the book from coming out?"

His eyes widened. "Victoria was murdered? I thought it was a car crash."

"It was," said Rem. "A deliberate one. Someone fiddled with her brakes."

"Someone fiddled with our brakes too," said Daniels. "But we got off lucky."

Rem pointed at his eye. "We escaped with just a few bumps and bruises, but whoever did this is going to spend a long time behind bars."

Carlo stood in silence. His gaze traveled down the hall, and he put his hand on the wall as if supporting himself. "My God." He dropped his jaw. "She's trying to..." His face furrowed and his expression darkened. "That bitch."

Before Daniels could stop him, Carlo headed down the hall just as Reinart and Parsons stepped into it with Isabella.

"Is that your plan?" he screamed at Isabella. "To pin this all on me?"

Isabella, who'd appeared reserved when she entered the hall, curled her lip at Carlo's advance. "Don't you touch me, you bastard. I'm going to tell them everything."

Parsons stepped in front of Isabella, but she moved around him. "They're going to know what a lousy father and husband you are."

Carlo rushed at her, but Daniels and Rem pulled him back. Reinart, her face still pale, took Isabella's elbow and steered her away from Carlo. "Stop it," said Reinart. She guided Isabella back to the living room with Parsons beside them.

"It's not going to work," yelled Carlo. "You can't pin this on me."

Daniels and Rem stayed with him as he followed Isabella. "Take it easy, Carlo," said Daniels. "What is she going to pin on you?"

They made it back to the living room but managed to keep Isabella on one side near the kitchen and Carlo on the other, near the coffee table.

"The murders," yelled Carlo. "Rowan's, Victoria's and almost yours." He waved a hand toward Daniels.

Isabella scoffed. "Murders? If I was going to kill anyone, it would be you, you asshole. I never should have married you."

"I know exactly why you married me," yelled Carlo. "You wanted to get back at Laroche and you used me to do it. You even went so far as to tell me that Mateo was mine."

"I thought he was yours," she yelled.

"Liar," he screamed. "You always knew, you conniving bitch. And you tried to murder me. Don't deny it. You were putting something in my drink."

She shot a finger at him. "It was sugar, you idiot."

"Sugar does not come out of a bag from your purse," he yelled.

"It does when I brought sugar with me to your mother's. That hag is always telling me to not to eat it."

"Since when do you care what she thinks? And she has sugar at her house."

"The sugar isn't for me, it's for her," yelled Isabella. "I put it in her tea when she's not looking."

Carlo hesitated. "You do what? She's diabetic."

"And she sneaks sweets all the time. The sooner the diabetes takes that ice queen, the better."

Carlo stepped toward her, but Daniels stepped in front of him.

Rem put his fingers in his mouth and whistled loudly. "Both of you shut up," he yelled. Carlo and Isabella went quiet, but Daniels could hear their heavy breathing.

"I told you she's a murderer," said Carlo. He eyed Daniels. "Aren't you going to arrest her?"

"There's no law against adding sugar to a woman's tea," said Daniels, wondering how they were going to keep these two from killing each other.

"You're assuming it's sugar," said Carlo.

"If I wanted that woman dead," yelled Isabella. "Believe me, she'd be dead."

"Be quiet, Isabella," said Reinart. "Both of you, take a breath."

Isabella turned and faced the kitchen, and Carlo paced again. Parsons' radio squawked to life. He responded and told them he and Jim were still on a call.

"It's okay. We can take it from here," said Daniels.

Parsons looked between Isabella and Carlo. "You sure?"

Isabella chuckled coldly. "What do you think we're going to do? Murder three detectives?" She scowled at Carlo and raised her voice. "Maybe I'll put sugar in their water and hope they collapse from hyperglycemia."

Carlo sneered back at her.

"It's fine, Parsons," said Reinart. "We got this."

Parsons nodded, responded to his radio call, and left the house.

Rem spoke to Carlo. "Are you capable of having a conversation and not a screaming match?" He looked at Isabella. "Are you?"

Isabella jutted her chin at Carlo. "If he'd stop accusing me of such absurd crimes, I'd happily sit and discuss our issues." She stepped back and leaned against the island in the kitchen.

"Carlo?" asked Rem.

Carlo whirled on Isabella. "You tried to poison my mother."

Isabella calmly crossed her arms. "She hates me, and you know it. The only reason she tolerates me is because of Mateo, and he's not even her grandson. She's lucky I even let her see him."

Carlo's face twisted. "Don't you dare threaten to take Mateo away from my mother."

Isabella smiled and Daniels could see how she easily manipulated and provoked people. "Don't worry, Carlo. I plan to take him away from you first."

Carlo called her another ugly name and launched himself over the sofa. Isabella screamed and darted around the island to get away from him. Reinart followed her and put herself between Carlo and Isabella just as Daniels and Rem got to Carlo and pinned him against the island.

Carlo raged, and Daniels and Rem struggled to hold him down. "You will never take him from me," he screamed. "Never. I'll kill you first."

Isabella stayed behind Reinart. "He's insane," she yelled. "If anyone's capable of murder, it's him."

Carlo stopped struggling, and Rem and Daniels held him down against the counter. "Stop fighting, Carlo," said Rem. "Or you'll force us to take you in."

Seeing they weren't going to get any helpful information out of either of them, Daniels spoke to Isabella. "Do you have somewhere you can stay with Mateo?"

"I'm not leaving," she yelled. "He is."

"It's my house," yelled Carlo.

"Can you go stay with your mother?" Rem asked Carlo. "Until you two can settle down and act like sane people?"

Carlo went still, but his gaze found Isabella's. She stared back with an expression of triumph, and Daniels almost told her to look somewhere else.

Carlo spoke calmly. "You think you've won, but you haven't."

She smiled bigger. "Haven't I?"

Carlo relaxed, and Daniels and Rem loosened their hold. He straightened and smoothed his shirt. "You forget who you're dealing with, Isabella."

Her smile fell.

"I've dealt with worse than you since I was a teenager. You can act smug and triumphant, but one day soon that grin is going to be permanently plastered on your face when they find your cold, dead body floating down the river." He grinned back at her. "And then Mateo and I will live a happy life without you."

Isabella's smile vanished and her face froze in place.

"That's a threat, Carlo," said Rem. "If you don't shut up, we'll take you in."

"Go get your things," Daniels told Carlo. "We're taking you out of here. Now. Before we arrest you."

"It's not a threat," said Carlo, his gaze never wavering from Isabella's. "It's a promise."

"That's it." Rem pushed him back toward the island. "Assume the position. You're under arrest for assault." He grabbed Carlo's arm and pulled it behind him. "You have the right to remain silent..."

Reinart took Isabella's elbow. "Isabella. Let's go to the other room. You can stay in there until he leaves."

While Rem read Carlo his Miranda rights and Daniels secured Carlo's hands, Carlo stared at Isabella and began to laugh.

Reinart walked around to the other side of Isabella and tugged her elbow again. "Come on."

Isabella didn't move. Rem pulled out his cuffs and Daniels reached for them when Isabella whirled around and pulled a large knife from a butcher block. Swinging it and shrieking, she launched herself at Carlo.

Chapter Twenty-Six

FROM THE MOMENT REINART walked into the Vespucci house, her skin prickled, and she flashed back to the day she and her partner were brutally attacked in another domestic altercation. She almost had to stop to gather herself, but if she had, she probably wouldn't have entered the home. Pushing forward, Reinart reminded herself that this situation was different. Isabella and Carlo were volatile but not impoverished drug addicts looking for their next fix. And if they hurt anybody, it would be each other.

Once inside, her stomach settled, but her heart hammered. Telling herself to deal with it, she'd mustered her courage and gone with Parsons to speak with Isabella.

Isabella had been agitated, but capable of discussing the situation with Reinart. That had all changed, though, when Carlo confronted her in the hall. Once they'd returned to the living room, Reinart doubted they'd get anywhere with the couple until they were separated. After Isabella made her threat and Carlo made his, Reinart sensed the shift in energy, but hadn't moved quickly enough to remove Isabella from the room.

Seeing Isabella reach for the knife, Reinart froze. Time slowed and within that split second, Reinart relived her near death at the hands of a murderer; she recalled the blood, the assailant's face, and her partner's collapse. In that second, she almost collapsed herself, until the glint of the knife caught her eye, and she tracked Isabella's movement. Isabella was aiming for her husband, but Daniels was in the way. In her frenzy to get to Carlo, Isabella would have to go through Daniels first.

Isabella's shriek snapped something inside Reinart, and she flung herself at Isabella, catching her around the waist and redirecting her away from Daniels and Carlo. The tip of Isabella's knife caught Daniels across the shoulder, but Reinart's counterattack knocked her and Isabella to the tiled kitchen floor. Isabella struggled against Reinart, but Rem grabbed her wrist and slammed it to the ground. The knife skittered across the floor as Isabella raged and cursed at her husband. Reinart secured her by the shoulders and, with Rem's help, they flipped her over and Rem used his handcuffs on Isabella's wrists instead of Carlo's. Breathing fast and her heart slamming against her ribs, Reinart stood and grabbed the nearest counter for support.

A little pale himself, Rem pulled Isabella to her feet. "You two okay?"

Reinart checked herself for injury, but couldn't find one. "I'm all right."

Daniels remained with Carlo, who was still leaning over the island, but blood seeped through Daniels' sliced jacket and ran down his arm. Carlo gaped at his wife, who continued to scream at him. "I told you she was crazy," he said, before Daniels cuffed him, too. He winced and glanced at his injured arm. "I'm okay."

"Is it bad?" asked Rem.

"Could have been a lot worse if it hadn't been for Reinart." Daniels met her gaze as she tried to catch her breath. "I'm pretty sure you saved my ass."

Isabella cursed at all of them, and Carlo snickered at her.

"We're not out of here yet," said Rem. "Let's get a patrol out here to drive these lunatics to get booked and take you to the hospital."

Daniels took hold of Carlo and guided him to the door. Before leaving, he stopped beside Reinart. "Nice tackle."

Her nerves rattled, and her fingers shaking, Reinart sighed and straightened. "Thanks," she said and, after a deep sigh of relief, followed him out the door.

· · • • · • • • · ·

Rem removed the second coffee cup from the vending machine and carried both cups into the waiting area of the ER. Reinart was sitting in one of the chairs, her elbows on her knees, staring at the ground.

After arriving at the hospital and waiting a couple of hours in the ER, a doctor had checked on both Reinart, who still appeared shaken, and Daniels, and had suggested Reinart take a mild sedative and get some rest. Reinart had declined the sedative, though, and while Daniels was getting stitched up, she and Rem had gone to the waiting room. Rem had updated Lozano, who'd obtained a search warrant for the Vespucci home and had sent a team to the house. Carlo and Isabella had been booked and asked for their attorneys and Mateo was being taken care of by his grandmother.

Rem had also reassured Marjorie that Daniels was fine and wasn't hiding a more serious injury to prevent her from worrying. She'd been ready to leave work and come to the hospital, but he'd convinced her that Daniels would be on his way home soon.

Carrying the coffees, he walked over to Reinart. "Here," he said, holding out a coffee, "I think you need this."

She looked up with weary eyes. "Thanks." She reached for the Styrofoam cup.

He sat beside her. "You sure you don't want that sedative? It might help you sleep tonight."

She straightened. "No. I'm good." She sipped some coffee and grimaced.

"Sorry. It's out of a vending machine."

"It's fine. I've had worse."

Rem sipped his drink and grimaced, too. "Not much worse." He sipped some more. "But I'll get it down."

She stared at her cup and didn't say anything.

"You did good, Reinart. Stop overthinking it."

Her jaw tightened. "I keep replaying it in my head. I should have seen it coming."

"We were all there. Any of us could have played it differently. Don't let hindsight mess with your head. Besides, you're the one who prevented disaster. Give yourself some credit."

She sat back. "I guess."

"I need to thank you too, for saving Daniels. Good partners are hard to find."

"I just did my job."

"And you could have easily let fear take over, but you didn't, and I appreciate it." He took another sip and made another face. The coffee tasted like what he imagined would be the flavor of burned rubber. "I take it back. This is officially the worst."

She ran her fingernail over the Styrofoam, making a crease in the cup. "It's always been in the back of my mind what would I do if I ever faced this situation again."

Rem settled back in his seat. "Well, now you know."

Reinart rested her head back against the wall. "You think Isabella and Carlo murdered Laroche?"

"After what we saw today, they certainly have the temperament for it. If Isabella can get that mad with Carlo, imagine how she must have felt about Laroche." He sighed and glanced at the doors to the ER.

"Their house is being searched as we speak, so if there's any evidence, we'll find it soon enough."

The electronic doors leading to the parking lot slid open and Lozano entered the hospital. Seeing Rem and Reinart in the waiting area, he walked over to them.

"Nice of you to join us, Cap," said Rem. He checked his watch. "It's late. You should have gone home."

Lozano grunted. "I'll get there, eventually." He sat beside Rem. "How is he?"

"He's okay. Still with the doctor, getting stitches," said Rem. "Any progress with the search?"

Lozano loosened his tie. "So far, they've found two unregistered weapons and a small amount of cocaine in an unlocked safe, plus a small bag of sugar in the kitchen, plus another bag of what appears to be sugar in the pantry. We'll check both to be sure."

"That backs up their stories," said Rem.

"Assuming neither of them is poison," said Reinart.

Lozano leaned back and crossed his arms. "We also found a desktop calendar in an office. The calendar has three dates circled. The date Laroche died, the date you had your accident, and the date Victoria died."

Rem sat up and Reinart looked over. "You're kidding," said Rem.

Lozano arched a brow at them. "Do I look like I'm kidding?"

Rem noted the deeper than usual creases around and under his captain's eyes. "You look like you could use a stiff drink and good night's sleep."

"If I had three wishes," said Lozano, "those would be two of them."

Rem almost asked what the third wish would be, but Reinart interrupted. "What do you think the circled dates mean?"

Lozano shrugged. "On their own, they mean nothing. Maybe Carlo and Isabella want to remember what dates to celebrate next year." He scratched his nose. "There was a note on the calendar with a name and number." Lozano shifted in his chair. "That's what's got me interested."

"Whose name and number?" asked Rem.

"Name's Burton Rimaldi."

"Who's Burton Rimaldi?" asked Reinart.

"I spoke to Mel and Garcia on the way here. They did some checking and Rimaldi is Isabella's younger half-brother. He was an art instructor at a community college but lost his job after getting arrested for drug possession. He also did time for fraud, larceny, and aggravated assault. He's been out a year and living in a decent apartment in a decent neighborhood."

"Is he working?" asked Reinart.

Lozano nodded. "He is. As a mechanic at a car dealership."

Reinart straightened. "So he knows cars."

"He sure does," said Lozano, "but he must have a side job, because a mechanic's pay wouldn't cover his decent rent."

Rem set his coffee cup on the table in front of him. "You think Isabella or Carlo hired him to do some extra work?"

Lozano smoothed his tie. "That's what I plan to find out. Mel and Garcia are trying to locate Rimaldi."

Hopeful, Rem bounced his foot. "Rimaldi could be our killer, and with his background, maybe he's connected to the forged tiger, too."

"But how do you explain the poison used to kill Laroche?" asked Reinart.

"If Rimaldi has connections," said Lozano, "maybe Isabella or Carlo asked him to buy the poison, but we can't rule out Carlo's mob connections. It's too soon to know for sure."

Rem scratched at a coffee stain on his pant leg. "I guess we shouldn't be surprised. He's a mobster, and she's a jilted lover and possibly a sociopath."

"We don't know everything yet," said Lozano. "We still have to find Rimaldi, but it's not looking good for Carlo and Isabella."

Reinart shook her head. "Poor Mateo. If it's true, he's lost his parents. Who's going to raise him?"

"That'll be for a court to decide," said Lozano. "But let's not assume anything yet. We need more evidence to lock this case up."

"You want us to keep digging into Evelyn Sinclair?" asked Rem. "We were planning on talking to her next."

"Right now, I want you to take Daniels and yourselves home. It's been a rough day. We'll see where we are tomorrow and go from there."

Rem reached for his coffee cup. "I won't argue with that." He sipped some more and almost spit it out. "I keep trying, but this is too awful to drink." He set the cup back on the table.

"I concur." Reinart set her cup next to Rem's.

The ER doors opened, and Daniels emerged, looking almost as tired as Lozano. He was holding his jacket and wearing his bloody shirt, but Rem could see a bandage through the hole in the fabric. "All done," he said.

"How many stitches?" asked Rem.

"Eighteen." He sat beside Lozano, rested his head back and closed his eyes.

"Does it hurt?" asked Reinart.

"Only when I move," said Daniels. He cracked an eye open. "I'm exaggerating. It's numbed up."

"Just wait till tonight," said Rem. "Did you get some pain pills?"

Daniels lifted his head. "Got a prescription, but I'll be fine."

"You and Reinart need to listen to the doctor," said Rem. "Take the pills if you need them."

Daniels sat up. "Says the man who stopped taking his antibiotics too soon and almost wound up back in the hospital with an infection."

Rem held his belly. "Those pills messed up my stomach."

"Better your stomach than flesh-eating bacteria taking your leg."

"It wasn't that bad."

Daniels narrowed his weary eyes, and Rem slumped in his seat. "All right," he said. "It wasn't great."

Lozano looked between them. "Since you're well enough to berate your partner's dumb decisions, care to hear the latest?" He filled Daniels in on what he'd learned about Carlo and Isabella.

Daniels dropped his jaw. "So we may have found our killer."

"I knew it all along," said Rem.

"Since when?" said Reinart.

Rem poked his temple. "It's been up here the entire time."

"At least something's up there," said Daniels. "Anything in that cavernous space that might help with who stole the tiger?"

Rem shook his head. "Not yet, but I'm working on it."

"That means no," said Reinart.

Daniels rested his head back again. "Careful, Reinart. You're starting to speak Remalla. Once you go down that road, there's no turning back."

Rem patted Reinart's wrist. "Don't mind him. He gets grumpy when I'm right."

Daniels snorted, and Lozano stood. "Get out of here and get some sleep. We'll make some decisions in the morning. I'll need your reports, too." He headed toward the exit. "Take it easy, Daniels."

Rem stood and stretched, and Daniels got up with a groan. "Will do, Cap."

Lozano left the ER, and Reinart got to her feet. "So our theory is Isabella and Carlo hired Rimaldi to kill Laroche, us, and Victoria and possibly steal the tiger?"

Rem twisted and cracked his back. "Something tells me we'll find out tomorrow."

"Let's hope we get lucky," replied Daniels, plodding toward the exit.

Careful to avoid Daniels' injury, Rem took Daniels' elbow. "Let's get you home before your wife yells at me. I think I'm more scared of her than I am of Isabella."

"With good reason," said Daniels.

Reinart stifled a yawn. "I need to meet this lady."

"When this is over, you're invited to dinner, Reinart," said Daniels. "You can meet the whole Daniels' clan."

"Don't forget me," said Rem.

Daniels scoffed as they left the ER. "Perish the thought."

Chapter Twenty-Seven

PHOEBE PULLED UP TO the curb outside Remalla's house. The front door opened and Remalla stepped out, holding a thermos.

"At least he's on time," said Daniels from the passenger seat. After leaving the hospital the previous evening, Phoebe had offered to pick up Daniels and Remalla the next day. With Daniels injured and Remalla driving a rental, it seemed time for her to take the wheel. She got their addresses and had gone home to get some sleep. She secretly feared Barry would be waiting for her, but thankfully, he hadn't shown or called.

Rem walked up and got into the backseat. "Thanks for the ride, Reinart." He shut the door and eyed Daniels. "How are you? Did you get some sleep?"

"About as well as expected. Thankfully, J.P. had a good night." Daniels moved his arm. "It's sore but bearable."

"Well, let's hope that's our last scare on this case." Rem sat back.

"I think we've hit our quota." Phoebe pulled away from the curb.

"Slight change in plans," said Rem. "Don't head to the station."

Daniels attempted to turn in his seat, but winced. "We are not going to the donut shop."

"No, we're not." Rem sat up again. "I got a phone call from Maria Rossi." He paused. "That's a sentence I wish I could have said when I was a teenager."

"I bet." Daniels glanced back. "What did she want?"

"She wants to meet. Said she needs to talk, but not at her place."

Phoebe pulled over until she could find out where they were going. "Why is that?"

"She was secretive about it and said she'd tell us more when we saw her. I suggested she meet us at that diner. I let Lozano know we'd be making a detour on the way in."

"What diner?" asked Daniels.

"You know. The place where we saw that guy do that thing."

Daniels arched an eyebrow. "The place that serves your favorite breakfast?"

"That's the one."

"Convenient."

"I thought so." Rem sat back again.

"So we're going to a diner that serves breakfast where a guy did a thing?" asked Phoebe.

"Yup," said Rem.

"Sounds good to me." She pulled back out onto the road.

Twenty minutes later, they pulled into a small parking lot of an equally small diner. Phoebe parked near the entrance. "Looks interesting."

Daniels unbuckled. "Let's hope Maria's not hungry."

"Stop complaining." Rem got out of the vehicle. "Thay have those bran muffins you like."

"I'm pretty sure I'm the only one who eats them."

"Wouldn't surprise me at all," said Rem.

Phoebe joined them on the sidewalk, and they entered the diner. Across from the entry was a short counter with four stools, booths lined the perimeter and four-top tables took up the rest of the space. A waitress with short blonde spiky hair, wearing jeans and a tight cleavage-revealing top with a white apron tied around her waist walked by carrying a pot of coffee. "Seat yourself," she said. She eyed Rem. "I'll bring you some coffee, sugar."

"Thanks, Marsha," said Rem.

Daniels stopped. "Marsha?"

"I'm a regular," said Rem.

"Obviously."

They looked around, and Phoebe spotted Maria in a back corner booth. "Over there." She headed toward Maria and sat beside her. Rem and Daniels slid into the opposite side of the booth.

"Thank you for meeting me," said Maria. She rested her forearms on the table and interlaced her fingers. "I know this must seem unusual."

Marsha, holding a mug and a pot of coffee, stopped beside the table. She placed the cup in front of Rem and poured him a steaming cup. "What can I get the rest of you?"

Phoebe and Maria ordered coffee, and Daniels ordered apple juice.

Marsha left, and Maria squirmed in her seat.

"Why did you want to meet?" asked Phoebe. "And why here and not your place?"

Maria hesitated. "I heard about Isabella's and Carlo's arrest. Did they kill Rowan and Victoria?"

"We're still trying to figure that out." Rem reached for sugar and creamer and added them to his coffee.

"Does this have something to do with them?" asked Daniels.

"I don't know." Maria shifted in her seat again. "The reason I wanted to meet here is that I've felt certain that someone's been watching my place." She looked around as if expecting to see someone.

Phoebe looked at the other patrons but didn't see anyone suspicious. "Why do you say that?"

Maria shook her head. "It's just a feeling I have, but I don't have proof. I think I see someone, but when I look, they walk on by or turn the corner. The other day I came home, and I swear someone had been in my apartment."

"Did you call the police?" asked Rem. He stirred and sipped his coffee.

"No," said Maria, "because I couldn't be sure. It was a little thing. I have a letter opener on my desk, and I keep it in the same spot, but the other day I came in and it was moved. Maybe I did it, but I don't know why I would have."

"Anything else disturbed or out of place?" asked Phoebe.

"My closet door was open, and I typically close it, but again, I may be misremembering." Maria rubbed her forehead. "It might be all the stress from Rowan's death and now Victoria's." She lowered her hand. "I haven't been myself."

"Have you seen a doctor?" asked Rem. "It might help with the anxiety."

She nodded. "I saw my shrink who prescribed something for stress, but it's not helping much."

"Is that why you wanted to see us?" asked Daniels. "Because you think someone's watching you?"

Marsha returned with two more mugs, a coffee pot, and a juice. She set the juice in front of Daniels and poured coffee for Maria and Reinart. "You ready to order?" She pulled out a pad and pen.

"I'll have my usual," said Rem.

"You got it, sugar." Marsha scribbled on her pad.

Daniels ordered a bran muffin, Reinart got a bowl of oatmeal and Maria declined breakfast, saying she wasn't hungry. Marsha took their orders and left.

Maria wrung her hands and stared out the window.

"What's bugging you, Maria?" asked Rem.

She looked back at them. "I guess you could say a guilty conscience."

"Guilty about what?" asked Reinart. "Victoria?"

Maria closed her eyes and shook her head. "That book caused all of this. I should have never agreed to participate."

"We read an early draft," said Daniels. "It wasn't flattering, especially to Rowan or Isabella and Carlo."

"You told Victoria a lot about her dad," said Phoebe.

"It was all true," said Maria. "I didn't lie about any of it."

"Are you saying someone did?" asked Daniels.

Maria tensed and shook her head. "I don't know."

Rem sipped more coffee. "Something tells me you do."

Phoebe added creamer to her coffee and stirred it. "Does this have something to do with the deal you made with Rowan? About holding off on publishing?"

Maria fiddled with her napkin but didn't answer.

"The early draft we read made some serious accusations," said Rem. "Who was Victoria's source?"

"I can't say for sure," said Maria. "Victoria talked to a lot of people. It could have been Rowan."

"So, Rowan contributed to the book?" asked Phoebe.

Maria sighed. "Maybe he figured it would be the ultimate revenge against Isabella. Isabella no doubt contributed a few things against Rowan, not thinking he would do the same to her."

"So everyone's turning on each other," said Daniels. "Nice circle of friends."

"I wouldn't call any of those people my friends, Detective," said Maria.

"Is that why you called?" asked Rem. "To ease your guilt?"

"It's more than that." Maria paused. "That book...it was just supposed to be a way to expose Rowan for his crimes, and he deserved that, but then it turned into much more. I think Victoria used it to blackmail people, and it may have gotten her killed."

"She got in too deep," said Phoebe.

Maria blinked back tears. "I warned her to be careful, especially after our deal with Rowan."

"Why?" asked Phoebe. "What did Rowan want that he was willing to pay so much for?"

Maria used her napkin to blot a tear from her eye. "It's what he didn't want. He asked Victoria to take out some of the more incriminating evidence against him."

"I can't imagine Victoria was okay with that," said Phoebe.

"She wasn't," said Maria. "But Rowan agreed to give her something in return, other than the money. Rowan wasn't stupid. He wanted to use the book against others. If he was going down, he was taking others with him."

"But Victoria already mentioned Carlo and Isabella," said Daniels.

"Not just them," said Maria. "Victoria wouldn't tell me more than that."

Daniels leaned in. "And you think that's what got Rowan killed?"

"Could he have said something about you?" asked Rem.

Maria shrugged. "He could have said whatever he wanted, but I think Victoria would have told me. I'm not a big fish, though, and attacking me wouldn't gain Rowan much."

"You accuse him of stealing and taking credit for your work," added Phoebe. "That's reason enough to come after you."

Maria wrapped her fingers around her coffee mug. "Maybe."

"That's not what this is about, though, is it?" asked Rem.

She stared resolutely out the window, nibbled her lip, then reached beside her and opened her purse. "The morning of Victoria's death, she sent me this via email." She pulled out a USB drive. "It's the latest version of her book. She asked that I keep it safe and not show it to anyone, but she wanted my opinion." Her breath caught. "I didn't see it until after I learned she was dead, and...and...I couldn't read it." She sniffed and handed the USB drive to Rem. "But you can. And if there's anything in there that points to her killer, I want you to use it."

Rem took the drive from her. "Thank you. This could be a big help."

"I hope it is." She sniffed again and dabbed her eye with the napkin. "If it soothes this gnawing guilt, then it's worth it."

"Are you sure that you're okay?" asked Phoebe. "Do you think your life is in danger?"

Maria shook her head. "I doubt it." She took a deep breath and wiped her nose. "I should go."

"Maria, if you're scared, we can help," said Daniels.

"I'll be fine." She picked up her purse. "I just want to get rid of that book. I don't want any part of it, and I hope it never gets published."

"If it's any consolation," said Rem. "Carlo and Isabella are behind bars, and if we get the information we're hoping for, they won't hurt anyone else."

"I hope you're right." She picked up her purse.

Phoebe slid out of the booth to let Maria leave. "You have our number if you need to reach us."

Maria stood. "No offense, but I don't want to see any of you again. I just want to put this all behind me."

"If this goes to court, you'll need to testify," said Daniels.

Maria clutched her purse. "Then I'll see you in court, Detective." She turned, and without looking back, strode out of the diner.

· · • • · • • · ·

Sitting in the back seat with the bag of food beside him, Rem stared out the window, thinking. After Maria left the diner, they'd hastily flagged down Marsha and told her they needed their orders to go. They were eager to get back to the station to read the latest version of Victoria's book.

Lozano had called on the way and while he and Daniels spoke, Rem considered Maria's concerns about being followed. Was she paranoid? Had the medication the doctor prescribed her made her overly suspicious? Was her guilt over Victoria causing her to see things that weren't there? Or was someone actually watching her and accessing her apartment? And if so, why?

Rem wondered if Carlo and Isabella had similar issues to Maria. Had they been followed, or had someone been in their home without their knowledge? Was the evidence against them too convenient? Or were they overconfident and reckless? What was Rimaldi's role in all of this? If he was involved, the logical conclusion was that Isabella killed Laroche and, with her brother's help, possibly forged and stole the tiger. Was Carlo telling the truth when he suggested Isabella was framing him? Based on Rem's experience with her, he wouldn't put it past her. It would be an effective way to get rid of a husband and protect her son. And what about Evelyn, James, and Robert? Was the killer stalking potential victims? Had he stalked Victoria? Had someone hired Rimaldi to do the stalking or killing, or both?

His mind whirling with potential scenarios, he came to the inevitable deduction that the simplest answer was usually the correct one. Isabella, possibly with her husband's and brother's help, had killed Laroche and Victoria, cut Rem's brake lines, and probably stole the tiger too. If Isabella wanted to stop Victoria's book, she might have told Rimaldi to follow Maria and search her place.

"Earth to Rem." Daniels glanced back. "You still there?"

Rem blinked and put his hand on the bag of food. The smell of his eggs, bacon and hash browns was making his stomach rumble. "Yeah. Still here. Just thinking. What'd Lozano have to say?"

"They're still looking for Rimaldi. He's not at his place and didn't show up for work."

Reinart pulled into the parking lot of the station. "If he's involved and heard about Isabella and Carlo's arrest, he may have taken off."

"It doesn't look good in terms of his guilt," said Daniels. "Innocent people don't run."

Reinart parked in an open space. "Even if we find him, all we have is his name on a desktop calendar. Our only hope is to get Isabella or Carlo to turn on him."

"Don't count on that," said Daniels, opening his door. "They're not talking either. Lozano said they'll both be arraigned today and likely make bail."

Rem imagined that scenario. "Depending on who's out first, they'll both head to Mateo. They could end up killing each other over him before we ever get this case solved." He grabbed the food and got out of the car.

"Wouldn't that be a cluster," said Reinart, joining Rem and Daniels on the sidewalk. They walked toward the entrance of the police station. "Let's pray Victoria's manuscript has some answers or we may never know who killed Laroche."

"Or may never be able to prove it." Eager to eat, Rem took the stairs two at a time.

"Detective Daniels?"

Daniels stopped on the stairs, and Reinart and Rem turned.

"Maurice?" asked Daniels.

Rem recognized Laroche's chef. He was leaving the station and holding a white box with a thin but colorful bow around it.

Daniels walked over, and Rem and Reinart followed. "What are you doing here?" asked Daniels. "Everything okay?"

Maurice held out the box. "I came to see you and your partners. I brought you those cookies I told you about. I made more batches than

I needed, so I thought I'd stop by and see how the investigation was going."

"Cookies?" asked Rem, stepping closer. "What kind?"

Maurice smiled. "Chocolate chip. My specialty."

"My favorite." Rem took the box from Maurice. "Thank you." Rem held the box to his nose and sniffed. "Delicious."

"You've officially made his day," said Daniels.

"You better share," said Reinart.

Rem held the box close. "Only if you're nice."

Maurice's smile softened. "I heard about Isabella's and Carlo's arrests. Did they kill Rowan?"

"We haven't gotten that far yet," said Daniels. "Right now, they're just charged with hurting each other, but we believe they have some involvement with what happened to your friend."

Maurice wrung his hands, looking like he wanted to cry again. "I'll sleep better when I know his killer is behind bars."

Rem thought of Maria. "Just out of curiosity, Maurice. Have you had any concerns about being watched?"

Maurice's smile fell. "No," said Maurice. "Why do you ask?"

"No reason. Just curious."

Reinart looked around as if double-checking they weren't being watched. "Since we're talking, would you mind telling us more about James? I know you two are no longer dating, but what do you know about his frame of mind?"

Maurice's expression fell. "Why? Is he in trouble?"

"No. Not at all," said Reinart. "But this case has taken a toll on all of you who were close to Rowan. If you've spoken to James recently, could you tell us if he's been acting out of character or done anything of concern?"

Rem figured that was a good question. If James was going to accuse Evelyn of acting strangely, they ought to confirm that James wasn't doing the same.

Maurice shook his head. "I've spoken to him a few times, and he's understandably upset, but shouldn't he be?"

"Of course he should," said Daniels. "But something like this can trigger odd behavior. We have to ask it of all our suspects."

"James is a suspect?" asked Maurice.

"Until we find our killer," said Daniels. "No one at that party is officially off the hook."

"I see." Maurice rubbed his shiny head. "I guess that includes me."

"Nobody here thinks you hurt Rowan," said Reinart. "But yes. You're not officially cleared."

Maurice held his chest. "I know you're just doing your job, but it's a shock to be thought of as a suspect." He took a breath and appeared to collect himself. "But to answer your question, no, I haven't felt that James is acting strangely. He's been his usual smug self. He's been a little stressed recently, but I think that's reasonable, considering the circumstances."

"Is he stressed over anything else?" asked Reinart. "How's his relationship with Evelyn Sinclair?"

Maurice frowned. "Miss Sinclair? It's fine, as far as I know." He paused. "I mean, he has the usual gripes and grievances, but that's just James."

"What gripes and grievances?" asked Daniels.

Maurice hesitated. "You know. The typical boss's behavior. James wants more and Miss Sinclair is hesitant to give it." He sighed. "I told him to expect this. He was just jumping from one fire into another, but he assured me he knew what he was doing."

"So he's been unhappy with his arrangement with Evelyn?" asked Rem.

"I wouldn't say unhappy. He likes Evelyn, but he's frustrated. He and I talked when he came by the house before the party. He was more open than usual and even in a good mood. He even brought me a gift." His smile returned. "James can be an ass most times, but occasionally his good side emerges. We talked, and he opened up about his concerns. I've been telling him he should take the leap and open up his own gallery but—"

Daniels raised his hand. "Sorry to interrupt, but did you say you talked to James before the party? You mean that same day?"

"Heavens, no. I was much too busy. I meant the week before. He stopped by to say hi and bring me a gift." He sighed softly. "I thought it was sweet."

"The week before?" asked Reinart. "What day was that?"

Maurice stared off. "Um, it was Saturday. The Saturday before the party."

Rem gripped the handle on the food bag. "James came to see you the Saturday before the party? Was Evelyn there?"

"No," said Maurice. "Just him."

"What did he bring you?" asked Rem.

Maurice put his hand on his heart. "He brought me a lovely painting. It was a seascape. He knows how I love the ocean."

"How big was the painting?" asked Reinart. "Was it framed?"

Maurice shook his head. "No. It was on canvas, and he'd rolled it up and had it in an art tube. He said I could get it framed, however I'd like, which is a good thing. His and my tastes rarely match."

Rem's mind raced. James had shown at Laroche's the day the security had gone down carrying an art tube that could have easily delivered the false tiger and removed the real one. Seeing Reinart's and Daniels' expressions, it was obvious they were thinking the same.

Daniels' cell rang, and he pulled it from his pocket. Staring at the display, he arched an eyebrow. "Excuse me a second." He stepped away and answered.

Reinart focused on Maurice. "You're sure about the date? There's no doubt when James was at the house?"

"No," said Maurice. "That's the day I spoke to the cake designer about the cake for the party. James arrived just as he was leaving." He clutched the edge of his jacket. "Is something wrong?"

"How was his demeanor?" asked Rem. "Did he seem nervous or anxious?"

"Not that I recall." He looked between the two of them. "Why? What's wrong?"

"How long was he there?" asked Reinart. "Were you with him the whole time?"

Maurice pursed his lips. "You're scaring me."

"There's nothing to be scared about but this information might help with the case," said Reinart. "This could be important."

"Just tell us whatever you can remember," added Rem.

Maurice stammered. "He…uh…stopped by after lunch. We chatted, and he gave me the painting."

"Was Rowan home?" asked Reinart.

"Um, no, he wasn't," said Maurice. He held his head. "I think that was when he went out to La Jolla to meet with a potential new artist. He was gone most of the day."

Rem's heart thudded. "What happened after James gave you your painting?"

Maurice stared off. "He left. No wait. He stopped by the gallery. He said someone had mistakenly delivered a package to Rowan instead of him and Rowan had asked him to pick it up."

"Package?" asked Rem. "Did he say what package?"

"How long was he gone?" asked Reinart.

Flustered, Maurice's gaze bounced between the two of them. "Not long, and I don't know about the package. I didn't think anything of it. Rowan and James were still friendly, and they occasionally met for business reasons. I stayed out of that stuff, though."

"Was it normal for him to go into the gallery alone?" asked Rem.

Maurice hesitated. "He actually asked me to go, but I wasn't going near that tiger. I told him he could get it himself." He put his fingers over his mouth. "Was that wrong?"

Daniels returned, holding his phone. "Can you do me a favor, Maurice? Can you call James and see if he answers?" His tone suggested he was concerned.

Maurice dropped his jaw. "What on earth? Is he okay?" He fumbled in his jacket pocket and pulled out his phone.

"I just need you to call him, please," said Daniels. He held his phone against his shoulder and Rem wondered who was on the line.

Maurice hit a button on his keypad and put his phone to his ear. A few seconds passed and Maurice shook his head. "Straight to voicemail." He lowered the phone and hung up. "What is going on?"

Daniels turned, spoke into the phone, and hung up. He turned back around and faced Maurice. "I want you to go home and we'll be in touch." He regarded Rem and Reinart. "We've got to go."

Rem raised the bag. "But our breakfast."

Daniels started toward the car. "Give it to Maurice. Let's go." He walked off with Reinart.

Hungry, Rem hesitated, but then handed the bag of food to Maurice with disappointment. "I hope you like eggs and bacon." He held on to the box. "But I'm keeping the cookies." Leaving Maurice on the steps, Rem turned and jogged to catch up with Reinart and Daniels.

Chapter Twenty-Eight

REINART PULLED OUT OF the lot as Daniels secured his seatbelt. "Evelyn was on the phone. Head to her gallery."

"What did Evelyn say?" asked Rem from the backseat.

"She arrived at the gallery to find her office ransacked, and James isn't there, nor is he answering his phone. I asked her if she felt safe and she said she was fine, but she looked outside and there's a car in the lot with someone at the wheel. It could be nothing, but I told her to lock up, and we'd be right there." Reinart picked up speed and turned at the corner. "I had Maurice call James just to be sure he wasn't ignoring Evelyn's calls."

"If he took the tiger, he may be on the run," said Reinart.

"Based on what Maurice said, James had means and opportunity," added Rem.

"We can't be sure if he did anything," replied Daniels. "Let's talk to Evelyn first. If James took the tiger, I don't know how she's not involved."

"You think she killed her rival and his daughter to protect her and James' secrets?" asked Rem.

"And if she did, where do Isabella, Carlo and Rimaldi fit into all of this?" asked Reinart. "Who came after us? And who is following Maria?" She sped by a car. "And why is she calling us if she's involved?"

Daniels held on to his armrest. "Maybe she's legitimately worried. She doesn't know James talked to us about her. If she is involved, it's a good way to incriminate him."

"Or, if she killed him," said Rem, "make herself look innocent."

"So, we have no idea what we're walking into?" asked Reinart.

"Not really," said Daniels. "Maybe something or maybe nothing."

Rem held on to the seat as Reinart took another quick turn. "If I hadn't missed breakfast, I might have some answers, but my brain cells haven't fully kicked in."

"I don't think that has anything to do with breakfast." Daniels pointed. "Take the next turn. You can bypass the main road leading to the gallery. Traffic's going to be heavy this time of day."

Reinart took the turn and sped down the street. They got caught at a couple of lights and hit some light traffic, but made decent time as they crossed the busy intersection and street near the gallery. Reinart pulled into the gallery's lot and parked in front of the entrance. Daniels looked around but didn't see any other cars.

Reinart undid her seatbelt. "Maybe the suspicious car was just a lost driver who needed directions."

"I'm going to tell Lozano where we are." Rem pulled out his phone.

Daniels opened his door. "Probably a good idea." He got out along with Reinart. They stepped onto the walkway and peered through the glass. Daniels could see the familiar artwork on display, but there was no sign of Evelyn. Nothing appeared out of place, and it was quiet.

"Maybe she's in the back office, waiting." Reinart peered through the glass, too. "Maybe you should call her and tell her we're here."

Daniels pulled out his phone. "I will." He dialed Evelyn's number and waited. It rang three times and went to voicemail. "No answer." He hung up, glanced through the glass again, and lowered his phone.

"That's strange," said Reinart. "Where is she?" She walked toward the front door as Rem got out of the car. "Lozano's updated," he said.

"He's putting out an APB on James based on what Maurice said. He also told me Carlo was arraigned and released on his own recognizance."

Surprised, Daniels swiveled in surprise. "Are you serious? No bail?"

Rem shrugged. "I guess that's the perks of being a mobster. You've got friends in high places. Isabella isn't due in court until later, and something tells me she won't be so lucky. Especially since one of those bags of sugar in their kitchen turned out to be poison."

Reinart dropped her jaw. "The same that killed Laroche?"

Rem joined them on the walkway. "They're not sure yet. I wish we'd known that before Carlo got released. The walls are definitely closing in on those two."

"It supports Carlo's story though, that Isabella was trying to kill him," said Daniels.

"Maybe, but who knows?" said Rem. "We'll have to track down Carlo again. And Isabella will probably have attempted murder added to her assault charge."

Reinart shook her head. "Isabella will be spitting nails when she learns Carlo is out and probably headed straight for Mateo. That should make him easy to find, though." She pulled on the door to the gallery, and it opened. "I thought you told Evelyn to lock up."

Concern rippled through Daniels. "I did."

Rem walked over and poked his head inside the gallery. "Hello? Anyone home?" He waited a second and entered.

Daniels and Reinart followed, and the door closed behind them.

"Evelyn?" asked Reinart. "Are you here?"

There was no response other than the motorized hum of the spinning mannequin.

"It's a good thing they turned that on." Rem eyed the mannequin and the rest of the gallery. "It's awfully quiet in here."

"It's an art gallery. What do you expect?" Daniels walked in the opposite direction of Rem.

Rem stopped beside a statue. "At least someone who might want to prevent us from stealing a painting."

Daniels gestured at the picture of the naked man with the sliced apple in his lap. "You want that? It's all yours."

Rem turned and walked toward the back of the building. "I'd rather have a velvet Elvis."

"That can be arranged," said Reinart, keeping her voice low. She moved quietly through the showroom. "I don't know about you guys, but I'm getting the willies."

"Me too." Rem stopped in front of a closed door marked *Office*. He stepped to the side of it and pulled his gun. "Care to do the honors?" he asked Daniels.

Reinart pulled her gun too and stepped to the other side of the door.

His heart thumping, Daniels walked closer. "She may have stepped out for some coffee."

"Or she, or James, could be dead inside this room." Rem gripped his gun.

His nerves taut, Daniels pulled out his own weapon. "You really need to work on your positivity."

"Happy to," said Rem in a whisper. "Once we leave here in one piece." He banged on the door with the butt of his gun. "Evelyn? You in there?"

Daniels stood next to Reinart and heard no response.

Reinart reached over, turned the knob, and pushed the office door open. Rem swiveled around, his gun aimed. Reinart and Daniels went in behind him, but no one was inside the office.

Daniels spotted a messy desk with a computer monitor and keyboard, a set of drawers and a bookshelf, but no Evelyn. "Where the hell is she?" he asked. A couple of desk drawers were open, and papers were on the floor.

Reinart walked over and touched a key on the keyboard. The screen flickered on, and Daniels could see a scenic picture of the ocean along with a password request. "If she left, why wouldn't she let us know?"

Rem went through the bookshelf. "Just a lot of books with fancy pictures."

Daniels tried to open a drawer, but it was locked. "First James disappears and now Evelyn. This is like that sci-fi show you watch, Rem, where all those odd things happen."

"You mean *The Twilight Zone*." Rem left the office. "Let's try down here." Holding his weapon at his side, he walked away. Daniels and Reinart followed him to the far side of the showroom, where less provocative paintings with smaller price tags covered the walls. "Check this out." Rem pointed at another door marked *Staff Only*.

Daniels paused next to it. "I'm game if you are." He stood to one side of it, Rem stood to the other, and Reinart came up behind Daniels.

"I'm ready," she said, pointing her weapon down with both hands.

Rem nodded and knocked again. "Hello?" he asked, his voice raised. "Anyone in there? Evelyn? James? It's the police."

When there was no response, Rem turned the knob as Reinart had done at the other door. He pushed it open, and Daniels swiveled around, his gun aimed. Reinart went in behind him and Rem took up the rear. They found themselves on a narrow landing in front of a staircase leading down to a basement. One illuminated light on the staircase gave the space a murky feel. "What the hell is this?" asked Reinart, looking down the stairs. They led to another small landing, where the stairs turned and descended in the opposite direction.

Daniels peered down. "Probably leads to a storage area."

Rem put a hand on the stairwell. "That's not creepy at all."

Daniels took the first step down. "And that's why you shouldn't watch those horror films." Holding his gun, he took another step. "Let's go."

"Right behind you," said Reinart.

Rem sighed, glanced back into the showroom, and then returned to the stairs. "Right behind you."

The three of them headed down, the light above growing murkier as they descended. As Daniels walked, he saw the ceiling open up, and another room came into view, also dimly lit. It was a sizeable space with ample room for storage, but Daniels didn't see many art pieces. He assumed a woman like Evelyn Sinclair would have amassed a lot of art over the years and this would be the logical place to put it, but all he saw were a variety of empty frames leaning against the wall, a few blank canvasses on easels, wooden crates on the ground and what looked like an artists' studio. There were tubes of paint and various sized brushes in containers, a couple of partially completed paintings, a table and shelf full of supplies, folded canvas tarps on the floor, and it smelled like turpentine.

Reinart and Rem made it to the bottom of the stairs. "Where are we?" asked Reinart.

Other than the stairwell light, there was a small bulb in the corner that offered only the barest of light.

"According to those movies I watch," said Rem, approaching a shelf containing a variety of paint tubes, "I'd say this could be a portal to hell."

Daniels sighed. "It's obviously a studio." He squinted to peer back into the shadows of the room and spotted folded chairs, more shelves, and another mannequin, only this one wasn't spinning and bore no clothes or jewelry. Her silent stare caused a chill to run up his spine.

Reinart stopped in front of a blank canvas on an easel. "It's not like any studio I've ever seen. It's too dark. Artists need lots of natural light."

"There's bound to be a light switch around here somewhere." Daniels holstered his weapon and headed to the wall to search for one.

"The sooner, the better." Rem approached the table full of art supplies. "Nobody's down here, so we should go."

Daniels walked farther back into the darker recesses of the room.

"Wait a minute," said Reinart, stopping beside an incomplete painting partially covered by a cloth. She pulled it back, and it fell to the floor. "Look at this."

Returning his gun to its holster, Rem walked over. "What is it?"

Daniels searched the far side of the vast space. His foot hit something solid, and he stopped beside it.

"This looks like a painting called *Portrait of Helene*." Reinart stood back from the canvas. "I can't believe it. This picture has been missing for years."

Rem eyed the picture. "Looks like? How can you tell in this light? And why is it half done?"

Reinart stepped closer and Daniels heard her suck in a breath. "Someone's duplicating it."

Daniels felt around the crate he'd bumped into and, finding the edges, pulled on the lid, stirring the dust into little whirlpools.

"Missing?" asked Rem.

"It was stolen, but now I'm trying to remember from who," said Reinart.

"I have an idea," said Daniels. He stepped back from the painting he'd revealed lying in the crate, recognizing the same figure only partially completed on the other canvas. His vision had adjusted enough to see the female subject of the portrait. She was facing away but glancing over her shoulder with an enigmatic expression. She wore a sexy red dress with one strap fallen over a bare shoulder and her red hair cascaded down her shoulders and back. The other canvas only contained an outline of the woman's body and face, and her dress was only partially painted.

"My God," said Reinart, walking over to Daniels. "This is the original."

"I think we found our fraudster," said Daniels.

Reinart squatted and touched the frame. "Why would Evelyn resort to this?"

"I think the word you're looking for is greed," said Rem. "Is it just her, though? We have to assume James is involved." He paused. "And what about Isabella and Carlo? What's their role in this?"

"The bigger question is, where is everybody?" asked Daniels. "If Evelyn is behind this, why contact me and disappear?" asked Daniels. "The last thing she'd want is for us to find this." He waved his hand toward the studio.

"Maybe there's more going on here," said Rem, looking around.

Daniels sensed Rem's anxiety. "Don't freak yourself out, partner. What do you mean?"

"What if...?" His eyes darted around the room.

"What if what?" asked Reinart.

"What if Daniels was right?"

"That's not uncommon," replied Daniels.

Rem didn't offer his usual sarcastic retort. "Remember what you said about Laroche having some sort of art cult?" He paused. "What if that's true? What if all these people are in on this? What if Carlo and Isabella killed Laroche, James and Evelyn forged and stole the tiger and Robert used Emily to explain the lost video footage?"

Daniels didn't buy that theory, but played along to help Rem get it out of his system. "You forgot Maria."

Rem stilled. "What if she's the ringleader of the whole thing, and we just walked into her lair?" His jaw dropped. "What if she's the one who killed Victoria, and she's been playing us all along?"

Reinart walked toward another crate. "Rem, I don't think—"

"And Maurice," exclaimed Rem, his eyes wide with worry. "What if he's part of it, too?"

"Ok, now you're getting way ahead of yourself," said Daniels.

Reinart passed the crate with the painting and stepped toward what looked like a small hall Daniels hadn't seen. "What's down here?" she asked.

"We need to get out of here," said Rem. "Right now."

"Rem, you're overreacting. This is not an art cult. I was just kidding." Daniels told himself that Rem was letting those movies he watched get to him, but in the back of his mind, he also understood his partner well enough to know that his insight and intuition were usually spot on. It might not always be a hundred percent accurate, but when Rem got a bad feeling about something, Daniels had learned to listen. His nerves jangling, he glanced at Reinart, who was staring down the hall. "C'mon, Reinart. It's time to go. We need to call Lozano."

Reinart gaped at something Daniels couldn't see. "Look at this." She pointed with her free hand.

There was a loud bang from above. Daniels jumped, Rem swiveled abruptly toward the sound, and Reinart sucked in a breath just as the lights went out.

Chapter Twenty-Nine

NOT ABLE TO SEE his hand in front of his face, Rem's heart rate soared. Nothing quite matched the feeling of vulnerability when you were stuck in a lightless, unfamiliar room. He considered himself a fairly courageous man, but in that moment, the fear hit him right in the gut and he had to take a second to collect himself.

"What the hell?" said Daniels.

Reinart cursed.

Remembering the flashlight on his phone, Rem fumbled for it in his pocket. "Use your phone flashlight," he said.

Something squeaked and Rem heard what sounded like a footstep. Telling himself that there wasn't a psychopath stalking him in the dark, he heard another footstep and then a click. Breathless, he pulled his phone out with one hand and his gun with the other. The display illuminated, and he swiped down and found the flashlight button just as Daniels found his. His face lit up with eerie shadows, and Rem jumped at the sight.

"It's just me," said Daniels.

Rem aimed his light toward the ground. "You scared me." He noticed Daniels was holding his gun as well.

"I'm not the one you should be scared of." Daniels moved his light around, but it only illuminated the few feet in front of him. "You see anything?" he whispered.

Rem turned in a circle. "Does it look like I can see anything?" He swung the light. "Reinart? Where are you?" He moved the light to where he thought she was. "Reinart? Now's not the time to go quiet." If she came at him out of nowhere, he'd likely punch her in the face. Aiming the light down the small hall she'd entered, he took a step closer just as the room lit up in bright white light. Blinded, he shut his eyes and cursed, and heard Daniels do the same.

"Rem?" asked Daniels. "You there?"

"Right here." Rem squinted. He shut his flashlight off, blinked and, his vision adjusting, slowly opened his eyes. Recessed lights in the ceiling brightened the entire space and he could see how big the area was, but all thoughts of exploring vanished when he saw Reinart standing down the hall, her back against it but her hands up. James stood in front of her with a gun to her forehead and she didn't move. Her gun was gone, and Rem saw James holding it in his free hand.

"Daniels," said Rem, holding his gun away so as not to appear as a threat to James.

Still squinting, Daniels blinked. "You find Rein—" He stopped when he saw James.

James shifted on his feet and his gaze darted between Reinart and Rem.

"Put your weapons down. Now." James' voice shook and Rem worried he'd fire from fear alone.

"James," said Rem. "Listen—"

"I said put your gun down," yelled James. He eyed Daniels. "You, too."

"Okay." Rem loosened his grip and let the gun swing from his index finger. He bent his knees and lowered himself enough to set the gun on the cement floor.

Daniels did the same. "James," he said. "Let her go."

Reinart stared at the gun, and her chest rose and fell with her breathing. Farther down the hall was an open door to a room none of them had seen in the dark.

"I'll let her go when I'm ready. Kick your guns over here, toward me." His hand holding the gun against Reinart's head trembled.

"No problem," said Rem. "Just take it easy. Nobody needs to get hurt." He kicked his gun down the hall, Daniels kicked his, and they skittered across the floor and stopped near James' feet.

Staring at Reinart, James took a step back but still aimed the gun. "Go stand with them."

Reinart hesitated, but took a small step away from him. Still holding her hands up, she took another step. Looking relieved to have the gun off her forehead, she moved slowly backward until she reached Rem.

"You okay?" asked Rem, staring at James.

Reinart released a shaky breath. "He came up on me in the dark. All I felt was metal on my head and heard the click of the safety disengaging. I froze, and he took my weapon."

Daniels stepped up beside her. "You made the right choice. He might have shot you."

Still holding Reinart's gun, James aimed his weapon at the three of them. "You three do what I say, and maybe you'll get out of this alive." He jabbed the gun in their direction. "Keep your hands up where I can see them."

Rem raised his hands along with Daniels. Reinart still held hers up.

"Where's Evelyn, James?" asked Daniels. "Is she okay?"

James' upper lip shone with sweat. "Be quiet. Let me think."

"Evelyn was here," said Daniels. "She called me."

James smiled. "I know she called. That was my idea."

Rem eyed the room with the open door. "Is she back there? Did you hurt her, James?"

James' smile fell. "She thought I was taking it too far. But Maria gave you the book and I couldn't risk you reading it and learning everything."

Rem frowned. "How do you know Maria gave us the book?"

James didn't answer.

"She said someone was watching her," replied Reinart. "Did that someone see us in the diner this morning?"

"Who is it?" asked Daniels. He paused. "Is he here?"

Rem thought again of the art cult. "Who's in that room, James?" His mind played out a variety of unpleasant scenarios, and he feared they wouldn't leave the basement alive.

James straightened his aim. "Back up. Move into the studio."

Rem didn't move, and neither did Daniels nor Reinart. "Did you kill Evelyn?" asked Rem.

James snorted. "No. I didn't kill her. Just shut her up before she told you everything."

"Did you kill Laroche?" asked Reinart.

James' fingers tightened around the gun handle. "You should shut up too."

"What's in Victoria's book?" asked Daniels. "What didn't you want us to learn?"

"I said to back up." James took a step toward them.

"Is it that Evelyn is running an art forgery scheme?" asked Daniels. "That she's been getting away with for years?"

"Did Laroche find out and tell Victoria?" asked Rem. "Is that why you killed her too?"

"I didn't kill her," James snapped. His upper lip shimmered in the light.

Rem noted how he didn't deny killing Laroche. "Listen, James. You need to think this through. You've got three detectives whose absences are going to be noticed pretty soon. Our captain knows where we are, and he'll send someone to look for us."

"You're just trying to scare me," said James.

"You should be scared," added Daniels. "You can't walk away from this."

The gun shook in James' hand. "I think I can."

"We talked to Maurice," said Reinart. "He told us you visited him at Laroche's on a day that the security went down." She paused. "Is that the day you took the tiger?"

James made an almost imperceptible gasp. "You know?"

"That the tiger is a forgery?" asked Reinart. "Yes, we know."

"It's a hell of a job too," said Daniels. "Whoever painted it is talented. You almost got away with it."

"But why forge and steal the tiger, James?" asked Reinart. "That's risky even for Evelyn, especially if she plans to sell it."

James snickered. "Who says we did it for money? Rowan Laroche stole that painting out from under us, so we did the same to him."

"So why kill him?" asked Rem.

"Because he deserved it. He was telling Victoria things to put in that book. His sole purpose was to ruin Evelyn and me, too. I spent years with him because he promised me more opportunities, but never followed through. And he loved to tell me how Maurice could do way better than me. The man was an asshole, so after I took the tiger, I decided it was time to deal with the bigger problem."

"You put the poison in his drink?" asked Reinart.

"I wasn't sure I'd have the balls to do it, but after he unveiled the forged tiger, he came over and laughed, telling me to enjoy the painting because I'd never see it again. Then he laughed at Evelyn, and I knew something was up. Evelyn went to talk to Victoria, who implied her father had contributed to the book as well, and I knew we were in trouble." He paused. "When the time was right, I dropped the poison in his champagne. I was careful, but when Evelyn saw Emily and Robert together, she saw an opportunity."

"She scared Emily enough to cause her to delete the video footage," said Daniels.

"It wasn't necessary," said James. "I know where the camera is and I waited until other guests blocked the view, but Evelyn wanted a back-up plan, and damn if it didn't work. There's a reason she is where she is...or was."

"How did Laroche know about Evelyn's schemes?" asked Reinart.

"Because of who he is," yelled James. "I know how he works, and he's as big a scam as Evelyn, but no one seems to care. But one word from Rowan that suggests impropriety or misconduct can ruin someone's career. He may not have had proof, but the mere mention of it would bring scrutiny we couldn't afford. Evelyn promised me I would get from her what I couldn't get from Rowan, and I wasn't going to let it all fall apart because of his and Victoria's stupid book."

"You confronted Victoria, didn't you?" asked Daniels. "On the day we stopped by to talk to her?"

James narrowed his gaze. "I was inside when you knocked. I suggested she not answer."

"Is that when you learned what was in her book?" asked Rem. "Did she blackmail you?"

"She was bold enough to ask me for a response to Rowan's claims about Evelyn's involvement in fraud and forgery. I told her it was all a lie and if she printed it, we'd sue her for everything she owned. She laughed at me though and said she didn't care what I did."

"Did you offer her something in return for removing the accusations against you and Evelyn?" asked Reinart.

James hesitated. "She suggested if I could give her something better, she'd consider it."

"And did you give her something better?" asked Rem.

James narrowed his eyes. "I told her I needed time to think about it."

"What was it, James?" asked Reinart. "What did you know that could change Victoria's mind?"

James expelled a shaky breath. "It doesn't matter anymore."

"Why did you cut our brake line?" asked Daniels.

James wiped his upper lip with the sleeve of the hand still holding Reinart's gun. "I didn't cut anything."

Rem kept his eye on the gun James was aiming at them. "If you didn't kill Victoria or cut our brake line, then who did? Who's working with you?"

"I'm not telling you anything. Now back up into the studio." He waved the gun.

Praying he wouldn't accidentally fire, Rem took a step back. "Take it easy."

Daniels and Reinart took a step back, too.

Rem kept talking to keep James distracted. "Carlo and Isabella have been arrested. We found poison in their house and there are some ugly things written about her and Carlo in the book, too. Are you all working together?"

"We also found Isabella's brother's name written on a calendar in her and Carlo's office," said Daniels. "We know her brother's history. Are you working with Isabella, and she pointed you in her brother's direction? Is he involved? Did he get you the poison?"

James' face fell and his gaze flicked toward the open door down the hall. "No." He sneered and raised his voice. "Now shut up and keep moving."

A man with tousled blond hair, broad shoulders, a narrow face, and thick eyebrows walked out of the back room. "You son-of-a bitch," he yelled at James. "What the hell are they talking about?" He stopped beside James. "How did they find my name at Isabella's? And why was

poison found in her house?" He glared at James and then directed his glare at Rem, Reinart, and Daniels. "What are they talking
about?"

"They're lying, you idiot," yelled James. "They're trying to pin
everything on you, and you're falling for it."

Rem guessed the newcomer was Burton Rimaldi. "We're not lying
about anything," said Rem. "Everything we said is true. Isabella is
currently under arrest for assaulting her husband and, because of
the poison, a murder charge isn't far behind."

The man gaped at them and pointed at James. "He's the one who
murdered Laroche."

"If Isabella helped him, that would make her an accessory, which
isn't much better," said Reinart.

The man's expression darkened, and he whirled on James. "You
set her up, didn't you, you bastard?"

James stepped back and raised Reinart's weapon at the man. "I
did what I had to do. She's just as vicious as Rowan was, and she's
married to a damn mobster. She'll be fine. And if they don't locate
you, they have nothing to connect her to Laroche, so stop worrying."

"What about the poison, you idiot?" The man took a step toward
James. "I'll kill you."

"Would you rather have them blame you, instead of her?" yelled
James. "You're the one who cut their brake lines," he nodded toward
Rem, Reinart, and Daniels, "and Victoria's."

"Because you told me to. You told me I was protecting Izzie."

"Victoria wasn't supposed to die."

"You said to do the same to her as I did to them." He waved a
hand. "You said scare them. I can't help it if she's a lousy driver.
But you never said anything about blaming this on Izzie." His scowl
intensified. "Did you actually direct the police to me and put poison
in Izzie's house?"

"He circled dates too," said Daniels. "Of Laroche's and Victoria's murders and the date of our accident. He's framing your sister, and you, to take the fall for all of it."

"You're Burton Rimaldi, aren't you?" asked Reinart.

"My sister is a lot of things," said Burton, "but she's not a murderer, and you know it," he yelled at James.

"Back off," said James, whose forehead was shimmering along with his upper lip. "I did what I had to do."

"Or what?" asked Burton. "You going to do to me what you did to Evelyn?" Despite the gun pointed at him, he entered the back room and pulled out an office chair with Evelyn Sinclair sitting on it. Her wrists were zip tied to the armrests and her mouth was duct taped. Her dark hair was ruffled, mascara ran down her cheeks and she was breathing hard through her nose. The chair rolled into the hall and stopped near Reinart.

"Sorry, James," said Burton, "but I'm not dealt with so easily." He held out his hands. "If you're going to shoot me, then do it. Have the balls to take responsibility for something."

"Whoa, hold up," said Daniels. "Nobody needs to shoot anyone."

Burton yelled at Daniels. "I'm not letting my sister take the fall for something she didn't do." Burton faced James. "What happened to us selling the tiger and disappearing on some Caribbean island?"

James took a deep breath. "That can still happen."

"What world are you living in?" asked Burton. "What are you going to do? Kill them? You can't kill cops."

"At least someone is thinking logically," said Rem.

Burton glared in his direction. "Don't make the mistake of thinking I'm on your side. I don't want to go to jail any more than he does. I'm just not partial to capital murder charges." He eyed James. "We can tie them up, like Evelyn, and then figure out what to do. And stop aiming that gun at me."

James hesitated, but took Reinart's gun off Burton and aimed it at Rem, Daniels, and Reinart.

Staring down the barrels of two weapons, Rem hoped Burton wasn't playing with them. "What exactly is your plan? Leave us behind and flee the country? And while you're at it, clear Isabella's name and sell the tiger?"

"We can sell the tiger after we're safe," said James.

"Not after today," said Reinart. "Once the FBI hears about the forged tiger, nobody will touch it. Not even on the black market. You'll have to wait months for the heat to die down."

"You're lying," said James.

"Her mother heads the FBI's art crime division," said Rem. "She's not lying."

"Son-of-a-bitch," yelled Burton. "You've totally screwed us."

"All of you shut up," yelled James. "We are not screwed. We can figure this out."

"Where's the tiger now?" asked Reinart. "If you turn yourselves in and hand over the real tiger, they might go easier on you."

Burton scoffed. "Who are you kidding, lady? I know how this works. You say one thing and do another. I don't trust cops."

"You can trust us," said Daniels. "We'll put in a good word for you. The DA will listen."

"The hell he will," said James. He eyed Burton. "We can still go. We'll just wait on the tiger for now and sell it later."

"And live on what?" asked Burton. "Your meager savings and my nonexistent wealth?"

"Your sister will help us."

"After you tried to pin a murder on her?"

Reinart took a tentative step forward. "Did you paint the forged tiger, Burton? If you turn yourself in, along with the legitimate tiger, that will show that you're willing to cooperate."

"You have some leverage," added Daniels. "You offer that, along with your cooperation, and you can testify against Evelyn and even Victoria and Rowan's schemes."

Burton crossed his arms. "I appreciate your positive attitude, detective, but I killed Victoria, and almost killed you three, and he killed Laroche. We could tell you when the next killer asteroid is going to hit this planet, and it wouldn't mean shit. We turn ourselves in, and we're going away for a long time." He looked back at James. "I say we tie them up, leave them with Evelyn, and get the hell out of here. We'll take our chances with the tiger." He pointed at Rem. "But you promise me my sister doesn't take the fall for this, or I'll come back and finish the job."

Rem kept his hands up and visible. "Tempting as it is to keep your sister behind bars, you have my word she will not go to jail for a crime she didn't commit."

"Mine too," said Daniels.

"Mine too," added Reinart.

Burton studied them as if to gauge whether they were telling the truth. "Get back into the studio. Stand against the wall." He spoke to James. "I'll get more zip ties."

"Move," said James. "Do what he said."

Rem debated whether to tell James that an APB had already been issued for him, but didn't want him to change his mind about killing them. He took a step back, along with Daniels and Reinart. If getting tied up by these two meant they'd get out of this alive, he was okay with that.

As they took slow steps back into the studio, James encroached with both guns still aimed. When he neared Evelyn, he put a foot on her chair and shoved her. Her chair rolled, and she sucked in a breath through her nose. Her chair narrowly missed the easel holding the partially completed *Portrait of Helene*.

Burton emerged from the back room, holding several zip ties. "Turn around," he said.

"There's something else you should consider before you do this," said Reinart.

"Yeah?" asked Burton. "What's that?" He pulled out a zip tie and set the others on a table.

"The curse," said Reinart. "That painting means certain death for whoever owns it, and right now, that's you two."

Burton lowered the zip tie and glanced back at James. "Is she serious?"

"Deadly serious," said Rem. "All of its previous owners are dead."

"Except that I killed one of them. Not the painting," said James. He eyed Burton. "Don't listen to them. It's a stupid story that papers love to tell."

Burton hesitated. "What happened to the other owners?"

James rolled his eyes. "We don't have time for this. We have to get out of here."

"You better not be bullshitting me." Burton turned back toward Reinart. "You first. Turn around."

Eyeing the gun, Reinart began to turn when audible footsteps sounded on the stairs, and a man's voice echoed from above. "Maybe you should listen to Detective Reinart. She knows what she's talking about."

The man reached the bottom of the stairs and came into view, and Rem gaped when he saw Hendrix.

Chapter Thirty

PHOEBE FAILED TO HIDE her shock when Hendrix stepped off the stairs and entered the room.

The color in James' face visibly drained. "What are you doing here?"

Hendrix slid his hands into the pockets of his pressed navy pants. He wore a brown turtleneck with a dark brown leather jacket and his perfectly cut, thick hair was smooth and shiny. Phoebe thought he looked like he'd just stepped off a private plane on his way to a fancy dinner in the city.

"I thought I'd check in on Evelyn." He walked toward her. "And it's a good thing I did. What are you up to, James?"

James stammered. "I, uh, I'm taking care of problems."

Hendrix glanced toward Rem and Daniels and walked closer to Phoebe. "What an interesting way to do it." He spoke to Phoebe. "Hello, Detective. Nice to see you again. I wish it was over caviar and champagne, but as usual, James screwed it up."

Phoebe itched to tell this guy what she thought of this situation, but decided it wouldn't help things. "Probably better we keep this professional."

Hendrix nodded. "Perhaps."

"Maria gave them Victoria's book," said James. "What was I supposed to do? Let them read it? And risk having them show up with an arrest warrant for all of us?"

Hendrix stepped away from Phoebe and spoke to Burton. "You must be Burton Rimaldi, James' buddy. The one he's been keeping so secret." He tipped his head. "You realize your friend betrayed you and your sister?"

Burton straightened. "Who the hell are you? The ex-boyfriend James keeps talking about?"

Hendrix raised his lip in amusement. "Hardly."

"He's the artist," said James in a rushed breath. "He painted the tiger. His name's Hendrix."

Phoebe stiffened. "You painted the forgery?" Rem and Daniels appeared equally surprised. "Why?" she asked.

Hendrix tensed, and his face furrowed. He offered James an expression that Reinart was happy wasn't directed at her. "Why Evelyn trusted her secrets to a such a pathetic excuse of a man, I will never understand." He turned toward Phoebe. "You want to know why? Money. That's why. It's a lucrative side gig, and what Evelyn does with the forgeries is not my concern."

"Why the hell do you need money?" asked Rem. "You're stinking rich."

"Don't believe everything you read, Detective." Hendrix took his hands from his pockets. "Life happens."

"Gambling debts," said James. "Hendrix sucks at poker. Rowan gave him a loan, but Hendrix defaulted on it. Nobody knows this, but Rowan was going to dump his ass, and Hendrix knew it. That's when he started working for Evelyn, but it still wasn't enough." He chuckled. "He stopped playing poker and ended up betting on the ponies instead and now he's in even deeper. That's the dirt I considered giving Victoria in exchange for me and Evelyn." He sneered at Hendrix. "And you call me a pathetic human? You should kiss my ass for taking care of this mess. If it were up to you, we'd all be in jail by the end of the day."

Hendrix looked like he'd gladly strangle James with his bare hands. "At the rate you're going, we'll all be in jail by this afternoon."

"Then get the hell out of our way and let us finish," said Burton.

"What are you going to do?" asked Hendrix. "Tie them up, take the tiger and leave town? Good luck. Maurice called me when he couldn't get a hold of you, James, and mentioned his conversation with the detectives." He glanced at Reinart, and a shiver ran up her spine. "My guess? There's already an APB out for you. You won't make it through an airport, train, bus station or border crossing without being tackled within three minutes, and that includes you too, friend." He eyed Burton. "And they'll confiscate that tiger along with the two of you." He scowled at James. "And based on how you run your mouth, you'll sing like a canary, which means you'll tell them about me." He paused. "And I am not going down with this dump of a ship."

James clenched his jaw at Phoebe. "Is that true? Are the cops looking for me?"

"Listen," said Daniels. "APB or not, after this, you will always have to look over your shoulder. And with that tiger, you'll never feel safe. Just turn yourself in. Don't make this harder than it needs to be."

"It's plenty hard already," said Burton. "I don't know how this could get much worse."

Hendrix slid his hands into his jacket pockets. "I do." He pulled out a small caliber gun and fired it at Burton.

Phoebe shrieked, and Evelyn jumped. James yelled, "No," and Burton fell to his knees with a bullet in his stomach. Blood stained his shirt, and he gripped his wound with his hands. "Shit," he whispered, before he fell sideways onto one of the crates.

"Son-of-a..." Daniels took a step forward, but Phoebe grabbed his elbow. Rem cursed but didn't move.

"What the hell have you done?" screamed James, aiming one of his weapons at Hendrix.

Hendrix aimed his gun at James. "Exactly what needed to be done, but you're not capable of doing." He took side steps and got behind James so he could aim his weapon at Daniels, Rem, and Reinart, too. "Now put your guns down and let's talk."

Burton groaned and clutched at his bloody stomach. Beads of sweat popped up on his skin.

"He needs a hospital," said Rem.

"Thank you for stating the obvious, Detective." Hendrix spoke calmly to James. "There's still a way out of this."

"You shot him," said James, breathless. He kept one gun aimed toward Rem, Reinart and Daniels, and the other remained on Hendrix.

Hendrix nodded. "I did. Where is the tiger, James?"

Phoebe's mind raced to figure out what Hendrix planned. "Don't listen to him, James. The only way out is for him to shoot you, too."

"And then shoot us," said Daniels. "We're witnesses."

James shook his head. "He can't get away with that."

"He can if he blames you for our deaths," said Rem. "After he shoots us, he'll put the gun in your hand and make your death look like a suicide. He'll have to kill Evelyn too."

Evelyn moaned, and fresh tears ran down her cheeks.

"But you can stop him," said Daniels. "You have to fight back."

Hendrix snickered. "Do you honestly think I'm going to kill three detectives? And you and Evelyn, too?" He bobbed his gun. "With this little measly weapon?"

James kept his gaze on Hendrix. Phoebe debated tackling him, but with Hendrix pointing his weapon in their direction, the risk was too great.

"Is that true?" asked James. "Are you going to kill me?"

Hendrix's eyes glinted in the light. "Where is the tiger?"

"What do you care?" asked James. "You can't sell it. Not after this. The cops know Laroche's is a forgery."

Burton groaned as his blood dripped onto the floor.

Hendrix's face fell. "That's unfortunate." He paused. "But I can make lemonade out of lemons. I'll simply return the real one."

"So you can look like the hero," said Phoebe, her heart pounding against her ribs.

"That would be nice, Phoebe, but my primary concern is that it's returned to the trust for sweet Mateo." Hendrix spoke to James. "Is it here? In the studio?"

James didn't answer.

"Knowing you, it's in the most obvious place." He paused and chuckled. "Is it upstairs in the office?"

James gritted his teeth.

Hendrix smiled. "That's all I needed to know."

"Since when do you care about Mateo?" asked Phoebe.

Hendrix shrugged. "Brian Klein contacted me. Imagine my surprise when he asked if I could manage Mateo's trust in the event of his death? Since Rowan and I were friends, he feels I'd be the next best choice that Rowan would approve of." He smiled. "Isn't that nice?"

Phoebe wondered if Klein had conferred with Dryer regarding the transfer of his trustee duties if he died. She questioned if it was as simple as naming Hendrix in his will, but doubted Hendrix knew that.

"It may not be that simple," said Phoebe. "Maybe before you assume anything, you should double check if Klein can do that."

Hendrix smirked at her. "What would you like me to do? Call him and confirm? And then let you all go? Nice try, Phoebe, but I'll take my chances."

Rem sucked in a breath. "You're going to kill Klein."

Hendrix flicked his gun toward Rem. "Not anytime soon. I'll wait for the appropriate time to pass."

"And then you can use the tiger to pad your pockets," said Daniels. "But that depends on if you can get away with all of this, which is doubtful."

"That means killing you, James," said Rem. "And Isabella will take the fall for Laroche, and maybe even Victoria."

James spoke with force. "It won't work, Hendrix. Isabella and Carlo will fight you every step of the way if you become the trustee. They hate you. And even if they can't stop it, they'll watch your every move with that tiger."

"Let them try. Isabella will be in prison, and Carlo will keep his mouth shut and let me do whatever I want."

"Carlo is in the mob. He can make your life miserable if he doesn't kill you first. Mateo's well-being and future come first with him," said James.

"Which is exactly why he'll do everything I say, unless he wants the truth exposed."

"What truth?" asked Phoebe.

Hendrix grinned like a man who was about to reveal a big secret. "Isabella didn't always hate me. There was a time when we both commiserated over Rowan's treatment of us and found passionate satisfaction together." His grin grew. "Mateo is my son, not Rowan's."

Phoebe couldn't believe what she was hearing.

"You're lying," said James.

Hendrix raised a brow. "Am I? You don't think when Isabella threw Mateo in my face in order to extort money out of me when she couldn't get it out of Rowan that I didn't demand a paternity test?" He shook his head. "Poor Rowan. He never considered for a second that Isabella betrayed him." He straightened his aim at James. "And if I don't become trustee, I'll use my clout as Rowan's friend and Mateo's father to use that tiger to my advantage. I forged it once, and I can do it again. Klein wouldn't know one tiger from another."

"You're going to take your son's inheritance away from him?" asked Reinart.

"Technically, it's not his inheritance," said Hendrix, lifting the side of his lip.

"Unbelievable," said Rem. "You think you've got this all tied up with a neat little bow, don't you?"

"You're not getting away with anything," said James.

"Aren't I?" asked Hendrix. "The only way to stop me is for you to shoot me." He straightened his aim. "Before I shoot you."

"James...," said Daniels. "If he fires first—" Daniels didn't finish his sentence and the room went quiet.

"We're in trouble," whispered Rem. "If we're going to do something, it needs to be now."

Prepared to counterattack despite the odds against them, Phoebe braced for the inevitable gunshot, praying it wouldn't hit one of them, when a wail shattered the quiet. Phoebe gasped in shock when Burton pushed up from the crate and, his hands and shirt bloody, launched himself at Hendrix.

Chapter Thirty-One

HENDRIX FIRED JUST AS Burton hit him and knocked him back into a crate. The shot went wide, and Daniels heard it whiz between him and Reinart. James bellowed, fired, and ran at Hendrix, but his foot caught on Burton, who'd stumbled to his knees. James' shot missed Hendrix, and Rem, Daniels and Reinart ran at the trio.

James fired again and Hendrix cried out when the bullet hit his shoulder, but he aimed his gun and fired back. Rem jumped out of the way but grabbed Hendrix's arm to prevent him from firing again and knocked him off the crate and to the floor. Daniels jumped on top of James, who fell to his knees and dropped Reinart's gun. Reinart rushed to pull Burton out of the melee.

James found leverage against a crate and pushed up, knocking Daniels backward. While Rem struggled with Hendrix, James swiveled and aimed his other weapon at Daniels, and Daniels leaped away as James fired. After getting to his feet, James fired at Reinart, who ducked behind a crate.

Rem had Hendrix on his back and had a hold of his wrist, but Hendrix still gripped the gun and fired again.

James ran toward the stairs, still shooting to keep Reinart and Daniels away from him. He reached them and ran up.

Reinart ran out from behind the crate and grabbed her gun. "Help Rem. I'll go after James." She darted toward the stairs.

Rem grunted as Hendrix connected his knee into Rem's ribs, but Rem held onto the gun. Daniels jumped up and ran over just as another shot discharged into the air. Daniels grabbed Hendrix's other arm with the wounded shoulder. Hendrix cried out and although he still struggled against Rem, some of the fight left him. Now having more leverage, Rem hooked a leg over Hendrix's midsection and yanked the gun from Hendrix's grip.

Unarmed and injured, Hendrix went limp. Rem moved back, and Daniels pulled Hendrix to his side and stomach. Hendrix moaned in pain and blood dripped onto the ground from his shoulder. Rem got one of Hendrix's arms around and Daniels the other and they cuffed him with Daniels' handcuffs.

Breathing hard, Rem jumped up and ran over to retrieve their guns while Daniels checked on Burton. He was bleeding profusely and holding his belly. Evelyn was crying and had pushed her chair out of the way to avoid being injured. Daniels ran over to her and pulled the tape off her mouth. "I need something to staunch his bleeding. Where can I find it?"

She coughed and spoke dryly, but answered quickly. "There are cloths in the drawer beneath the supplies. Bottom right."

Daniels ran over, found what he needed, and ran back over to Burton. He packed the wound as best he could. Rem squatted beside him. "How is he?"

"Losing a lot of blood."

Rem glanced back at Hendrix, who was handcuffed and lying on his stomach. "Where's Reinart?"

"She went after James."

Pulling out his cuffs, Rem ran over to Hendrix. He pulled him to his feet and brought him over to the stairwell where he sat him down. He secured one end of his cuffs to the link between the cuffs around Hendrix's wrists and the other to a rail on the stairwell.

A gunshot rang out from above them. Daniels and Rem looked up and Rem pulled out his phone. "Hendrix isn't going anywhere."

"Neither is Evelyn." Daniels leaned close to Burton. He grabbed Burton's hand and put it over the cloths covering his wound. "Keep pressure on it and stay still. We'll get you some help." He stood and Rem handed him his gun.

"Let's go," said Rem, and they ran up the stairs as another shot rang out.

·· • • • • • • • ··

Phoebe ran out the door and into the gallery. Not seeing James, but knowing he had a gun, she ducked behind a statue of an angel holding a bow and arrow. The gallery was quiet, and she wondered where James had gone. She felt certain she would have spotted him run out of the gallery if he'd made it to the front door.

Stepping out from her cover, she saw James dart out of the manager's office with a long art tube with an attached strap draped over his shoulder. Realizing he likely had the tiger, she raced toward him when he turned and fired at her. She ducked back down, and the bullet struck the pedestal of the statue behind her. Peering out, she saw James running for the front door. "James. Stop." Hoping to prevent him from escaping, she ran out from cover again.

Before he left, he fired once more, and she dropped low behind a glass cabinet of small figurines. The glass shattered and rained down on her. She shut her eyes to protect them and when she opened them again, she saw Rem and Daniels running toward her. They stayed low and squatted next to her in the glass.

"Where is he?" asked Rem.

"Front door," she said, shaking glass off her sleeve. "He's got the tiger."

"I called it in," said Rem. "Help is coming."

Daniels peered out. "Let's go."

He ran out and Phoebe followed, with Rem behind her. They got to the front door and ducked back in case James was ready to fire again if they exited the gallery.

"Where is he?" asked Rem.

"We can't let him escape," said Phoebe.

Daniels pulled the door open and peeked out. "There. Across the parking lot." He raced out, and Phoebe followed. She saw James sprinting away with the tube bouncing against his back and the gun still in his hand.

"James. Don't," she yelled. Daniels and Phoebe broke into a run, with Rem right beside them.

James glanced behind him just as he reached the busy street. A low rumble alerted Phoebe to an approaching delivery truck heading toward the design district. In a split second, she watched in horror as James raced into the street just as the truck shot past the gallery. James saw it too late, and the truck hit him head on. James' body went airborne; his gun went one way, and the tube went another.

"James!" screamed Reinart. The truck's brakes engaged, its tires squealed, and the truck went into a skid, its backside swinging back and forth. The driver got it under control and it came to a screaming stop in the middle of the road.

Daniels raced up to it, and the driver jumped out of the van. "I didn't see him." He held his chest. "He came out of nowhere."

Reinart ran into the grass where James had landed.

"Police." Daniels flashed his badge. "Stay with your vehicle." He ran into the grass to join Rem and Reinart. "How bad is it?"

Reinart stared in shock at James' body. His head and face were bloody, his neck and leg were lying at wrong angles, and his eyes were open in a lifeless stare.

"Not good," said Rem, still catching his breath. He squatted and put his fingers on James' neck. "Looks like the tiger claimed its next victim." He looked up at Reinart and stood. "He's dead."

Disgusted by the outcome, Reinart felt sick to her stomach. "All of this, over a stupid painting."

Daniels jogged over to a brown patch of grass, picked up the art tube and brought it over. He opened it and pulled the canvas out far enough to identify the painting. "It's the tiger." He slid it back in. "I'm halfway tempted to throw it in the trash." He handed the tube to Phoebe as sirens wailed in the distance. "I'm going to talk to the driver."

Rem glanced back. "I'll go check on Burton and the other two."

Phoebe nodded. Spotting James' gun nearby, she walked over and picked it up.

"You okay?" asked Rem.

Deflated despite finding their perpetrators, Phoebe sighed. "Yeah. You go. I'll meet the cavalry and send the EMTs when they arrive."

Rem returned his gun to its holster. "It doesn't always go the way we want, does it?"

"No, it doesn't."

After a pause, Rem jogged off, and with one last look at James, Phoebe swung the tube over her shoulder and headed toward the parking lot.

Chapter Thirty-Two

REM LICKED HIS FINGERS after picking another rib clean. "You've out-done yourself, Daniels. How come you don't grill ribs more often?" He picked up his beer and had a drink.

Daniels set a rib bone down. "It's for special guests only and your specialness ran out a long time ago."

Reinart smiled. "I'm flattered to be considered special." She wiped her greasy fingers on a napkin. "And Rem's right. The ribs are delicious, and so is your potato salad, Marjorie."

Marjorie took a sip of wine. "Thank you, Phoebe. It's my mom's recipe." She raised her glass. "And thank you for the wine. It's very good."

Phoebe picked up her glass. "It's even better that we get to share the bottle since these two are drinking beer."

Marjorie smiled and had another sip. "My sentiments exactly." She set her glass down. "I'm so glad you could come over. Gordon has told me so much about you, I worried Rem might be replaced."

Rem paused in mid chew. "He'd never make it without me, Marge."

"Says who?" asked Daniels. "I think Reinart and I would make a great team." He bit into another rib.

Rem narrowed one eye. "As far as that goes, she and I would do pretty well, too."

Marjorie laughed. "I never thought I'd see the day when these two would fight over another potential partner. You must be pretty exceptional, Phoebe."

Phoebe shook her head. "They're just being nice. Believe me, I have my flaws."

"Don't we all?" asked Daniels. He eyed Marjorie. "Just ask my wife. She could tell you a few things about me." He chuckled at Rem. "And don't even get me started on him."

Amused, Rem wiped his mouth with his napkin. "I don't know what you're talking about. I'm about as flaw-free as you can find."

"Is that so?" asked Daniels.

Rem pointed a greasy finger. "I had the whole Laroche thing figured out at the end."

"Too bad it couldn't have been at the beginning," said Daniels. "That would have helped." He frowned. "And aren't you the one who suspected it was an art cult? When we were in the basement?"

"That's right," said Reinart. "You thought everyone was in on it." She smiled. "You were worried they were all in that room, weren't you?"

"Hey, the art cult thing was his idea." Rem tipped his head at Daniels.

"I didn't expect you to take it seriously."

Filling up fast and with a stack of rib bones on his plate, Rem sat back. "Yeah, well, I wasn't that far off."

"How do you figure that?" asked Daniels. "It was Hendrix, James, and Burton. You had Maria as a ringleader and Maurice involved, too."

"Don't forget Evelyn," said Rem. "And Isabella and Carlo were already suspects, so it wasn't that crazy of an idea."

Daniels smirked. "You see what I deal with every day?" he asked Phoebe.

Phoebe swallowed and stabbed some of her green salad with her fork. "I do. And you two are pretty lucky, comparatively speaking."

Making eye contact with Daniels, Rem knew that despite their poking fun at each other, Reinart was right. "Any word from Barry?"

Chewing, Reinart shook her head and swallowed. "No. I haven't spoken to him since our encounter at the station." She paused. "It's hard though. Despite what I know about him, I still catch myself missing him."

"It's funny how the heart can want what we know isn't good for us," said Marjorie. "But it gets easier with time."

"That whole time thing is tough," added Reinart.

"Tell me about it," said Rem, thinking back. "But Marge is right."

Reinart nodded. "I talked to my captain and when Barry returns to work, he's being reassigned to another division."

"Is that a good thing?" asked Marjorie. She took a bite of potato salad.

"It is," said Reinart. "But even if he hadn't been, it wouldn't matter." She set her fork down. "I've applied to the FBI. I have an interview next week."

Surprised, Rem sat up. "That's great news, Reinart."

"So you decided what you wanted?" asked Daniels.

"I did," said Reinart.

"What about your mom?" asked Daniels. "Any concerns there?"

Reinart shrugged. "I haven't told her. I want to do this on my own merits and not be given special treatment because of her."

"She's going to find out," said Rem.

"I know she will, and when she does, we'll talk." She picked up her wineglass. "I'll be honest in my interview about my plans and my history, and I'll let them decide, hopefully without my mom's involvement."

"What made you choose to do it now?" asked Daniels.

She sipped some wine. "After this case, and everything we did, and working with you two, I realized how I was letting what happened to me stop me from so much. I finally talked to my captain, and he told me he'd never doubted me, and I realized that all those limitations and doubts were self-imposed. For the first time in a while, I feel like myself. That's when I knew the FBI was the next step for me." She paused. "And I think I'm ready."

Rem smiled. "Good for you, Reinart. I expect you'll be an agent soon. They'd be lucky to have you."

"Thank you. I appreciate that."

"What about the Laroche case?" asked Marjorie. "Do you have any loose ends to tie up, or are you free to leave, Phoebe?"

Phoebe glanced at Rem and Daniels. "We've wrapped most of it up, but I'll be around if these two need anything from me."

Daniels licked a finger. "Isabella and Carlo still have their domestic issues to deal with, but as far as Laroche and Victoria are concerned, they're cleared of those charges."

Marjorie sucked in a breath. "I forgot to ask. Did you ever read Victoria's updated book?"

His stomach full, Rem blew out a satisfied breath. "Sure did, and it's no wonder she had everyone upset. She outed Evelyn as the ringleader of an art forgery scheme, and James as her right-hand man. Isabella was labeled as a money grabbing cheater who used her pregnancy and marriage to manipulate Laroche, and Carlo as a mobster and abusive husband. Victoria had plenty against Laroche, but mainly the stuff about Maria Rossi and his shortcomings as a father, so he got off pretty clean."

"Victoria took it easy on him and removed the Toby LaRue stuff," added Daniels. "I guess becoming Laroche's beneficiary swayed her."

"What about Hendrix?" asked Marjorie.

Daniels ate a bite of potato salad. "He was in the book, too. Laroche told Victoria plenty. Hendrix's drinking and gambling were mentioned and his debts, but nothing about his involvement with Evelyn." He pushed his plate back. "And nothing about him fathering Mateo."

"So Robert is Laroche's only living heir?" asked Marjorie.

"Sure is," said Rem. "He and Emily should live a happy life together. Maurice is moving forward with opening his own restaurant and Maria is giving up her swanky apartment and moving away. I think the guilt is still eating at her and she's ready to move on."

"And once Burton is out of the hospital, he'll face his own music," added Daniels. "For what happened to Victoria and almost happened to us."

"And Hendrix will be right behind him," said Rem. "But Evelyn's smart. She agreed to cooperate and testify against Hendrix and Burton, and James' schemes. She might get out in twenty years if she's lucky."

"What's the story with James and Burton?" asked Marjorie. "Were they a couple?"

Daniels ate the last bite of meat off another rib. "According to Isabella, they met when James still worked for Laroche and Laroche and Isabella were still together. Burton stopped by to see his sister, and I assume he and James hit it off. They must have stayed in touch or reconnected after James and Maurice broke up."

"Burton was trying his hand at the *Portrait of Helene*," said Reinart. "I guess Evelyn was on the lookout for new talent."

"Incredible." Marjorie shook her head. "I still don't understand how she got away with selling all that forged art."

"She sold it on the black market," said Reinart. "Several years ago, she had a break-in at her warehouse and lost several works of art. Insurance covered her losses and despite the FBI's search, they never recovered the pieces." She glanced at Daniels and Rem. "The *Portrait of Helene* was one of them."

"But Gordon said she had the original," said Marjorie.

"She did." Reinart picked up the wine bottle and added more wine to her glass and Marjorie's. "That's because the robbery was a scam.

She robbed her own warehouse. The public thought it was stolen, she forged it and sold it to secret buyers and kept the originals."

Marjorie dropped her jaw. "My old art professor did that?"

"She sure did." Daniels tossed his napkin on the table. "It was a pretty lucrative business."

"Until she forged the tiger and stole it with James' help," said Rem. "That was her mistake. She got greedy and the tiger's curse was her undoing."

"She took the tiger just to get back at Laroche?" asked Marjorie.

"That was the original plan," said Daniels, "but Victoria's book caused more problems, and James took matters into his own hands. Before Evelyn knew it, she was in too deep." Daniels set his napkin on his plate. "When she called me that day, she was ready to tell us everything, but James intervened. If Hendrix hadn't interrupted, James and Burton would have left us in that basement and taken the tiger."

"Did they really think that would work?" asked Marjorie.

"Nobody said they had brains," added Rem. He drank some beer. "That's one thing Evelyn screwed up on. Picking her partners."

"James did an impressive job stealing the tiger," said Daniels. "He used Maurice as a pretense to visit, managed to disable the security system so he wouldn't be on camera when he switched out the paintings, and left with the tiger tucked under his arm. That's pretty slick. Plus, Evelyn picked Hendrix," said Daniels. "That was pretty smart."

"The guy who sells all those landscapes actually painted the forged tiger?" asked Marjorie. She regarded Daniels. "Don't tell my mom, honey. She'll be so disappointed."

"According to Evelyn," said Reinart, "the minute she learned Laroche had purchased the tiger, she asked Hendrix to paint it. That's why he was in Europe. He never used her studio, but didn't need to. He has studios of his own. Once he finished it, he mailed it to her."

"He must work fast," said Marjorie.

Reinart finished her last rib and set it on her plate. "It took almost a month for the auction house to deliver the painting after Laroche bought it. Between that time and when James stole it, it was over two months. For a man with Hendrix's talents, that's enough time."

Marjorie set her napkin down and shook her head in disbelief. "And how did Isabella wind up with poison in her house?"

Daniels pushed his plate back. "James stopped by to see her the day before her blow up with Carlo on the pretense that he'd heard about the will and wanted to see how she was doing. Isabella said they'd forged a tentative friendship while she was with Laroche, so didn't think it was too strange. Carlo wasn't home, and she had to put Mateo down for a nap. It was more than enough time for him to plant the poison and mark the calendar."

"This whole thing is baffling," said Marjorie. "And all of it over a tiger?"

"And greed," said Rem.

"And revenge," said Reinart.

"You really think that tiger is cursed?" asked Marjorie. She stood and picked up her plate.

"It certainly didn't do anyone who owned it any favors," said Rem. "Let's just hope when Mateo gets it, he has better luck. For now, though, according to Klein, it's going into storage for the foreseeable future." He wiped his fingers again, stood and took Marjorie's plate. "You sit. Daniels and I will clean up."

Daniels stood too. "You two ladies enjoy your wine."

"Thanks, guys," said Marjorie, returning to her seat. "So no one knows Hendrix is Mateo's father?"

"Isabella and Hendrix know," said Daniels, picking up Reinart's plate. "And whether she tells Mateo or Carlo is up to her, unless it comes out at trial." He headed into the kitchen with Rem.

"I made brownies, Rem," said Marjorie.

Rem spoke from the kitchen. "You're lucky Daniels married you, Marge, or I'd have stolen you from him."

Daniels scoffed. "Marjorie's standards are way too high. You'd have never made the cut, partner."

Rem added his plates to the sink as Daniels turned on the faucet. "How'd you manage it then?"

"Bribery," said Marjorie. "And those eyes of his."

Daniels blinked with emphasis at Rem. "When you've got it, flaunt it."

Rem snorted.

While Rem and Daniels cleaned up, Marjorie and Reinart talked. Just before dessert was served, Marjorie started a pot of coffee and Reinart excused herself to get something from the car.

As the coffee percolated, Marjorie patted Daniels on the arm. "I'm going to check on J.P. Be back in a sec."

Daniels squeezed her fingers. "Hopefully, he's sleeping peacefully. The stuff for his teeth is in his room if he needs it."

Marjorie headed up the stairs. "Okay."

The front door opened and Reinart returned holding two wrapped gifts.

Rem widened his eyes. "What are those?"

Reinart returned to the table and sat. "I wanted to give you guys something to say thank you."

Daniels sat beside her, and Rem pulled out his chair and sat across from Reinart. "You didn't have to do that," said Daniels.

Reinart handed Rem his gift. "It's not much. Just a gesture of appreciation."

Excited, Rem ripped open his gift. He chuckled when he saw the velvet painting of Elvis. "I love it, but are you sure you want to give this away?"

"I completely understand why," said Daniels.

Reinart smiled. "I think it's better in your hands. If things work out with me the way I hope, I could end up moving and this guy," she gestured at Elvis, "could end up in a box."

"Perish the thought," said Daniels.

Rem smirked at his partner. "You're just jealous." He raised the painting. "I'm putting him in the guest room, so whenever you stay over, you'll see him."

Daniels rolled his eyes. "Lucky me."

Reinart handed Daniels his gift. Daniels took it and opened it. It was another picture, and Daniels went still when he saw it. "Reinart, this is beautiful."

Rem leaned in. "What is it?"

"I know you said you like landscapes," said Reinart, "but this is pretty close."

Daniels turned the portrait toward Rem. It was a charcoal sketch of a man and a child fly-fishing in a river. Their backs were to the viewer, and they were amid a serene setting of trees and water.

"You're right. It's beautiful," said Rem. "Who's the artist?"

"Me," said Reinart. "I dabble, but just for fun."

Daniels widened his eyes. "You drew this?" He turned the picture back around.

"You're a woman of many talents, Reinart," said Rem.

"I love it," said Daniels. His eyes watered. "It reminds me of my grandfather."

Reinart's eyes rounded. "Oh, no. I didn't mean to upset you."

"It's okay," said Rem. "You just caught him at a difficult time. He found out last week that his grandfather died."

Reinart sucked in a breath. "I'm sorry. I didn't know."

"Don't worry about it," said Daniels. "This just hits home because when I was a kid, I'd go see him in the summers and we'd fish in the river that borders his property. We were estranged for years, and this brought up some old memories." He held up the picture. "This is very special. Thank you."

Reinart smiled. "I'm glad you like it. And my condolences. Losing a grandparent is hard."

Daniels shrugged and set the sketch on the table. "It is, but I hadn't seen him in a while. I regret that, but there's not much to be done about it now."

"He left you his house," said Rem. "Maybe that was his way of making it up to you."

"Maybe," Daniels said with a sigh. "I guess I'll never know."

"He left you his house?" asked Reinart. "Are you moving?"

Daniels shook his head. "No. He lived in a small town called Dumont. From what I hear, grandad's mind wasn't what it once was, and he was a hoarder in his later years. His place is literally full of stuff. Marjorie and I have decided to sell it."

"Makes sense," said Rem.

"We'll have to clean it out, but the extra money will come in handy." Daniels stood as Marjorie came down the stairs.

"That will be a big job." Rem went into the kitchen to grab the coffee cups.

"The little man is sleeping fine," said Marjorie.

"Great," said Daniels. "Sorry you couldn't have spent more time with J.P., Reinart, but he missed his nap today and for all our sakes, it was better to put him down early."

"That's fine," replied Reinart. "I hope I'll get to visit again."

"You're welcome anytime." Marjorie grabbed the brownies and brought them to the table. "At least you got to hang out while Uncle Rem played trains with him. What's this?" She picked up the sketch.

Daniels showed off Reinart's gifts.

Marjorie admired the Elvis picture and the sketch, and Rem set the coffee cups on the table and started filling them with coffee. After setting the sketch on the front entry table to be hung later, Marjorie brought some forks and plates and set them on the table.

While enjoying dessert, they talked more about Reinart's art background and Daniels' grandfather, and Marjorie mentioned an upcoming girls' trip.

"Gordon and I will go up to Dumont the week before I leave to do some cleaning and get some time away."

Daniels added more coffee to Reinart's mug. "It's sort of like an extended honeymoon, since we didn't get much of one."

Rem swallowed a bite of brownie and drank some coffee. "That's a great idea. You two deserve it."

They ate brownies and drank coffee until Reinart had to go. After thanking her again for the gifts and planning to do dinner again in the future, Daniels and Rem waved as she drove away. Rem stayed a few extra minutes to help clean up after their brownies and take a few home with him, and Marjorie said her goodbyes and headed upstairs.

Daniels followed Rem out to the front porch. "You know," said Daniels. "Why don't you come up to Dumont after Marjorie leaves and help me finish with the house? We can do some fishing and hiking and get some fresh air."

Rem hesitated. "Tempting as it sounds, you know how I am about the great outdoors."

"The great outdoors would be good for you. Other than some long weekends with Jacobs, you haven't taken a serious break since, well, since before Jennie died." He paused. "Maybe it's time to give yourself a break from the grind."

"I like the grind."

Daniels gave him a dubious look. "No. You like to immerse yourself in work to distract yourself. I get it, but now I think you could use the time off. Cut yourself some slack, partner."

Rem tried to think of the last time he'd had a serious vacation. His chest tightened when he recalled the week off he'd taken with Jennie two months before she'd died. "Maybe so, but Dumont? How little is it?"

"It's quaint, just like most small towns are."

Rem questioned the word quaint. "Is there takeout? Are we within a reasonable range of civilization?"

Daniels threw out his hands. "We're not going to Timbuktu."

"How big is your grandad's house? How messy is it?"

Daniels rolled his eyes. "It'll take a couple of days, tops. Besides, Marjorie and I will get some of it done before you get there."

"If this is a second honeymoon, you better not be spending all your time working unless it's in the bedroom."

Daniels smiled. "We're taking J.P. so our couple time will be limited. Plus, we're in a hurry. The sooner we get this done, the better."

Thinking it might be good to get a change of scenery, Rem tucked his brownies and painting under his arm. "I guess it sounds somewhat appealing."

"Don't get too excited."

"Lozano will have to approve my time off. I can talk to him tomorrow."

Daniels patted Rem's shoulder. "Already took care of that. I spoke to him this morning. We're both good to go."

Rem narrowed his eyes. "You had this planned all along." He pointed. "You even waited to spring this on me when I'm leaving, so I won't have time to argue with you."

Daniels tapped his temple with his finger. "It's called strategy, partner."

"I'm glad I'm finally rubbing off on you."

"I was trying to prevent it, but my stamina wore out."

Wondering what Daniels had roped him into, Rem stepped off the porch. "If this turns into a fiasco..."

"It'll be great. You'll thank me later. I promise." He paused. "And getting away will help mend some cracks."

"Cracks?"

"In your heart. I know they're there, and spending all your waking hours working won't fill them. Taking time for yourself will. And one day, you'll meet someone special who will help you fill the rest."

The grief bubbled up yet again. "I can never replace Jennie. I learned that with Jacobs."

"Jacobs helped heal a crack or two. And no, you'll never replace Jennie. That's impossible. But you're not the same guy anymore, Rem. Whoever you find will be the perfect fit for you now, not the you from the past."

"Well, whoever I am, I don't know if anyone can heal my cracks. They run pretty deep."

"It'll happen when you're ready. One step at a time."

Rem smiled softly. "Famous last words."

"We can get that tattoo whenever you want."

Nodding, Rem turned and stepped away. "I'll let you know when I'm ready." He waved and glanced back. "Thanks for dinner... and everything else."

"That's what friends are for, right? And next time you're cooking."

"You're on." Grateful for the friend who'd helped him through so much, Rem waved. "Night, Daniels."

"Night, Rem."

Reaching his car, Rem waved the Elvis painting. "And this is available for loan whenever you want it."

Daniels' face fell. "You can bring it to my grandad's house. There'll be plenty of trash and we can add it to the pile."

Chuckling, Rem got in his car and drove away.

What Happens Next?

As their series unfolds, Daniels and Remalla battle psychopaths, unexplained evil and unsolved cases. In book one, *Haunted River*, Daniels and Rem travel to Daniels' grandfather's cabin in Dumont, where the ghost of a woman murdered twenty-five years ago haunts the small town where she lived and died. When a second woman's body turns up dead on Daniel's property, the detectives become suspects, and the next targets.

Enjoy an excerpt below.

Want more from J.T. Bishop?

Want to know what happened when Daniels and Rem interviewed the sumo wrestler mentioned in Chapter Eleven?

Sign up for J.T. Bishop's newsletter at jtbishopauthor.com to get that bonus scene, plus the Daniels and Remalla prequel novella, *The Girl and the Gunshot*, along with excerpts, fun promos and opportunities for **free** books.

Already a subscriber and want access to the bonus scene?
Go to https://BookHip.com/QXCGDNR, enter the email you subscribed with, and enjoy!

Discover how it all began...

Daniels and Remalla first appear in *The Family or Foe Saga*. This set of four books follows the trail of a murderer determined to exact revenge on the family he believes wronged him. But there's more to the story when his secrets reveal unexpected connections, and shocking revelations come to light.

Discover *The Redstone Chronicles*

Meet the Redstones. Introduced in Of Breath and Blood, book two of Daniels and Remalla, Mason Redstone, a former Texas Ranger, and now paranormal investigator, works alongside his sister Mikey and partner Trick. They investigate the cases others won't and risk their lives to ensure the living, and the dead, get the justice they deserve.

Note: *Daniels and Remalla* and *The Redstone Chronicles* share an overarching story, and the characters from each are mentioned or appear in all the books, so reading both is ideal. The books published alternate between both series. A list of books in chronological order follows below.

Do you like light sci-fi suspense with urban fantasy and a delicious romance thrown in?

Discover Bishop's first series, *The Red-Line Trilogy*. One woman's startling transformation holds the key to unlocking a secret that will ensure the survival of a secret community. One man, assigned to protect her, will risk everything to keep her alive, but when he falls for her, will their destiny be enough to save them both?

And the *Red-Line* series continues with the sister series to the trilogy, *The Fletcher Family Saga*. A distant but deadly threat risks the lives of three unique siblings, but life can't stop because of who they are. They'll endure love, loss and a dangerous enemy determined to destroy them.

Either the trilogy or sister series can be read first. Take your pick. Boxed sets are available, too!

A Note from J.T.

Murder Unveiled came as a surprise to me. I was busy writing the next book in *The Redstone Chronicles* when I got inspired to write a Daniels and Remalla novella about a murdered art dealer, a cursed painting, and a myriad of troubled and unusual suspects. I told myself it wouldn't take long to write and could get it published fast.

Well, that novella turned into this novel, and it took twice as long to write and publish as I expected, but here it is.

I made it a prequel because I thought it would make a nice introduction into the series and it could work together with *Haunted River* and the *Family or Foe Saga* (which precedes *Murder Unveiled*) to welcome readers into the world of Remalla and Daniels. They're a fun partnership to write about and I enjoy diving into their background and history. The more I know about them, the more I like them.

I think this book will be enjoyed by those familiar with Rem and Daniels because they know what's coming up in *Haunted River* and beyond. The books and novellas I've written regarding their back story provide compelling glimpses into their unique bond and friendship. It's what I like best about these guys. Their banter, vulnerability, and love for each other make this series tick, and whether or not a story is your favorite, that bond never changes, and I hope I do it justice with each tale I tell.

And while many of my books contain aspects of the paranormal, this one is light on that element. I loved the idea of a cursed painting, and it worked well but I left it at that on purpose. Not all stories with Rem and Daniels will contain the paranormal unless it calls for it. Forcing it never works. But if you like the paranormal, then stay tuned, because there's plenty coming up.

I hope you liked this next installment of Rem and Daniels. It's a labor of love for me and one I love sharing with you. As you likely realize, reviews are a big help for an author, and for potential readers. I would welcome it if you could take a couple of minutes to leave a quick review for *Murder Unveiled*. And if you'd like, please leave a few comments, too.

As always, thank you for your time and readership. It is deeply valued and appreciated.

Now, on to the next book!

Books in Chronological Order

Although recommended but not required, in case you like to read in order...

Prelude to The Shift, a short story (subscribers only)
Red-Line: The Shift
Red-Line: Mirrors
Red-Line: Trust Destiny
Curse Breaker
High Child
Spark
Forged Lines

• • • • • • • • •

The Girl and the Gunshot, a novella (subscribers only)
A Hamburger Christmas, a novella
The Magic of Murder, a novella (subscribers only)
First Cut
Second Slice
Third Blow
Fourth Strike
Murder Unveiled
Haunted River
Of Breath and Blood

About the Author

Award-winning author, J. T. Bishop, is a writer of mystery thrillers with a paranormal edge. Growing up, she read Stephen King, Mary Higgins Clark, and Dean Koontz, devoured every episode of *The X-files* and watched plenty of TV shows with great partnerships that leave you wanting more. She loves tangled relationships, unexpected twists and turns, heart-stopping love stories and the complications that come with all the above. Throw in a little supernatural fun and she's hooked. Her evil plan is to hook you, too.

She's the author of *The Red-Line Trilogy* and its sister series, *The Fletcher Family Saga*, which features touches of urban fantasy, light sci-fi, and paranormal romance. She's also happily writing mystery thrillers featuring two charismatic detectives who may occasionally encounter a supernatural villain or two, and a crossover series which follows the exploits of a gifted, but troubled, paranormal P.I. and his spunky sister.

All the above keeps her busy, but in her spare time, she loves good movies, tasty food, an unfortunate sugar addiction, and traveling.

Acknowledgements

Another book is complete, and again, I have many to thank. This doesn't happen alone, and I am indebted to family and friends for their help, support, and encouragement. It is truly appreciated.

I also want to thank my Beta and ARC teams. You guys keep me on my toes, ensure I write a great story, and help with early reviews. Thank you for being honest and offering your guidance.

I love writing about the bonds between loving family, deep friendships and the ties that hold them together. Plus, my fascination with the unknown thrown into the mix makes for a satisfying story and hopefully, adds a little more thrill for my readers.

I especially want to thank my fans. Hearing from you and knowing that you're enjoying my books makes all the hard work worthwhile. None of this would matter without your tremendous support. If I can help you escape from this crazy world for a short period each day, then I've done my job.

Here's to more stories, more fun, and more time for yourself. If you can have a little of that each day, you're on the right track.

Enjoy an excerpt from Haunted River, book one in Detectives Daniels and Remalla

DETECTIVE AARON REMALLA STUDIED his phone, wondering where to take the next turn. The farther he drove, the worse his cell phone connection became, and he cursed his partner. The woods were thick, and the roads were narrow, and despite his ability to handle the most violent of criminals, at this moment, nature seemed far more dangerous. He'd take a cabin within a thirty-minute drive of a decent restaurant any day, but this was different. He'd driven through a small town about twenty minutes earlier that he'd almost missed entirely if not for the gas station on the corner. He'd stopped to fill his tank but had only filled it half-way when the creepy attendant with long, uncombed hair, dirty clothes, and stubbled face started to stare at him from the door to the station.

His partner had told him the place was rustic, but Rem would obviously have to explain to him the definition of rustic. There was civilization rustic, and there was the movie *Deliverance* rustic, and this was borderline *Deliverance*.

Coming to a fork in the road, he cursed again and pulled over to the side. He shook his cell phone, hoping for reception. He thought he was supposed to go right, but he couldn't be sure. The house had to be close, but he had no desire to get lost. He'd rather face a gang of armed street thugs. Visions of being stranded and spending the night in his car made him break out in a cold sweat.

He hit a button on his phone, hoping it would connect. He heard a click, and then nothing, and almost hung up, when he heard a static-filled "Hello?"

Rem didn't mince words. "What the hell have you gotten me into? Do you know I am driving through wilderness right now? A Bigfoot probably has me in his sights and he's anticipating dinner. I thought you said this place was near humans?"

More static, but he heard his name. "Rem? Where are you?" He recognized his partner's voice.

Rem groaned. "That's why I'm calling you. Cell reception here sucks. I'm at the fork in the road. Which way do I go?"

He heard a snort. "The one less traveled."

"What?"

More static. "Go right." His partner's voice continued but Rem only heard bits and pieces. "house...across...mile...white post...right side." The call cut off.

"Shit." Rem tossed the phone into the passenger seat and made a mental note to request a partner transfer when he got home.

Feeling reasonably comfortable that he'd heard to go right at the fork, he put the car into drive and started to hit the gas when movement on his left caught his eye. Turning in his seat, he saw a woman walking down the side of the road.

Frowning, he looked around. Where had she come from? He'd seen no houses, and the small town was a good distance away. More concerning is what she wore. It looked like a white dress, but the dirt on it gave it a beige, dingy color, and it was ripped at the hem. Her wet, tangled, long hair ran down her back, and she was barefoot.

Rem knew trouble when he saw it. The day was warm but as the sun descended, a chilly breeze blew, and that dress was not suitable coverage. And considering the rocky ground, she should've been wearing shoes.

He rolled his window down and stuck his head out. She'd passed his car and had not looked his way.

"Ma'am, are you okay?"

She did not acknowledge him but kept walking.

"Ma'am?"

Again, she ignored him and continued to walk.

Rem huffed. He couldn't leave this lady out in the middle of nowhere. Something was wrong, and all his cop instincts told him she needed help. He unbuckled his seat belt and grabbed his phone. He considered turning the car around but didn't think driving up next to her would be smart. It might make her run if she was scared and thought he might hurt her.

He popped the car door open and stepped out. Maybe if he called to her from the road, but kept his distance, she'd be less frightened of him. Standing and swiveling back to find her, he searched, but his mouth fell open when he didn't see her.

Scanning the road and trees, he took several steps down the pavement. "Ma'am?" he yelled. "Hello?"

Nothing. The woman was gone. Had she walked into the woods? Had he scared her off when he'd left the car? Granted, he was wearing his favorite baggy and ripped jeans, his dark hair hung down to his shoulders, and his Metallica T-shirt didn't scream policeman, but he figured compared to gas station guy, he couldn't look that bad. He jogged slowly down to where he'd last seen her, checking the surroundings. Where was she? He called again, but there was no answer.

A gust of wind blew, the branches swayed, and he listened, but didn't hear anything, not even the sound of a bird. Everything seemed eerily quiet, except for the sound of the leaves rustled by the breeze. A shiver ran through him, and the hair on his neck stood on end. Imagining a Bigfoot hiding in the brush and watching him, he turned and ran back to his car, got in and locked the door.

His heart racing, he started up the engine, offering a silent prayer of thanks when it turned over so that he could get out of there. He hit the gas and took the right fork.

·····•••••··

Detective Gordon Daniels put the phone down, shaking his head.

"Who was it?" His wife, Marjorie, entered the kitchen, putting on an earring. Her smooth blonde hair brushed her shoulders. "Rem?"

Daniels chuckled. "He's on the road and bitching up a storm. Thinks he's lost."

Her earring secured, she smoothed her T-shirt. "You can't be surprised. You didn't exactly give him the full story."

"I hadn't been here since I was a kid. I told him what I remembered."

"We've been here a week. You've had ample time to give him an update."

Daniels shrugged. "And ruin a perfectly good opportunity to get him away from the city for a bit?"

She stood up on her tiptoes and gave him a quick kiss. "You mean have him help you get this place out in the middle of nowhere cleaned up and sellable? Does he know that part?"

"He knows I need to get it ready to put it on the market. I figure we can hammer out the rest of the details once he's here."

"Uh-huh. Is he actually lost?"

"Not really. He's at the fork in the road."

"Where we took the wrong turn on the way in?"

Daniels sighed. "We weren't lost. I just wanted to get the lay of the land."

She frowned. "Sure you did. And J.P. wasn't crying, he was just curious about how to make water come out of his eyes."

Daniels smiled and pulled her into his arms. "I think J.P. is curious about a lot of things."

She hugged him and rested her head in the hollow of his neck. "I'm sure. Like how to get fed, cleaned, and entertained. Not unlike his father."

"J.P. asleep?"

She nodded against him.

He rubbed his jaw against her hair. "Care to be entertained?"

She squeezed his waist and laughed. "Rem will be here any minute."

"You're a lot more confident than I am. I give him an hour, at best."

"If he's at the fork, he's just down the road."

"I know."

Smiling, she looked up. "I'm going to miss you." She squeezed his arm. "And your sexy muscles."

Daniels kissed her forehead. "You've been looking forward to this trip for a while. It will be fun. You need to hang with the girls." He flexed a bicep. "My muscles will still be here next week."

"They better be." She rested her hands on his chest. "You're sure about this? You think Rem will mind helping you with J.P. for the week?"

"Mind? Nah. He's looking forward to it. Plans to teach J.P. how to throw a curve ball and make a hot dog."

"He's eleven months old."

"No time like the present."

"Well, if you need anything..."

"We won't need anything. We'll be fine. Go on your girls' trip and relax. Rem and I will get this place into shape, and I'll get it on the market. I'll meet you back home next week, with J.P. and Rem right behind me."

"You sure you can handle it?"

Daniels rubbed her shoulders. "He's my son, babe. Of course, I can handle it."

"I was talking about Rem."

He grinned and stepped back. "I've survived this long."

She opened the fridge and grabbed a bottled water. "How's he been? Any better?"

Daniels grabbed a banana from the counter. "Still has his moments, but he's hanging strong."

"Good. After everything that's happened, I was halfway wondering if he'd go off and become a mountain man somewhere."

"Rem?" asked Daniels. "He can barely handle a salad, hates sleeping bags, and jumps when he sees a bug larger than a fly. I don't think mountaineering is in his future, much less leaving the comforts of home."

"He still seeing the shrink?"

Daniels peeled the banana. "Up until the last month or two. Don't think he's seen him since."

She twisted the cap and drank some water. "As long as he's still talking to you. When that stops, then I'll worry."

"No need. I won't let it get that far anyway. I can tell when he's getting stressed, which he hates."

She reached over and took his hand. "Be careful he doesn't bite."

"Oh, he bites, but so do I. I just need to be sure to talk to him when he's not hungry. Then it might get ugly."

Marjorie nodded. "I know. That's why I feed him so often. Have to make sure to keep you safe."

"And that's why I love you." He squeezed her fingers and took a bite of the banana.

She checked her watch. "I should get going. I don't want to leave too late. I don't like driving around here at night. Feels spooky."

"You're right. I don't want you to rush. What time is your flight tomorrow?"

"Bright and early. We leave at eight a.m."

"You'll meet at the airport?"

"I'll meet Melanie there. We'll have dinner tonight at the airport hotel and head out in the morning. We'll meet the rest of the ladies when we get to Fort Lauderdale."

"It'll be a blast."

The doorbell rang and Daniels heard a yell from the front. "Anybody there?" The bell rang again. "Daniels? Marjorie? Satan? Bigfoot?"

"Guess who?" asked Daniels.

"I think he found us." She poked him in the arm. "There's still time. You can leave him on the front porch."

Daniels put his banana down and headed toward the door. "I'd only find him babbling on the steps tomorrow morning. It's not worth the cost of the straight jacket I'd have to buy."

"Good point."

Daniels reached the door and opened it. Rem stood on the other side, his long black hair disheveled and his face white. "Where the hell did you invite me? I'm halfway expecting the name of this place to have something to do with a Black Lagoon."

Marjorie joined Daniels at the door. "You're close. We're actually on the Black River."

Rem's jaw dropped. "You're kidding?"

Daniels swung the door wide. "Nope. She's not. Come on in."

Rem stomped in, wearing hiking boots and carrying a backpack and duffel bag. He dropped them on the floor. "Were you aware of this, Marjorie? I expected more from you. You're supposed to warn me when Daniels is keeping secrets."

"Sorry, Rem," said Marjorie. "But I needed your help with J.P. I figure it was worth a few spiders and a potential Bigfoot sighting." She raised a brow when he jumped and brushed something off his sleeve. "I hope I can still consider you a friend."

Rem glared. "You're lucky I like you, and you're cute. You, on the other hand," he pointed at Daniels, "are not so attractive."

Daniels raised his hands in mock seriousness. "Ah, come on, partner. Consider it an adventure. It's nice to get out in nature. Good for the soul. Besides, it's not like we're camping. We've got bathrooms and showers. How's it any different than Lozano's cabin?"

"Adventure? We deal with enough adventure in our jobs. And Lozano's cabin is half an hour from civilization. What's wrong with a sandy beach and five-star service?"

Daniels closed the door. "How about this? Once we get this place cleaned up and ready to sell, we'll look online at some five-star resorts, then we can pretend we're there."

"Online?" Rem shook his head. "How do you plan to look online when you have no Wi-Fi?"

"Details," said Daniels.

Rem's eyes widened. "Details? I was just kidding. Do you seriously not have Wi-Fi?"

Marjorie patted Daniels chest. "I think that's my cue. I need to hit the road."

Daniels hugged her and gave her a quick kiss. "You got everything?"

"It's all in the car. Just need my purse."

"You know where you're going. Got your cell?" asked Daniels.

"I got it," said Marjorie, grabbing her purse from a chair beside the door.

"What good is a cell out here?" said Rem. "Might as well use it as a paperweight."

Daniels ignored him. "Call me when you get to the airport."

"I will," said Marjorie. "Call me if you need anything. Love you."

"We're not going to need a thing," said Daniels. "Rem and I are going to be fine, and so's J.P. Love you, too."

"Take it easy, Rem," Marjorie said as she opened the door to leave. "Try to have fun. Take care of J.P. and don't let him catch too many fly balls or eat too many hot dogs."

Rem swiped at his pant leg. "I'll try, but no promises. I see a creature or something with too many legs, it's every man or baby for himself."

Marjorie bit back a smile, and Daniels shook his head. "I'll walk you to the car."

"Keep an eye out for a woman in a white dress on the way out," said Rem.

Marjorie stopped, and Daniels looked back. "What?" he asked.

Rem took his jacket off and shook it out. "I saw her near the fork. Tried to help her but she disappeared into the woods. Just goes to show how crazy this place is. God knows what she's running from. The lady looked in distress, plus she was all wet, like she'd fallen in your Blue River."

"Black," said Daniels.

"Whatever," said Rem.

Marjorie shot a glance at Daniels. "Did you say a woman in white?" asked Marjorie.

"On the road?" asked Daniels. "Near the fork?"

Rem paused. "Did I stutter? Yeah. Just now. On the way in." He narrowed his eyes. "What? Something wrong?"

Marjorie held her chest. "Oh, my God. You saw the Lady of Black River."